fathermucker

Also by Greg Olear

Totally Killer

fathermucker

a novel

Greg Olear

HARPER

NEW YORK • LONDON • TORONTO • SYDNEY

HARPER

HarperCollins books may be purchased for educational, business, or sales promotional use. For information please write: Special Markets Department, HarperCollins Publishers, 10 East 53rd Street, New York, NY 10022.

FIRST EDITION

Designed by Justin Dodd

Library of Congress Cataloging-in-Publication Data
Olear, Greg.
Fathermucker : a novel / Greg Olear. — 1st ed.
p. cm.
ISBN 978-0-06-205971-0
1. Stay-at-home fathers—Fiction. 2. Parenting—Fiction. 3. Marriage—Fiction. 4. Political correctness—Fiction. I. Title.
PS3615.L426F38 2011
813'.6—dc22 2010054575

---

11 12 13 14 15 OV/RRD 10 9 8 7 6 5 4 3 2 1

For Stephanie

&

For Dominick & Prudence

Before I got married I had six theories about bringing up children; now I have six children and no theories.

—John Wilmot,
Second Earl of Rochester
(1647–1680)

Mommy's alright,
Daddy's alright,
They just seem a little weird.
Surrender, surrender,
But don't give yourself away.

—Cheap Trick
(1974–present)

PART I

what to expect when
you're least
expecting
it

Friday, 10:37 a.m.

Fatherhood is fear. Fatherhood is disappointment. Fatherhood is anger and envy and lust. And the surest guarantee of fatherly success is a Spock-like mastery of those base emotions. Mister Spock, not Doctor.

Good fathers conquer fear. They become One with their phobias. Like the Buddha. Or Patrick Swayze in *Point Break*.

Good fathers manage their expectations. They do not expend perspiration on small stuff, and they recognize, like the Zen masters that they are, that all stuff is small. That nothing is worth sweating over. Not even punishments cruel and unusual, tortures that violate the Geneva Conventions: sleep deprivation, emotional blackmail, *Go, Diego, Go!*

Good fathers temper their anger. They don't snap, they don't yell, they don't call the douchebag in the BMW who just cut them off a *fucking asshole* when children are in earshot, they don't smack, and they sure as hell don't spank. Love is their sole instrument of discipline.

Good fathers combat the Seven Deadly Sins with the Seven Cardinal Virtues: humility, charity, kindness, patience, temperance, prudence, and, oh yes, chastity. Good fathers emulate good fathers of another kind, priestly, offering blessing and balm, repressing carnal yearnings, sacrificing their own desires for the salvation of others.

That's what good fathers do.

I strive to be a good father, but when your three-year-old daughter won't stop kicking you, and your five-year-old son swats at you with his fork when you try to take away his Lego catalog, and the two of them come to blows over matters of great import, such as who gets to play with the *Us Weekly* magazine insert they found on the mildewy floor near the toilet, this can be a challenging—nay, an impossible—duty to uphold.

Which calls to mind another axiom of my austere and lonely office:

Fatherhood is failure.

"I DON'T KNOW HOW TO TELL YOU THIS," SHARON SAYS, HER EYES wide with concern, "so I'm just going to tell you."

It's Friday, twenty minutes before eleven (eleven *a.m.*, I might add; unless one of the kids wakes up with a nightmare, I'm toast by eleven at night). We're at Jess Holby's house—Emma's mommy's house—on our weekly playdate. Jess and Sharon and Gloria and me, the on-duty parents of three-year-olds. As usual, I'm the only male in the room (not counting Gloria's son, Haven, although he is often mistaken for a girl, on account of his Bret-Michaels-circa-1989 locks).

We're in the well-appointed kitchen, Sharon and I, availing ourselves of another hit of that parental crack-cocaine that is freshly brewed coffee. The others are in the great room, beneath the vaulted ceiling. I can see them through the archway. Gloria is blowing bubbles; the cavorting kids watch rapt as the glistening spheres float heavenward and burst into nothingness, exploding like so many childhood dreams. Although my daughter is the youngest and smallest of the bunch, she runs roughshod over the others, leaping over backs to have at the bubbles like an undersized power forward vying for superior position on a rebound. Maude, the tough broad: a thirty-pound freight train, three yards and a cloud of (Pixy Stix) dust. She has my father's face, only she's pretty. Wouldn't have thought that was possible before she came along, but here she is, a cute, miniature My Dad. Wait . . . what did Sharon just say?

I don't know how to tell you this, so I'm just going to tell you.

A line copped from God knows how many *Lifetime* movies of the week, on hackneyed par with *It was all a dream.* Which does nothing to dispel its harrowing efficacy. Unlike the other mommies—and I include myself in that group—Sharon, as far as I know, is not prone to melodrama or gossip. Which means bad news coming down the pike.

Dynamite. I could always use more bad news.

I stop my pour with the cup half empty, coffee sloshing over the rim and burning my thumb. The coffee pot (Krups; we don't fuck around with our Moka Java) trembles in my hand.

"O-*kay* . . . "

Sharon doesn't say anything for a moment, as if reconsidering. I can see the struggle in her eyes (which, incidentally, are quite lovely; big, brown, and bright, like a NASA image of binary planets in some faraway galaxy). In the living room, Maude squeals with delight as another bubble bursts.

"Maybe I shouldn't," Sharon says, turning away. A piece of soap-opera blocking to go with the soap-opera dialogue. "It isn't really my place."

Her thick, baggy sweater, the kind with the way-too-big turtleneck, obscures her lithe frame and breasts that are sneakily perky (I only know this because I saw her last summer in a one-piece at Moriello Pool). She's probably a knockout, Sharon, when dolled up for a night on the town. But mothers of three-year-olds don't tend to dress that way. Not in New Paltz, anyway. Function trumps form, sure as a full house beats three of a kind. There's a reason mothers wear baggy clothes and cut their hair like Simon Cowell. Why my own hair is military short. Why I've worn the same pair of jeans every day for two weeks straight.

"Sharon," with some difficulty, I jam the pot back into its hot-plated nest, spillage sizzling on the metal, and try to keep my voice level, "just tell me. It's okay. Whatever it is, it's fine."

This is what she's after—my blessing to continue, a tacit promise not to kill the messenger, absolution in advance. She opens her mouth (her best feature; her plump lips are what Hollywood surgeons are going for when they inject the collagen) but before she can say anything, Iris plods into the room.

"Mom-*mee*," Iris says. Her dark hair is bobbed, the comically short bangs intended to cutely channel Louise Brooks, but more suggestive of Mo of *Three Stooges* fame, to whom, truth be told, the girl bears a striking resemblance. Iris is the Alexa Joel of New Paltz—one of the prettiest mommies in town, and she's the spitting image of her ho-hum old man. Genetics is such a crapshoot. "Mom-*mee*."

"What's the matter, honey?"

"Mom-*mee* . . . Mom-*mee* . . . "

Iris stammers her way into requesting a cookie from the pile of Stop & Shop specials on the plastic tray before us—this takes almost three full minutes; I time it on the coffee-pot clock—leaving me to suffer in purgatory. From *purgatorio*, I think, root word of *purge*. The sloughing off of old skin. At night, Iris sleeps in Sharon and David's bed. Always has, since infancy. There isn't even a bed in her so-called bedroom, I've heard, just a Dutalier glider and a grand assortment of (wooden; nothing that bleeps, nothing that's fashioned from that Devil's clay, plastic) toys—the whole Melissa & Doug catalog. The appeal of co-sleeping, to me, is right up there with castration. While there are undoubtedly moments of sweetness—parents and child lovingly nestled together, like so many puppies in a basket—the family bed is like Iraq: there's no exit strategy. Once embedded between Mommy and Daddy, the kid remains there till the troops come home. She's there until she starts dating. And this must pose problems for the co-sleeping parents. How can Sharon and David possibly get it on with a permanent chaperone heaving and snoring and sucking up space in the middle of their mattress, like a goiter in human form? But maybe that, too, is by design. Sharon and David, I can't quite figure them out. He's a good twenty years her senior, and not particularly attractive, in terms of either looks or personality. The pairing is something of a head-scratcher about town—not exactly Anna Nicole Smith and her decrepit oil heir, but still remarkable—but no one knows her well enough to broach the subject of how she wound up with a late Boomer my wife calls Old Man River.

As Sharon bends down to present Iris with a cookie (health-food-brand, retrieved from a Ziploc baggie in her canvas handbag, and not from the Stop & Shop stack, as if that makes it nutritious), her baggy sweater hikes up, offering a glimpse of a tattoo I didn't know she had on the small of her back (an ornate scorpion, red and black) and the satin hint of her panties (also ornate, also red and black), and I feel an unfamiliar twinge down below. A rumble in the dormant volcano. For the first time, the parental wool is lifted from my eyes, and I see Sharon not as Mother but as Woman. This is someone I've known socially for almost two years, and only now does it occur to me that Sharon is *gasp* kind of hot. I've always known she was *pretty*, of course, but in the same way I recognize that, say, my friend Meg's daughters are pretty, or my sister. Like I'm watching her on the Disney Channel of my mind. Only now, only this morning, does my inner remote control change the channel to Skinemax. Only now does it dawn on me that sex with Sharon would be *oh man* highly enjoyable. The road to Damascus is Emma's mommy's kitchen.

Most guys, of course, would have recognized this as soon as she walked into the room with her aging, balding dud of a husband. But most guys are not stay-at-home fathers of two young children. Men in my station must, by necessity, divorce ourselves from our carnal impulses. Lust, you see, is a pernicious weed that grows in the (kinder) garden. As soon as it rears its ugly head, it must be *ahem* whacked away. It wouldn't do for me to be at the preschool, at the playground, at the Little Gym (where Maude spends most of the forty-five minutes in my lap), formulating fantasies of fucking Sharon Rothman. Bending her over the dining room table, ripping off those sleek panties, putting my thumbs on either side of that tattoo, and—

Not that Stacy and I don't have sex. We do. But the night in Capri on our honeymoon, when we drank two bottles of wine apiece and tore at each other like animals in heat . . . those days are over. Not *over*; that implies they will never return, and they will return, I know they'll return. But at the moment, they feel as distant as retirement. If the full moon, when the freak comes out, represents the reckless abandon of the weeks after your wedding—the *honey*moon, if you will—Stacy and I now find ourselves under the darkling sky of its antagonist, the black and hopeless night of the new moon. That she has been in Los Angeles all week, on an interminable business trip the purpose of which I cannot hope to divine, does not help matters. When I think about this, it upsets me, so I try not to think about it.

Cookie successfully won, Iris tub-thumps on stout little legs back to the living room, where the bubble mosh-pit has found new life. Sharon stands up straight and glances at me, her eyes reassuming their wide-with-concern look; I avert my gaze just in time to avoid getting busted for ogling. And just as suddenly as they appeared, my lustful urges vanish, as I recall her words, the preamble to what are sure to be tidings of discomfort and *oy*.

I don't know how to tell you this, so I'm just going to tell you.

"Sorry," she says, gesturing toward the living room. A beat, an awkward grin, and then: "So . . . "

"So . . . "

She takes a deep breath, maybe for dramatic effect. "It's about Stacy," she says.

"What about her?"

"She's . . . oh, Josh, I hate to be the one to tell you this. I think . . . I think she's having an affair."

This is the opening to a dialogue that could last hours, but parents can never depend on the luxury of time or undivided attention necessary to converse intelligently for more than sixty seconds. We've been in the kitchen for five minutes, Sharon and I, bullshitting about nothing, about how the mayor is an idiot, how the metered parking in the muni lot is killing downtown, but no sooner does she lay this bombshell in my lap—before I can process it; before the news can even generate the ineluctable psychosomatic response in my stomach—than Maude trips over Emma's foot while going for a bubble, smacks her head on the corner of the coffee table, and bursts into throes-of-death tears.

"Hold that thought," I tell Sharon, and I'm in the living room before I even realize I'm moving.

I scoop up Maude, shower her with kisses. I hate to see her cry, of course, especially from injury, but boy does she look cute when she's upset. Her features scrunch up just so, and a single line of stubborn displeasure runs from one eyebrow to the other, across the bridge of her nose. Maude is so theatrical—histrionic, even—there's not much separating her *I'm-hurt* cry from her *Roland-took-my-toy* cry. The main difference between kids and adults—other than the fact that adults can have sex and can wipe their own asses after using the bathroom—is that the former have not yet learned to pick their battles, so they get upset over *everything*. Yesterday, for example, Roland flew into a rage because Maude wouldn't let him see the poop she just made in the toilet. That's maybe not something a grown-up would get riled up about. To the preschooler, every conflict is a life-or-death struggle. It's all do or die. Sometimes I think that my main job as a father is to show them how to manage disappointment. I get to teach them the all-important lesson that most of the time, life kind of sucks. Lucky me.

There's a little red knot on her forehead—bumps on the head tend to balloon, I've learned, and often appear worse than they actually are—but she calms down after I smother her with kisses and give her a pacifier. She loves the "passie." To Maude, it's like having a cigarette. I'll be shocked if she doesn't wind up smoking in college. If they're still distributing cigarettes in 2023. Or bachelor's degrees.

I take her into the kitchen, away from the tumult. Cradling her like a giant football in my right arm, I get some ice cubes from the ice maker with my left. Maude will accept ice on her skin for fifteen seconds, tops. I don't know why I bother, other than it's what you're supposed to do, and maybe if she gets used to it now, she won't mind it so much later on. After approximately five Miss'ippis of ice time, she starts flailing around, her patience for my ministrations at an end, and she yells, "Put me down," and I do—if she's not the most willful kid on earth, she's certainly in the top three, and I don't know who the other two are—and she bounds back into the fray like a wide receiver returning to the field after a vicious hit, Ford tough, like nothing happened. I half expect to hear Pat Summerall saying, "And look at this—here's Maude Lansky, coming right back into the game," followed by John Madden extolling her rough-and-tumble virtues and concluding, "You know what? There's not a tougher player in the National Football League than Maude Lansky."

Only now can I turn my attention to the your-wife-is-having-an-affair business—which, right on cue, is starting to generate the obligatory wave of nausea—but Sharon isn't in the kitchen anymore. I go back into the living room; no sign of her there, either. But there is the sickening smell of shit (which doesn't help the nausea), and one fewer body in the bubble mosh-pit, so I put two and two together. Iris, not yet potty-trained, must have taken a monster dump.

I head to the foyer, and the stairs leading to the bedrooms on the upper level, where Sharon probably went, but before I can advance, the front door opens, and Meg comes in with the twins. Meg is my closest friend in New Paltz. I met her in the waiting room of the Barefoot Dance Center, where Roland and Maude take Creative Movement class with Beatrix and Brooke. The first day there, as we sat with nine other parents—eight mommies, two of whom were nursing infants, and a stray daddy with oniony body odor—all of us idly discussing the scintillating topic of how to introduce new foods to a child's palette, someone complained about her daughter's hyperactive gag reflex, and Meg quipped, "Beatrix is like that, too. She pukes at the drop of a hat. She's a bulimic's wet dream." The others all looked at her like she'd just broken wind, eating disorders being beyond the pale as comic fodder, but I laughed, and I knew she wasn't like the other New Paltz moms, and that we would be friends. And so we are. Although at this point—mostly due to the tacit taboo against married men getting too chummy with married women; it wouldn't do for me to say, *Hey, Stacy, Meg and I are going out for a drink*, even though there would be nothing remotely untoward about us doing so—she's closer with my better half than she is with me. When she calls the house, if I happen to answer the phone, she asks, *Is your lovely wife there?*

Meg adroitly doffs the twins' coats, adding them to the pile on the floor, and gives me a hug and a peck on the cheek. "Big fun," she says, rolling her eyes, as Brooke (at least I think it's Brooke) makes for the seductive hoopla of the bubble mosh-pit. I can tell from the eye-roll Meg's pissed about something.

"You okay?"

"I'm married to a doucheface."

Something I love about Meg is that she drops *bon mots* like *doucheface* while one of her impressionable daughters is clinging koala-like to her leg.

"Soren went out last night," Meg tells me. Her voice is low, and she speaks slowly and not quite loud enough, like she's stoned to the gourds. Which she is often enough, although not as much as she'd like; she's lived here all her life, and, much to her annoyance, she still doesn't have a good pot hook-up. "With Peter Berliner, who *by* the way *still* hasn't realized that Cynthia's shacking up with Bruce Baldwin, even though, like, I'm pretty sure it was in the *paper*, so many people know about it."

The realization that I might share common ground with Peter Berliner, the town cuckold—that my friends and neighbors might speak in hushed whispers about me, if they are not already doing so, while I pass them in the Stop & Shop, obliviously stocking my cart with YoBaby six-packs and organic Spinach Munchies—cranks the nausea up to eleven. It's all I can do not to hurl my Moka Java all over Meg's Uggs.

"We were *both* supposed to go," she says, "but he was in charge of finding a sitter, so of course we couldn't get one, because he didn't call Abby till like *five* o'clock. Then he stays out till like two in the morning, and he comes home totally trashed, and he pukes all over the bathroom, and now the whole house smells like alcohol and vomit. It's dis*gust*ing. *He's* disgusting."

She looks down and appears to notice, for the first time, the barnacle of Beatrix lodged on her left leg. "Come on, dude," Meg says, more to herself than her daughter, giving the leg a shake. No dice. She turns back to me. "And then this morning, he's all whining about being hungover. Boo fucking hoo. He has to drive to Pawling today for some photo shoot. It's near Danbury, so I'm making him stop at Trader Joe's. The dick." With a sudden kick she detaches Beatrix from her leg, gives her a little spank on the behind. "Go play now, Trixie. Leave Mommy alone."

But Beatrix (so it *was* Brooke who already left!) just stands there. Twins—identical twins, at that—and they couldn't be more different. No two snowflakes and so forth. Parenthood would fill your heart with wonder if it weren't so fucking exhausting.

"There's bubbles."

"Bub-uhz?" Thus duped, Beatrix half-skips into the living room (one of her legs is slightly shorter than the other, giving her an odd gait).

"Well played," I tell Meg.

"So what's the deal with *Rents?*"

"How did you know about that?"

"Facebook."

"Oh. Right." I'd updated my status in the early morning hours, before my coffee had kicked in, and Meg had LIKED it. (Soren's crack-of-dawn Facebook update—CAN'T REMEMBER LAST NIGHT—now makes perfect sense.) "No, it's not quite that exciting. They liked my pitch."

"What was it?"

"You know how they do the Q&As? With celebrity parents? Well, I told them I could get Daryl 'Duke' Reid."

"He's that punk guy, right?" She says *punk* like Pat Robertson would say *gay*.

"Yeah. His daughter's, you know, in Roland's class at Thornwood."

Remembering, she nods. "Does she get services, too?"

"I don't know. Probably not. I mean, not everyone there does. It's an integrated program."

She contemplates this, moves on. "You think you can get him?"

"There's a field trip this afternoon. Pumpkin patch. He should be there. Hopefully. He usually comes to parent stuff."

"That's awesome, Josh."

At the moment, nothing feels particularly awesome, other than the weight of the world on my flimsy shoulders—figurative weight, as I'm able to shrug. "I guess."

"You need me to watch Maude?"

"Vanessa's coming over."

Meg, who used my babysitter once—*once*—laughs. "I repeat: you need me to watch Maude?"

On cue, Maude wanders into the foyer, a pissed-off look on her face, the fine white-blonde curls of her hair giving her head the aspect of a fluffy dandelion. "Daddy, I want to go home," she says, in her patented half-whine.

"But Beatrix and Brooke just got here."

"Because . . . because . . . " Her face contorts into a mask of almost parodic pissed-off-ness. "I don't *like* Bee-uh-twix and Bwook."

"Yes, you do."

"I want to go home!" And then she commences the subverbal wailing. Which, come to think, pretty much sums up my own feelings right at the moment.

I know you're not supposed to let the kids boss you around and all that, but one of the lessons I've learned the hard way is if your child wants to end the playdate, what you need to do is end the fucking playdate.

"Okay, honey. Let's get your coat."

"No! No coat!"

"We can't go without your coat on. It's chilly outside."

"No coat! No! Noooooooooooooooooooo!"

And she has a full-fledged temper tantrum, right in the foyer. A little early for her sporadic nap, but she hasn't been sleeping well lately, and she's probably tired.

"Well," says Meg, unfazed by my screaming banshee of a daughter, "have fun, kids. I better go pretend to be a good mother before one of the twins breathes on Haven funny and Gloria has a fucking cow."

I scoop up Maude—thirty-two pounds of fist-flying fury—and throw her over my shoulder like a sack of wriggling and violent potatoes, trying to position her so her flailing feet don't knock off my glasses, or the row of framed photographs of Emma Holby in various stages of development hanging neatly and chronologically on the foyer wall. Then I bend my knees, lowering myself, and with my free hand, snatch up her coat.

And that's when Sharon appears at the top of the stairs, Iris in one hand, a tied-off plastic Shop & Shop bag in the other. Reusable bags are great for Mother Earth and all, but disposable plastic is not without its uses. "You going?"

"Looks like."

"Shit. Sorry. I . . . "

"It's okay."

She extends her thumb and pinky, folding up the other fingers, and holds her hand to her ear—*I'll call you*—but the gesture looks ridiculous because there's a plastic bag dangling from her pinky with a poopy diaper inside it. Shouting goodbye and thank you to Jess and the others, I carry Maude, kicking and screaming and still coatless, into the minivan.

Friday, 3:33 a.m. (seven hours earlier)

I WAKE UP FEELING RESTED AND THEREFORE HAPPY—WHICH IS what happens when you awaken under your own power, to the rhythm of your own biological clock, taking the requisite time to ease from the nebulous realm of the subconscious into the real world *tiptoeing your sweet-ass way into a frigid lake*, rather than being yanked from your dream *pushed unsuspectingly into that same cold water* by the sudden and piercing cry of a child, and having to abruptly shift from navigating the soft, cloudy corridors of dreamscape to the sharp, unforgiving corridors of a darkened house *one minute out cold, the next splashing around for dear life*—but the blissful feeling fades when I become aware of the scratching.

Two baby monitors transmitting the dulcet din of dueling noise machines—white noise in Roland's room, steam train in Maude's—plus the metallic clang and watery rumble of the baseboard heater, but all my ears register is the scratching. The foreign sound, the intruder's noise.

October, and the mice have returned.

Damn it all.

We've lived here four full years now, so I'm familiar with the seasonal changes to the house. I know there are mice in the walls. I know they can't get out. I know that if they ever do get out, Steve will kill them. Look, there he is at the closet door, waiting in that infinitely patient, *Manchurian Candidate* way that cats do, for the damn thing to stop scratching and show his conical face. But the mouse—or the mice; they travel in packs, the fuckers, like gypsies—won't come out. He'll scratch, and he'll bang around, and he'll race up and down the gap in the floorboards, but he won't come out. He can't come out. He's trapped in there. He'll die in there—they always do—he'll die of hunger, of thirst, of feasting on the poison I dumped in the abyss beneath the vanity in the upstairs bathroom, and then his rotting corpse, his tiny decomposing mouse cadaver, will stink up our bedroom for the next two weeks. An awful smell, the pungent reek of death, but there is something about it that I sort of like (as the aroma of my own flatulence is vaguely intoxicating), because the smell of dead mouse means, at last, that the mouse is dead.

I am terrified of mice. I hate them. Everything about them. But especially I hate the noise. The scratching, the banging in the walls. Like fingernails on a chalkboard, but much, much worse. Whoever came up with the *quiet-as-a-mouse* simile was also probably the astute author of *slept like a baby.* Mice are fucking *loud*, you dipshit, and while we're at it, babies wake up all night long. As I well know.

When I first heard them in the walls, for a good month I was paralyzed with fear, like something out of Poe. I slept with the light on whenever Stacy was away. I made sure Steve was nearby, preferably curled up at my feet, for protection. On more than one occasion I actually did whisky shots to calm my nerves (not recommended: instant headache, and I had to get up three times during the night to pee).

Over the years, I've become more inured to the mouse problem. The scratching is more expected, and therefore not as debilitating. My musophobia has gone from a ten to maybe an eight-point-five. I can function now, when I hear them. But it's difficult, almost impossible, for me to relax. Because as soon as I hear a noise, any noise not immediately identifiable, even if it isn't mouse-generated, even if it's the heater and I *know* it's the heater, I start, every fiber of my body standing at attention. And should the source of the noise be confirmed as rodentine, heaven forbid, this triggers the burglar alarm in my soul. Adrenaline surges through me, the fight-or-flight enzyme or whatever it is, and, although I'm vaguely hard of hearing most of the time—to the degree that Stacy gets annoyed with me almost every day because I can't hear her from down the hall when she asks me to take out the garbage, check on Maude, feed the cat—I'm suddenly a sophisticated sonar device. The navy could install me on a submarine. And I lie there, on Def-Con One, unable to stop myself, and I listen. And when you're on guard like that, good luck sleeping.

Yes, I know. Mice are harmless. Mice are cute. Mice are mammals, like us. They care for their young and blah blah blah. This is presumably why children's literature is populated by—we might even say *infested with*—so many mice. Mickey, Minnie, Mighty, Maisy, Jerry, Wemberly Worried, Stuart Little. Hickory, dickory, dock, the mouse ran up the clock. Goodnight little house, and goodnight mouse. Not a creature was stirring, not even a mouse. Leaving crumbs much too small for the other Whos' mouses. Would you eat them in a house? Would you eat them with a mouse? No fucking way, Seuss—and what kind of doctor are you, tormenting me like that?

One time Stacy and I were driving up near Woodstock—this was before we moved upstate—and we came around a bend to find a deer on the highway. I was behind the wheel, doing sixty-five at least, and the deer was directly in our path. Cucumber-cool, John

Wayne in a showdown, I looked that deer straight in the eye and said *Don't you move now*, and I swerved around him, and we were all fine. Me, Stacy, the deer. All safe. But Stacy was in the passenger seat screaming. Two hours later, she was still freaked about the near miss. My pulse didn't even quicken. I don't know why or how, but I *knew* I wasn't going to hit the deer. I wasn't afraid at all, not even a little bit, and I probably should have been. My theory is that people who have extreme phobias, like me, they take all the excess fear they repress from instances when they should be scared, and they transfer all of it onto the object of the fear. So I wasn't scared about almost dying in a car crash, just like I wasn't scared on the streets of lower Manhattan on 9/11, or on the plane to Paris when lightning struck the wing and even the flight attendant puked. All of the residual fear that a normal person would experience at those perfectly appropriate moments, all of that, for me, is thrust on the miniscule shoulders of the *Mus musculus*—the tiny, harmless rodent who wants nothing more than a few crumbs of bread and a warm place to make a nest for its young. The brown mouse, my green Kryptonite.

Mice brought Stacy and me together. Sort of.

After years of secondary-citizen status in Hoboken, I was finally living in Manhattan, in my own shithole studio on Twenty-eighth Street and Lexington Avenue, right above two bodegas. (If I got home late enough, I could see the end-of-shift hookers buying bagels at the corner deli—Twenty-eighth and Lex was, unbeknownst to me, a prime spot for streetwalking.) My apartment, as it turned out, was a fucking mouse BQE, a West Side Highway of little furry critters. I didn't know this consciously, not at first, but I *knew*. Mice scurried about my subconscious, squeaked into my dreams. My dormant musophobia, which I'd acquired as a child, went into overdrive. But I never heard them, never found droppings, nothing. Then one night I came home late—it was almost two—and saw a couple of them flitting around my floor lamp. And I flipped out.

Panic attack, or close to. I almost passed out. I wouldn't have fled the apartment faster if there'd been a dead body in the room, leaking blood all over the area rug. I hopped in a cab, went to Stacy's place in the East Village, rang her buzzer, and pleaded with her to let me spend the night. I was crazed. I must have sounded like a lunatic. We were dating, by then we had even dropped the L-bomb, but this was still early enough in the relationship that it could have deep-sixed the whole thing. Who wants a partner who's *that* afraid of a measly mouse? She let me in, God bless her, and I climbed into her queen-sized bed, flanked by her two cats—Steve and the dearly departed Joni—and I've been there ever since. The turning point in our relationship, really. Because of a mouse.

When I confessed my musophobia to Rob, our erstwhile therapist, he suggested that the next time I hear mice in the walls, I imagine myself in their shoes. If, you know, they were wearing shoes. I've tried that. The mouse I imagine is wearing a leather jacket and a fedora and carries a whip, like Indiana Jones. He's navigating the warren of passageways in the bedroom wall, trying to find his way out. Rounding a corner, he finds an enormous chamber, like one of the anterooms in the bowels of the Great Pyramid. And in this chamber is a towering pile of mouse skeletons. All of his predecessors, their decomposed arms still scratching futilely to freedom, still searching for the elusive way out, for the Ark of the Covenant that is the portal to the bedroom proper. And that mouse knows his time is up. He knows he's a goner.

So here I am, exactly three thirty-three in the morning, the dark night of the soul and all, lying on my back, covers wrapped around me like Kevlar, listening to the mice scratch, and Steve the cat scratch back, and I'm trying to focus on the lead rodent dressed like Harrison Ford, which should be a comical enough image to soothe most people, but no, I'm a wreck.

I hate being awake in the middle of the night when the kids are asleep. I hate being awake in the middle of the night *period*, but when I'm not up to fulfill fatherly duties, that *really* drives me bonkers. It's like I haven't had sex in months, and then suddenly I'm in bed with a naked and nymphomaniacal Kardashian sister (preferably Kim, but any of them would do; even Khloé, although she sort of looks like a guy in drag), but I've just whacked off, so I can't get it up. The opportunity is blown—and nothing else.

Speaking of whacking off and a naked and nymphomaniacal Kardashian sister . . . my wife is in L.A. I have the bedroom to myself. I'm free to make like Bloom at Sandymount Strand. Should I take the situation in hand and fight fear with lust? I don't often have the opportunity to rub one out right before bed, like I did every day of my life between age twelve, when that seminal gift of the gods was bequeathed to me, and the day I moved in with Stacy fifteen years later. Sweet release might calm my nerves . . . but no, I'm not feeling it. There are two essential ingredients for a climactic climax: 1) a backlog of shall-we-say raw material, and 2) an inspirational scenario to fuel the *come on baby light my fire* imagination. I beat off six hours ago, so my reserves are depleted. But even that was a chore—my imagination and last week's *Us Weekly* (thanks for the memories, Heidi Montag) only go so far. There is nothing happening to feed that part of me, nothing at all. I'm a summer house that's been shut down for the winter. I'm a fallow field. I'm dull roots and dried tubers.

Meanwhile the mice keep scratching.

Stacy has vivid dreams almost every night, the sort of crazy, densely packed-with-detail dreams on which Jungian disciples—like Rob—could write full dissertations. Every morning (as I'm pouring my second cup of coffee, but before the caffeine from the first has completely kicked in) she tells me, "Oh my God, I had the *craziest* dream last night." And every morning she's right, because each succeeding dream is, in fact, far loopier than its predecessor. As if the inner director of her subconscious—a cross between Fellini and David Lynch, but under the influence of some

CIA lab–concocted hallucinogen—were constantly trying to one-up herself.

If her dreams are *8½* and *Wild At Heart* on industrial-grade acid, mine are unedited raw footage of a C-SPAN feed from the Senate floor on a slow day. They could not be more dull. The palette is all earth tones: browns, grays, faded blues; the color scheme of a Banana Republic catalog from the late eighties. I'm usually a) wandering lost around some Manhattan-that-isn't-really-Manhattan, trying to meet friends who never appear, b) in the HR-office-that-isn't-really-the-HR-office of News Corp., my old place of employ, where I have not set foot in almost five years, fretting about a job posting that I've done incorrectly, or c) stepping away from whatever lame-ass dream-action might be happening in order to find the men's room and relieve the Johnstown Dam–like pressure in my bladder, only to find new ways to have this mission thwarted (urinal is too small, bathroom is locked, stage fright brought on by professional wrestler standing next to me impedes flow, etc.). Most of the time I don't remember my dreams at all, and when I do, they're not worth remembering.

But check this:

I'm in a living room—it's supposed to be the green room on some talk show, *Colbert* I think, or maybe *Letterman* . . . I'm the guest, *Babylon Is Fallen* has been made and is a surprise hit, I'm a Golden Globe screenwriting nominee, maybe even an Oscar contender, I'm vaguely famous, way more desirable than in real life; it's the (ha ha) Dream Me—but it's actually the den at Meg and Soren's house. There are two couches, not matching, at a ninety-degree angle, one on each wall. I'm sitting by myself on the longer couch, all the way to the right, in the corner of the room. On the other couch are a few people, girls I think, whom I can't identify. Maybe they're the *Suicide Girl*–pictorial SUNY coeds, all piercings and tats, who work the counter at the Convenient Deli. I'm not sure. But they all rise as this stunner makes a grand entrance. The newcomer has long blonde hair, straight with bangs, like Jenny Lewis, or Feist, or perhaps Janel Moloney from *The West Wing*, but she's not someone I recognize. I can't really see her face. She sits down next to me in such a way that her skirt—a short skirt, off-white—hikes up, and I can see her white silk panties and her white silk stockings, and the thin white line of the garter running down six inches of bare white leg. I reach out and touch what I see, and I can feel everything—the smooth, almost-cold silk, the heat radiating from her leg, the little ridge where the strap bisects the warm peach-pink flesh. She lifts herself up slightly, so my palm can further slide beneath her ass, and lets out a soft moan. I lean closer to her, my eyes not straying from that glorious patch of leg.

And then, *story of my life*, I wake up. Or rather, am woken up.

"States!" comes the voice from the baby monitor, holding out the long *a* as if singing. "Daddy! I need my states!"

I squint at the clock: 5:03.

Jesus Fucking Christ.

I must have fallen asleep, mouse soundtrack or not. The way I feel—hung over, but without the preceding alcoholic reverie; headache, dry mouth, general lethargy—I almost wish I hadn't.

"States!"

I drag my ass out of bed and haul it up the stairs. Our house is a Cape Cod, with the master bedroom at ground level. Both kids sleep on the second floor, separated by a tiny hallway and bathroom; the noise doesn't travel much from room to room, and Maude has slept through fireworks displays, but I hustle anyway so she doesn't wake up. One kid this early I can handle. Two? Please God no. I burst into my son's bedroom.

Roland sits on his bed, legs crossed like an Oxford undergraduate's, his left foot rotating like a ceiling fan in one of his *Lamps Plus* catalogs, reading a thick grown-up architecture tome I bought him last year at Barnes & Noble, *A Field Guide to American Houses* (which *American Libraries* hails as—get this—"the definitive field guide to American homes."). His hair, now at the midpoint between the white-blond he was born with and the sandy brown it will one day become, and cut in the pixieish style popular in our crunchily hip town, poofs up to such a degree that his (handsome, much more so than his old man's) face appears too small for his head. The light by the door is on, as usual—he won't sleep without a light on anymore; monsters—but the pendant light over the bed (a present for good behavior) is still off, so he's reading small print in the dark. Spread out in front of him on the bed is an oversized Rand McNally road atlas of the United States. What he likes to do is cross-reference; he matches the location of the houses in the *Field Guide* (as he calls it, with emphasis on the second word)—Cleveland, Ohio; Louisville, Kentucky; New Albany, Indiana; Rolla, Missouri—to the respective dot or yellowed area on the roadmap.

He won't turn five for two more months.

Littered about the room, among pages torn from the *Field Guide* and various lighting catalogs and maps, as well as countless pieces of myriad toys—Lincoln Logs, Tinkertoys, Legos, bristle blocks, Trios, Thomas tracks, Thomas engines, Playmobil accessories, and a few neglected dolls we got him to encourage pretend play—are foam-rubber pieces from a giant puzzle of the United States (for purposes of scale, Wyoming is about the size of a Pop-Tart). Roland is obsessed with states in general, as evidenced by his cross-referencing game, and these states in particular. He plays with them as if they're dolls—"What are you doing there, Connecticut?" he'll ask. Texas and Alaska, I notice, are now stuffed into the bedroom of one of his dollhouses. He sleeps with the states at night, like Maude does with her stuffed animals. On those rare occasions when he actually assembles the puzzle, he insists on placing the states in alphabetical order—Alabama is first, then Alaska, and so on—and he'll often stack them that way. He knows them in that order because my sister sang a state song for him, two months ago, that rattles off all fifty in alphabetical order. She couldn't have sung it more than a handful of times—she was only up for the day—but he knows it cold. He never gets the order wrong, never even pauses to think about what comes after Delaware.

"Some of my states are downstairs," Roland says, by way of greeting. His eyes are aimed in my general vicinity, but he's not really looking at me. "Louisiana, West Virginia, Maryland, California . . ."

Florida. That's what comes after Delaware: Florida. There are no "E" states.

"And this was worth waking me up for?" I say this for my own benefit; he doesn't pick up on sarcasm. One of the useful symptoms of his complaint, for a father who likes to crack wise—I don't have to worry about him catching on.

"Maude brought down Maryland," he informs me. "I brought down Louisiana and California. Then Maude brought down West Virginia."

"I have to get my coffee," I tell him, tiptoeing my way across the tornado's-been-through-it mess of his room and flipping on the pendant lamp. "You have to put the light on when you read, okay? It's bad for your eyes to read in the dark."

If he hears this, there's no indication. "And the states!" At last he looks me in the eye, although there's something ever-so-slightly off about his gaze; making direct eye contact for him is the equivalent of me holding a difficult yoga pose. "Bring the states, you stupid Daddy."

I should probably reprimand him for calling me stupid, but he doesn't really mean it, and I'm too tired, and anyway, he's not exactly wrong.

"Relax, would ya? Keep it down. I'll bring the states, I'll bring the states."

I go back downstairs to the living room, where, in a sloppy half-pile on the couch, I find California, Louisiana, West Virginia, and Maryland. I bring them back to his room, where I leave Roland, now quiet and clam-at-high-tide happy, with fifty-four puzzle pieces (forty-nine states plus five Great Lakes; Massachusetts went missing last week, probably due to his habit of hiding pieces in his room and promptly forgetting where he's put them). My brain attempts to formulate a joke about how, since my son is such a "statesman," that must make me a Founding Father, but without the caffeine, it just won't come.

THE WORST PART ABOUT WAKING UP LIKE THIS IS NOT BEING ABLE to lie in bed for the nine extra minutes alarm clocks allocate for snoozing and reflect on my dreams. While my dream life, as mentioned, is about as rich and fulfilling as my sex life—so much for compensation—if I'm not consciously aware of what my subconscious was working out when I pass from one state to the other *I couldn't pee because the urinal was in a little room with a four-foot ceiling and I couldn't stand up, right, now I remember, let's move on*, I am left with the naggingly unpleasant sensation that I've forgotten something important, and, often, a headache that all the coffee beans in Colombia can't dislodge.

This morning, in particular, I'd like to process my dream. Who was the woman in white? Why were we at Meg and Soren's house? Wherefore the fixation on the garter? And, most importantly, what does it all mean? If I were still seeing Rob, I'd bring this to the next session, but if there is to be a next session, it will be next month, next year, next decade, some magical time when the Lansky ledger is back in the black—and frankly, when the Lansky ledger is back in the black, I don't think I'll be needing therapy. No, I'm on my own with this one.

Josh's Law of Dream Analysis, which stunning accuracy belies its illicit birth as a dormroom joke, goes like this: if your dream is about sex, it's *not* about sex; if it's *not* about sex . . . it's about *sex*. Because, you know, your subconscious likes to fuck with you. But Josh's Law does not apply here. My subconscious is not fucking with me this time. Sex is as sex does. The cigar in this dream, Dr. Freud, is just that: a big fat Romeo y Julieta maduro clamped between the yellowed and feral chompers of Fidel Castro. The cigar is a cigar.

. . .

***Soren Knudsen** can't remember last night.*

He updated his status at 4:08 a.m. EST—a little over an hour ago. Already he can't remember? How much hootch did he drink?

***Ruth Terry** great article*

with a link to Bob Herbert's latest *Times* diatribe.

I'm gonna go out on a limb here and predict that Bob Herbert is grousing about Republicans.

***Gloria Gallagher Hynek** and **Brady List** are now friends.*

Here's what you're in for, Brady List, whoever you are: liberal use of the LIKE button, oft-shared YouTube links to grainy live sets by unloved grunge bands, and frequent updates involving Haven that speak of the towheaded lad as if he were the Messiah. Enjoy.

In addition to tending to the insatiable needs of two preschoolers (sippy cup of watered-down apple juice, Z-bar and/or bagel with cream cheese, Noggin On Demand) and a vociferously greedy and shrill cat (Friskies Buffet, release into the pitch-black yard), the following elements comprise my pre-dawn hours: coffee, Facebook, fetch the newspaper (if it's there), horoscope, more coffee, e-mail, glass of water, bathroom, more coffee, bagel, another glass of water, Facebook, e-mail, bathroom, shower. The order sometimes changes, and the shower is often sacrificed for expediency, especially when Stacy is away, as she is, for the fifth *Fifth! The very word screams for hard liquor* morning in a row. But coffee is always first. Coffee is paramount. When parents pray to the God of Easy Mornings, the burnt offerings are roasted coffee beans.

Ceramic tiles cold on my bare feet, I scoop the ground manna into the Proctor Silex, pour the water (the dishwasher attachment doohickey saves me the trouble of first filling the pot), hit the magic button. There is a timer mechanism, but any time I've tried to use it, I've set it for the wishful-thinking hour of six o'clock, only to have to start it manually well before that; setting the timer on the coffee maker is the wake-up equivalent of mentioning a no-hitter in the seventh. I stumble into the bedroom, fall into my faux-leather desk chair, and return to the laptop.

Jennifer Hemsworth is in a relationship, and it's complicated.
That's understating things.

Mike DiLullo became a fan of The Colbert Report.
Wow, Mike, way to take a stand.

Simone Smithson hope heaven is peacefully cause I'm sick of crap.
I'm right there with you, Simone, [sic] and all.

Outside the window, a black abyss. Only my faint reflection in a pane well-fingerprinted by tiny hands. Steve is still asleep, curled into a ball—a hairball, if you will—at the foot of the bed. The mice, mercifully, have moved on. Through the baby monitor I can hear, in the "East Wing" of the upstairs, Roland banging around with some or other toy, probably his Thomas tracks, judging by the clatter and the proximity to the microphone; in Maude's room, all quiet on the Western Front. I should probably jump in the shower now, while I have a fighting chance, but no, not without the coffee.

Sharon Rothman was tagged in an album.
Wow. Her hair was big, back in the day.

Matt Harris just barely has enough sense to not download and start playing a new video game at 2 a.m.

Michelle Strange just beat Laurence Rand in Three Towers Solitaire.

Unless you have a Sibylline personality disorder, how can you beat someone else in solitaire? It's been a while since I took French, but doesn't *solitaire* imply *solitude*? Isn't the point to beat yourself? (Right-click, hide updates from Three Towers Solitaire. I'm a big fan of the HIDE feature, a huge concession in the historic treaty that ended the *Mafia Wars*.)

Eugenia Last is a syndicated astrologer. In the picture they run with her column in the *Poughkeepsie Journal*—which won't be deposited on my driveway until six thirty or so; I'm on her website now—she is attractive, with long, kinky blonde hair and the Slavic features (wide, flat face; tiny eyes) she shares with Debbie Harry, Neko Case, Michelle Pfeiffer, and my friend Meg. Eugenia's New Age bona fides are impeccable. Every morning, she offers up her oracular wisdom, and, while lesser pliers of the zodiacal trade fall wide of the mark, damn if she's not bang-on most of the time. When Eugenia Last proclaims a five-star day, the heavens will smile upon you . . . but if she metes out the minimum two, you'd best go back to bed.

Raising the ceramic chalice of the Mud of Christ to my unworthy lips, I take my first sip of coffee—a perfect blend of Fair Trade Organic Kenyan Gold, light cream, and Splenda, in a well-stained Clifford-the-Big-Red-Dog-sized World's Greatest Dad mug—scroll down the page, and receive cyber-auspices from my kinky-haired prophetess:

> SCORPIO *(Oct. 22–Nov. 21): You will have difficulty following through with your plans. Expect disruptions, delays and last-minute changes. A change in the way you feel about someone can lead to a breakup. You will gravitate toward someone more compatible and less restrictive. Two stars.*

Okay, then. A suck-ass blurb *and* two stars. For the third day in a row, I might add. Fucking bonanza. On the plus side, both Roland and Maude (and Stacy, because the two ladies in my life are both Virgos) have four stars. Twice my celestial bounty. Perhaps their luck will rub off on me? If not, there's always *the sun will come out* tomorrow, which, after three two-star days in a row, is almost guaranteed *bet your bottom dollar* to yield five stars. All I have to do is survive today, and I'll be alright. *It's only a day away.*

Stacy Ferguson Lansky *Zzzzzzzzzzzzzzzzz . . .*

Well put, honey. Updated at 2:03 a.m. Just after eleven, California time. Right after we last spoke.

Todd Lander *became a fan of Duran Duran.*

Sue Wilson Amorosi *is glad to see wonderful postings from friends today, including this one that I need to remember: Let all bitterness and wrath and anger and clamor and slander be put away from you, along with all malice. Be kind to one another, tender-hearted, forgiving each other, just as God in Christ also has forgiven you. Ephesians 4:31–32*

Easier said than done, St. Paulie Boy. Easier said than done.

As I polish off the first cup of coffee, I set about composing my own status update, a practice I regard with the same solemnity that Obama does the drafting of an executive order.

Josh Lansky *has a two-star day. I hope Eugenia Last is wrong.*

Josh Lansky *up at 5:03 am. Again.*

Josh Lansky *Day Five of The Ordeal.*

No, no, no.

I hate when I want to update my status and can't figure out what to say. They should have a Sniglet for that. Wait . . .

Josh Lansky *Not Necessarily the News.*

Definitely not feeling it this morning. Chalk one up for Eugenia.

Again I consider a shower—almost-scalding water streaming down the back of my pinkening neck is the closest I'll get to a spa vacation until Maude is at Vassar, or whatever overpriced liberal arts school she winds up majoring in English at—but I decide that caffeine intake is more exigent on the priority list, so I pour a refill. Why does the second cup never taste as good as the first? Would it help if I made a fresh pot? Or used a fresh mug? Diminishing returns.

Half past five now. Still pitch black outside, not even the hint of morning. Nosferatu still on the clock, and Bill from *True Blood.*

Emily Hoyt *killed Nya in Vampire Wars. Emily has a kill record of 83.*

I wonder if eighty-three is good or bad. There's no context for us non–vampire warriors. It doesn't *seem* impressive . . . unless, of course, Emily has staked the hearts of eighty-three real people.

Becky Stack *If my liver survives this week, I'm totally taking it out for beer.*

It would prefer a Jack and Coke.

Jessica Holby *Up early with Emma and Maddie & looking fwd 2 the playdate.*

Better hit the LIKE button. Facebook etiquette. Emily Post would advise hitting the LIKE button when the hostess of a playdate you're attending updates her status to trumpet said playdate. Even if the hostess is too lazy to write out "to."

• • •

I open Outlook, another of my constant companions. I am a compulsive inbox checker. I pound the SEND/RECEIVE button like a Skinnerian rat on the plunger in one of those Eisenhower-era, pre-PETA psychology experiments in which many animals were harmed. More e-mails! More messages! More information! More more more! But when I get actual notes from people, from friends I haven't heard from in a while, from my drinking buddies in New York, from my housemates from college, I let them twist in the inbox wind. I fail to respond. I have a mental block about writing back—probably because I have nothing to say, no self-aggrandizing news to share, no humble pie to serve up. Invariably they ask how the screenwriting "biz" is doing (in no other line of work do people employ that term), if I've sold another script, when we might see *Babylon Is Fallen* playing at a theater near you. While my stock reply—*George Clooney is interested*—is not completely untrue (although the *is*, by now, is probably more accurately expressed as *was*), what I don't elaborate on is that his interest is—that his interest *was*—directly proportional to the willingness of a studio to pour tens of millions of dollars into the project. Actors are the face of Hollywood, but they don't call the shots, literally or figuratively. They're like the British royal family—all pomp, no power. But this is moot. I haven't even opened Final Draft, my screenwriting software, in a good year, and that was to try my hand at a vampire thriller, an exercise in cranking out schlock. What can I tell my friends? That I've given up the ghost? No, better to stay silent, cultivate some mystique.

The hamster spins in the wheel of my aging laptop, and Outlook finally opens. Unlikely that I've gotten any notices since I last checked, what, six hours ago . . . but no, I'm wrong. Not one but *two* new messages. Two! Jackpot. The first one is . . . an offer for *c!@lis*? Jesus. How does this shit make it through the spam filter? And why? Does anyone really open the e-mail, or, God forbid, click the link? Let me rephrase: is anyone stupid enough to click the link? Odds are, this isn't a legitimate offer for knock-off Cialis, but a Trojan horse virus from some bellicose Bulgarian computer programmer, some rogue Russian cyberterrorist, al-Qaeda online. The Biblical tale of Judith, reenacted virtually. An offer of e-sex yielding only e-STDs. The thing is, I don't want Cialis, generic or otherwise. I'd be more interested in the anti-Cialis, the un-Viagra, a magic philter that compels the snail to retract into its shell, that transfers the frequent flier miles of my carnal desire to other, more useful, accounts. *Origen*, call it. Wisest philosopher in all of history. Now this is enlightenment: lust is a waste of time.

***Lawrence Richards** Lawrence has been to Des Moines on the Cities I've Visited travel map.*
I can't think of a less interesting piece of information to share.

***Christine Rowan** needs a sublettor at her UWS apartment for January, February, and March.*
Ah, to sublet that apartment! To return to the city! Upper West Side, Upper East Side, Red Hook, Bed fucking Stuy. Anywhere but here. Just me and the undersized refrigerator like the one in my apartment on Twenty-Eighth Street that froze its contents solid in a few hours. That made Diet Coke cans explode. That laid waste to yogurt. Would have to bring Steve with me, though, to ward off the mice. Maybe New York is not such a good idea. There are no snakes in Ireland, they say. Is there a place on earth devoid of mice? Antarctica, maybe? Greenland? Death Valley?

***Meg Stein Knudsen** became a fan of Deborah Schneer for Ulster County Judge.*
Updated a minute ago. Not quite six a.m. She's up early. And Meg is *not* a morning person. Which, coupled with Soren's drunk-dialed update, can only mean one thing: trouble brewing *chez* Knudsen. Juicy gossip for later, perhaps?

Behind Door #2, an electronic mail message from . . . Christine Keeslar? Holy shit. Christine Keeslar is the editor-in-chief of *Rents Maga-*

zine. Rents, a slangy truncation of *Parents*. I pitched her a story a few days ago—a stay-at-home dad's take on playdates, I think it was . . . or maybe a memoir on why we decided not to circumcise our son, despite pressure from my mother and the medical community. I've pitched her so many stories, I've lost track. Freelancing is the only way I could possibly eke out a living up here without going back to school. In typical me fashion, I'm trying to jumpstart my freelancing career at the exact moment when half of the country's seasoned journalists have all been laid off and are doing the exact same thing. How does Eugenia Last put it on her website? *Psst . . . the Secret to Success, Wealth, and Happiness is . . . Timing.*

I don't know why I bother trying; it's not like Christine Keeslar bothers with rejection letters. So far, she's just ignored my e-mails. And I certainly didn't expect her to acknowledge my existence this time. What the hell did I even pitch? I honestly can't remember. Elimination communication? Free-range parenting? My short-term memory is fried. I blame the kids.

Hi, Josh.

We'd love to run an interview with Daryl "Duke" Reid. Will be interesting to get his take on parenting, as he seems an unlikely candidate for Father of the Year.

Keep it to 500 words. We need it by November 14, and we can pay $300. Please let me know if you accept.

All best,
Chris

Christine Keeslar
Editor-in-Chief
Rents Magazine

Oh, right. Daryl "Duke" Reid. Now I remember.

November 14. My thirty-seventh birthday. A little gift from the gods! Take those two stars, Eugenia, and stick 'em where the sun don't shine.

I write back at once, something to the effect of *Thanks, I accept, looking forward to working with you*. While the e-mail constitutes good news, for sure, this particular rose at my doorstep comes with a fresh thorn of a problem: how to get access to Daryl "Duke" Reid. Just because he lives in New Paltz and both of us have kids at the Thornwood Education Center doesn't mean he'll grant me an interview. Or acknowledge my existence.

But hey—at least I know WHAT'S ON YOUR MIND:

Josh Lanksy Rents Magazine accepted my pitch!

Within seconds, Meg Stein Knudsen, Jessica Holby, and Gloria Gallagher Hynek all LIKE THIS.

WE MOVED HERE DURING BUSH'S SECOND TERM, WHEN TENSIONS between the Blue and the Red were at their peak. We didn't know a single person in New Paltz, but we moved here anyway. It was a long time coming. When we lived in the East Village, Stacy and I, like most New York City Bohemians (or wannabe Bohemians; New York hasn't been a true boho town since the heyday of the Yiddish theater on the Lower East Side; thirty dollars hasn't paid the rent on Bleecker Street in my lifetime, Paul Simon), operated under the assumption that, with the possible and debatable exceptions of Los Angeles and San Francisco, the part of the United States extending beyond a twenty-mile radius of Union Square was populated in the main by subliterate, slack-jawed, Walmart-shopping, country-music-listening, Jesus-loving, gay-bashing hicks. The old saw about what happens when you assume applies here. Kingston, the artsy Ulster County seat, is Williamsburg without the hipsters, and the eighty thousand people who flocked to Central Park to see Garth Brooks a few years ago were not all from out of town. There are cool people beyond the boundaries of Manhattan, just as there are plenty of New Yorkers, Lord knows, whose coolness is in short supply (we have a name for them up here, über-urbane urbanites who assume the rest of us are rubes: *citiots*). We just didn't acknowledge this when we lived there.

Or maybe we did, and chose to ignore the signs. In order to accept the dreary and oppressive conditions of life in Manhattan, or even Park Slope or Astoria—in a city where five million dollars is not enough to buy an apartment all that much bigger than the one you live in—you need to drink the Big Apple–flavored Kool-Aid. You must bow to the false idol that is the god of Gotham. As Born Agains evince a faith in Christ's salvation that borders on the delusional, so a not terribly successful screenwriter-cum-HR-generalist and a not terribly successful actress-cum-marketing-manager who pay two grand for six hundred square feet of squalid living space five elevatorless flights above the ground-level grime must rationalize this prohibitive expense by believing absolutely that New York is an Artist's Paradise, and the rest of the nation so many benighted circles of Limbaughian hell.

It took the birth of our son for us to see things for how they really are, to recognize that the Empire State emperor was, and always had been, butt naked. In just six weeks—six cold, dead-of-winter weeks—we went from *We could have two kids in this apartment* to *Let's get the fuck out of here*. Roland was born on Christmas; by Valentine's Day, we were househunting in New Paltz. The charms the city offered, so alluring to us as childless thirty-somethings—conveniently placed casting calls, movies opening two weeks earlier than anywhere else, the theater, fine dining, the only-in-New-York personalities teeming into the IRT, the ability to drink copious amounts of alcohol without having to worry about driving home—held no appeal for us as new parents. To raise kids, you need space, safety, good schools, fresh air, and a roomy car, none of which are readily or cheaply available in Gotham. When you're wearing your infant son in a Baby Björn, the only-in-New-York subway lunatic becomes not so colorful.

My friends were stunned when I relayed the news. *We're moving to New Paltz*, I told them, my group of New York drinking buddies, a hodge-podge of comrades from high school, college, and the city, loosely affiliated by a bi-monthly beer night. They didn't get it. Noo Yawkers never do, especially residents by choice rather than birth. I should know; I was just as gung-ho once, the notion of escaping just as unfathomable to me. Why would anyone want to leave nirvana? Aside from, you know, the crime and the grime and the mice and the noise and the price tag and the claustrophobia and the all-permeating negative energy, the volcanic Bad Vibe that seems to seep up from the abysmal warren of overheated subterranean tunnels. *The snow doesn't stick on the streets of New York . . . because it's so close to Hell.* I could have told my friends I was leaving to enter rabbinical school; they wouldn't have been more shocked. They were still in Lady Liberty's dastardly and delusional thrall.

And none of my city friends had—or, indeed, have—kids. Some of them aren't even married. It's impossible to adequately convey to someone on the outside the radical level of change that takes place when you cross that threshold from childlessness to parenthood, especially to someone living in the bubble of arrested adolescence that is the East Village. Every aspect of your life is altered, forever. It's like pre-9/11 and post-9/11. Nothing—*nothing*—remains the same.

New Paltz? Why there, *of all places?* That was the next question, once it sunk in that I wasn't pulling their collective leg, that my intention to skip town was sincere. Start with this: a rare combination of affordable houses and nationally ranked schools. Vibrant, activist, communal community. Top-notch restaurants. Plus, this is a college town—SUNY maintains a campus here known for its fine arts program—and college towns always have a youthful energy. But the clincher was that, at the time, then mayor Jason West, of the Green Party, was performing same-sex marriages at Village Hall, in blatant disregard for state and federal law. We figured that any town whose mayor could so audaciously, and in our view so heroically, champion gay rights—heck, any town that installed a member of the Green Party in City Hall to begin with—must have a low hick-factor.

And so it does. In New Paltz, pretty much everyone drives a Subaru with at least one sticker of leftist sentiment crookedly festooned to its bumper. This is a bluer locale than even Manhattan, which is, at last, a city of bankers. Where better than Crunchtown to wait out the last days of Bush-Cheney? To wit: in the election returns last November, Obama smoked McCain by 5,360 to 1,274. Had Gore gotten anything close to those results in a few precincts in Florida or Ohio, the world would be a vastly different place.

But it was not to be. The alternate reality where Gore takes the White House feels as distant and foreign as the alternate reality where Stacy and I are childless residents of the East Village. The former never existed, thanks to the Supreme Court; the latter may as well not have.

"DADDY," COMES MAUDE'S STENTORIAN VOICE FROM THE MONItor, just as I'm about to step into the shower, "I want to watch TV." She has the personality of a despot, at times, and the voice to match.

Although Maude speaks well for a three-and-a-half-year-old—her prosody and vocabulary are excellent—she resists dropping the vestigial whine of her toddlerhood. *Daddy, I want to watch TV* is delivered in a voice halfway between a baby's bawling and the King's English, as if her native and preferred tongue, Crying, manifests itself in an accent she can't quite shake, like Keanu Reeves trying to play an Englishman in *Bram Stoker's Dracula*. As with Reeves, the effect is grating.

Another facet of Maude in the morning: she doesn't wake up gradually. When she comes to, she's as alert as I would be after three cups of coffee. She's like a laptop on sleep mode—flip it open and the applications are still running, Firefox displaying the Facebook feed, iTunes paused in the middle of "Rehab," unfinished Solitaire game going: just how you left it. If you tell Maude before she goes to bed that she can have a lollipop if she has a good night's sleep, the first thing she'll say when she opens her eyes ten hours later is *Where's my lolly?* Nothing gets past her—nothing. She could work the homicide desk with McNulty and Bunk. This is in stark contrast to Roland, who will put a *Lamps Plus* catalog on the table in front of him, pause to look out the window, and then start crying because he can't find the *Lamps Plus* catalog.

I jump back into my sweatpants and run up the stairs. By now, Maude's whine-accented speech has reverted to outright crying, and Roland is banging on his door to get out (we have these child safety thingamajigs on the knobs so they can't open their doors, or the lunatics really would run the asylum). I open Roland's door, switch off his noise machine—he bounds into the hallway—open Maude's door, switch off her noise machine, and scoop her up.

"Daddy," she says, and her eyes meet mine so directly, her gaze so intense, she may as well be trying to hypnotize me, "I want to watch TV."

"Good morning to you, too. What do you want to watch?"

"Ummm . . . ummmm . . ." She does this a lot, filling in the space as she decides.

"*Yo Gabba Gabba!*?"

"No! Not *Yo Gabba Gabba!* I don't want to watch *Yo Gabba Gabba! ever again*."

Kids have no concept of time. *Ever again, forever, yesterday, tomorrow, last year, next month*—none of these terms have any real meaning to a child, especially a three-year-old. Sometimes you can use this to your advantage. *Sure,* you can say, *we'll go there tomorrow.* Or, *We'll buy the new Lego set next week*. So few arrows in the parental quiver—important to use the full comportment of weaponry at your disposal, however meager their power (and however deceptive their advertising).

"But Daddy," says Roland, "*I* want to watch *Yo Gabba Gabba!* What's for me? *What's for me?*"

"We'll watch something you both want to watch," I tell him.

This isn't good enough. He spins around, rage ruddying his cheeks, and swats at me with both arms. "No! I don't like that. I don't like sisters. I don't want Maudes. No Maudes allowed here. I'm *mad* at her!"

He swoops by her like a bird of prey, arms extended, smacking her on the head as he races by.

"Roland," I holler. "Stop it. Jesus Christ."

My swearing has increased both in frequency and severity with each day of Stacy's absence. Today's over-under on "F-bombs With a Child in Earshot" is five. Especially if we drive around a lot. The whole "blinker" concept is not much known in these parts.

"Stupid Christ," he shouts, as I suppress giggling at his botched attempt to swear. Then he gets one right: "Stupid Daddy."

Ignoring him—this is, after all, not unusual behavior—I turn to Maude. "*LazyTown*?"

"No. I want to watch . . . ummm . . . *Max & Ruby*."

Figures she'd pick the show I dislike the most. That's her job as a kid, right, developing tastes antithetical to mine? Rankling my sensibilities? I shudder for the teenage years. I really hope the whole tattoo fad is done by then. "Does that work for you, Roland? *Max & Ruby*?"

He lets out an exaggerated sigh, but calms down, like a possessed villager post-exorcism. "O-kay," he says.

Catastrophe averted.

"Let's go down. I'll make bagels."

"I don't like bagels!"

Noggin, the more or less commercial-free cable station programmed for little tykes *it's like preschool on TV*, in an apparent attempt to assuage your guilt for plopping your pride and joy in front of the zombie box, displays, before each offering, infographics that extol the educational virtues of the show you're about to suffer through.

Max & Ruby, for example, which concerns the diurnal goings-on of a pair of corpulent bunnies, a bratty two-year-old (the former) and his prissy seven-year-old sister (the latter) who doubles as his de facto legal guardian, *enhances preschoolers' understanding of* INTER- *and* INTRAPERSONAL DYNAMICS.

LazyTown, featuring the athlete/superhero Sportacus, Iceland's second most important export after Björk, *enhances preschoolers' understanding of* KINESTHETIC SKILLS *and awareness of* HEALTHFUL BEHAVIORS.

Yo Gabba Gabba!—the title refers to the incantation D. J. Lance Rock, the orange-garbed host, intones at the top of each episode to bequeath life to his five deformed playthings—*enhances preschoolers'* SOCIAL SKILLS *and* SELF-AWARENESS *and uses interactive games to expand their* MUSICAL *and* KINESTHETIC SKILLS.

And *Olivia*, a show about a family of pigs whom I can't tell apart, and who look, to my jaded East Village eyes, like the blown-up photographs of late-term aborted fetuses the pro-life crazies used to wave around at tourists in Washington Square Park . . . *Olivia*, for the love of God, *enhances preschoolers' understanding of the* CREATIVE THINKING *and imaginative* PROBLEM-SOLVING *that support imaginative play and the development of* INTER- *and* INTRAPERSONAL AWARENESS.

I've heard the porcine program also turns loaves into fishes and helps O. J. find the real killer.

There is a pervasive belief among parents, particularly crunchy parents, which constitute an overwhelming majority in New Paltz—mommies who subscribe to both *Mothering* magazine (*Judgmental Mothering*, as Stacy calls it) and the doctrinaire philosophies therein; mommies who eschew diapers for Elimination Communication; mommies who practice Attachment Parenting; mommies who "fight through" a baby's natural instinct to wean and continue breastfeeding until Little League—a tenet clung to with such zeal that it may as well be a Zen koan, a papal bull, a lost commandment, that TELEVISION IS BAD. High-fructose corn syrup for the eyes. Unfiltered Luckies for the brain. KILL YOUR

TELEVISION is a popular bumper sticker around here, and an even more popular sentiment. *TV, or not TV: that is the question*. When chatting casually on the subject with other Hudson Valley parents, I find myself qualifying, if not outright apologizing for, our decision to let our kids watch TV. If I permit such deleterious activity, you see, I must at least recognize its inherent and unequivocal evil. (Tacit disapproval is still disapproval, and often harder to counter than the explicit variety.) So, the obligatory caveat: I don't think kids should watch adult programs, commercials especially, and I don't think they should spend all the livelong day in front of the boob tube. But I don't see the harm in my kids catching a little Noggin while I gird up for the grueling day. It amuses me to wonder, when Roland wakes up particularly early—four o'clock, three thirty early, as he occasionally does; Asperger kids require less sleep—how these über-parenting zealots would handle him, without the Athenian aid of the TV. What would these Kill Your Televisionaries, what would Gloria Hynek, do with Roland? A fucking *craft*? She would sit and make beaded fucking bracelets with my boy for the three hours till the sun came up? Really?

The truth is, my kids could spend the next half-hour watching the *South Park* movie, and I wouldn't mind, as long as I got to take a shower and they didn't memorize the words to "Shut Your Fucking Face, Uncle Fucker." If that makes me a shitty parent, well, alert Child Services. *That's U-N-C-L-E-Fuck-You*. The number's in the book.

ON THE TOILET, I FLIP YET AGAIN THROUGH LAST WEEK'S WELL-worn *Us Weekly*—the new issue should arrive this afternoon; one of the (sad) highlights of my (pathetic) week—hoping to discover a page that I've missed during seven days of heavy bathroom perusal, but I keep coming back to the same full-page HOT PIC of Gwyneth Paltrow strolling down an unnamed London street, hand-in-hand with her two sickeningly adorable kids, that I've seen about a thousand times since last Friday.

Study these pages long enough, and you discover certain trends. For example: although there are a fair number of Tinseltown Ethans and Madisons, celebrities as a rule prefer outside-the-box names for their spawn. And if you read the tabloids as religiously as I do, you know that there's a fine line between *outside-the-box* and *ridiculous*. Like, Nicolas Cage, who was rumored for years to be playing the eponymous role in a Superman movie, has a son named Kal-El—the Man of Steel's name on the planet where he (and, by all indications, Cage as well) was born.

Kal-fucking-El!

Nicole Kidman and Keith Urban have a daughter named Sunday; she was born on a Saturday. Jenna Elfman has a son named Story. If Story grows up and has a son with the same name, the little guy won't be a junior, but a Second Story; you might say Jenna's getting in on the ground floor. Jason Lee's little lad is named Pilot Inspektor. Spelling it with a "c", one assumes, would just be too conservative.

"*Dad*-dy," comes Maude's trumpet-like voice, all singsong, "another *Max & Ru-by*!"

"Be right there," I tell her, also in singsong. "I'm in the bathroom."

The daffiest of all celebrity baby names, it says here, belongs to Paltrow's daughter, Apple. Apple! Forget, for a moment, the fact that she's named for a either a monopolistic corporation or a piece of fruit, or that the word itself is ugly; Apple's old man—the father whose eye Apple's the apple of—is Chris Martin, Coldplay's front man, whose surname she shares. What that means is, Apple Martin is one "i" away from being a Happy Hour special.

"Another *Max & Ruby*," Maude again demands, her tone less musical, more Mussolini.

My (long deceased) grandparents, born before Philo T. Farnsworth's groundbreaking gadget, didn't watch *Dr. Quinn, Medicine Woman* and *Murder, She Wrote* on weekend nights because they enjoyed programs with strong female protagonists and commas in the title; those shows just happened to be on when I was staying there. They watched television *all the time* because, on some level, they were amazed that such technology existed. If you stop and think about it, TV is a marvel—a miracle, really—unthinkable to, say, Napoleon, who was chilling on Elba a mere two centuries ago, a blink of an eye in the history of humankind. My mother has a similar if less reverential relationship with the VCR (already usurped by the DVD player). You can watch movies *without going to the cinema!* You can tape shows, *and watch them again!* You can *fast-forward through the commercials!* This sense of astonishment explains why she and Frank, her husband, rent so many egregiously crappy movies (their Netflix queue is unspeakable). I feel the same awe toward the home computer, my portal to the wonderful World Wide Web. At thirty-six, I'm old enough to remember when computers were not ubiquitous, when correspondence was done by post, when classifieds and want ads were the primary means of communicating for-sale items and job openings and potential romantic encounters, when news came in fixed cycles, when the telephone call was not an anachronism, when you had to stop at a gas station to ask for directions, when you had to listen to the radio to hear that hit song you couldn't get out of your head. Those analog days are gone. TiVo, Craigslist, Gmail, Facebook, GPS, YouTube, iTunes, and CNN.com have made moot the need to wait. Almost anything I wish to know can be found out in minutes, if not seconds, with a few keystrokes and mouse clicks. *That actress looks familiar; what else has she been in?* IMDB will tell me. *What is Tupac saying in the last part of "Hit 'em Up"?* A snippet in the Google search bar reveals the garbled lyrics ("My fo-fo make sho all yo kids don't grow"). And if I want to compare "We Are the World" with "Do They Know It's Christmas," or revisit old *SNL* sketches, or listen to new bands before investing in the album, YouTube's got the hook-up. To me, this is wonderful, in the pure sense of the word; the novelty might never wear off completely. But Roland and Maude have never known a different world. At a moment's notice, they can watch what they want to watch, hear what they want to hear, read what they want to read, and the longest delays they have to endure are the (interminable) menu intros on the *Thomas the Tank Engine* DVDs. "Again!" Maude will demand when *Little Bear* ends, and I have to tell her that it's *regular* television, not DVR, and therefore I cannot process her request. Which of course she doesn't understand. Technology that seems magical to me is the norm for Roland and Maude, horse-and-buggy stuff, coal-powered machines. Our society places a premium on *not wasting time.* Almost every technological breakthrough in the last century is just another milestone in our eternal quest for instant, if not perpetual, gratification. Brave new world, indeed. How can I teach children born into such a you-snooze-you-lose world the virtue and value of patience? I'm not sure if I understand it myself.

Leaving the magazine next to the his-and-hers bottles of Tums on the vanity, I go downstairs, fire up another *Max & Ruby*, check on the progress with breakfast—Roland's eaten most of his bagel, Maude half of hers—and retreat to the bathroom to try again to shower. I need to shave—Maude told me so last night—so I'll be in there a good ten minutes. With any luck, they won't kill each other while I'm indisposed. Or if they do, it will be quick, painless, and easy to clean.

No sooner does the hot water jar me into some semblance of higher awareness than I remember that Roland's class has a field trip this afternoon. Vanessa, our hapless but always-available babysitter, is coming at noon to stay with Maude—after the playdate at Jess's—and I will be joining the Thornwood preschoolers for the annual foray to the pumpkin patch. Last month, when we went apple picking, pee-wee Zara Reid—whom Roland has a thing for, as best as I can tell; he tends to like littler girls—was accompanied by her notorious old man, erstwhile lead singer of the seminal D.C. punk band Circle of Fists. It was his incongruous presence at the apple orchard, in fact, that prompted me to pitch the interview to *Rents* in the first place. So Chris Keeslar's note was well-timed. It may well be that I will encounter Daryl "Duke" Reid this very afternoon. And what better place to approach him about a parenting interview than a preschool field trip? He might not show, of course. But if he doesn't come, his wife—the Québécoise model Céline St. Germain, whose *Sports Illustrated* swimsuit issue pictorial, although a good ten years old, remains the stuff of masturbatory legend—probably will. And I could ask her. Although frankly, Reid is less intimidating. Either way, better brush up on my Circle of Fists trivia before the pumpkin patch. I'm at best a casual fan; I only have the one album, the one with "My Heart Is Hydroplaning" on it, *The Worst Crime*, the same one everybody else has. I don't know if I can even name a "classic" Fists song, one from the vault that predates their signing with Universal, learning how to actually play their instruments, writing melody lines with hooks. Talent and musicality are anathema to punk, and knowing more than three chords akin to selling out, so a generation of early Circle Jerks turned on the band when "My Heart Is Hydroplaning" came out. A shame, really. It's a catchy tune, so much so that I find myself engaged in the time-honored pastime, singing in the shower:

You're wet you're wet you're wet you're wet
Cuz love love love is raining
Inside inside
I slip and I slide
Yeah my heart is hydroplaning

My face is full of lather—or rather, the left half is; the right is already smooth, give or take a stray graying whisker—when the phone rings. No way to get it in time, not with the shave half complete, so I don't try. But whatever momentary peace I'd derived from the gallons of almost-scalding water on the back of my neck evaporates, and the curiosity eats at me, and a I feel a tinge of distress *who could be calling at this hour?*, so I finish up as quickly as I can, nicking my upper lip in the process. Ablutions as unsatisfying as the previous evening's self-generated orgasm. A cold shower of a hot shower.

Puddling water on the cheap hardwood floor in the bedroom, I check the message. Stacy, on the voice mail. Early in Los Angeles—

half past four, there. Jet lag, five days in?

The recording begins with an intake of breath, as her messages always do, and then she speaks:

Hey, Josh, it's me. Woke up really early for some reason, so I figured I'd try you before the day gets away from me. You're probably, I don't know, maybe you're in the shower? That's probably good if you are. Are you asleep? Shit. I hope you're not asleep. No, it's seven thirty there, there's no way. Anyway . . . really miss you guys. It's nice out here, but I really can't wait to come home. It's time. Too long, too long to be away. I'm going to try and go back to sleep, I think, so . . . yeah, I'll just . . . I'll call you later, okay? Hope the drop-off goes okay. Love you. Miss you. Bye.

She called, what, five minutes ago, so it's probably okay to call back, but before I can dial, Maude summons me again—"Daddy! Another *Max & Ruby*! Another *Max & Ruby*!"—and I'm back to the basement, still in my towel, to play yet another new episode, or, rather, an episode they've watched a million times but not yet this morning (they didn't finish the last one; it was rejected as too familiar). What can you do. At least those rotund rabbits are enhancing my children's understanding of INTER- and INTRAPERSONAL DYNAMICS.

Then Maude says she's hungry—in her whine-infused accent—and I come upstairs to find a banana, and I'm just about to peel it when she starts wailing, and when I get back down, now wearing only boxer briefs, Roland is on top of her, and they're wrestling on the sofa, what probably began as play fighting—both of them like physical contact; Maude like a power forward who bangs under the boards, Roland delighting in the tactile stimuli until all of the sudden it becomes too much and his faulty sensory processing systems overload—and I have no idea how this started, or who started it, or why, and it's a good fifteen minutes before I can separate them and restore order, and by then, it's too late to return Stacy's call.

While this is all happening the episode plays on a loop on the TV, the insidious theme song burrowing its way into the recesses of my brain:

Max and Ruby . . .
Ruby and Max.
Max and Ruby . . .
Ruby and Max.
Max and Ruby . . .
Ruby and her little brother Max . . .

(The melody is almost as inventive as the lyrics.)

TIME WAS, MY INTEREST IN MY APPEARANCE WAS MORE THAN cursory. Not that I was ever a clothes horse, but there was a certain artsy look I tried to cultivate. In New York, this was easy to achieve; I simply wore the customary East Village uniform: black shirts, black sweaters, black Doc Martens, (not black) jeans. However hackneyed the ensemble, my clothes communicated what I wanted them to communicate, namely, *Please do not mistake me for a banker, stockbroker, or lawyer.* When we moved up here, where no one would ever mistake anyone for a banker, stockbroker, or lawyer—even Gloria's husband Dennis, who *is* a lawyer, dresses like a high school English teacher—I resolved to "go native," as it were, and began wearing *say it ain't so* colors. Black, after all, is for the clergy, and, for obvious reasons, I felt a priestly look would be inappropriate attire for someone who spent the lion's share of his time with small children. When Roland was still an infant, I took a trip to Woodbury Common, the celebrated outlet mall, and splurged on new shirts, new jeans, new sneakers, new Doc Martens that were brown, not black; hanging all the bags on the handle of Roland's Maclaren stroller until the damned thing threatened to topple over. Notwithstanding the stray online T-shirt impulse-purchase, I have not expanded my wardrobe since. For the last four years, I've pretty much punted on fashion. There's just no point. We seldom go out, and what's the use of blowing fifty bucks on a swanky DKNY shirt if the principal activity I'm engaged in while wearing it involves wiping someone's ass? I have a pair of jeans that I wear every day. This is not an exaggeration—I wear the same pair of jeans *every single day*, only changing to sweatpants during the fortnightly washing. I think they're stylish, these jeans, as they sort of look like what the dudes from *The Hills* wear in the *Us Weekly* layouts, but I have no real way of knowing, no touchstone of chic. What I do is, I pair those jeans with a T-shirt—I have a drawer stuffed with them, most procured from that vaunted boutique of cutting edge *couture*, Target—and if it's cold, as it is today, I first throw on a lined long-sleeved white undershirt. In the summer, I substitute shorts for the jeans, and brown Crocs for brown Docs. This combination is what I've worn for probably 1,585 of the 1,600 days we've lived in New Paltz. Carson from *Queer Eye* would take one look and turn into a pillar of salt.

I've just pulled on today's T-shirt—a blue-on-blue number bearing the inscription NEW JERSEY: THE ALMOST HEAVEN STATE over a line drawing of my home state, which I bought to honor my son's latest obsession, and also because the indeterminate irony of the sentiment amuses me—when Roland meanders into the bedroom, running a Matchbox car along the wall as he walks, and stands at attention next to me, or as close as he can to attention, which involves a considerable amount of spinning, rocking, and the making of odd hand gestures. He comes up to my belly button, tall for his age.

"Daddy," he tells me. "I'm bored of watching TV."

His gaze meets my own, but unlike his sister's, there is no intensity to it. His eyes look like mine must look when I'm getting my hair cut, and my glasses are on the table next to the brushes and combs, and the cute stylist pauses in her ministrations to offer some pithy comment, glancing at me in the mirror, and I direct my myopic gaze to where I think she's looking, but I am physically incapable of making genuine eye contact.

"Oh, really."

"And what shall I do now?"

We have the same conversation every morning—repetition is key for Roland; once something works its way into his routine, the habit becomes difficult, if not impossible, to dislodge—so I know where he's going with this, but I try and draw him out, have him articulate his needs explicitly, rather than in this indirect way, despite his employment of grown-up words like *shall*, that frustrates his ability to get what he wants. Roland often speaks in riddles, coming off like a pre-K sphinx.

"I don't know. What would you like to do?"

"Something else," he says.

"Like what?"

"Something that begins with 'c.' "

I pause, pretending to contemplate this. Part of the game. "Cat? You want to play with Steve?"

A broad smile breaks across his face. He really is a handsome devil. He's got that going for him, at least. "Nooooo."

"Car? You want to ride in the car?"

"No. It starts with 'c' and ends with 'puter.' "

"Cat-puter?"

"No!"

"Car-puter?"

"No!"

And I pretend to have an epiphany. "Ohhhhh. You mean the *computer*?"

"Yes!"

"Okay."

We go back in his room, and I set up the old laptop. Roland and I used to peruse the real estate websites together—he likes looking at pictures of the interiors of houses, especially if chandeliers are involved—and one day I got so bored of this that I showed him how to click around. *Teach a man to fish.* The first day, I had to help him every few minutes, but by the second day, he'd gotten the hang of it. The third day, I went to check on him, and found him on Google, his *Field Guide to American Houses* open on the desk next to him, trying to type "Louisville" into the search engine bar (there are a number of lovely old homes in Louisville; it's his second favorite city after Cleveland). He also enjoys surfing through the various lighting sites—*Lamps Plus, Shades of Light, Capitol Lighting*, and so forth—and checking out the torchières and the floor lamps, the sconces and the accent lights.

"What do you want to look at?" I ask him.

"I don't know," he says. "You pick."

He says this, but I know he knows what he wants; he just won't come out and tell me.

"Lamps?"

"No. No lamps."

"Houses?"

"Okay."

I go to the real estate subsection of pluggedincleveland.com, and click on the SHAKER HEIGHTS link. Presto, rows and rows of listings, in neat little boxes, each box a portal to dozens of images—enough to keep Roland busy until it's time to go to school. The flip side of Asperger's: if he's doing something he finds "interest," as he puts it, he'll amuse himself for hours. Sitting down, his ass halfway off the chair, he falls under the spell of the photographs of dining rooms and master baths, eat-in-kitchens and finished basements, and I leave him in peace.

ROLAND PLUGGED IN TO CLEVELAND, MAUDE IN THE BASEMENT with her animated bunny chums, I have a moment to relax. I'm sprawled on the bed, a beached starfish. All I want to do is surrender to the Sandman's call *it's a Sand*woman, *not a Sandman, and not a call but a siren song, she's Salome dancing the dance of the seven veils, half-naked and writhing on a pole, her heart-shaped ass plainly visible behind the gossamer, primped in a gesture of promise, anything I desire, anything at all, to lure me to the Land of Nod,* but I can't, because if I fall asleep now, only to wake ten, eleven, twelve minutes later, the fatigue will be *worse*, if that's possible; the aching in my bones will intensify, the dull headache *cavalry stampeding in the space behind my eyes* will magnify, the nausea will become unbearable, and I cannot fathom how anyone, surgeon, midwife, mother offering newborn child her chapped nipple, can function under such dire conditions without breaking down and falling apart sooner or later *I can't go on I must go on I will go on* but I *do* understand, with hi-def clarity, the efficacy of sleep deprivation as a method of torture, the hard-on it gives Dick Cheney, because if I were an al-Qaeda operative at Gitmo—me, Josh Lansky, how I feel at this precise moment—and some G-man in mirrored shades entered the oubliette and promised me twelve hours of undisturbed sleep if I named names, names would be named, *habib*; every last name I knew, one long litany of guttural utterances, of Abduls, Muhammeds, and Ibrahims, of Osamas, Khalids, and Anwars, and when every last morsel of so-called intelligence was extracted from my weary head, I would lay it on the pillow, or the cold, pig-blooded cement floor, and *Allahu Akbar* resume relations with Salome the Sandwoman, who after all is not unlike one of the virgins promised me in my thwarted martyrdom, and I would sleep soundly and without remorse, *al-salatu khayru min an-nawm* be damned.

Two minutes later, the patter of tiny feet, and I feel Maude standing by the side of the bed.

"Daddy," she asks, with almost comic politeness, her voice containing a slight Continental lilt, "would you please help me pyoo-pee?"

Thus continues the shitty morning.

Friday, 8:42 a.m.

THE USUAL CHAOS, GETTING THEM INTO THE CAR. CHECK THAT, the *minivan*: an '07 Honda Odyssey, Bali blue, leased before fall of Lehman and the global economy and therefore overpriced at $389 a month, MOMS ROCK! bumper sticker just below the left rear taillight (as if driving a minivan were not sufficiently emasculating), the whole of the floor from cockpit to hatch strewn with Cheerios, Late July cheese crackers, Veggie Booty, cold French fries, old gum, desiccated pieces of bagel and crusts of bread, straw wrappers, lollipop wrappers, gum wrappers, yellow-and-orange cheeseburger wrappers, the dried-out husks of juice boxes and Poland Spring bottles, spent Diet Coke cans, used napkins, used Kleenex, used baby wipes (used on dirty faces, not dirty behinds), used socks (Old Navy or Circo, snowflaky in their stubborn inability to find a match), pennies, nickels, dimes, quarters, Chuck E. Cheese tokens, mud, sand, pebbles, rocks, crumpled pages from Lego catalogs and real estate leaflets, torn-off pages of the original copy of *A Field Guide to American Houses*, forgotten Happy Meal toys, lost Lego bricks, and countless smaller particles of indeterminate origin, and the interior giving off an odor, faint but foul, best described as a Mayor McCheese fart. And that's just from the past week; I spent forty-five minutes vacuuming the car out last Friday.

So: the usual chaos, getting them to the *minivan*, to the impossible-to-be-more-appropriately-named Odyssey. Fifteen minutes or so to cool them both down, Maude locked in her room, banging on the door, yelping like a caged animal, Roland in my lap in the glider, both of them crying for their mother. I squeezed him to calm him, balance out the sensory input. Like wrapping him in a blanket to set the heat at a more constant rate. Then, when we finally made it downstairs, Roland put on Maude's shoes, and Maude put on his . . . and then mine . . . and then Stacy's knee–high snow boots. All of which is funny enough, downright adorable if you're in the right mood, a low-grade Mack Sennett act—certainly they both found it riotously funny—but not when I've been up since five and I've still somehow managed to be late getting out the door. When they finally have the proper footwear on, Roland decides that he's hungry, even though he's already eaten an entire bagel, half a box of dry cereal, and a good pint of milk. When I turn my back to fetch two bags of Pirate's Booty—a snack food manufactured by Robert's American Gourmet that is said to be healthy but could, for all I know, contain some highly addictive chemical compound whose eventual release into the bloodstream of children across America will herald the initial phase of some nefarious plot to take over the world; it is *Pirate's* Booty, after all—Maude's done something to spark Roland's wrath. I'm not sure what, but it could range from hitting him to pushing him to standing there minding her own business, as Roland's fits are Pompeian in both their unpredictability and their fury. So they're both upset, again, and the Pirate's Booty, booty though it may be, isn't sufficient treasure to console them, so I have to break out the big guns to lure them to their carseat confinement. *Who wants a lollipop?* Like an incantation, a magic spell. *Dum-Dum-bledore.* No more tears. They're in the back now, strapped in, slurping hypnotically. Too much sugar for the morning, yes, but once the boy is at school, it's not my problem. Roland flips through the "car copy" of his *Field Guide*—the aforementioned remains of the first purchase of said book—and Maude clutches tightly her precious stuffed froggie, a glazed look on her face.

The popularity of pirates among the preschool set *a bottle of rum to fill my tum* baffles me. Sure, the eyepatch and Jolly Roger and squawking parrot and the "ahoy, matey" accent have obvious *that's the life for me* appeal, as does the swashbuckling strut of the well-mascara'd Johnny Depp. But pirates are thieves, pillagers, vandals, murderers, outlaws—*I jumped aboard a pirate ship and the captain said to me* the baddest of bad guys. Thomas Jefferson's administration waged war against pirates; Obama's has contended with them as well; still they troll the *this way that way forward backward over the* Somali coast. Yet somehow (the peg leg, perhaps?) the notion persists that pirates are cute. Three-year-olds take up the skull and crossbones for Halloween, and the winsome visage of Jack Sparrow winks from lunchboxes the world over. Two hundred years from now, I wonder, will there be a *Serial Killers of the Caribbean* ride at Disney World? Will our children attend masquerade parties in rapist costumes? Tasteless jokes, horrible even to contemplate. And yet pirates—for whom murder is part of the job description, and rape a reward for a hard day's work—are *over the Irish Sea* let off easy, their abominable behavior tacitly condoned. Never mind that walking the plank is the original form of waterboarding.

"Music!" Roland orders, and I feel the staccato kicks of his feet on the back of my seat, like a massage chair eight settings too strong.

"Is that how we ask? And stop kicking me."

"Sorry," he says—the correct rejoinder, but he inflects it as if he were telling me to fuck off. This is part of his complaint; for all his 800 Verbal vocabulary, he has difficulty with linguistic subtlety. He can come off rude, but the truth is that he doesn't know any better. The easier-said-than-done trick is to not take it personally when he's mean—he doesn't *intend* to be rude; he legitimately can't help himself. "Daddy, I have something important to tell you. Daddy . . . can we have music please Daddy," he says, with emphases on the wrong syllables. *Can we have music please Daddy*. He often sounds like a bad actor, like Keanu Reeves in *Point Break*: *I am an FBI agent.*

(I have Keanu on the brain this morning. I think it's because there's a picture of him in the STARS: THEY'RE JUST LIKE US! section of *Us Weekly*—disguised by a baseball cap and a full dark beard, he's purchasing DVDs at a West Hollywood Best Buy—that I've been flipping past all week.)

"Yes," I tell him. I turn on the stereo.

"States!" Roland cries.

I know what he means, but I press him. It's good for his development, to make him explicitly and politely *ahem* state his needs. "I don't understand you."

"I . . . *want* . . . STATES!"

"You mean you want *The States Mix*?"

"Yes."

"Then say so."

"I . . . want . . . *The* . . . *States* . . . *Mix*."

"Please, Daddy."

This time he yells each word with equal emphasis: "*I . . . want . . . The . . . States . . . Mix . . . please . . . Daddy!*"

Not perfect, but as good as I'll get under the circumstances. We're already late, and I don't want him screaming his head off all the way to school.

The States Mix, as the name suggests, is a compilation of songs in which one or more of the fifty states are prominently mentioned in the lyrics. It was harder to compile than you'd think—in pop music, cities tend to be referenced more often than states; California and New York are over-represented, and, owing to my HR background, I sought diversity (although I don't think Roland cares); furthermore, some obvious choices—"Mississippi Queen," "New York State of Mind," "Carolina in My Mind"—flat-out suck. After some tweaking, here's what I put together:

1. "Sweet Home Alabama," Lynyrd Skynyrd
2. "School Days," Kate and Mary McGarrigle
3. "Hotel California," Eagles
4. "The Devil Went Down to Georgia," Charlie Daniels Band
5. "If Heaven Ain't a Lot Like Dixie," Hank Williams, Jr.
6. "Pigsknuckle, Arkansas," Circle of Fists
7. "Kentucky Woman," Deep Purple
8. "Long Vermont Roads," Magnetic Fields
9. "Portland, Oregon," Loretta Lynn with Jack White
10. "Rocky Mountain High," John Denver
11. "Take Me Home, Country Roads," John Denver
12. "America," Simon & Garfunkel
13. "Oklahoma," 1998 London revival, featuring Hugh Jackman
14. "California Girls," The Beach Boys
15. "West Texas Teardrops," Old 97's
16. "Rock'n Me," Steve Miller Band
17. "Private Idaho," The B-52s
18. "Going to California," Led Zeppelin
19. "Theme From *New York, New York*," Frank Sinatra

I'm starting to tire of many of the songs on the *States Mix*, especially the Steve Miller. But, while some might argue otherwise (and argue convincingly, if not incontrovertibly), three minutes of Steve Miller is preferable to the same time allotment of a loudly displeased Roland.

The first track begins with the familiar guitar riff, and when I'm told to *Turn it up*, I do. Thornwood is a fifteen-minute ride from our house, give or take; we usually arrive during the dueling guitar outro of "Hotel California." If we're running late—caught behind a school bus, say—I skip past the Charlie Daniels (a song I used to play all the time at parties in college, but which I never want to hear again as long as I live) and the Hank Williams, Jr. (ditto). Unlike most of these tracks, C of F's "Pigsknuckle, Arkansas" grows on me the more I hear it, and Roland finds it incredibly "silly"—a word he employs when his feelings about something exceed his precocious lexicon—that the gruff, scowling baritone raving about hard love is his friend Zara's daddy.

A COP IS PERCHED ON THE SIDE OF THE ROAD, NEAR THE AUXILiary firehouse on Henry Dubois Drive, camouflaged by political signs: a Dodge Charger'd leopard poised to pounce. Thirty-five in a thirty, failure to yield. SUNY campus police, looks like; you can tell by the orange detailing on the car. State troopers, technically. My hearts skips a beat—although I'm a law-abiding citizen and have never gotten a ticket in my life, police officers tend to dislike me, and the feeling is mutual—but I'm well under the speed limit. Lots of cops in New Paltz, surfeit of boys in blue: campus police, town police, state police, DEC, Ulster County Sheriff's Office, and I've even seen state park rangers in their white SUVs, now that the Walkway Over the Hudson's opened in Highland. With respect to ratio of number of patrol cars to population density, the Village of New Paltz might be the most overpoliced municipality this side of Singapore. There are days when driving through town feels like passing through a checkpoint on the Gaza Strip. Although when some tardy student is tailgating you on a slush-strewn street, behind the wheel of a fiberglass deathbox not equipped with all-wheel drive, yammering on her cell, that's when the pigs are taking a powder. Or a powdered donut, as it were.

As I pass him, taking care to put both hands on the steering wheel, a wave of lightheadedness comes over me, along with the dull timpani roll that is the crescendoing overture to a Mahler symphony of a headache, and I realize that, in my haste to rally the troops, shower, mainline caffeine, and manage my e-mail, I've neglected to eat so much as a Clif Bar.

So once again, for the *shit* fourth morning this week, I pull into the McDonald's. Although *mea culpa* I enjoy their fare, I'd rather go somewhere else, believe me. Oh, to sit and savor the breakfast special at Main Street Bistro, to banter with Carly, the hip waitress who calls everyone *hon*, and sip cup after cup of burnt coffee! But the genius of McDonald's—and any Fortune 500 company whose workforce comprises mostly minimum wagers is, undoubtedly, genius—is that they equip the place with a drive-thru window. Before I had kids, I thought drive-thru windows were for gluttons too lazy to drag their fat asses out of their fat-ass SUVs. Now I understand that they are intended for parents, who can quickly procure McNuggets, ketchupless cheeseburgers, Apple Dippers, juice boxes, kid-sized cups of ice cream, even *toys*, without having to de-carseat their young charges and navigate them through the perilous parking lot. One day, as God is my witness, when my kids are older and can make their own culinary decisions, I will make the healthy choice and eschew Big Macs and Quarter Pounders with Cheese for the "afforda-bowl" at Karma Road, the vegetarian place where the ice cream parlor used to be. Never again, for the remainder of my (compromised because of so much McDonald's food; there's a reason they call the goop they fry the fries in *shortening*) life will I introduce this processed, saturated-fat-filled, cholesterol-loaded, super-fucking-delicious crap into my digestive system. In the meantime, however, I view the Golden Arches as a temple of miracle and wonder to which I make frequent pilgrimages—Lourdes with *special sauce lettuce cheese pickles onions on a sesame seed bun.*

It's the same woman manning the drive-thru window. She works the breakfast shift, I guess. I'm a regular here, but she never seems to recognize me, or if she does, she pretends not to. Not that she's unpleasant, or even cold; she's all-business, no-nonsense, good at her job, a job I had in high school, a job whose duties involve doing six or seven things at the same time, as rapidly as possible, without fucking up, a job that is, for all its lowly societal status and meager pay, difficult. I admire her work ethic: the fluidity of motion as she takes my ten-dollar bill with her left hand and hands me my Diet Coke and straw with her right, the smart efficiency with which she returns my change, the crispness of the fold when she seals my bag, the curt-but-not-rude way she wishes me a good day, as if she'd love to stay and chat if there weren't two guys in hunting gear in the Durango behind me waiting on their Sausage McMuffins with Egg.

She's Latina, is my guess, and of indeterminate age—she could be in her thirties, she could be in high school; it's hard to tell. She's petite, and her ramrod posture gives her uniform a military feel. Her long, dark hair is bound tightly in a ponytail, but the few strands that fall into her face are dyed an alluring magenta. There is a thick silver ring on her thumb, the sort of thing you buy from sidewalk vendors on St. Marks Place, and a silver stud on the right side of her face just above her chin. A labret, I think it's called. Amy Winehouse has one in the exact same place.

"Have a great day," she tells me, no trace of Hispanic origin in her unaccented voice, and as I thank her and return the well-wish, I drink in her image—I've seen her on dozens if not hundreds of occasions, and four times this week alone, but it's hard to get a good look at someone in a drive-thru window—and I realize that she looks a bit like a waifish Rosaria Dawson. If you plucked her from the New Paltz Mickey D's, let down her hair, decked her out in whatever "frock" *Us Weekly* asked a hundred people in Rockefeller Center who wore best, and trotted her out on the red carpet before the Golden Globes, you'd never know she wasn't a secondary player on some new MTV reality show. Her name is Wendy, according to the plastic tag on her (small but perky) left breast. Wendy? Not a Latina name at all—and an ironic choice for an assistant manager (I'm giving her the stripes on account of the uni and the comportment) at a McDonald's.

I wonder what her story is, how she came to be employed at the McDonald's in New Paltz, New York. I wonder if she has kids.

I wonder if she has a boyfriend.

The cars crawl along Main as I wait to turn. The kids immediately complain that we've been stopped too long—red lights and stop signs, waiting of any kind: the bane of childhood. I take the opportunity to unsheathe my Egg McMuffin, take a big bite, and am on the verge of concocting a fantasy, perhaps sufficient for this evening's onanistic fodder, involving Wendy's labret-adorned mouth, a tub of hot fudge, and the McDonald's break room—the lightbulb has gone on in my brain, but the electrical surge has not yet coursed down the length of my spine—when a familiar hunter-green Subaru Forester drives by, its rear panel, like the Tattooed Man, almost completely covered in bumper stickers (KILL YOUR TELEVISION, WELL-BEHAVED WOMEN SELDOM MAKE HISTORY, COEXIST, GOD BLESS THE FREAKS, GODDESS BLESS, OBAMA/BIDEN, HOME BIRTHS, PRACTICE POLITICAL COOPERATION: I'LL HUG YOUR ELEPHANT IF YOU KISS MY ASS, END THE WAR, a red-white-and-blue Deadhead, and a good half-dozen more), and Gloria Hynek—the über-est of über-moms and driver of said Subaru-cum-billboard—sees me pulling out of the (evil) McDonald's, my face stuffed with (evil) Egg Mac, and I'm pretty sure, although not certain, that she shakes her head at me and scowls in tsk-tsk disapproval. Busted by the Crunch Patrol! Because, you know, how dare I eat food that isn't organic and locally produced. She's sure to give me shit at the playdate. Worse, I've forgotten to skip the post–"Hotel California" tracks, and Charlie Daniels is now sawing at his fucking fiddle and playing it hot.

Gloria exhibits the gamut of infuriatingly crunchy behaviors known to the New Paltz parental demographic. To wit: attachment parenting. When Haven was an infant, Gloria adhered strictly to this draconian practice, the central tenet being that a baby, like a consecrated American flag, should never touch the ground, lest the momentary separation from the parent, and the resulting feeling of abandonment, scar him for life. Instead, he should be *worn*, in a sling or a Baby Björn, while the mother goes about her daily routine. It's sort of like being pregnant for four extra trimesters, except the infant is heavier, cries a lot, and needs to be fed and changed—although in Haven's case, diapers were not involved, not even the unbleached Seventh Generation kind, because Gloria also practiced elimination communication. (*EC*, as its zealots call it, is a potty-training technique in which the infant uses "baby signs" to indicate a need for going wee-wee or poo-poo, at which time the vigilant parent transfers his or her behind to a potty, toilet, or roadside shrub. While EC does work after a few short years, and it's environmentally laudable, is it really worth the effort and extra loads of laundry to teach your tyke the toilet a few months before the next kid?) The most prominent advocate for attachment parenting—a technique imported from China, the country that popularized foot-binding, lead-painted toys, and female infanticide—is one Dr. Sears, a pediatrician and author who specializes (as too many famous pediatricians do) in making mothers feel bad about themselves. Dr. Sears claims to have employed attachment parenting on all of his own children. He has eight kids, so either his wife is a kangaroo, or he's full of shit. You can't fit eight kids in an Escalade, let alone a Baby Björn.

So: Gloria is a proponent of attachment parenting, and elimination communication, and she breastfed her son until he turned three, and she doesn't let Haven's precious, unsullied eyes gaze upon screen images of any kind, nor does she let him play with plastic toys, or toys that require batteries, or toys that bleep. When she and Stacy go out for drinks, however, she complains and complains and complains about how *hard* it is to be a mother, seemingly unaware that she is herself multiplying the degree of difficulty by being such an inflexible ideologue. Yet Stacy continues to go out with her, because Gloria can be really fun. One-on-one, she's a hoot. But Haven's presence turns her into a deranged, hypermaternal Ms. Hyde. She's one of those people who are great when alone, but insufferable when with her kid.

The other issue with Gloria is that she's a stay-at-home mom—a *SAHM*, as they call themselves on the comment boards at the Hudson Valley Parents website—to a single child. With the first kid, you want everything to be perfect, and you tend to rail against the many forces at work to corrupt the pure, blameless creature in your care. *Little lamb, who made thee?* Once a sibling enters the world, you stop drilling the first kid on his ABCs and his multiplication tables, and charting when they feed and sleep and poop, and you chill the fuck out at playdates.

Gloria is a SAHM. That makes Haven a Son of SAHM.

And it makes me SAHD.

Friday, 9:26 a.m.

AUTISM IS A GROWTH INDUSTRY. FIFTEEN YEARS AGO, ONE IN TWO thousand children was diagnosed with an autistic spectrum disorder; now it is one in 170, and the numbers keep increasing every year.

No one can adequately explain this unprecedented surge. The consensus is that autistic spectrum disorders are caused mostly by genetic factors—although what those factors are and how they are passed on remain anyone's guess—triggered by changes in the environment. These environmental triggers are just as murky as the genetic factors. Exposure to mercury, lead, Thiomersal, Tylenol, pesticides, ultrasound; deficiencies in vitamin D, in folic acid, in female hormones; complications from "leaky gut" syndrome, viral infection, fetal testosterone, thyroid disorders, gestational diabetes; age of the mother, age of the father, stress, depression, even rain—rain!—have been bandied about as environmental triggers of autism.

When one of these theories finds legs, parents of autistic children hop on the bandwagon. We want to believe that autism is caused by sonograms, by heavy metals in the drinking water, by noxious additives in MMR vaccines, by undetectable by-products in plastic containers, by chocolate shakes from McDonalds—by something external, something tangible, something upon which we can heap blame. This is why the vaccine theory became so popular in the nineties. It made intuitive sense (autism rears its antisocial head around age three, roughly coinciding with the first MMR inoculations), it was refuted by the mainstream media (it's a conspiracy!), it fed into Gen-X skepticism of modern medicine (we're injecting our kids with poison! This must be stopped!), and it was adopted as a *cause célèbre* by the rubber-faced goofball who lit his farts on fire in *Dumb and Dumber.* Never mind that the theory had as much statistical heft as the "Nigerien yellowcake" case for WMDs in Iraq. We still haven't found the nukes in the Babylonian desert, or the cause of the autism spike.

Cambridge University autism researcher Simon Baron-Cohen—it's hard not to picture him as Borat; Sacha is, in fact, his cousin—is the author of the "extreme male brain" theory of autism. Men, as we know from decades of scientific (and millennia of anecdotal) evidence, are not as strong as women with respect to relating to other people (if you're an *Eat, Pray, Love*–reading manhater, feel free to replace "relating to" with "giving a shit about" in the preceding sentence). This is hard-wired, apparently, from the days when we had to bludgeon cute animals to death before ripping them apart and feasting on their bloody innards, a process which, while necessary for survival, can be traumatic if you feel sympathy for the cute animal in question. Baron-Cohen calls this ability to interrelate—"the drive to identify another person's emotions and thoughts, and to respond to these with appropriate emotion"—*empathizing.* Generally speaking, testosterone is to empathizing what a bottle of Jim Beam is to driving. What men *are* good at is what Baron-Cohen terms *systemizing*—"the drive to analyze or construct systems that follow rules." This is why, if you need to repair a wireless router, or change your oil, or build an aqueduct, the person whose aid you enlist tends to have a Y chromosome. If men are, generally speaking, strong systemizers and so-so empathizers, autistics are uncannily strong systemizers (*hyper-systemizers*, in Baron-Cohen's jargon) and extremely deficient empathizers. The inability to discern what other people are thinking, feeling, implying, and so forth, Baron-Cohen calls *mind-blindness*.

Roland has Asperger's syndrome, not autism proper, but per the DSM-V (to be released in 2012) he'll be classified as "high-functioning autistic." The dreaded A-word, a worse scarlet letter than the one worn by Hester Prynne.

The Thornwood School is an early education center for preschoolers with disabilities. The progressive thinking goes that, rather than segregating these children in "special" classrooms, they should be integrated with kids who don't have disabilities—*typicals*, as they're called, in the oh-so PC parlance. Thirty years ago, when the school was established, the focus was on Down syndrome, mental retardation, speech defects, and other disabilities common at the time. These days, "spectrum" kids comprise the lion's share of non-"typical" enrollment.

My son has a love/hate relationship with his school. He likes the other kids and the teachers, and he likes the toys and the books, and he especially likes the rigid structure. But during free periods, such as when he first arrives, he can get a little nutso. He'll race into the room like a Thoroughbred at the gate, his head tilted back, and spin around, taking it all in, everything from ceiling to floor, like a sophisticated surveillance camera. He'll run his fingers along the wall. He'll tap his cubby, the table, the chair, the walls, the other kids as they come in, some of whom recoil from him with unvarnished aggravation. He'll chatter nonstop, excitedly providing the play-by-play, like Marv Albert calling a Knicks game. *Here comes Olivia. Hi, Olivia. Olivia has a pink shirt on today. She wore that shirt last Friday. She wears pink on Fridays. Oh, boy! Olivia's going to wash her hands. Now she's sitting in her spot for snack. She's sitting next to Tyler!*

Dropping Roland off at school is the most nerve-wracking part of the day for me. Like Marlin releasing Nemo from the anemone, I'm forced to expose him to the outside world. I'm never able to predict how he'll do, if he'll integrate seamlessly into the pack or fall by the wayside, if he'll put away his backpack and lunchbox like he's supposed to or run around like a maniac, pushing the other kids and knocking over their block towers and ripping stuff off the walls. Sometimes he has a great early morning, only to get to school and have it unravel. Sometimes he wakes up pissed off and crabby, only to recover by the time I drop him off. There's no discernible rhyme or reason to it (although if Eugenia Last gives him five stars, he does tend to have a five-star day).

But my deepest fears are not realized, not this morning. Without saying goodbye, or even turning back to me and Maude—if Orpheus had Asperger's, Eurydice would have made it all the way back from Hades—Roland stows his bag in his cubby, takes out his lunchbox, heads to his appointed seat at the table, and begins speaking with Lenore, the prettiest of the aides. The topic: floor-plans.

"Bye, Roland," I tell him, although he isn't paying attention. "See you for the pumpkin patch."

In the back of the room, I notice, Zara Reid is drawing something with an oversized purple crayon. She's always here when I get here, even when I get here a few minutes early. I've never seen her parents at drop-off or pick-up, not once. Does a nanny take her? An au pair? A Circle of Fists fanatic?

In the hall, I bump into Roland's teacher, a white-haired battle-ax named Mrs. Drinkwater. Sounds like the name of a Vonnegut character, Drinkwater, but according to census data, there were approximately fifty Drinkwater families in the United States in 1920. The surname, according to Ancestry.com, "may have been given in irony to a noted tippler." Like calling a fat guy Skinny. If her ancestors were noted tipplers, the alcoholic gene seems to have bypassed Mrs. Drinkwater, who is as sober as they come, although dealing with Roland every day would give her temptation enough to drink more than water.

"Oh," she says, "Mr. Lansky. Hello."

I've told her ten or fifteen times to call me Josh, but she's too old-school to switch to the familiar form; most of the other teachers are younger, and go by their first names.

"Mrs. Drinkwater. Hello."

"Have you by any chance noticed a change in Roland's behavior of late?"

"Not that I know of. Why?"

"He seems . . . *off* this week. Moody. Distracted. More prone to tantrums than usual. More prone to violence. On Wednesday, he told Irene he was going to 'weapon her with Alabama.' Yesterday he told Lenore that he wanted to 'kill her and cut her up and eat her arms and legs.' "

"Well," I say, suppressing a smile, "he says stuff like that sometimes. He doesn't mean it. It's just that, you know, he can't edit himself. He can't filter his thoughts. It all comes out."

"Oh, I know," she tells me, although there are times that I question the depth of her Asperger's knowledge; the disorder has only been on the books since 1994, and Mrs. Drinkwater's been teaching special ed since the *Titanic* went down. "I wondered if something might be going on at home. I thought his behavior might be due to external causes."

"Well, Stacy's away this week. So . . . I mean . . . "

"Yes, that could be it. Roland does not take well to change."

"That's putting it mildly. But I know he's looking forward to the pumpkin patch."

"Will we see you there, Mr. Lansky?"

"You will."

She nods approvingly, her enormous teeth giving her a bunnyish look. "It's so wonderful when parents attend the field trips. Roland does love it so."

"You don't happen to know if Daryl Reid will be there, by any chance?"

"Zara's father? I'm not sure," she says. Mrs. Drinkwater, I'm fairly certain, has no idea that Daryl "Duke" Reid is anything more than a well-inked behemoth who is the father of one of her tiniest students. "In all likelihood. He usually does attend—he or his wife. She's so lovely."

"That she is."

I give Maude, who is clinging to me, her face buried in my neck, like a tiny vampire feeding, a little shake. "Okay, Maude. You ready to go to Emma's house?"

"No," she shoots back, her voice surprisingly loud for someone who appeared catatonic a moment ago. "I don't *want* to see Emma *ever again.*"

I had to ask.

Back in the Honda, I call the exterminator (Joe Palladino, Paladin Pest Control) on my cell phone. He answers on the first ring, and agrees to come to the house this afternoon to, as he puts it, "rid your dwelling of rodent life once and for all."

The best-laid schemes of mice and men.

MOST OF THE HOUSES IN NEW PALTZ ARE ON THE SMALL SIDE. Cape Cod, bi-level, split-level, ranch, raised ranch, Craftsman, and what Roland's *Field Guide* would characterize as "folk style," but what I call—and my term is more accurate—shoeboxes. Three bedrooms, two baths, flood-prone basement, dilapidated detached garage, small rutted yard of equal parts crabgrass, rocks, and weeds. As you get further away from the Village—toward the low-flung valley of Gardiner, over the wooded hills of Esopus, and across the Wallkill toward Mohonk and Lake Minnewaska, where the vacation homes of well-to-do weekenders lurk behind trees and beyond dells—the size of the lots increases, the view of the rough-hewn Shawangunk Ridge becomes more dramatic, and the landscaping shows more care. The few new developments in New Paltz can be found here, on the outskirts of town. Giant manses raising their bulk over the gentle green slopes like something out of Melville, each house visible to every other; unguarded, vulnerable to attack. Long, meandering driveways of still-sticky asphalt baking in the still-warm October sun, Palladian windows gleaming uselessly. A paucity of trees; instead, vast verdant lawns, upon which swing-and-slide sets, built to the same mammoth scale as the planet-sized houses they orbit, their tall turrets shaded by red-blue-and-yellow tents, slowly decompose.

The Holbys live in a McMansion in one of these developments, south of New Paltz proper, off Yankee Folly Road (the pervasive rumor that Derek Jeter owns a house on this oddly named street proved, alas, apocryphal). Their McMansion is the smallest McMansion in the neighborhood—no ostentatious stone façade, no bonus room above the garage, no shrubbery flowering gaudily around the perimeter—but it's still big and cold and museum-like.

Time was, I abhorred architectural monstrosities like this. But after spending the last five years in our thirty-year-old Cape Cod—and a small fortune on windows that don't let the bugs in and the heat out, and appliances that work properly, and toilets that flush, and a new water tank, and a million other things—with no central air, and no garage, and mice amassing their squeaky forces behind the walls, I'm beginning to come around on the whole McMansion thing. Yes, the cycloptic window over the door is purely cosmetic, illuminating an unused upstairs alcove, and for something born of form not function—a vestigial descendent, in fact, from Diocletian's Palace, an architectural masterpiece beloved by Robert Adam, on whose eighteenth-century designs modern McMansions are based—an abject failure. Yes, it screams nouveau riche to have twenty-five-foot ceilings in the great room—or, for that matter, to have a room that deserves the "great" prefix in the first place. Yes, it's soulless and boring. But who cares? Everything is brand-spanking-new, the washer and dryer are right off the kitchen, there's a mud room, and walk-in closets, and a Jacuzzi tub with jets, and a yard that isn't built on a sixty-degree incline.

Put it this way: I don't think I'd ever *buy* a McMansion, but for playdates, there's no better venue.

Jess Holby greets us at the door. She's a twig of a woman, as curvy as a stick figure—in fact, the stick-figure drawing her daughter, Emma, made of her, the one magneted to the stainless-steel refrigerator door, is a pretty good rendering of her actual shape—and not much taller than Emma, who is at the moment helping Gloria's son, Haven, into a pink faerie dress complete with gossamer wings, a duplicate of which she already has on. Just what the poor boy needs. The costume, it must be said, becomes Haven more than it does Emma.

Although Jess has two kids, a part-time job in the admissions office at the Culinary Institute, and a home almost as big as the Vanderbilt Mansion to maintain, she always looks put together. I've never seen her without her (fake, but expensively so) blonde hair flawlessly done, her make-up perfectly applied, and her dressier-than-the-occasion-calls-for outfit (today: black cardigan sweater over white blouse; smart gray slacks; tasteful black pumps) amply (and not untastefully, if you're into that kind of look) accessorized by earrings, bracelets, rings, necklaces, and unseen clouds of perfume (the brand escapes me, but it's one of the good ones, although to me it is redolent of little old ladies, and Jess is only thirty-four). "Why, hell-*o*, Maude," she says, in an exaggeratedly kind and slow voice adults often use when addressing children not their own. "Emma and Haven are playing dress-up. Would *you* like to play?"

Maude, smiling, fixes her eyes on the floor and does her little shyness dance, holding my hand and using my right leg as a peek-a-boo prop. Then she laughs, chomps hard on her pacifier, and takes cover behind the tail of my untucked T-shirt.

"Still with that binky, huh?" Jess says. "Isn't that for *babies*?" She's talking to Maude, and she's teasing, and she's also right, but it's hard not to take this as a judgment, especially when Jess makes the same damned comment every week, usually followed by an aside that too much pacifier now means orthodontia bills out the wazoo in ten years. Also—and this is a pet peeve, I realize—I hate that she calls it a binky. *Binky* sounds like a slang term for oral sex, if you ask me. *Gonna get me some binky.*

Maude peers from my shirt-tail to address this last point. "It's not a binky; it's a *passie*," she says, as if Jess were a complete idiot, and tauntingly chomps on the pacifier for effect. (This is one of those moments when I could just about burst with parental pride.) Then Maude hands me the passie and makes for the next room, where the faerie versions of Emma and Haven flit about, as Gloria implores her androgynous son to *be careful*, a sentiment she delivers so often, and in so many benign situations (such as now, when he's six inches away from the corner of a coffee table he's a good foot taller than), that she may as well just ignore him altogether. Aesop for the twenty-first century: *The Mom Who Cried Be Careful.*

"How are you?" Jess asks, hugging me firmly and pecking my cheek. "You look tired."

"I feel tired."

"There's fresh coffee," she says. "Catskill Mountain, Moka Java blend. When did Stacy leave?"

"Monday."

"Oh, you poor dear. Maybe you'd prefer a beer?"

"No, coffee's good. If I have beer, I'll sleep, and I'm not allowed to sleep."

"Just as well. The only beer we have is this weird microbrew stuff Chris is into. Fin du Monde. There's so much alcohol in it, you're better off doing tequila shots. I had half a bottle over the weekend, and I swear, I had a headache for like two days." We process through the kingly archway into the kitchen, and she takes out a cup—an oversized thing with the insidious face of Mickey Mouse on it; I can't escape rodents this morning!—and pours me a generous helping. "When's she back, tomorrow?"

"Yeah."

There's a crashing noise, and Haven starts whimpering. Leaving the coffee, Jess and I race to the next room to see what happened—and to make sure that our respective charges aren't the ones responsible for upsetting the little crybaby. I won't say Gloria is overprotective, but she makes the Secret Service look like a bunch of art school dropouts at the Phish Halloween show. Check that; I'll say it: she's overprotective. If she would just take a chill lozenge, these little gatherings would be a lot more . . . I hesitate to say *fun*, because I'm not sure the bonhomie derived from a good playdate constitutes fun, exactly . . . but the time would go by faster. And for all the horseshit about *socialization* and *learning to share*, that's the real purpose of playdates: to kill time. You know how if you go to a really awesome party—one without kids, I mean; a wingding in, say, a two-bedroom apartment in the West Village—and you get there at nine thirty, and you start drinking and dancing and schmoozing, and the next thing you know, you look at your watch, and it's two in the morning? That sort of thing rarely happens to me these days. Almost never, in fact. Parenthood is like prison in that regard. I'm always aware of the hour, aware of the fact that it's always earlier than I'd hoped, aware of the vast and intimidatingly vacant Sahara between now and the undependable oasis that is the kids' bedtime (a bedtime that may turn out to be a mirage!). Gloria, at times, can be a cellmate from hell, a fellow-traveler in the desert who grouses about the heat and bums water from your canteen.

Neither Maude nor Emma is responsible for Haven's agony, thank God. What happened was, he dropped the toy he was playing with—an oversized plastic Thomas engine that bleeps and chuffs and plays the irritating theme song *they're two they're four they're six they're eight*; at home, he doesn't have toys like that, so it's a playdate novelty—on the floor, and was spooked by the noise *shunting trucks and hauling freight* when it hit the polished hardwood. Rather than redirect him by introducing a new *red and green and brown and blue* toy, or a new activity, a new anything, or just ignoring his blatant attention-grab, Gloria's reacted in the worst possible way, which is to say, like Jackie Kennedy in Dealey Plaza.

"What's wrong, Haven?" she cries, cradling him in her arms (the tableau of mother and woman-haired child suggests a pietà, only with a midget Jesus wearing a hipster Nirvana T-shirt). "Oh, it's so *awful* that that happened. You must be *so* upset!"

Even Maude and Emma, who are closer to three than four, regard Our Lady of the Sorrows with puzzlement. Even the preschoolers know that Gloria, like the plastic surgeon who did Heidi Montag's boobs, is blowing things way the fuck out of proportion.

Before Gloria begins rending garments, Jess, who has *two* kids and therefore understands the Parenting 101 concept of redirection, intervenes. "Maybe it's time to have a snack. Who wants some cookies?"

This snaps Haven out of his sympathy ploy. At once he stops with the histrionics, breaks away from his *Mater Dolorosa*'s tentacles, and follows Jess into the kitchen, a spring in his step, leaving me alone in the great room with the forgotten Thomas train and Gloria. She arches her eyebrow and gives me a sly grin. "So . . . McDonald's?"

Rather than defend my choice of restaurant—in three weeks, I'll be thirty-seven goddamn years old; do I really need to justify my decision to have an Egg Fucking McMuffin?—I fib. "I needed more coffee."

"They have coffee?"

"They have coffee. It's pretty good." I give the Thomas train a kick. "Not as good as Dunkin' Donuts, but better than Starbucks."

This is a mistake. Although New Paltz has a McDonald's, a Burger King, a Subway, a Blimpie, and the two aforementioned coffee places, our many and vocal radical-Leftist citizens, veritable Jedi knights in their opposition to Evil Empires, are particularly outspoken about their contempt for chains of any kind. Chains, you see, are the bonds of our corporate oppressors.

"I get my coffee at Mudd Puddle," Gloria says. "Fair trade."

"McDonald's has fair trade coffee," I tell her. I don't know if this is the case—it's probably not; McDonald's would buy coffee beans picked by orphaned Sumatran child prostitutes if it were half a cent cheaper a bushel—but I'm banking on the fact that she won't know enough or care enough to call my bluff. My stratagem works.

"I'll have to keep that in mind," she says.

"They have Apple Dippers, too. Pre-packaged, pre-sliced apples. You know. For the kids."

"Haven, honey, no mouth. No mouth!"

Her pride and joy has *Ecce Homo* returned, cookie in hand, but it's one of his long tresses that has found its way into his hungry maw. *I'll cut his hair when* he *wants to cut it*, Gloria'll tell us, although it's pretty clear to me that he'd at least appreciate a trim. He's forever blowing his stray hairs away from his nose or pushing them out of his face or putting them in his mouth and slurping on them, like he's doing now. Sometimes my crotchety neighbor, Bill—a divorced man in his late fifties who still has his McCain/Palin sign on his lawn, although that ill-matched tandem flamed out almost a year ago—will neglect to cut his grass in a timely fashion, probably because it's difficult to navigate his John Deere tractor around the ancient BMW carcass rusting on his lawn, and I have a powerful urge to get my own mower going and cut it myself. I feel the same way about Haven's hair. It's all I can do not to drag him to the bathroom right now and shave his head with one of Jess's Lady Schicks.

"Haven, I said *no mouth*!"

As I said before, the difference between Gloria Hynek and the rest of the moms (and dads; fuck, I just referred to myself as a mom; maybe I should sample one of Chris's microbrews, after all) is that Gloria only has the one child. If she had two kids, or three, like Cynthia Pardo, she wouldn't give a shit about one of them chewing on some hair. Although if she had more kids, she would keep Haven's hair short, because short hair is easier to maintain and harder for ticks and lice to hide in.

Jess returns, bearing a platter of Stop & Shop cookies (which, incidentally, are baked on the premises and quite tasty) and my cup of coffee. Thanking her, I take the cup and three chocolate chips. She then offers the platter to Gloria, who waves it off.

"They look delicious," she says, "but I can't." When no one asks her why she can't, she supplies the reason herself. "Isagenix."

"Isa-who?"

"Isagenix. The cleanse? Sounds crazy, I know, but it totally works. I've lost four pounds, and I've never felt better."

Gloria is short and curvy, with fair skin, strawberry blonde hair, pendulous breasts and a booty that would "spring" Sir Mix-a-Lot. Even at her slenderest—at age twenty-five, the magical and well-chronicled year she spent in Portland, dabbling in a raw foods diet and sleeping with both of her housemates—she wasn't slender, but she gained twenty-seven pounds when she was pregnant with Haven, twenty-seven pounds she's been unable to shed in the intervening three-plus years. It's not from lack of trying; she's gone on every fad diet, and attempted every fad exercise, known to man—South Beach and Crossfit, Zone and yoga, Weight Watchers and "willPower & grace," Atkins and hooping—but the excess poundage remains intractable. Never mind that she looks great, that she wears the weight well (despite what the kingmakers in Hollywood believe, most straight guys prefer curvy women; whenever a Lindsay Lohan or a Kate Winslet starves away her God-given boobs and butt, rendering her figure as flat and uninteresting as Justin Bieber's, men the world over rend their garments). She's forever beating herself up for being beefier than her old friend Jess Holby, next to whom skeletons appear plump.

"Isn't that the starvation diet?" Jess wrinkles her nose. "Ruth told me about that."

"Not starvation." Gloria produces a barrette from her pocket and puts it in her son's hair, unobstructing his line of sight but making him look even more like a girl. "I mean, fasting is *part* of it, but it's all about, you know, purifying the body. You should *see* the stuff that comes out of your body. Disgusting."

"Where *is* Ruth?" I ask, not wanting the conversation to veer into the scatological, which with Gloria, it would. Gloria is the Queen of TMI. She'll tell you *anything* about herself, no matter how private. This can be amusing when she's discussing clit piercings and Oregonian three-ways, but when the subject is odd chunks of green matter in the stool, it's best to change the subject. "Is she coming?"

"She can't," Jess says. "Sarah has a stomach bug."

"Bummer."

"She thinks she got food poisoning from that batch of yogurt she tried to make from her breast milk."

Before I can ask for elaboration on the breast-milk-yogurt story, on the other side of the (great) room, Emma whacks Maude in the arm, the first salvo in what will probably be a playdate-long battle over the former's coveted possessions. All necessary to their development, this child warfare, in some weird, twisted way that the Creator should probably have spent a bit more time thinking through before dickering around with marsupials and trigonometry. (Maybe a full day of rest on Sunday was too generous—I mean, would the extra half-day of work have killed Him?) Spiritual growth, in its simplest form, and in every major religion, concerns the transition from selfishness to selflessness. *The meek shall inherit the earth.* Unfortunately, the world remains under the sceptered sway of the selfish. *The kingdom the power and the glory are someone else's now and forever.*

Before anyone can react, the girls settle it themselves. Ah, progress. Maybe we all *can* just get along.

"Hey," Jess says, finishing the last of her cookie, "did you guys hear the latest Cynthia Pardo dirt?"

Cynthia Pardo: New Paltz's most successful real estate broker and most notorious adulteress. *Her vagina*, Meg once quipped, *is an open house.* Impossible to attend a social gathering these days and not have her name come up.

"I heard she almost got arrested," Gloria says, "but I didn't get the whole story."

"Arrested?"

"Oh my *God. Wait* until you hear." Jess sits on the couch and takes a long sip of coffee, reveling in the dramatic-effect attention. "So, you know how she and Bruce Baldwin like to have sex"—she mouths the word *sex*, in case kids are in earshot; they aren't; they're in the spare bedroom now, playing a laughably uncompetitive game of hide-and-seek—"in public places?"

Jess happens to be looking right at me when she ends the question, so I nod. This is common knowledge. Meg, with whom Cynthia had a recent falling out, delights in regaling us with juicy tidbits of where the two lovebirds roosted. Last week, the tryst went down in one of the homes for which she has an exclusive listing.

"Well, they were in Beacon last week, at Dia? You know, the art museum?"

Sure—the art museum built in the abandoned Nabisco factory, specializing in the exhibition of modern-art installations too large for MoMA, such as the piece Roland and Maude were drawn to during our one ill-fated visit there, the untitled sculpture Stacy dubbed *Enormous Pile of Broken Glass on the Floor.*

"Apparently," Jess says, "there's this like big exhibit in the basement. These sort of big steel mazes?"

"Yeah," I say, "they're really something."

"Well, they were there on this like rainy day, and it wasn't crowded. So they went into one of these mazes, right, and they decide to, *you* know."

The steel mazes comprise a permanent part of the collection, a Richard Serra installation of massive sheets of gray-brown steel, the kind used to make ships, twenty-some-odd feet high, heavy as fuck, arranged in spiral patterns. Roland was fascinated by them. You walk into the things—there are half a dozen of them, I think—and the effect is spooky and disorienting. Like getting lost in a steely corn maze. You don't see them; you *experience* them. The last thing that would be on the mind of any sane individual interacting with that installation is, *Wow, this would be a great place for some afternoon delight.* I mean, there's nothing remotely aphrodisiac about them. "They did it *in* the installation?"

"Um . . . *yeah.* And when they get it on, they don't go halfway, so Cynthia's skirt is all hiked up, and Bruce's pants are around his ankles, and she's loud, louder than she should be, and it echoes off the steel walls . . . and that's when the cops show up."

"No shit!" Gloria says, and immediately covers her mouth and scans the room for Haven, lest his immaculate ears be adulterated by her potty mouth.

"Apparently there's a surveillance camera down there, so there's like a *tape* of this."

"Is it on YouTube yet?"

"Wouldn't *that* be a fun link to discuss on Hudson Valley Parents," says Gloria, and we all laugh. She can be very witty, Gloria, when she's not crimping her son's playdate style. "So what happened?"

"What happened is, museum security called the police, and the officer who responded, he trains with Bruce at the gym, so they got off . . . "

" . . . in more ways than one . . . "

" . . . with a warning. But, Jesus! That's only a misdemeanor, but it would have been in the police blotter if they got busted . . . "

"Oh, they got busted, alright."

" . . . and Peter would . . . "

"He'd find out."

" . . . find out. But isn't that *gross*? I mean, why would you *do* that?"

"Well," Gloria says, batting her eyes as she always does when she's about to reveal information more personal than any of us wants to know, "sex in a public place can be *intensely* erotic."

"This isn't on the *beach* or whatever." Jess wrinkles her nose. "Or the Mile High Club. It's an *art* museum. *Kids* go there. It's like so disgusting. She's such a skanky skank. It makes my skin crawl."

"She *is* kind of a succubus."

"The only reason you'd have sex at Dia:Beacon," I offer, "is because you want to get caught."

"That's what *I* said," Jess says. "She wants out of the marriage, but she doesn't want to be the one who leaves. She wants him to find out."

"Unfortunately, he's oblivious."

"Or in denial."

"How do you know about this?" I ask.

"She told Mike DiLullo, who told Cathy, who told Ruth, who told me."

"Jesus."

"I know, right?"

"Poor Peter," I say.

"And the kids," says Gloria.

"All three of them," adds Jess.

If there *were* a thread about Cynthia Pardo on the Hudson Valley Parents website, most of the comments would harp on the fact that Cynthia has three kids, and that her abundant offspring makes her indiscretion even more abominable. This is the tack most people take when the subject comes up. How could a mother of all those children—not to mention the doted-upon wife of Peter Berliner, a nice, non-abusive, faithful guy with a steady job and top-drawer fathering skills—stray so brazenly, so wantonly, so self-destructively? Sure, Gloria is not the paradigmatic wife, but next to Cynthia Pardo, she looks like Donna Reed. Donna Reed with genital piercings, but still.

"Seriously," Jess says. "She skeeves me out."

A few years back, on one of those rare occasions when Stacy and I went out with a group of people—and one of the not-rare occasions when we were in the middle of a bad patch—a bunch of us went to Eighties Night at Cabaloosa, and as we formed a crude circle, I found myself dancing next to Cynthia (Peter, it should be noted, wasn't there; he's kind of antisocial and doesn't get out much, unless bowling is involved). As I watched her shake it to Cyndi Lauper, I remember thinking, *This is someone you could have an affair with. She has three kids. She'd never break up her marriage, so you wouldn't break up yours. Discreet encounters in far-flung motel rooms. The occasional clandestine rendezvous at the house, when Stacy's out of town. We'd use the futon in the basement. Look at her move. You* know *she's good in bed. She probably hasn't had a good fuck in almost a decade. And when's the last time someone's face was buried in her thighs?* Looking back at that night at the dance club, I see that Cynthia was putting out a distress call, and I merely picked up on it. She wanted out, period. She was a princess locked in a tower, and it didn't really matter who came to the rescue: me, Bruce Baldwin, Prince Charming, Shrek; it was all the same to her. If I had pursued her that night, or soon thereafter, I might be the one schtupping her in art museums, the trending topic on the mental Twitter feed of moms all across town. Whenever her name comes up, then, I breathe a sigh of relief. Her name, like some secret incantation, makes me swell with contentment at my own marriage, and renews, in some hard-to-define way, my own wedding vows.

"Oh, totally," says Gloria, with a sanctimonious nod of her head.

"I'm going to check on the kids." I mosey down the hall, peek into the spare bedroom—Maude and Emma are playing with dolls, while Haven is jumping up and down on the bed, a dangerous and reckless act whose discovery would give Gloria a conniption—and then head to the bathroom.

What gets me about the Cynthia Pardo business is that I *like* Cynthia Pardo. Not in a sexual way—that urge in the dance club proved fleeting—but as a friend. I haven't hung out with her as much, but I enjoy her company more than Jess's or Gloria's. I like her . . . but I don't understand her. There are better ways to extricate yourself from a dead marriage, ways that don't involve crimes and misdemeanors, ways that aren't as humiliating for her husband, the poor sap, who, whatever his flaws may be, doesn't deserve to be treated like this.

As I shake off the last of my coffee-fueled piss—one of the greatest challenges of stay-at-home fatherhood, for me, is coordinating my bathroom breaks; I have the bladder of a nine-months-pregnant woman—I happen to glance out the window just in time to see a shiny black BMW X-5 pull into the shiny black driveway. In West Hollywood, where my wife is now holed up, every third car is a BMW; not so in New Paltz, where Subarus, Honda CR-Vs, or pickup trucks dominate the roads. A BMW here is like a Bentley in L.A. Who belongs to the Beamer? Ruth isn't coming, and Meg drives a beat-up Jetta.

I wash my hands for longer than necessary, holding them under the hot water as long as I can stand it, letting the heat radiate through my body. The face in the mirror—Jess was right—looks tired. The gray at the temples has begun to migrate in all directions, like the mint plants in our backyard. Gentrification of gray. Conquest of age. Bags under my eyes, hidden by the rim of my glasses, but Jeff Van Gundyan in their depth and darkness. The only hint of youth in the entire expanse of weary visage, the last vestige of my teenage self, is the dime-sized zit forming painfully above my left eyebrow.

I'm mildly and not unpleasantly surprised to find Sharon Rothman in the great room when I return, an oversized water bottle in one hand, her daughter's hand in the other. The playdate roster, like a basketball team, has nine members, five of whom (Jess, Gloria, Meg, Ruth Terry, and me) are starters, with the other four substituting every so often (and some of the fringe players, it must be said, are not crazy about a father encroaching on their mommy time; the inverse of pro athletes made uneasy by female reporters in the locker room). But Sharon is not one of the regulars; this is the first time she's come to one of these things, or the first time *I've* seen her at a playdate, anyway. In my limited dealings with her—at a birthday party at Meg's, at Hasbrouck Park, at the healthfood store—she strikes me as more East Village than New Paltz, and although she's quiet, she's fun to talk to, if only because I'm not yet bored of her. She's intriguing, her sad eyes bespeaking unknowable depth. And I have this strange feeling that I already know her, although I can't for the life of me figure out how.

"Oh, hey, Sharon. I didn't know you were coming."

"Good morning, Josh."

We don't know each other that well, so we do an awkward dance, neither of us sure if we should shake hands, embrace, kiss the other's cheek, or all three, and we wind up going full-on awkward and kissing half on the lips. And me with my coffee breath. Should have brought the Altoids from the minivan.

"What are you drinking? Margarita?"

"I wish. It's a protein shake."

"She's doing Isagenix, too," Gloria informs me.

"Too bad," I tell her. "The cookies are really good."

"These shakes, I gotta say, they're not that bad," Gloria says.

"I wish I could have cookies," Sharon says. "Sugar gives me a migraine. It's a curse."

Sharon taught at the Montessori school until the big scandal—a sex offender was discovered to be living in a house adjacent to the school grounds; it subsequently came out that the school not only knew about this and didn't disclose it, but said sex offender was one of the school's initial investors—when all of the teachers quit en masse. I'm not sure what she's up to these days—last I heard she was training to be a yoga instructor . . . or was it an astrologer? Maybe both. "I'm still finding myself," she told Stacy one time. From the looks of the BMW, it doesn't appear she's in a hurry to locate her self, or a gainful job.

"I'm sorry to hear that."

The kids run in from the other room to greet Sharon's dumpling-shaped daughter, Iris. They don't say hello, as such, just jump around happily as the dynamics shift. Gloria takes a seat on the ottoman near the fireplace. "Look what I found," she says. "Bubbles!"

Maude, Emma, Haven, and Iris jump up and down even more furiously, bouncing to the fireplace and the bubbles like so many hopped-up kangaroos.

I find my Mickey Mouse mug and notice, to my dismay, that it's empty.

"I'm going to get a refill. Anybody want some coffee?"

"I'll go with you," Sharon says.

"Help yourself," says Jess. "There's light cream in the fridge."

"How decadent."

"I know how to live."

Sharon and I move through the archway into the kitchen.

"Are the shakes really tasty, or is Gloria just saying that?"

"They're supposed to be chocolate flavored," Sharon says, "but they actually taste like carob. I really hate carob."

"The cubic zirconium of dessert flavors," I say, and she laughs, although it's not a particularly good joke. "So how are you doing? How's David?"

"He's fine. He's been really busy at work."

"Yeah, Stacy has, too."

"Is she having fun in L.A.?"

I'm a bit surprised that she knows my wife's whereabouts, but then, it's not exactly a state secret, as it's been all over Facebook.

"I think she's too busy to have much fun. She said she'd rather have gone to Dallas. The conference rooms are the same everywhere, but Dallas at least is a much shorter flight."

"Where'd she fly out of? Albany?"

"Newark."

"That's far."

"Yeah."

Sharon pours coffee into the same oversized Disney mug that I have, only with Minnie Mouse instead of Mickey. "I went to town this morning. I swear. Have you used the muni lot since they put in the meter machine?"

"No."

"It used to be so easy to park," she says. "Now, it's this big hassle. The lot used to be full, and now it's practically empty. People are afraid of the meter machine. They'd rather not use it."

"Yeah, it's been a *great* way to increase revenue. Another genius decision by the mayor."

"I know, right?"

"Woodstock has a free muni lot. Rhinebeck has a free muni lot. Poughkeepsie has free muni lots. And New Paltz doesn't? What sense does *that* make? They basically removed an entire parking lot. How does that not hurt local businesses?"

"Exactly."

"What'd you do in town?"

"Yoga."

"How's that going? You're training to be an instructor, right?"

"I was. I quit. It wasn't right for me. I don't know."

Sharon sips her coffee and moves aside—our forearms glance as we switch positions—and I begin to refill my cup. The clock on the coffee pot, I notice, reads 10:39. Not even eleven yet. A whole lot of day left. *Miles to go before I sleep and miles to go before I—*

"I don't know how to tell you this," Sharon says, her eyes wide with concern, "so I'm just going to tell you."

PART II

where the wild things are

given services

to prepare

them

for

kindergarten

Asperger's: A Chronology

ROLAND WON'T SLEEP WITH US. HE'S BEEN CRYING FOR A SOLID hour, lolling his tongue over Stacy's breast, not hungry, just upset. We bring him to the bed, a double because anything bigger won't fit in our miniscule apartment, not particularly roomy but more than adequate for man, woman, and child. We lay him down between us. We pat his head, his back. We sing him lullabies. We sing "Silent Night" and "Little Drummer Boy" and "Greensleeves," because he was born on Christmas.

He flails around. He punches. He kicks. He cries. He won't sleep with us. We want him to share the bed, want this glorious product of our love between us. But he'll only sleep in the crib, by himself.

He's four months old.

Martin Luther, the famed theologian, encounters a twelve-year-old boy who cannot speak, shuns contact with other people, and is chronically stricken with odd compulsions to twitch his body this way and that. The great Christian leader determines that the afflicted child is a victim of demonic possession and recommends immediate suffocation.

Soon after, Johannes Mathesius, Luther's biographer, will publish the account in his *Table Talk of Martin Luther*—the first recorded course of treatment for an autistic child. It is 1540.

Roland is in the driveway. His fat-diapered bottom is perched on a railroad tie, legs extended into the bed of mauve-toned rocks some artless landscaper has dumped on the side of the house. He leans over, picks up a rock. He flicks the edge with his thumb. He holds it up to me.

"Is rock?"

I'm sitting Indian-style on the asphalt, zoned out, enjoying the warm sun on my face and arms, the soft breeze blowing through the leafy trees all around us. We've just moved here; country living is still a novelty. I don't say anything. He repeats himself, with more urgency. "Is rock?"

"Yes," I tell him, for at least the ninetieth time. "That's a rock."

He flings the rock across the driveway, almost to the tire of the newly leased Honda Odyssey. There are many rocks scattered about the driveway. More rocks on the driveway than in the bed of rocks, where the black plastic liner is visible beneath the dirt. Later I will rake up the rocks and replace them. Again.

He leans back into the bed, picks up a new rock, holds it up to me. "Is rock?"

"Yes, that's a rock."

He flings it toward the minivan.

He is sixteen months old.

In a village in the Scottish Stewartry of Kirkcudbright, Hugh Blair, scion of a well-to-do family, is sued by his younger brother John, on the grounds that he, Hugh, is unfit for marriage and land ownership.

As the testimony plays out, Blair's eccentricities come to light:

He does not answer questions, instead looking away to avoid eye contact. On those occasions when he does reply, he repeats the question rather than supplying an answer.

He is religiously religious, sporting a perfect attendance record at church. He always sits in the same pew—he cannot abide someone else taking his seat—and recites the entire Mass verbatim, from memory, but without inflection.

He is closer to animals than people.

He enjoys futile activities such as gathering stones in a pile, moving the pile, and then returning the stones to the river bed, or watching water drip from his wet wig.

Hugh Blair is stripped of his wife and his inheritance when his eccentric patterns of behavior are found by a magistrate to be evidence of insanity.

It is 1797.

A hippie friend of Stacy's who lives in a yurt outside of Arcata, California—a crunchy town similar to New Paltz, albeit with the advantage of medicinal marijuana—gifts Roland a book called *Zen ABC*. Written and illustrated by a mother-daughter team who live not far from here, the book, as the title suggests, pairs letters of the alphabet with matching Buddhist words. A is for Awareness, B is for Buddha, C is for Cadence, and so forth.

Zen ABC is one of Roland's favorite books. He knows all the letters, and he knows the matching Buddhist words. Point to "O" and he will say, in his high-pitched, cherubic voice, "One *Mind*." This delights my mother, who announces that he is a genius.

He is eighteen months old.

In 1797, a feral boy emerges from the woods outside of Saint-Sernin-sur-Rance, in the Aveyron *département* of southern France.

Victor, the Wild Boy of Aveyron—as he is called in the press—has lived for ten of his twelve years in the woods. Although he is not mute as such, he does not speak, and is more comfortable among animals than people.

A medical student named Jean Marc Gaspard Itard adopts Victor, working with him as a deaf-mute. During the Age of Enlightenment, Victor is hailed as a "noble savage," and is known the world over.

He likes to spin things. Bottle caps, Tupperware containers, lids, Frisbees, quarters. Anything that can be spun. A flick of the wrist and he whirls them around like tops. He hovers over his spinning objects like Samantha Ronson at the DJ booth.

I've tried to duplicate the feat. I can't. It's much more difficult than it looks.

He can even make square objects spin. I didn't think that was possible in the realm of physics, but Roland can do it.

He sits on the ceramic tiles in the kitchen, presiding over his round plastic lids, while his newborn sister sleeps in her detachable carseat. We don't find anything unusual with his uncanny knack for spinning. We're proud that he's so good at it.

He is twenty months old.

The term *autism*, a derivation of the Greek *autos*, or *self*, first appears in a paper on the symptoms of mental illness by a Swiss psychiatrist named Eugen Bleuler. It is 1910. The term is used to describe the lack of empathy in certain of his patients—an "autistic withdrawal of the patient to his fantasies, against which any influence from outside becomes an intolerable disturbance."

Autistic is adopted as a synonym of *schizophrenic*.

. . .

Roland started preschool. He's the youngest child there. When they go outside to the playground, the other kids run around, play tag, climb on the playground equipment. He sits in a corner, picking up stray woodchips and rubbing them on his cheek.

"He groks that," Stacy jokes.

We still joke. We still see nothing unusual, only the seeds of genius, just like my mother said.

He groks that. Stranger in a strange land.

He just turned two.

A research paper called "The Schizoid Personality of Childhood" presents a study of six boys with eccentric patterns of behavior and unusual and rigid habits. It is 1926. Because this paper is written in Russian, and is published in the Soviet Union at the time of Stalin's ascendancy—and by a *woman*, no less; a neurologist's assistant named Eva Sucharewa—its findings, which comprise the first record of patients with what will be called Asperger's syndrome, are ignored.

Jess Holby brings her daughter Maddie, whom Roland has known most of his life, to our house for a playdate. Usually they get along swimmingly, but not this time. Roland is mean to her. When Maddie tries to play with one of his Thomas trains, he attacks her. He hits her. He pulls her hair. He tries to bite her, but Stacy separates them in time.

Subsequent playdates are even worse.

We stop organizing them.

"All kids go through that phase," friends of ours, parents of older children, assure us. "All kids hit and bite. Don't worry; he'll outgrow it."

But other kids don't hit, other kids don't bite. Not like that.

We don't see Jess or Maddie for months.

He is twenty-eight months old.

At preschool, he misbehaves. He's difficult, the teachers tell us. Prone to tantrums. Prone to hitting. He likes to knock over towers that other kids have made of blocks. He'll race across a crowded room just to knock over a big stack of blocks some other kid has spent fifteen minutes carefully constructing. He circles the room like an eagle, looking for towers to knock over. He taps other kids on the head. He makes other kids cry. He doesn't get upset when they cry. He just retreats to a corner and spins things.

All kids go through that phase. Don't worry; he'll grow out of it. We cling to this like a nun to her rosary beads, repeat it as a novena. But we don't believe it anymore.

Despite his shortcomings, the other kids seem to like him. Or so we're told. *He wants to play with the other children, but he doesn't know how.* The teachers seem to like him. *He has a pleasant personality. He's such a nice boy.* They try and feed his brain. *We have to get puzzles from the Blue Room. He can already do all the puzzles here.*

"You should really get him evaluated," his primary teacher, Gina, tells us. "He might have to go to a special school. He might need services."

The thinking is that he might have a sensory integration issue, but nobody really knows for sure.

Hans Asperger of the Vienna University Hospital borrows Bleuler's *autistic* coinage to describe a specific neurological disorder that would eventually bear his name. It is 1938. *Autistic psychopathics*, he writes, demonstrate a pattern of bizarre behavior, including "a lack of empathy, little ability to form friendships, one-sided conversations, intense absorption in a special interest, and clumsy movements."

He calls these children "little professors."

. . .

During the summer, we visit friends and family. Short day trips. *Fun car rides*, is how we bill them, to sell Roland on the concept, although he's always enjoyed the Sunday drive. We hit the neighboring states: Connecticut, New Jersey, Pennsylvania. When we arrive at my brother-in-law's house, my mother's house, Laura's house, Roland follows the same routine. First, he walks the perimeter of the building, hand-in-hand with me or Stacy, taking careful note of window placement. Then he tours the inside of the house, matching the windows on the inside with the corresponding windows on the outside. Then he circles the house again from the outside, and has us tell him which rooms the windows belong to.

"That's the kitchen," I'll tell him. "And that's the dining room. And that little window is the bathroom."

He takes this all in.

He can do this for hours. He'd do this all day if we obliged.

"See? I told you—he's a genius," my mother says.

He is two and a half.

Leo Kanner, a Ukraine-born doctor at Johns Hopkins University Hospital and the world's first child psychiatrist, publishes the landmark study "Autistic Disturbances of Affective Contact."

It is 1943. This is the first modern use of the term *autism*.

Roland has invented a game. He pokes you in the eye with his index finger, *Three Stooges*' style, and yells, "Boook!"

Boook rhymes with *spook*. It's a word he invented. He often invents words. For example, when he wants to express *no* emphatically, he will say *nokes*, or, sometimes, *nars*.

I mention this at the special ed meeting.

There are more people in this meeting than there were at the closing on our New York co-op. All here for a kid who won't be three till December. In attendance are the district psychologist, who doubles as chair of the Committee on Preschool Special

Education; the Ulster County Department of Education representative; Gina, his teacher from his first preschool; a "parent advocate"; the therapist who evaluated him at the Saint Francis Hospital Preschool program; and of course Stacy and I.

We mention his use of the word *boook*. The county rep laughs. She says, "Kids don't make up words. They get them from someplace else."

"Well, our kid does."

We talk about the diagnostic report. About a delay in social play skills. In fine motor skills. In pragmatic language development. In articulation. Stacy mentions his sensory integration issues. She can barely get the words out. She's already starting to cry. I take her hand under the table, squeeze it tightly, as if this can make the issues go away, as if love were enough.

He can't be autistic, Stacy says. *He's a big mush. He loves physical contact.*

We want this to be sensory, something he'll grow out of, something we can repair. We don't want it to be something else. Something we don't even want to utter.

He can't be autistic, Stacy says. *He has a sense of humor. He tells jokes.*

"We know he needs services," the psychologist says, evading the A-word. "We just don't know which services he needs. Does he need speech? Does he need OT? Does he need a SEIT? We don't know."

He recommends we see a diagnostic pediatrician. He recommends further evaluation. Stacy leaves in tears.

Hans Asperger argues that his "little professors" should be spared from Dachau-style extermination, on the grounds that their unique genius might be useful to the state. It is 1944.

"We are convinced, then," he writes in *Die "Autistischen Psychopathen" im Kindesalter*, his doctoral thesis, "that autistic people have their place in the organism of the social community.

They fulfill their role well, perhaps better than anyone else could, and we are talking of people who as children had the greatest difficulties and caused untold worries to their care-givers."

Before bed, Roland sits in my lap in the glider, and we work our way through one of his astronomy books, all of them written for elementary or middle schoolers: *Stars & Planets*, with its mythological renderings of the planet names; the *The Usborne Complete Book of Astronomy and Space*, complete with maps of the various constellations; *The Solar System*, which, despite the finite title, is about the whole of the universe.

He can identify all nine planets by sight. He can name some of the moons—Charon, Pluto's lone satellite, being his favorite—as well as comets and the Oort cloud and the Kuiper belt. With some prompting, he can go through the twelve signs of the zodiac.

We haven't observed the actual night sky, because we've only been reading the books during the late summer, when it gets dark long after he goes to sleep, and already bright when he wakes up.

One morning in the late fall, just before Thanksgiving, I bring Roland out as dawn is breaking to gaze upon a gorgeous heavenly conjunction: against a backdrop of still-visible stars, the planet Venus rests in the lap of the crescent moon (this identification of the planet Venus is the sort of thing I knew nothing about before Roland evinced an interest, and my subsequent subscription to *Sky & Telescope* magazine). You can see it perfectly from the front steps. It's like an IMAX movie playing just for us.

"That's the moon," I tell my son. "And that's Venus."

I lived in New York City for ten years; the only star I saw in all that time was Cindy Crawford, so the wonder of a glimpse of a different kind of heavenly body has not worn off.

After a few minutes, I bring him into the dining room, where Stacy is drinking her coffee. "Tell Mommy what we saw," I tell him, strapping him into his booster seat.

"Saw Venus," says Roland. "The moon . . . and Virgo."

"Virgo?" Stacy says.

I shrug. "Don't look at me. I didn't say anything about Virgo." I dig the latest issue of *Sky & Telescope* from beneath a stack of *Poughkeepsie Journals* on a stray dining room chair, and flip to the "Map of the Sky" section. The stars that formed a backdrop to the Venus and moon conjunction, the stars that to my eyes looked like patternless white dots, were part of a constellation. The constellation of Virgo. Which Roland somehow recognized and identified (or managed to guess correctly).

He is not quite three.

Hans Asperger opens a school for "autistic psychopathic" children with the help of a nun, Sister Victorine.

Just months after opening, the school is destroyed by a stray Allied bomb. Sister Victorine is killed, and all of Asperger's early research is consigned to the flames.

It is 1944.

Roland likes Thomas the Tank Engine, a creepy anthropomorphic train who, with his creepy anthropomorphic-train accomplices, chuffs hither and yon across the mythical Island of Sodor, doing the bidding of Sir Topham Hatt, his bloated, bald overlord, who bears a passing resemblance to the monocled plutocrat of Monopoly fame. I think the original concept was to teach British children to bow to the king.

Roland knows the names of all the engines, but he's more interested in the tracks than the trains. He makes me construct elaborate tracks. Eventually he builds them himself.

He also enjoys dollhouses, but does not care for dolls.

He needs to work on his pretend play, Gina says.

He is three.

• • •

The child psychologist Bruno Bettelheim, a professor at the University of Chicago, invokes Freud, suggesting, in his influential book *The Empty Fortress: Infantile Autism and the Birth of the Self*, that the eponymous complaint is the fault of the mother. Autistic children are hapless victims of early rejection from the women who gave birth to them—*refrigerator mothers*, as Bettelheim calls them. To prove his point, he conducts a study and finds that mothers of autistic children show higher instances of stress and depression than mothers of neuro-typicals. (It does not occur to him that it is the autistic children who cause the stress and not the other way around.)

"The difference between the plight of prisoners in a concentration camp," he writes, "and the conditions which lead to autism . . . in children is, of course, that the child has never had a previous chance to develop much of a personality."

Bettelheim is himself a survivor of the Dachau camp.

It is 1967.

The diagnostic pediatrician is based in Woodstock. Roland and I drive up one afternoon. The thermometer on the dash reads ninety-eight degrees.

On the way there, he wets himself. Pees right through the diaper (he's one of the few kids in his class not yet potty trained). I have to change him from his shorts to the only other clothes in the car, a pair of heavy sweatpants.

The diagnostic pediatrician, Dr. Archer, looks more like a baby-boom poetess than a physician. She wears a long flowing skirt and a beaded necklace.

She takes us into her office, a small room stocked with toys and books. She watches Roland play. She has him do puzzles, which he completes quickly. She asks him questions, which he mostly ignores.

He is not quite three-and-a-half.

She recommends speech therapy and occupational therapy. She recommends the Thornwood School.

She doesn't say he's autistic. She diagnoses him with Asperger's syndrome.

I don't really know what that means.

Leo Kanner concurs with Bettelheim's refrigerator-mother theory, remarking to an interviewer, in his thick Freud-like accent, that autistic children are the sad result of their parents "just happening to defrost enough to produce a child."

A syndrome, I learn from Wikipedia, is "an association of several clinically recognizable features, signs (observed by a physician), symptoms (reported by the patient), phenomena or characteristics that often occur together."

Asperger's has four such signs, according to the book *Asperger Syndrome and Your Child*:

1. Impaired social interaction
2. Impaired communication
3. Unusual responses to stimulation and environment
4. Repetitive or odd patterns of behavior or interests

Roland demonstrates the first three, I begrudgingly admit, but odd interests? Wikipedia says: "Pursuit of specific and narrow areas of interest is one of the most striking features of AS. Individuals with AS may collect volumes of detailed information on a relatively narrow topic such as weather data or star names, without necessarily having genuine understanding of the broader topic. For example, a child might memorize camera model numbers while caring little about photography."

Well, I tell myself, he doesn't do that. Dr. Archer must be mistaken. It's a sensory issue—that's all.

Although Roland's fascination with astronomy is, I allow, cause for some concern.

. . .

I'm changing the door knob in the bathroom. My father, who owned an auto body shop, had a gift for this kind of thing, but I have not inherited his mechanical inclination. I'm puzzling over the jangly pieces included with the actual knob—I had no idea there were so many!—and quickly become frustrated. I take a break, walk to the kitchen, have a glass of water.

I come back to the bathroom to find that Roland has taken the latch piece out of the box and inserted it into the proper hole in the door. Correctly.

It skips a generation.

He is three and a half.

In her 1981 work *Asperger's Syndrome: A Clinical Account*, Lorna Wing, a British physician and mother to an autistic daughter, is the first to attach Hans Asperger's name to the disorder he described.

Her intention is to make a clear distinction between Asperger's syndrome and mental illness.

We're at a red light on the corner of Main and North Manheim. Roland asks, "Why does that sign say 'No Turn on Red'?"

Only after I answer him do I realize that he just read the sign.

He is three and a half.

At the sixty-first annual Academy Awards, *Rain Man* wins for Best Actor in a Leading Role (Dustin Hoffman), Best Original Screenplay (Barry Morrow and Ronald Bass), Best Director (Barry Levinson), and Best Picture. It is 1989.

The character of Raymond Babbitt (the titular "Rain-man") is based on Kim Peek, a Utah-born "megasavant" with an astounding memory. Diagnosed with Opitz-Kaveggia syndrome, Peek had no corpus callosum connecting the two halves of his brain, and was, emphatically, not autistic—unlike Babbitt, who is described in the film as an *autistic savant*.

Nevertheless, *Rain Man* becomes, and remains, autism's cultural touchstone, and it is presumed that all autistics can count a pile of toothpicks.

A Pottery Barn catalog arrives in the mail; years ago, I bought someone's wedding present there, and because I may do so again one day before my demise, they keep me on their mailing list. Roland pulls the catalog out of the recycling bin (which is more a huge pile of cardboard boxes than a bin). Perusing the catalog, he is fascinated by the chandeliers. He has me read him the names of the various styles: Edison, Camilla, Armonk, Verona.

I sing him a silly song (I am a veritable Rodgers and Hammerstein of silly songs):

Verona chandelier,
Verona chandelier,
Hi-ho, the derry-o,
Verona chandelier.

Soon he graduates to catalogs that feature lighting exclusively: *Lamps Plus*, *Shades of Light*. He has me read him the various styles. The model names. The features. He knows the difference between a floor lamp and a torchière.

Odd interests? Dr. Archer, it seems, was on the money.

She was right, Stacy says, her eyes moist. Then she locks herself in the bathroom.

He is three years, nine months old.

. . .

The developmental psychologist Uta Frith, of University College London, translates Hans Asperger's *Die "Autistischen Psychopathen" im Kindesalter* into English.

It is 1991.

Later, studying two-hundred-year-old court documents, which provide her ample testimony from a host of character witnesses, Frith concludes that the eccentric Hugh Blair was, in fact, autistic.

I buy a children's atlas of the world. We spend hours reading it, at Roland's insistence. Continents, countries, states, cities, flags: he commits them all to memory.

He is not quite four.

Asperger's syndrome is included in the tenth edition of the World Health Organization's diagnostic manual, the ICD-10, published in 1992.

Two years later, it is appended to the *Diagnostic and Statistical Manual of Mental Disorders*, fourth edition (DSM-IV).

There is a loud crash, so I run to his room to investigate. His torchière—which is a floor lamp with the concavity pointed upward, like a bird bath—has toppled to the ground, thick chunks of frosted glass on the carpet. More distressing is that Roland is playing with the lamp. He's taken out the lightblub, and is unscrewing the on-off knob.

The lamp is still plugged in.

"Oops," he says, without looking at me. "Sorry, Daddy."

I don't want to stifle his mechanical creativity—being able to assemble a torchière, unlike being able to recite its model number from the *Lamps Plus* catalog, is a useful life skill—but I don't want him to die, either.

"Roland," I tell him. "You're not allowed to play with your lamps. But if you do—you have to unplug them, okay? Seriously. It's not safe when they're plugged in."

I'm not sure if he understands.

A week later, he breaks his sister's floor lamp.

He unscrews the lightblub.

The lamp is still plugged in.

Maude, a precocious two, is crying.

The writer Liane Holliday Willey coins the term *aspie*, meaning someone who, like her, has been diagnosed with Asperger's.

It is 1999.

For Christmas, which is also his fourth birthday—and which, to my mother's extreme annoyance, we observe—Roland gets some puzzles of the United States, including the foam-rubber one that will emerge as his favorite toy.

New Year's Day, my sister is on the floor with him, doing one of the puzzles. Laura attempts to place Nebraska directly over Oklahoma.

Roland snaps at her. "No, you stupe! Kansas goes *there*!"

Stacy hollers at him to be nice, but her heart isn't it in.

Christopher John Francis Boone, the fifteen-year-old narrator of Mark Haddon's novel *The Curious Incident of the Dog in the Night-Time*, attends a special-needs school. He is smart but has difficulty reading faces, and he cannot function in the outside world. Although his formal diagnosis is not revealed in the novel, and Haddon himself does not elaborate, the book jacket describes Boone as having Asperger's.

It is 2003.

An international bestseller—and the choice for the maiden *One Book, One New Paltz* event—the novel serves as the (somewhat misleading) introduction of Asperger's to the popular culture.

Thornwood prepares an IEP—an Individualized Education Program—with specific goals for Roland's development. He is four years old.

Roland is expected to *appropriately attend to speaker-listener responsibilities for five verbal exchanges*, and during those five exchanges, to *control vocal intonation and body language to accurately match the intent of the message—e.g., to smile when conveying good news*. To help him do this, he will *practice with various conversational scripts to maintain a normal exchange*.

As for fitting in with his classmates, Roland will *play and engage in activities near other children*. He will *play spontaneously with other children*. He will *participate in small-group activities with an adult present*. When approached by others, he will *respond in a socially acceptable manner*. He will *appropriately display affection toward another child*.

Periodically, we get reports of his progress.

Most of his "grades" are NPS—*Not Progressing Satisfactorily*.

When we get these reports, Stacy cries at the dining room table. She stops eating. Her left eye starts to twitch, her face breaks out in acne.

Eventually she stops reading them.

It is 2004. Amy and Gareth Nelson found an advocacy group called Aspies for Freedom. Its aims are: to erase the "disability" stigma affixed to people on the autistic spectrum, to have them recognized as a minority status group, and to eradicate the notion that autism is a disease that must be cured.

Within three years, the group accumulates twenty thousand members.

Among the treatments and techniques used by the teachers at Thornwood to help Roland: physical therapy (for gross motor development), occupational therapy (for fine motor development), speech therapy (for what's called *pragmatics*; knowing what to say at appropriate times, how not to interrupt, how to feign empathy, and so on), music therapy (stimulates the right half of the brain), counseling (oh to be a fly on the wall; I'm pretty sure he just talks about states and lamps the whole time), brushing protocol (in which they brush his arms, legs, and back with a soft brush for two minutes every hour, to balance his tactile stimuli), hippotherapy (where he rides a bus to a nearby horse farm and then rides an old nag named Pal), wearing a weighted vest (an L.L. Bean fisherman's vest, cute as can be, that weighs about five pounds), and good, old-fashioned removing him from the classroom when he gets out of hand. The last technique—call it what it is: a Time Out—is the only thing that reliably works.

The goal of this early intervention is to prepare him for kindergarten. Enough prep, the thinking goes, and he won't be as disruptive to his classmates, who will be learning their letters, numbers, and colors, knowledge Roland mastered years ago.

The 2012 edition of the DSM-V will eliminate the "Asperger's" diagnosis, lumping it in under the more catholic heading "autistic spectrum disorder."

The consensus among aspies is that this will only add to the confusion.

• • •

Although his "refrigerator mother" theory was debunked years ago, Bettelheim was right about one thing, as current studies clearly and repeatedly validate: Parents of autistic children are more likely to suffer from depression, from parental stress, from psychological stress.

Parents of autistic children are also more likely to split up.

The divorce rate for these parents is eighty percent, is what I hear.

Ernest, one of Cynthia Pardo and Peter Berliner's three children, is autistic.

Stacy and I haven't had sex in . . . how long has it been? A while. It's been a while.

Shit.

Friday, 10:51 a.m.

GOOD LOVE IS HARD TO FIND.

"You Got Lucky" is on the radio as I start the car after our abrupt playdate exit. I'm not a big Tom Petty guy, but this song is innocuous enough, and anyway Maude's stopped crying and has that distant look on her face like she's about to fall asleep, so I don't change it. Good love *is* hard to find. So say the Heartbreakers, who know.

I'm a good half-mile down Yankee Folly before I realize that the tune has a newfound and unwelcome significance. Check that: *potential* significance. If Sharon is right. If Stacy is—

In February, we'll have been together ten years; Roland is almost five. His arrival into our world, and the subsequent migration of said world from the city to the marchlands to the north, marks a distinct midpoint of our union, a delineated shift from Act One to Act Two *from the original blockbuster to the watered-down sequel.*

The first half of our relationship was spent in New York and the various indulgent vacation spots—Napa, New Orleans, New

Mexico, Nice—we periodically flew to from JFK. We both had jobs—not dream jobs, but real jobs, with salaries and benefits and personal days. We had free time, lots of free time, although it may not have felt that way back then, and the option to call in sick and sleep till noon if circumstances demanded it. One New Year's Eve—the year after the bathetic Y2K ballyhoo, if memory serves, as it doesn't as often as it once did—we got hammered at a friend's party, literally dancing the night away, and didn't get home till dawn. When we finally rolled out of bed on January first, it was three o'clock in the afternoon. The cats kept checking on us, rubbing whiskers on our cheeks to gauge for signs of life, puzzled looks on their feline faces, and we blissfully ignored them. Three in the afternoon!

Those first five years were our Gay Nineties; Roland's birth, the Zimmermann Memo heralding a half-decade dug into the Great War foxhole of parenthood. No money, no travel for pleasure, no drinking to excess, no raucous parties, no sick days, no sleep-ins. No let-up. No relent. New Paltz is our Flanders, and our charge is to remain in the trenches and hold our ground until the Armistice Day that is . . . what? Kindergarten? College? Death?

You got lucky, babe.

Yes, Stacy is unhappy. Not *depressed* unhappy, *worn down* unhappy. But unhappy just the same. Unhappy enough to trade foxhole for rabbit hole and vanish into a wonderland of wanton wander-lust? I don't believe so . . . she's not the cheating kind, I'd like to think . . . but I don't know. I mean, it's possible. Certainly I've let her down enough these last five years.

She turned forty last month—the Big Four Oh, which is a bigger deal for women than it is for men, I've the hard way learned—and I totally botched the birthday. Not that I dropped the ball, as such—I organized a well-attended surprise breakfast and the obligatory spa mani-pedi, and we went out to dinner at Hokkaido, her favorite sushi restaurant—but something was missing from the festivities, and we both knew it. *My birthday was just an item on your to-do list*, she groused afterward. *You didn't really care about it at all.* She wasn't right about the second part, but she was bang-on about the first. I did care, of course I cared, but I didn't have the resources—financial or emotional—to pull out all the stops. Had she turned forty after the kids were old enough to stay with her mother . . . after I'd gone back to work . . . after our credit card bills were not all on the brink of being maxed out . . . and not on a fucking *Wednesday* . . . I would have made the requisite fuss. But this year? I just didn't have it in me. The timing was bad. Her milestone birthday was one of countless fatted calves we've sacrificed at the altar of parenthood. And Stacy's fed up with it. She's worn out, to the point where she's starting to break. She's *unhappy.*

Unhappy enough to stray?

The weeks after her birthday were the frostiest in all the time we've been together. Unable to focus her anger on the actual source—the kids; or, rather, the at-times suffocating restrictions raising kids has imposed on us, as hands-on parents—she took it out on me. You know how a baseball team that can't trade all its players instead fires the manager? I was Team Stacy's Billy Martin. The question is, was I irredeemable enough to replace?

Maybe I deserved what I got. If not the ax, at least the hostility. Maybe Stacy's lame fortieth birthday was a passive-aggressive way for me to lash out at her. Maybe she's not the only one who's angry. Maybe I'm just as unhappy as she is. This would be prime fodder for couples counseling, but we stopped going to Rob in July because her insurance doesn't cover mental health, and we can't cover the out-of-pocket expense.

Things reverted to normal by the end of September . . . but could that be because she found satisfaction elsewhere? No, no, that's not right—she was miserable then, too. It was around the first of October, I think, when I came home from the dentist and found her in tears. *My life is a steaming pile of shit*, she told me, *and I hate everything right now. I've spent the last two hours with Maude, giving her every single ounce of my soul and it's still not enough. I'm tired, I'm getting sick, I have SO much work to do. Help.*

Unhappy enough to stray.

Period, full stop.

This would be the part in the movie where the jilted husband flies to Los Angeles on the next available flight—a cute and kindly stewardess would help him bypass airport security—to have it out with the cheating wife. He'd interrupt the business meeting, he'd yell and scream and embarrass her, he'd call her a whore and throw water in her face. Then he'd fly off into the sunset with the cute stewardess. But I can't imagine reacting that way. I'd rather crawl under the porch and await the *coup de grâce*, like a dying cat. The very idea of confrontation—and therefore confirmation—makes me ill. Hot bile churns in my gut, a toxic stew of hurt pride, sadness, humiliation, and dread that cannot be healthily expressed, but cannot be tamped down. Some of the coffee comes back up my throat, bitter and acidic—why did I drink so many cups!—but I'm able to roll down the window and spit, and thus avoid retching all over my jeans (although I leave a trail of brown caffeinated spew along the side of the minivan).

How will I react when I know for sure? Hard to say. But the Not Knowing is eating me up already. It's a monster, an apparition in human form; faceless like my wife's potential lover, but powerful, relentless; a ring wraith—or, perhaps, that legendary faceless Hudson Valley bugbear, the Headless Horseman (or if he *is* Stacy's lover, the Headless *Whores*man)—riding roughshod over the broken landscape of my mind, haunting me.

I should probably call her, check in, ask her even, although I'm the sort of guy who will go to great lengths to avoid confrontation, particularly confrontation whose outcome I won't like no matter how the cookie crumbles, as this sort of half-baked Lorna Doone is sure to. I should call her, yes, but what would I say? *Hi, honey, I know you can't talk long, but I was wondering . . . um, are you perhaps cheating on me?* If Sharon's information is bad, and Stacy has been true, I look like a dickhead for not trusting her. And that's the *best*-case scenario! No, I can't bring it up. Not now. Not until I talk to Sharon, find out what she knows.

And the Headless Whoresman gallops on.

. . .

When I found you.

Ten days until Election Day, and political posters have popped up everywhere, like so many red-white-and-blue zits: defacing the lawns, street corners, highway overpasses, storefront windows (the "T" where Main Street intersects the Thruway exchange suggests one of those Midtown plywood walls where the POST NO BILLS directive has been ignored)—blue for Democrat, red for Republican, although Ulster County lists so far to the left that the latter tend to be coy about their party affiliation. One of my little driving games involves trying to forecast a winner based on the volume of signage. Gilpatric, it appears, will cakewalk to a seat on the state Supreme Court. I've yet to see a single sign for his opponent. I don't even know who's running against him. In the race for county clerk, on the other hand, Nina Postupack and Gilda Riccardi appear headed for a photo finish—the number of lawn signs suggests a dead heat. I wonder who they are, these hopeful and perhaps gullible municipal candidates, who permit their names to be printed on posters all over town. Ronk, Zatz. Deborah Schneer. Hansut, Maio. And my favorite pair of names, Bartels & Hayes. *We thank you for your support.* As an American, I'm supposed to take pride in this ardent display of civic duty. Democracy in action and yadda yadda yadda, the stuff of Alexis de Tocqueville's wet dreams. But the signs tend to depress me, this morning especially. I feel bad for the losers, even the Republicans; their banners will remain on those lawns, street corners, overpasses, storefront windows, for days and sometimes weeks (and, in the case of my never-say-die McCain/Palin-supporting neighbor Bill, years) after Election Day, battered by the elements, faded like the glow of campaigning, like the hope of reform, torn from their metal frames, blowing in the wind like monogrammed flags of plastic surrender. What a humiliation it must be, losing an election. Public flogging. Tar and feather. I don't know how you come back from that. Look at Al Gore, that poor sap, vanishing into a beard and twenty pounds of post-election padding. How did he recover from that mortifying "defeat" in 2000?

Well, it probably helped that Sharon Rothman didn't tell him at a playdate that she thought Tipper was having an affair.

On that fateful Tuesday eight years ago, after the first plane hit the World Trade Center, we gathered in an office to watch history unfold on TV. One plane, one black hole, one tall tower. An accident—this is what everyone thought. Some dimwitted pilot had managed to fly his Cessna smack dab into *the largest building in North America.* What a dope! But when the second plane hit, we knew at once, all of us knew, that this was not the case. We knew it was *intentional*, an act of terror, an act of war. The newscasters knew it, too. Immediately, we were informed of commercial planes unaccounted for, lost in the wild blue yonder. There were six of them, like bullets in a chamber, heading toward other targets: the White House, the Capitol, the Sears Tower, the Golden Gate Bridge, LAX, the Empire State Building. And although I was stunned that this had happened, some small part of me—God, it pains me to admit this—*wanted* those six planes to hit those targets, just to see *what would happen.* I wanted to witness the apocalypse. I wanted to watch the world end, and with a bang, not a wimper. That base and shameful inkling proved short-lived; I came to my shell-shocked senses well before the first tower collapsed. But I cannot deny the frisson of thrill I felt that day, standing in that office, listening to the newscast, as I contemplated the coordinated destruction of Life as We Know It.

If I'm honest with myself, I recognize that the part of me that *isn't* devastated, that *isn't* overcome with anxiety and dread, feels the same way now. My marriage, my family, my entire life could tumble like those skyscrapers, leaving a gaping, smouldering, noxious hole where something tall and proud once stood. Those are the stakes—nothing less. And yet some small and obviously deranged part of me craves this outcome.

Why do I want to witness my own destruction?

As my son well knows, not to mention every producer in Hollywood, it's fun to watch shit blow up.

My throat is burning and I swallow hard, sending the Moka Java sluicing back from whence it came. *Easy, Josh. We don't know anything yet. Don't freak out.* The best recourse is to approach this as a mystery, I tell myself, like an episode of *Law & Order*, or a game of Clue, or an Agatha Christie novel. *Ten Little Huguenots.*

Okay, then.

For the sake of argument, let's accept Sharon's premise that Stacy is cheating on me. That begs three more questions: when, for how long, and with whom? We don't exactly have surplus hours to while away, not with two high-maintenance preschoolers, not with Maude's obstinacy and Roland's special needs; how exactly did she manage to sneak in an affair? Is this a long-term sort of infidelity, one of those *Same Time, Next Year* situations, or a relatively recent infatuation? And who the fuck is the Other Guy? Stacy rarely goes to the city, so it would have to be someone up here. Someone local. But who? A colleague at IBM, maybe? A trainer at the gym, like Cynthia Pardo's paramour, Bruce Baldwin? One of the other daddies? Chris Holby? Dennis Hynek? David Rothman? Soren?

My mind is blank. There are no usual suspects to round up. It really is an Agatha Christie book: *everyone's a suspect.*

I check the rearview—Maude is passed out, her head dangling off to the side like a broken bobblehead doll. On the radio, Tom Petty gives way to a guitar riff as familiar as "Twinkle, Twinkle, Little Star," and then the swaggering vocals kick in:

I can't get no . . . sat-is-fac-tion

My finger wavers toward the preset, but the familiarity of the song soothes my upset stomach, and I've always liked the line about not smoking the same cigarettes as me—it reminds me of my father, who loved the Stones, who would blast *Exile on Main Street* at the body shop *Is this a sign? Is he watching over me right now?*—and instead of turning it off, I find myself turning it up.

As an anthem for the stay-at-home dad, you could do worse.

. . .

STACY IS THE MARKETING MANAGER FOR ONE OF IBM'S SOFTWARE products. I should probably know which product it is, since my wife is in charge of its promotion, and my ignorance of such a basic piece of information does not speak well of her faculties in that regard, but the name keeps changing, and the departments keep shifting, and there are so many mergers and acquisitions and staff reductions that it's difficult for me to keep track. In my defense, she rarely talks about work. Big Blue has been good to her, she likes what she does well enough, and she's made some decent friends in the office, but it's hardly her life's calling.

She's uncomfortable with "marketing manager" as her primary social identity; when conversationally challenged guests ask her at parties what she does for work—the grown-up equivalent of *What's your major*—she visibly deflates. Sure, she can explain that she's a classically trained actress who works at IBM to make ends meet, but is that really what the partygoer is after? And why should she, or anyone else, have to justify her existence because some schmuck has no imagination, no gift for gab?

We were watching this Bill Hicks video last year, and the late comic greets the audience with, "Does anybody here work in marketing?" and to the sources of the scattered applause in the live audience, he deadpans, "Please kill yourself now." I don't think I've ever seen Stacy laugh like that. She howled so hard she wept. I mean, she *crossed over.* Tears were streaming down her face, her cheeks glistening with the changing colors of the TV lights.

During the Oscars, when Hilary Swank and Reese Witherspoon and Kate Winslet snivel and gasp for composure and neglect to thank their husbands, an awkward silence passes between Stacy and me. Although the subject is never broached—hence the pause—we both know damn well that Stacy belongs in that city, at that auditorium, on that stage, buckling under the bald statue's shiny encumbrance, resplendent in a designer gown that would charm the editors of *Us Weekly*, basking in earnest applause and the warm glow of affection from her peers, her esteemed colleagues in the Academy of Motion Picture Arts and Sciences, and not in an upstate outpost with two needy preschoolers, an unemployed husband (stay-at-home moms are *homemakers*; stay-at-home dads are *lollygaggers*), a salaried position at International Business Machines, and nary a role in a community theater production to her credit in the seven years since she last graced the stage, in a lamentable off-Broadway production of *Taming of the Shrew.* Catering, auditioning, catering, auditioning, cateringauditioningcatering-auditioning—the acting cycle was killing her, the IBM gig fell into her lap, she jumped and never looked back. That's the party line, anyway, but what is left unspoken . . .

Reese Witherspoon, she'll snipe during the Oscar telecast, *has an enormous chin.* That's as close as she comes to giving voice to her justified bitterness (unless someone mistakes her for Mary-Louise Parker, that is; but that's a whole other ball of Madame Toussaud's wax), but it's there. It's there. How could it not be?

The actor's road makes for difficult hoeing because acting is such a dependent art form. Actors need directors, they need writers, they need make-up artists and costumers and set and lighting designers, they need performance spaces, they need box offices and ticket sellers, they need audiences. What do I require? A laptop and Final Draft. If my script becomes a movie *if my bill becomes a law*, of course, many more dashes of spice will be added to the cinematic Bloody Mary before it is served with the requisite celery garnish to the moviegoing public. By then, though, the heavy lifting is done. The money is in the bank. *Babylon Is Fallen*, original screenplay by Josh Lansky. Optioned by the Freeland Group for three-quarters of a million dollars, which sounds like a lot of clams until you realize that you only get the whole pot if they *opt* to make the picture. Hence *option.* Like a non-guaranteed contract in the NFL. Sounds great on paper, but the real number is ten percent of the option. Seventy-five grand up front *money from the sky, manna from heaven* less the agent's cut and the tax hit, and what you're left with is just enough scratch to put a down payment on a house upstate, pay the movers, and buy some furniture. Then you're up here, and back to Square One. You've moved Square One ninety miles up the river, basically. Meanwhile the script gathers dust in some Hollywood vault, like an ancient relic, the Maltese Falcon, the Shroud of Turin . . . no, it's not as special as all that . . . like one more ducat on the corpulent dragon's swollen horde. Six years and counting in that gilded tomb, and I don't think it will ever see the (green) light of day. Optioned? Rendered unto Caesar. I've written two more scripts since then—*Quid Pro Quo*, a thriller about a crooked employment agency, and *Coronation*, a rom-com about three disparate candidates running for the office of county coroner—but the last two years have yielded nothing but the insipid vampire project, which I didn't even bother finishing. Writer's block seems to be a by-product of fatherhood.

And here we are. Back at Square One—or Square One-A, I suppose. In bluer-than-blue New Paltz, New York, home of Mohonk Mountain House, historic Huguenot Street, and more massage therapists, per capita, than anyplace else on the planet.

Maude is snoring, her breaths almost in time to the steady snare drum. I'm on North Putt now, driving past Woodland Pond, the massive assisted living place that opened six weeks ago. During the past year, every senior citizen in town has put a house up for sale, it seems, glutting the market with excess inventory just in time for property values to plummet by twenty percent. Shitty timing, really. Two years ago, their Village shoeboxes were worth almost four hundred large. No more. A sucky time to retire: shrunken 401(k)s, shriveled pensions, hollowed husks of real estate paydays. The poor fuckers. But then, I'd have more sympathy for them if they didn't keep voting down the school budget.

When we moved here, we were city transplants, with a colicky baby and two cats. I left my benefits job at News Corp., and after a few harried months of maternity leave, Stacy returned to work at IBM, this time in the Poughkeepsie office. Slowly but surely, we accumulated a circle of friends, all of them the parents of similarly aged children, most befriended by Stacy during her second pregnancy and leave of absence. That's who we see socially: Stacy's mommy friends and their (generally blah) husbands. Which puts me in the somewhat ghostly position of being one remove from the action. I know all of the Divine Secrets of the Ma-Ma Sisterhood—the salacious details of Gloria's adventures in polyamory, of Ruth Terry's bisexual forays, of Meg's habit of swapping nude photos with well-hung black guys via a secret Hotmail account—but all of this dirt comes from Stacy. *This place*, she'll say as she slings the gossip. *The more you dig, the more you find*. I don't know if Gloria or Ruth Terry or even Meg knows how much I'm privy to, so I don't bring any of it up. I play dumb. I'm already at a distance, as the only guy in the group, and this illicit harboring of secrets forces me to be even more aloof.

Five years upstate, and I'm a stranger here. I may as well be walking the streets of Skopje or Baku or Košice, lost and alone *he doesn't speak the language he holds no currency*, an expat, an exile, a man without a country. This is my own fault, I realize. The energy needed to cultivate new friendships, to get to know people, to establish an identity apart from sad-sack SAHD, is beyond what I'm able to muster. As with the planning of Stacy's bathetic birthday, I just don't have it in me. I'm too fucking *tired*, too beaten down. When the phone rings, it's almost always for Stacy, and when it's for me, it's either my mother or my sister. Pathetic.

Not that I can complain. I signed up for this, when I agreed—heck, when I *lobbied*—for us to leave New York, to quit my suck-ass job (which in retrospect seems not so suck-ass), to abandon my friends, to decamp even farther away from my family, from my comfort zone. My exile is self-imposed, and necessary. And yet I miss my old life. I miss my friends. I miss my sister. I even miss my mom. They all think, *He's busy; I don't want to bother him; he'll invite us for a visit when he wants to see us*. Not so! What I want is for *them* to take the initiative, to call me up and say, "Josh, I need to see you, I'm coming up, and I won't take no for an answer." I want someone else to take the lead, because I don't have the giddy-up to do it myself. But no one does. Instead, my friends pull away. The relationships fester—it depresses me, when I think about it, so I try not to—leaving me alone *he is a foreign man*, a stranger in a strange land. I observe, I take note, but I do not engage. Easier that way.

And what a spectacle! *The more you dig, the more you find.* Enough drama for a reality show: *The Real Housewives of Ulster County*. The relationships overlap and blur together like a Seussian fever dream, an X-rated *One Fish Two Fish,* until a grand design can be read into the nonsense. *From there to here, from here to there, funny things are everywhere.* Begin with Bruce Baldwin, the muscle-bound personal trainer at Ignite Fitness, and his affair with Cynthia Pardo. This is not a quiet, discreet, Don Draperian sort of arrangement; everyone in New Paltz knows about it, because Cynthia Pardo has a big mouth ("She could deep-throat Seattle Slew," as Meg so colorfully put it), *one fish two fish red fish blue . . . Bruce Baldwin* and because, as the Dia:Beacon incident demonstrated, they have eschewed lovemaking in the relative privacy of motel rooms on 9W for boisterous romps in public places within biking distance of their houses—*we see them come we see them go* the Wallkill Valley Rail Trail, the old stone houses, the hiking paths at Lake Minnewaska, unlocked bathrooms at various watering holes. Plus, everyone knows who Cynthia Pardo is, even if they don't know her; as a broker with Coldwell Banker *Oh! What a house!*, her comely visage smiles at you from FOR SALE signs on every third yard in town. She sold us our house, in fact, although we didn't meet her socially until later. Cynthia is married (for the time being) to Peter Berliner, a manager at Ulster Savings and, as I said, a nice guy, if something of a schlemiel *a Wump with just one hump.* They have three kids—a son in fourth grade; a daughter in second; and a five-year-old, Ernest, a high-functioning autistic who, like Roland, gets services at Thornwood. Peter Berliner is an avid bowler *I like to bowl how I like to bowl.* His top score is 285. He's a fixture at HoeBowl in Kingston, a legend of the local leagues. Meg's husband, Soren, also bowls, not avidly, but enough to have formed a friendship of convenience (that is, another guy with whom to have the odd beer and take in the occasional movie; what in Hollywood is called a *bromance*) with Berliner, who happens to live on Cherry Hill Road, a few houses down from Meg and Soren. Meg and Cynthia are BFFs—or were, until the latter's affair with Bruce *and some are very very bad*, a New Paltz native and Meg's date to a senior prom from hell (she thought about pressing charges; things got that ugly)—put a strain on the relationship. I struck up a friendship with Meg, as mentioned, in the waiting room of the Barefoot Dance Center, where I enrolled the kids at the suggestion of Gloria Hynek, whom we met through Catherine DiLullo, our doula for Maude. Cathy's husband *we like our* Mike has a thriving acupuncture practice (New Paltz is renowned for its healing arts). We saw a lot of Mike and Cathy when we first moved here, but they sort of fell off the grid when they adopted two children from Ethiopia to complement the two they'd already adopted from China. Mike DiLullo is part of an informal clique that meets for drinks every week or two (usually at the Gilded Otter, a brew pub), a group that also includes Jen Hemsworth, who left her husband and her two young children *I do not like this bed at all* to live with her lover, also named Jen, a nineteen-year-old student at Bard College; Paul Feeney, a goateed graphic artist whose "art" hangs in coffee houses, and whose slatternly ex-wife Felicia hangs in wine bars, all over the Hudson Valley; Ruth Terry, who had an affair with her au pair (an *au fair?*) Gretchen, a twenty-year-old from Austria with enormous boobs, only to send the poor girl packing when it ended in tears *all I like to do is hop from girl to bop to girl to bop*, which didn't stop her from putting the moves on the next one, who was flat-chested and from Colombia; and the ubiquitous Cynthia Pardo *not one of them is like another.* Meg used to hang out with the group, too, until Cynthia started up with Bruce, precipitating their falling out. Gloria, like Meg and Ruth and Jen Hemsworth and more married mothers than you can shake a stick at, also splashes around in the same-sex kiddie pool *hop hop hop,* although she primarily schtoops guys (including Paul Feeney *jump on the hump of the Wump of Gump*, one of her regulars) with the full consent of her husband and Haven's father, Dennis, an attorney at a Poughkeepsie law firm. Dennis doesn't care, though; it turns him on to see other men and women have at his wife *at our house we play out back*—some dudes are into that, apparently; it's kind of a thing—sometimes, he even finds lovers for her. Gloria spends a few nights a week at Paul Feeney's house, although they tell Haven she's away on business (even though she doesn't have a job), because they want to keep their son's home life as normal as possible—an uphill battle, given Gloria's inability to keep anything secret: the nature of her *if you never did you should* genital piercings, the battery-powered accoutrements of her *these things are fun and fun is good* experimentation-crazed sex life, the cock-size of her numerous paramours *I wish I had eleven too* and whether or not they are "cut." In addition to practicing law and complacent cuckoldry, Dennis (seven meaty inches; mushroom head) plays bass in a (beyond lousy; off-the-charts bad) cover band called String Cheese; Paul Feeney is the drummer (which must get awkward, I'd imagine), but the band's front man and driving force *my Ying can sing like anything*, Chris, is Jess Holby's husband. Chris teaches at the Culinary Institute in Hyde Park, but his wife does the cooking at home *and I get fish right on my dish.* The Holbys have not, to the best of my knowledge, cheated on each other, although in this place, nothing would surprise me *and some are slow.* Dennis and Chris know each other through their wives, who were freshman-year roommates at Skidmore College. The String Cheese keyboard player—an important member, as their repertoire is heavy on pre–*Glass Houses* Billy Joel *we are not too bad you know*—Ken, is a science teacher at Rondout Valley High, whose own marriage ended a few years back when he was caught in the marital bed *I will sleep with my pet Zeep* with his personal trainer at Ignite Fitness, none other than—ta da!—Bruce Baldwin. And thus the circle of incestuous sex fiends comes full circle.

BUTTHEAD

(snickering)

Heh heh heh heh. "Comes." Heh heh.

Is this game of spousal musical chairs played in towns all across America, I wonder? Are housewives everywhere this desperate? Or is there something in the air up here, some peace-love-and-happiness/anything-goes Woodstock state of mind that has made New Paltz a veritable Divorcerama? Certainly I don't see residents of my buttoned-up New Jersey hometown cruising the same-sex highway (*bi*cycling, if you will). But it doesn't matter what they're doing in Livingston, or Peoria, or ports of call even more starboard-listing. Nor do the exploits of Cynthia Pardo or Gloria Hynek or Meg or anyone else amount to a Bogartian hill of beans. It's what Stacy's up to that counts.

Speaking of which . . .

Active bisexual. Could the affair be with another woman? Stacy's never gone that route—although she's kissed girls before, on stage, in plays, and at parties, on dares, in college—but she's not adverse to the idea, as she's told me on numerous pillow-talk occasions (she can be quite inventive and exploratory in the bedroom, befitting her actorly talents). And, as evidenced by the melodramatic plotlines of *The Real Housewives of Ulster County*, anything's possible. I can totally imagine Gloria hitting on her; in fact, I'm convinced Gloria's been wanting to get in Stacy's pants since the day we met; all it would take is Stacy to give her the green light. It's easy to picture: they're at Bacchus, they've had a bit too much to drink, the conversation takes a kinky turn, as it tends to do when Gloria and alcohol are involved, and the next thing you know . . .

The Stones roll mosslessly off, and the bombastic announcer comes on. *You're in the middle of a rock block*, he informs me, in the sort of voice that implies the Rapture has come and I'm one of the Chosen Ones. *Nine songs in a row! Every hour! Guaranteed!* Like my optioned screenplay, this sounds like a pretty sweet deal until you do the math—nine songs times three minutes per song equals twenty-seven measly minutes; not quite half an hour of guaranteed music every hour, plenty of space left over to trumpet the once-in-a-lifetime sale going on *right now* at the Poughkeepsie Price Chopper.

Usually they lead off with a decent song after the nine-songs-every-hour boast. Not this time.

Shot through the heart and you're to blame . . .

My finger goes for the preset button so quickly it's almost involuntary. Half the reason I left my native state was to escape the well-manicured clutches of Jon Bon Jovi. Also, I'm not in the mood to hear about the tarnishing of love's good name. The next station is the one that plays *the best of the eighties, the nineties . . . and today.* The fawn-like Taylor Swift, the Romeo and Juliet song, whatever the hell it's called, the one that sounds like a book report that fetched probably a C+. Maude digs it, but she's asleep. Too bad for her. And on the third preset—

Good love is hard to find . . .

Same song. Same *spot* in the same song.

Coincidence . . . or the Universe is trying to tell me something?

I hold with the latter.

Score another point for Eugenia Last.

INT. BACCHUS, NEW PALTZ, N.Y. – NIGHT

STACY and GLORIA, both dressed for a night on the town, are tucked into a dark booth at this, their bar of choice. Six empty bottles of La Fin du Monde ale sit on the table; both women are a bit loopy.

STACY

I still can't believe you did that.

GLORIA

Why not? It feels good.

STACY

Yeah, but someone had to *do* it.

GLORIA

Someone had to pierce your nose. Didn't stop you.

STACY

A nose is not a clitoris.

GLORIA

Thanks for clarifying.

STACY

You know what I mean.

GLORIA

Look, I'll admit, it was a little embarrassing, but it's not like the chick was *offended*. She does clit piercings all the time. It's not like I got my *mom* to do it or something.

STACY

(shaking head)

I don't know. I couldn't do it.

GLORIA

Sure you could. It's *so* worth it, Stace. Best money I ever spent. I can orgasm from *running*. Think about that for a second. Orgasms are a terrific motivation to hit the gym.

STACY

No, no, I get it. I understand the appeal. I just couldn't *do* it. I don't have it in me.

Break in the conversation as both women drain the last of their fancy, super-high-alcohol-content beers. As they do, they move closer together in the booth; they are sitting like lovers now.

STACY

Does it ever get in the way?

GLORIA

In the way?

STACY

When you're . . . *you* know . . .

A beat, then another. "She's Losing It" by Belle & Sebastian starts up on the sound system. Gloria leans in close, whispers in Stacy's ear.

GLORIA

You wanna feel?

Stacy says nothing, but does not protest. Never breaking eye contact, Gloria takes Stacy's hand off the empty bottle of beer and leads it under the table. Then she wiggles around a bit.

STACY

There it is.

GLORIA

There it is.

STACY

You're . . . um . . .

Gloria kisses her greedily; Stacy responds in kind. Their hands never emerge from underneath the table. Finally, the kiss ends.

GLORIA

I've wanted to do that for the longest time. You have no idea.

STACY

Oh my God.

GLORIA

You're such a good kisser.

STACY

Oh my *God.*

GLORIA

You wanna go back to my place?

Stacy nods vigorously; Gloria signals for the check.

FADE OUT

O-R-D IS ALL THAT REMAINS ON THE REAR PANEL OF THE BATtered pick-up in the driveway. An "F" used to precede the trio, making the letters into a harmonious quartet, just as the truck itself was once white, and not a mishmash of faded eggshell paint, gray putty, and brown rust. A sign is attached crookedly to the driver's-side door—PALADIN PEST CONTROL, it reads, in boldface Comic Sans, above a cartoon termite being dispatched by a cartoon knight in armor that is no longer shining. Leaning against the front fender, fiddling with a BlackBerry, is the owner and sole employee of Paladin Pest Control—the paladin himself, you might say—one Joe Palladino, a shortish guy about my age with linebacker shoulders and a ballerina waistline, his triangle-shaped torso suggesting something from the *Baby Einstein* "Shapes" video. His form-fitting black shirt is tucked into his white painter's pants and cinched by a weave belt, and in the center of the mess of Brillo about his mouth that might generously be called a goatee, a toothpick teeters this way and that, chomped between a set of crooked yellow teeth.

When he sees me, he tucks the BlackBerry into a clip on his belt. I'm not even out of the minivan when he starts talking, his voice as loud as a TV set at a nursing home. "So the mousies are back, huh?"

Maude hears him in her sleep, starts. The pacifier falls out of her mouth, but she doesn't wake up. I alight and close the door gently behind me.

"Yup."

"Good to see you, Josh." Joe gives my hand an authoritative shake, like he's the commander of a battleship and I'm his new XO. He spent time in ROTC, I think, although he never saw active duty. "You know, if you'd let me put those traps down, like I wanted to last year . . . "

"Yeah," I tell him. "You were probably right."

"Don't worry," he says, patting me on the back. "We'll do a number on those little critters."

"Great."

We stand there for a moment in silence. Joe likes to talk, and his line of work doesn't allow for many opportunities to chew the fat. He notices the sleeping Maude in the carseat.

"Wow," he says. "She's getting big."

"Yeah."

"How old is she now?"

"Three." I'm about to add, "and a few months," but Joe doesn't really care, so I withhold that detail.

"Wow." He takes the toothpick out of his mouth and grins. "So, just you and the kid on a Friday afternoon. A little Mr. Mom duty today, huh?"

In the five years that we've been here, Joe Palladino has been to the house more than a dozen times, to do battle paladin-style with wasps, carpenter ants, and, on one occasion, a plague-sized swarm of ladybugs that turned our front porch into a Hitchcock set. On every visit, without fail, he makes a reference to that ridiculous and dated Michael Keaton picture—his subtle way of asserting a claim to alpha male-hood. Because, you see, it's much more manly to cavort with insects than spend time with your daughter. But I indulge him. I laugh at his sorry excuse for a joke. It's either that or knock the fucking toothpick down his throat.

"Yeah, I'd like to have kids someday," Joe tells me, as if this sentiment is one that no one else has ever before considered. "Have to find the right gal first."

I twirl my keychain around my index finger, hoping he takes the hint. "You'd be a wonderful father," I tell him, and Stacy would be proud of the acting it takes to sell the sincerity of the line. I move toward the front door.

"Well," he says, "you would know, right?" He follows me, peacocking his chest. Joe is the sort of guy who feels the need to constantly project his manhood, especially around an obvious inferior like me. Usually I find his compulsion toward machismo amusing. But today I'm in no mood. He derides my fatherly duties, the implication being that I'm less of a man than he is, because his line of work is predicated on my primal fears . . . but it's more than that: he owns his own business, draws an income, makes a decent living—and I don't. No matter how certain I am that stay-at-home fatherhood will benefit my children more than a few extra dollars in the bank, no matter how evolved and twenty-first-century my thinking, the fact remains that masculinity—and by extension virility—is inextricably linked to money. We men are *supposed* to bring home the bacon. Whether this role is innate or learned, nature or nurture, Stanislavski or Stella Adler, we've been playing it for millennia. A few piddly decades of Women's Studies programs, of CEOs in skirts, of Sandra Day O'Connor and Sally Ride and Sarah Palin, can't undo a million years of rigid, inveterate gender dynamics. Money begets power, power begets sex appeal. No one wants to fuck Mr. Mom—not even Mrs. Mom. And yet, taken in strict biological terms, what is more manly than procreation? Animals fight to the death for the right to sire brood, to continue their bloodline. I have kids; Joe Palladino has bugs. Scoreboard, Joe. Scoreboard.

"So I'll let you in," I say, "and then I have to, you know, take care of my daughter."

"Oh, yeah, right." Joe scratches his scruff as he watches me fumble with the lock. "So I went on a date last night that was kind of promising."

I don't say anything.

"Match.com," he continues. "Slim pickings up here, but she seems pretty cool."

"Good for you."

"I'm not one of those guys who operate well in bars, you know? I'm not down with that scene. I mean, I have a beer here and there, but I'd rather do other things. Hiking, climbing, fly-fishing. We went to a bar for the date, though. A wine bar, actually. New place. 36 Main? Down by Snugs? Her idea. She seemed to know the bartenders really well. I think it's where she, like, hangs out."

Finally the lock gives, and I push the door open. As soon as it does, Steve bounds out, dashing through my legs and down the steps.

"He's not doing his job," Joe quips, watching my cat vanish into the woods across the street. He's a barrel of laughs, this guy. A date with him sounds like a fucking Sartre play; *of course* the girl met him at a bar; she'd have to ply herself with cosmopolitans to get through it. "He's gotta earn his keep."

"You know where the basement is, right?"

But the Comic Sans paladin won't take the hint. "She's pretty hot, though. You know, for an older chick. Great legs. I'm kind of a leg man. Not bad upstairs, either. She knows her way around a cocktail dress, that's for sure. And she puts out. On the first date! Not all the way—she probably would have, but you know, I didn't want to push it. Maybe I should have. I don't know. She gives great head, though"—his voice gets softer, like a stage actor's *sotto voce*, even though there's no one within five hundred yards of where we're standing other than a napping three-year-old—"and dude, she *swallows*."

The urge to knock the toothpick down his throat returns. In addition to being contemptibly crude—be grateful you found someone to take you in her mouth, you scumbag, and keep yours shut!—the spit-or-swallow dialectic has always struck me as ridiculous. How could any man, in the throes of hummer-fueled climax, so much as ponder the final resting place of his manufactured goods, let alone genuinely care?

"She's divorced, is the only problem. Not that it's a problem, really. I mean, *I* don't care. We all make mistakes, right? The guy lives in New Paltz"—he pronounces it *Nu Paul's*, like the natives do—"though, so it could be a bit awkward. He's an artist or something. One of his murals was hanging over the bar, she said. Bunch of squiggly lines, looked like to me. Modern art, you know. I don't get it. Was pretty funny, though. 'I can't get away from the guy,' is what she said."

Felicia Feeney. Paul Feeney's lush of an ex-wife. As many notches as Paul has on that legendary bedpost of his—Gloria is not his only lover—Felicia has even more. It's like they broke up and now try to out-slut each other. Like rival siblings, vying for the bigger pile of toys, the more voluminous Christmas-morning haul. Which is curious because the Feeneys, alone among adults in our extended social circle, don't have kids. Paul shoots blanks, is the word on the street. An impotent Don Juan; oh, the irony. I decide not to relay any of this information to the gallant beneficiary of Felicia's swallowing, who, if the rumors are true, may have to contend with bugs of a different kind in a few days.

This is the traditional white American straight man! *This* is who the beer companies make their ads for.

"Well, it sounds like you found yourself a keeper."

He's about to continue, but I cut him off. "Sorry, dude. I have to get my daughter."

"No problem," he says, punching me a bit too playfully on the upper arm, "Mr. Mom."

• • •

When I get back to the minivan, Maude is screaming her head off. Her cries give way to gentle sobs as I extricate her from the five-point harness and carry her into the house.

"Are you hungry? Do you want lunch?"

"No!"

The grimace on her face is so over-the-top that I actually break character and laugh. "Okay, crabcake."

"Lollipop," she barks.

"What?"

"Lollipop! I want a lolly!"

This is where the political component of fatherhood comes into play, where I become Obama in the Situation Room, weighing the pros and cons of military response to this brazen act of defiance. Should I draw a line in the sand and take up arms against the Kandahar lollipop rebels, or simply cave to their modest demands, buying myself a few moments of peace? Key word in the decision-making process: *simply*. Like the American public with respect to Iraq and Afghanistan, I don't have the stomach for further acts of war. Sugar on a stick is a small price to pay for *Pax Lanskya*.

"If you sit quietly and watch something," I tell her, "you can have a lolly."

Yet another banner moment in my campaign for Father of the Year. Alert *Parenting* magazine while I clear a spot on my mantel for the bronze plaque.

I carry her downstairs, set her on the sofa. *Bob the Builder*, a show about a Playmobil-shaped carpenter who speaks in a vaguely marijuana-addled voice—not unlike a male version of Meg—comes on just as I flip on the TV. Twelve o'clock, on the nose. High noon. The theme song, call and response:

Bob the Builder, can we fix it?
Bob the Builder, yes we can!

The most successful political slogan since "Tippecanoe and Tyler, Too," purloined from one of the more irritating kids' shows of all time. *Yes we can!* When Obama contemplates the big decisions, does he then *sit back in his Thinking Chair and think . . . think . . . think*? Perhaps this is what he meant in his Inaugural when he said it was time to put away childish things.

"Lolly," Maude reminds me, as if I could somehow forget the terms of our historic peace treaty.

"Relax, would you? I'll get it."

I take the steps two at a time, find a vitamin C, health-food-store lollipop, unwrap it, and bring it back downstairs.

"I don't want that lolly," Maude says. "I want a *blue* lolly." A Dum-Dum. Can't blame her. The health-food lollipops *ahem* suck.

"We don't have any more blue lollies."

She considers this. Now it's her turn to be Obama in the Sit Room. *Think . . . think . . . think*. She's about to whine again, but the prospect of the prize in hand is too tempting. *We can do . . . any-thing . . . that we wanna do*. Already she's more clever than the fabular dog staring at his reflection in the lake. She grabs the treat, inserts it in her mouth, and eases into the couch and the show.

I retreat upstairs on the double, lest she tack on an eleventh-hour amendment to the bill. She has a bad habit of deciding she wants something on a whim and then demanding it over and over, in increasingly loud and sharp tones, until said object is produced, or she is locked in her room.

It's noon, I've been up for almost seven hours, and all I've eaten is an Egg McMuffin and a few chocolate-chip cookies. Which explains the lightheadedness. The refrigerator offers few tantalizing options. Yogurt, leftover ravioli, Kraft singles, a few bottles of Magic Hat #9, a jar of pickles from the Rosendale Pickle Festival. The Pickle Festival was almost a year ago. Probably should throw those away, but that's a task for another day. Digging in the meat drawer, I unearth the last of the Polish ham I bought on Monday. Is it still good? What's the shelf life on deli meat? Five days is a while to be in the fridge, but then, processed cold cuts are chock-full of preservatives and salt. In theory, they should last forever. Nuclear holocaust might destroy all life on earth, but cockroaches and deli meat would endure. I sniff the plastic. Doesn't smell rank, although this is really Stacy's area of expertise. She's the Anton Fig of the house. I throw the remaining ham—four thin slices, no longer pink; almost Seussian in ham hue, when held to the windowpane light—between two pieces of half-stale whole-wheat bread, add a Kraft single and some (low-fat; it's not *all* bad) mayo, and bring my delectable *répas* to my desk.

In the unfinished part of the basement, by the boiler and the oil tank, Joe Palladino, fresh off his Felicia fellatio, bounds around with an extra hop in his step. A good blow job will do that. Ah, blow jobs. Ah, the warm, inviting mouth slurp-slurping my swelling—

Oral sex sort of falls by the wayside when you have kids. But then, so does sex-sex. You know how, in lieu of birth control that actually works, some couples employ the Rhythm Method? Stacy and I use the Ferber Method—or, more accurately, we have applied the concept of this rather ham-handed sleep-training technique to a different kind of bedroom. When you Ferberize a toddler, you put him in the crib and let him cry for, say, five minutes. Then you go back in and comfort him, before leaving him to cry again. The second time away, you wait ten minutes, then fifteen, then twenty, and so on, until the toddler finally falls asleep on his own. Over time, and in theory, the toddler learns to fall asleep without the visit from Mom or Dad. With intercourse, it works the same way. You go a few days, then a week, then three weeks, then a month, then . . . you get the idea. The Ferber Method doesn't really help crying toddlers sleep through the night. It's even less effective weaning horny adults from their basic need of wet and wild whoopee.

Any new e-mails? Just a note from my sister detailing her Italian vacation and a reminder from Discover that my minimum payment is due. (Next week I'll have to look into the credit card choreography, see if another *pas de chat* in the *danse macabre* of the balance transfer is in order.)

It's not that I don't find Stacy sexy—she remains as alluring as the first time I saw her, in a play in the East Village ten years ago—or that I don't want to screw more often, or that we both don't really dig it when we do. Parenthood saps your energy, and sex—not just sex; lust itself, the primal urge of all creation—requires energy to sustain. Shit, even *God* had to rest after six days of intense creativity. Look, it takes an hour and a half to put the kids to bed every night. An hour and a half! Woody Allen movies aren't that long. Ninety fucking minutes. Every. Fucking. Night. If we devoted half the time we spend reading aloud the work of Dr. Seuss and Kevin Henkes and Ian Falconer, and singing bedtime songs in the rocking chair, and washing hands and faces, and brushing teeth, and preparing sippy cups, and going downstairs, and coming back upstairs because the sheets aren't tucked properly or the noise machine stopped or the ceiling fan cast spooky shadows . . . if Stacy and I devoted just half that time to foreplay, to pleasuring each other with Caligulan abandon, we would be the most sated couple in upstate New York. We would be the Ice-T and Coco of New Paltz. But we don't *turn on* each other; we turn on nightlights and noise machines.

The ham, while not spoiled, is stringy and flavorless. *I do not like them, Sam-I-am.* I choke it down with a big swallow of not-cold-enough Diet Coke.

Furthermore, there's something antithetical to the copulatory act in the drone of the noise machines, the framed photos of the kids on the dresser, the stray Legos in every conceivable nook in the house. *There must be thousands of Legos under our baseboards alone; how many must there be in the world? More than there are grains of sand? More than there are stars in the sky?* Less of a headache to repress the carnal yearnings, to tamp out the need for intimate sexual contact, to whack off every few days with the same utilitarian detachment with which I mow the lawn, to empty my reserves as stolidly as I empty the dishwasher, than to—

Not that I'm complaining. *A time to reap, a time to sow.* That's just how it is at this stage of the game. *A time to cast away stones.* Stacy and I thoroughly enjoyed our period of unbridled, impromptu, kink-infused sex. We experimented with cock rings and

French ticklers, handcuffs and nipple clamps, role play and *Kama Sutra* poses, porno films and costumes, tantra and *soixante-neuf.* We really went to town. But that was then. We're in a different phase now. *A time to gather stones together.* And this phase, like its steamier, wrapped-in-a-brown-paper-bag-after-its-purchase-at-a-store-on-Eighth-Avenue predecessor, won't last forever.

But if Sharon's right, *turn turn turn* Stacy has already turned the page.

For a moment, I'd forgotten. But no, the Headless Whoresman has not given up the chase. His sudden ghostly appearance makes the ham taste like it has, in fact, gone bad. A metaphor for my marriage?

If Sharon's right, my inner Fish in the Pot reminds me. *If.*

SHARON ROTHMAN. AN ODD MESSENGER, TO BE SURE. JOAN-OF-Arc odd. Out of the mouths of babes.

Of the half-dozen mothers in our loose little clique, Sharon is the most mysterious. She moved here last January, when the hyperactive Iris outgrew the family's two-bedroom in Park Slope. But to date, none of our sources of parental gossip—Meg, Jess, Gloria, Ruth Terry—have gotten close enough to Sharon to figure out what the deal is with her and Old Man River, as Stacy calls him. The grapevine has yet to bear fruit. We don't know that much about her. Which makes it even stranger that she would be the bearer of such bad news. Because when you get right down to it, it's an enormous responsibility to reveal someone else's infidelity. Heck, it's an enormous responsibility to know in the first place. Or it should be.

Time to put on my Philip Marlowe hat—a fedora, I suppose—and do a little gumshoeing. Choking down the rest of the ham sandwich, I open Facebook. At the top of the news feed is this:

> ***Gloria Gallagher Hynek*** *and Haven had a great playdate with Jess, Josh, Sharon, Meg, Emma, Maude, Iris, Beatrix and Brooke. So wonderful to spend time with good friends!*

A by-product of our gadget-mad age: users have developed distinctive Facebook styles. Gloria's updates, for example, almost always concern the quotidian, which she tries to spin in the shiniest, happiest way possible. Her house could be burning down and she'd talk about *the pristine beauty of the lapping orange flames*. She's also fond of sharing YouTube links, which I am not fond of following.

Jess Holby only talks about her kids. Her profile picture is of her daughter, Maddie (note: I hate when people do this). She also posts a photo album every other day—a good three quarters of my photo tags are from her. But her husband never writes about his kids, or his wife, or his job at the Culinary Institute. Chris is all about promoting his band, String Cheese. They're playing at Market Market. At the Rosendale Rec Center. At Snug's. At the Muddy Cup.

Catherine DiLullo's news feed doubles as a Google alert for midwifery.

Mike DiLullo is all about the perniciousness of vaccines, high-fructose corn syrup, and Fox News.

Peter Berliner inserts lyrics from classic rock songs and old movies.

Cynthia Pardo isn't on Facebook. Neither is Bruce Baldwin. Although both could wind up going viral any day now.

Meg's updates are snarky. Soren doesn't update often; only when he's drunk, usually.

Stacy posts about food.

As for me, I tend not to divulge day-to-day news—does anyone really care if I'm heading to Meadow Hill Farms this afternoon, or eating a spoiled ham sandwich for lunch, or on Day Five of my ordeal?—and I almost never post links. I only update if I have something important to share, or come up with a plum witticism worth repeating. Which is to say, I post rarely. Twice a week or so.

Sharon hasn't updated her status in almost a month (but I notice that she's untagged the photo from this morning, the one of her with the big hair).

Sharon Rothman is in a Sylvia Plath sort of mood.
September 30 at 1:16am

Sharon Rothman is sunshine & lollipops.
September 21 at 10:54am

Sharon Rothman Iris got a new haircut . . . she's so Louise Brooks.
September 19 at 3:14pm

Not much to go on there. Same profile picture she's had for ages, the shot of her and the infant Iris at the beach. Cape Cod, I think. Wellfleet. She's wearing a straw hat and those giant Nicole Richie sunglasses; you can barely see her face. She could be anyone. Iris, similarly bundled to ward off the sun's nefarious rays, could likewise be any baby, could be a doll for all we know. It's as anonymous a profile picture as you can have without opting for the generic blue silhouette.

Her info page is just as sanitized:

About me
Sex: Female
Birthday: November 2
Relationship status: Married
Interested in: Men, women
Networks: Poughkeepsie

Work & Education
Vassar College, 1997
Poughkeepsie, New York
Scarsdale High School, 1993
Scarsdale, New York

Quotations
"Is there no way out of the mind?" —Sylvia Plath

No photos. No further information, not even a short "likes" list of foreign films or indie bands or thick novels translated from the Russian.

A blank slate. A placeholder page. An ID card purchased in Times Square for ten bucks.

Call her—that's the next move. So I look at our phone list, which Stacy has typed up neatly and magneted to the fridge, but Sharon's number isn't on it. Nor is it contained in the CONTACT INFORMATION on her Facebook page.

So much for that idea.

I click PROFILE and, once there, the link to Stacy's page.

Stacy Ferguson Lansky *Scones here not so bad.*
4 hours ago

Scones not so bad? Come on, now, people! Is that really the status update of an unfaithful wife?

I'm about to laugh the whole thing off—until I check her Wall.

Chad Donovan *Don't be koi.*
15 minutes ago

Chad Donovan? She didn't mention anything about seeing Chad Donovan. And what is the meaning of that cryptic wall post?

And then it hits me. The rumored affair. The weeklong "business trip." Los Angeles. Chad Donovan, her first love; Chad Donovan of the killer backhand and the washboard abs . . .

"Daddy," says Maude in her half-whine, plodding into the office, "I want to watch music."

"Not now." The *Pax Lanskya* sure didn't last long. "Where's your lolly?"

"I ate it."

"What about *Bob the Builder*?"

"I want to watch *music*," she says, more sharply.

What she means is, she wants to sit in my lap and watch videos on YouTube. This is one of the few ways I can get her to sit still. Sometimes she even falls asleep doing this, if she's tired enough—although the early car nap probably blew any chance of that happening now. Fuck it. I'd rather watch music videos than, say, *Little Bill*.

"What do you want to watch?"

"Ummm . . . Mickey Winehouse."

That Maude's managed to conflate two personalities as antithetical as Amy Winehouse and Mickey Mouse never fails to amuse me. Even now, under duress, I can't help but smile. I scoop up my daughter, nestle her in her usual spot on my right leg. She melds her small but powerful body into mine—at moments like this, her tough-guy exterior is revealed as façade—and settles in. With a few short clicks of the mouse—that word again!—I navigate from Chad Donovan's territorial pissing on Stacy's Facebook page to the FAVORITES tab on YouTube, a motley hodgepodge of the Monkees, the Velvet Underground, Celtic Woman, Mad Donna, and braying toddlers singing the ABC song, and on comes the troubled Brit with the soulful pipes, the equine face, the ugly tattoos, and the alluringly deep and deeply alluring cleavage.

Chad Fucking *Donovan*?

I say no no no . . .

There *is* a way out of your mind, Sylvia. Stick your head in the oven.

STACY IS A SERIAL MONOGAMIST. WITH PRECIOUS FEW INTERREGnums, she's had one consort or another seated at the throne next to hers since she started "going out" with Dave the Rock Star her sophomore year of high school. Dave the Guido followed Dave the Rock Star, only to be usurped by Michael-Don't-Call-Me-Mike, who took her to her senior prom even though he'd already graduated. When she got to college—the Carnegie Mellon School of Drama; nothing to sneeze at—Michael-Don't-Call-Me-Mike was replaced by Jason the Mason, a sculptor and her deflowerer, who was in turn dumped for the aforementioned Chad Donovan, a varsity tennis player with a suntan and a six-pack gut who looked, in photos from that era posted to Facebook in which she's tagged, like Sookie's brother Jason on *True Blood*. Hot, in other words. Although he was fifth in an uninterrupted series, Chad was Stacy's first true love. They had one of those college relationships where they sleep in the same bed every night, where they behave like an old married couple and finish each other's sentences, where circles of friends orbit around their starry coupling.

Chad was at Tepper, the business school, and although he had no interest in or aptitude for acting, he grew up in Brentwood, and had industry connections. For spring break her junior year, he brought her to Los Angeles to meet his parents, although the Donovans are cut from the *Less Than Zero* cloth, so they weren't around much. Chad knew somebody who knew somebody, and on a lark, Stacy went to an audition for a pilot—a sitcom based on the movie *The Goonies* (unsurprisingly, it never aired). She didn't get the part, which was just as well, but she managed to impress an influential casting director who is, in the field, well known, but whose name always escapes me. You can probably find it on the bowels of IMDB.

A few weeks after she returned to Pittsburgh, this casting director wanted to bring her back to audition for a part in a film he was working on. He couldn't promise her the leading role that he envisioned for her, *You'd be perfect for it; perfect*, but he had the juice to get her at least a supporting part. Or so he claimed. Casting directors make such promises. The catch was, she had to leave for California immediately. Like, the next plane out. She was in the middle of the spring semester, and leaving would have meant withdrawing from a full slate of classes, surrendering unrefundable tuition, and jeopardizing her future in the Drama School, with only the promise of a small role in a film. There were other mitigating factors as well: her father, with whom she was quite close, suffered a brain aneurysm the day she got back to campus after spring break in L.A., and two days after that news broke, Chad very classily broke up with her—the only time in her history of dating that she'd been given the heave-ho (she started seeing Jeremy, one of the few straight guys in the drama program, eleven days later). After hemming and hawing for a day or so, she opted to stay at school. She'd already made the contact with the casting director, she figured; she could get a small role in a film after she graduated.

Her calculations were off. Miffed, the casting director declared her *persona non grata*—apparently he'd already greased the wheels with the producers, gushing about her, and by bailing she'd made him look foolish—and blacklisted her. And that's how the part of Ruth in *Fried Green Tomatoes* went to Mary-Louise Parker and not Stacy Ferguson (or *Stacey Ferguson*, as her film credit would have read, her birth name having already been claimed at SAG by the erstwhile child actress who now goes by Fergie and fronts the Black Eyed Peas).

The decision still haunts her. *It was the chance of a lifetime*, she's told me, on more than one occasion, usually after a few drinks, *and I blew it. I fucking blew it.* I talk her off the ledge, explain that it was an assessment of risk and reward, like all big choices in life, and the reward—a small chance of a big role in a medium-sized movie—was by no means assured. The likelihood is that she would have gotten a bit part, maybe one without dialogue, and left with a few more relationships and some points toward her Guild card. Would that have been worth wasted semester of school that put her degree in jeopardy? Would that have been worth being in Hollywood the night her dad died, instead of by his side? No and no, I tell her. And even if she'd won the part, and been Taft-Hartleyed by the Guild, and turned in a bravura performance—which she would have, if given the chance; that much was certain—that would not have come with guarantees either.

I think she made the right call. *Unhappy enough to stray*. But I'm not the one who has to live with it.

EXT. MULHOLLAND DRIVE, LOS ANGELES - NIGHT

Top down, a red Porsche 911 is parked on the side of the road, affording a dazzling view of the lights of Los Angeles. In the driver's seat sits CHAD DONOVAN. A form-fitting V-neck T-shirt highlights his buff physique. His powerful right arm rests on the back of the passenger seat, in which sits a rightly impressed STACY. "L.A. Woman" plays on the radio.

STACY

It's beautiful.

CHAD

I know, right? Never gets old.

STACY

I'm really glad you called. It's been *so great* to reconnect. And I've always wanted to go to Koi.

CHAD

You've *got* to do Koi when you're in L.A. Especially when you've never been.

He moves his arm a bit; now he's touching her back.

CHAD

You look *great*, you know? Really. No way would I have thought you had two kids.

STACY

You're just saying that.

CHAD

I'm not even joking. You look hotter now than you did in college. And you were pretty fucking hot in college.

STACY

Now you're being ridiculous.

CHAD

(*unridiculously*)

No. I'm not.

Pause as they take in the view. She's looking at the lights, but his eyes are trained on her.

CHAD

You know, I never should have broken up with you. Biggest regret of my life. I was young, I was stupid. Man, I wish I could take that back.

STACY

Well, what's done is done. It was a long time ago.

CHAD

Is it? I never stopped loving you, you know. Look at me, Stace.

She looks at him.

CHAD

I *never* stopped loving you.

STACY

I know. Me neither.

CHAD

What are we going to do about it?

STACY

I have some ideas.

He pulls her close; they kiss passionately.

CHAD

I love you.

STACY

I love you, too.

We pan back, and Stacy disappears below the dashboard. We hear the CLANK of a belt. On the radio, the song has slowed down; Jim Morrison is singing "Mr. Mo-jo Ri-sin."

STACY

(*off-camera*)

Holy shit. I forgot how *big* it is.

Chad cranes back his head, lets out a loud moan, and we . . .

FADE OUT

SEX WITH BABYSITTERS: THE TRIED-AND-TRUE MALE FANTASY. AN unlikely, if not outright unattainable, brass ring. Like scoring with a bethonged bartender at Coyote Ugly, or a miniskirted hair stylist at a swanky salon. Mostly it's movie stars who boink babysitters. Or so *Us Weekly* would have us believe, as every issue, it seems, breaks yet another babysitter sex scandal. Although they usually put a favorable spin on it and call them *nannies*. Because fucking a *nanny* sounds less sleazy. More upscale. That's something millionaire playboys do. Jude Law fucked his nanny, after breaking up with his movie-star mistress. Ethan Hawke fucked his nanny, and then *married* her, after divorcing his movie-star wife. (They're still together, Hawke and the nanny. We saw them once, up in Woodstock. They looked really happy.)

If Jude Law and Ethan Hawke met our babysitter, however, Sienna Miller and Uma Thurman would seem as attractive to them as they do to the rest of the red-blooded, straight American male population. Although Vanessa is not uncute *per se*, there is something off, very much so, about the sum of the parts. She has a tattoo on her lower back—an ostensibly sexy "tramp stamp"—but it's of a butterfly, and so poorly rendered it looks like something one of Roland's classmates might draw up in Magic Marker. Her low-rise jeans—also ostensibly sexy, especially when paired with the peek-a-boo tat—reveal her ass crack in a way that is less *Keeping Up with the Kardashians* and more *I'm here to snake your clogged drain*. And her eyes, while deep and blue, stare so vacantly, she may as well be Bambi gazing into the angry headlights of an oncoming tractor-trailer. In short, Vanessa, although old for a college student at twenty-six, is such a child that the very idea of banging her is simply unimaginable, quite like the notion of shagging a unicorn, or a My Pretty Pony.

Vanessa is a senior at SUNY New Paltz. She's been a senior for a few years now. She keeps switching majors. First it was psychology, then sociology, then English, then back to psychology. Now she's majoring in ceramics *What does one do with a major in ceramics? Work at Pottery Barn?*, which involved taking a slew of fine arts prerequisites, ceramics not having much overlap with other fields of study.

I made a joke once about kilns. Vanessa stared at me blankly. She appeared not to know what a kiln was.

Back in June, I asked Vanessa if she'd seen *Star Trek*—this was after she'd professed her love for the TV show, so asking about the new movie version was *ahem* logical—and she said, with total candor, "No. I only see movies at drive-ins."

Another time, she was staying at the house while the kids were asleep. She planned to cook mac and cheese for dinner. She asked us if we had, and if she might borrow, a pan, water, and salt. The way she phrased it, she seemed pleasantly surprised that her request could be accommodated.

If that is not enough of an indictment, neither Maude nor Roland particularly care for Vanessa—a big red flag for a babysitter. But she's cheap, and she's reliable insofar as she shows up when she's supposed to most of the time, and unlike the dour young lesbian couple we used briefly last year who spoke condescendingly about "wanting to work for a family that shares our values," while grimacing at our television set and boxes of non-organic cereal—

Maude still recalls, with horror, her two miserable afternoons with Dark-Haired Amy—Vanessa is not judgey. Plus, we don't really use babysitters very often. (This irked Vanessa when she applied for the job, as she'd demanded twenty hours a week of steady work, as if babysitting were the same thing as working the cash register at the Kingston Plaza Fashion Bug.)

"I have to ask you something?" Vanessa's standing at the door, but lacks the initiative to open it. Her shorts are Richard Simmons–short—again, that should be sexy, but the sight of her beefy, overexposed thighs makes my skin crawl.

"Shoot."

"I started a new hobby," and her voice changes, as if the next word is from a dead language, an arcane reference a provincial rube like me couldn't possibly be hip to. "Smoking?"

"Smoking? Like, as in cigarettes?"

"Yes," and she's surprised that I'm down with such subversive activities. I open the screen door to let her in.

"Okay . . . "

"And I'm sort of into it now, and I'm wondering if it's okay to take like a smoke break while I'm here? I'll go outside, of course."

"Of course." I really need to find another babysitter. "But you're only here for a few hours. You don't think you could, you know, maybe wait until I get back?"

"I've developed a habit," she says, shrugging. Now that she's standing next to me, I can smell the reek of cheap cigs on her clothes and frizzy dirty-blond hair. Sometimes cigarette smoke can be a pleasant, aphrodisiac scent. Not with her. My stomach lurches, the bad ham drowning in a sea of hot bile and Diet Coke.

"Well," and I can see I'll have to punt on this afternoon, and post an ad at SUNY for a new babysitter ASAP, "you have to do what you have to do. Just don't do it in front of Maude."

"Thanks."

Clomp-clomp-clomp on the basement stairs—footsteps too heavy to belong to a barefoot three-year-old; Maude has returned to the basement and the Noggin programming; I can hear Moose and Zee, the cartoon station hosts who kill time normally reserved for commercials, singing about an aversion to candy corn—and Joe Palladino powers into the living room. "All set," he says. "Give it a day or three, and those critters are *toast.*"

"Thanks."

Noticing Vanessa, Joe flashes his most winsome smile, which involves a lot of yellow. "Hiya, honey." *Honey?* And he wonders why he has to resort to Match.com in a town where the single-male-to-single-female ratio is so staggeringly in his favor. "Who's this?" he asks me.

"Vanessa, Joe Palladino. Our exterminator."

"Paladin Pest Control." He fishes around in his shirt pocket, produces a crinkled business card, hands it to her. "Call me if you're ever in need of my services." He gives the last word an emphasis that's a bit too creepy for my taste, but I'm pretty sure the erotic subtext goes right over Vanessa's big-permed head.

"Thanks," she says. "I sure will."

"I'll be seeing you," he says to me, but his wide arm gesture takes in the babysitter, too.

"Good luck with Felicia," I tell him. "She sounds like a keeper."

He's halfway down the front stairs before he realizes he never told me her name. I watch him stop in his tracks, consider backtracking to ask me about it, decide against it, and head back to his ORD.

The appearance of Joe Palladino has apparently sparked something in Vanessa's dim memory. "I was watching a show on cable television?" she says, "with my roommate? I can't remember the name of it. It's about this woman, this mother? And she lives in this great big house somewhere in like California I think? And she like deals in marijuana? Because her husband is dead, and she doesn't have a job? The guy, the big goofy guy from *Saturday Night Live*, you know, Hans and Franz? He's in it, too."

"*Weeds.*"

Her eyes light up like I've just revealed to her a forgotten detail about her childhood, or disclosed one of her most precious and closely held secrets. "That's it! Have you seen it?"

"Once or twice."

"Well, the woman on that show? The mother? She looks, I mean, she looks *exactly* like . . . "—trying to recall the name; failing— " . . . like Maude's mom. I was watching it the whole time thinking it was actually her."

Stacy is often mistaken for Mary-Louise Parker, or was, when we lived in the East Village. I understand why strangers, and why buffoons like Vanessa especially, insist upon a resemblance, but I don't really see it. Stacy's prettier, for one thing, her figure less waifish, her nose less *retroussé*, her voice less grating. Stacy is also five years younger, and looks it. If she has a doppelganger Parker, it's Posey, not Mary-Louise. But Mary-Louise Parker is what Stacy always gets, and this never fails to unnerve her, if not outright piss her off, because she *loathes* Mary-Louise Parker. Whatever regrets she has about her short-circuited acting career, she holds Mary-Louise Parker to blame. Whatever vile stew of negative energy that bubbles up inside her when she contemplates opportunities missed, roads not taken, chances lost, she directs at Mary-Louise Parker. Stacy is not by nature a vindictive person—she's *nice*, for lack of a more Kaplanesque word—but when talk turns to Mary-Louise Parker, oh brother, the claws come out. *I can't believe they gave her a Tony for that stinking turd of a performance*, she'll say; *and are we really expected to believe that she can do advanced mathematics?*, even though she never even saw *Proof*. *People think it's acting, but all it is is her trying to wipe that idiotic look off her face*, she'll offer, if anyone mentions the HBO version of *Angels in America*. And forget about *Weeds*. If Stacy were here now, she might bite Vanessa's head off for referencing the W-word. When *Us Weekly* ran the story about Mary-Louise Parker, then seven months pregnant, getting dumped by longtime beau and baby-daddy Billy Crudup, Stacy actually cackled. I mean, she sounded like the witch from *The Wizard of Oz*. It was enough to make me believe in demonic possession. As far as my wife is concerned, the Devil has a face, and it is the (comely) face of Mary-Louise Parker.

"Yeah, she gets that a lot." I put my keys, my phone, and my wallet into their respective pockets. "Maude's in the basement. I'll be back by three."

"Bye, Maude," I shout down the stairs. Am I a shitty father for not going down there again? Screw it. My daughter's had plenty of time, quality and otherwise, with her old man today. "Vanessa's here. Roland and I will be back in a bit."

Maude raises her voice to express her displeasure at this state of affairs, but before she can get into the meat of her argument, I'm out the door.

One of the most salient benefits of moving here from the city, where we paid $175 a month to Russian mobsters for the right to park our car in an ill-maintained lot, is that our driveway is enormous—plenty big enough to accommodate a Honda Odyssey, a beat-up pick-up, and Vanessa's gold Escort, and yet she's managed to park in such a way that it takes an extra five minutes for me to back out.

The clock on the dash, which runs a bit fast, reads 12:43. The first time all day I've been alone. I switch from the radio back to CD, and from the *States Mix* to what Stacy calls the *Testosterone Mix*. Jane's Addiction, Red Hot Chili Peppers, Metallica, Rush, Fugazi, Green Day, and my favorite song *du jour*, "Hit 'Em Up" by 2Pac & the Outlawz.

"Hit 'Em Up" must be the angriest song of all time. You know how Kurt Cobain is pissed off about being *alienated*, and Rage Against the Machine and Circle of Fists are pissed off at *the system*, and Metallica is pissed off at Napster? Here's why Tupac Shakur is pissed off: the Notorious B.I.G. *tried to have him killed*. Attempted murder trumps ennui as a reason to get one's dander up. What happened was, Biggie (allegedly) arranged for some goons to blast Tupac's car outside a Vegas nightclub. 'Pac took five bullets, but didn't die. Instead, he recovered . . . and then wrote a song about how he planned to exact his revenge. The rage is so evident in his voice, especially at the end, that he sounds like he's going to blow a gasket. It's awesome. It's also a catchy tune musically. And I really enjoy the irony of blasting it at top volume from a Honda Odyssey with a MOMS ROCK! sticker on the bumper.

The minivan rolls down Plutarch Road, and 2Pac rolls in his early grave. Heavy bass comes in, and I hit the gas until I'm doing fifty in a thirty-five—the Odyssey has sneaky torque—and I roll down the windows and bang my head to the beat. I rap along with 'Pac, my voice almost a scream, and it feels so good to let loose this way:

First off, fuck your bitch, and the clique you claim,
West Side, when we ride, come equipped with game
You claim to be a playa, but I fucked your wife . . .

Shit.

I kill the stereo.

Now all I can think of is Chad Donovan, from the "West Side" of the United States, and *very* well-equipped with game, taunting me about fucking my—

I ride the rest of the way to Thornwood in silence, my mind so fraught with activity it's blank, like my old desktop frozen by too many open applications. I get there a few minutes early, so I try Stacy's cell. Straight to voicemail.

Then I call up our landline voicemail and listen to her message from this morning. It's all I can do not to read confession and guilt into her choice of words, her vocal inflections, her uncanny ability to call at the only time I was not able to get to the phone:

Hey, Josh, it's me. Woke up really early for some reason, [because Chad's hard cock pressing against my ass-cheek stirred me] so I figured I'd try you before the day gets away from me [because I'm going to stay in bed all day fucking

Chad]. You're probably, I don't know, maybe you're in the shower? That's probably good if you are [because I couldn't bear to actually speak to you after what I've done]. Are you asleep? Shit. I hope you're not asleep. [I feel guilty for taking Chad's meaty cock, but I'll pretend my guilt is for maybe waking you up]. No, it's seven thirty there, there's no way. Anyway . . . really miss you guys [because seeing you will help relieve my guilt]. It's nice out here [especially when Chad leads me to multiple orgasms], but I really can't wait to come home [I really mean "come again," not "come home," but maybe you won't notice]. It's time [to fuck Chad again—he's waking up now and already hard as a rock and his cock is . . .]. Too long, too long to be away. I'm going to try and go back to sleep [or, rather, to bed, where Chad awaits], I think, so . . . yeah, I'll just . . . I'll call you later, okay [because if you call now, the phone might ring with Chad inside my wet box, and that would be really awkward . . . and also would ruin my orgasm]? Hope the drop-off goes okay. Love you [like a brother]. Miss you [but not that much]. Bye [gotta go hop on Chad].

And this sends my overtaxed brain back to the world of Seuss, to the bedtime book I read Maude last night:

Dad is sad.
Very, very sad.
He had a bad day.
His wife is fucking Chad.

Friday, 12:58 p.m.

***Daryl Wade "Duke" Reid** (b. March 3, 1965, in Charlottesville, Va.) is the American bass player, singer, and principal songwriter for the alternative rock/punk band **Circle of Fists**.*

Here's what I'm able to glean from the rest of his Wikipedia page, which I printed out this morning, and which now rests on the steering wheel, and which I'm forcing myself to read to get my mind off the topic of Chad the Cad:

After forming in Greenpoint, Brooklyn, in the late eighties—back when Greenpoint was still Warsaw West and not yet Hipster Central—the band moved to Washington in 1989 and was a major player in the renascent punk scene there. Their debut album, *3301 Waverly Drive*, was released in '91 on Dischord Records. Their sophomore effort, *Saved By Demon Song*, featuring "Crystal Meth, Dance of Death," a minor hit on college radio, came out to much fanfare in 1993, leading to a deal with I.R.S., which put out the band's commercial magnum opus, *The Worst Crime*, in 1995.

"My Heart Is Hydroplaning," reviled by many fans as a "sell-out" track, enjoyed considerable play on MTV and rose to #34 on the *Billboard* chart in November 1995, and is often used in movies and TV shows (although you never hear it on the radio). The three-piece band broke up in 1997 after the death of drummer Bernie Mash in a drunk-driving accident.

Reid occasionally tours with other disbanded D.C. punkers, most notably the legendary Ian MacKaye, but has not released an album since 2003's mellower solo effort, *The Dark Undone*. He was engaged briefly to actress Rose McGowan, who ditched him for Marilyn Manson. He lives in New Paltz—in one of the mansions in the shadow of the Ridge, is what I've heard—with his swimsuit-model wife and their two children.

There are two more pages—early life, early career—but it's time to fetch Roland.

The Thornwood classroom is cozy—too small, really, for the twelve students and three teachers it contains at any given time. To the right as you enter are the cubbies, crammed into a narrow corridor that fills up like a rush-hour subway platform when the kids arrive or depart. There are three tables—Rectangle, Square, and Circle—where the children take their lunch, and shelves teaming with art supplies, puzzles, toys, and games. In the back corner of the room is a padded mat, the stage for the daily soap opera that is Circle Time. The walls are adorned with various collections of art projects, handprints and snowflakes and the like, and on the back wall, a collage of the students' names (twenty total, counting the part-time kids: Tucker, Tyler, Taylor, Walker, and Parker; Aidan, Ethan, Jaiden, Jayden, and Hayden; Jake, Max, Olivia, Isabella, and Emily; Reeve, Caleb, Joey, Zara, and Roland). The trend in the twenty-first century is to name your kid for an obsolete line of work. A *walker*, for example, was, in a certain part of Great Britain, the same thing as a fuller: a dresser of cloth (cloth had to be trampled upon in cold water, hence *walk*). A *reeve* was a kind of steward; a *tyler*, a maker of tiles. Will preschoolers of the twenty-third century be named Webmaster, Shortstop, Cashier, and Coldcaller? Time will tell.

When I get to the classroom, the kids are all sitting on the floor in a sloppy semicircle around Mrs. Drinkwater, with Roland occupying the lap of Lenore (Roland prefers to be cared for by beautiful people; hence his unvarnished disdain for Vanessa). As the parents begin to make their entrances, chaos reigns, the kids popping out of position, exclaiming "Mommy! Mommy!" or "Daddy! Daddy!" while Mrs. Drinkwater, Lenore, and another aide, Irene, struggle to maintain control.

No sign of Daryl "Duke" Reid or his knockout wife, but Zara is here, tucked away in the Circle Time corner, hiding behind the pleats of Mrs. Drinkwater's long skirt. Zara's long brown hair is cut in crooked bangs over her eyes, revealing an elfish-looking face and small but shiny brown eyes. She's wearing a blue-on-blue Hanna Andersson dress, white leggings, and Dora the Explorer sneakers—not at all what you'd expect of the child of a punk god and a model—and she can't weigh more than forty pounds. She looks a little bit like Pinkalicious, of the eponymous children's book.

Usually Roland mentions his classmates only as part of an indistinguishable group. "I want to see my friends," he'll say. Or, if I asked him whom he played with that day, he'll reply, "Friends." "Which friends?" "All of them." Rarely does he talk about any one individual. The exception is Zara. He seems to genuinely like Zara. Like, romantically. Once he told me, "I like her even more than Cleveland," which, for him, was quite the confession.

Roland, noticing me, bursts forth from Lenore's clutches and takes a long detour around the room, bouncing off classmates and parents alike, until he barrels into me with such force he almost knocks me over. "Daddy!" he says. He wouldn't be more excited if I'd rescued him from Gilligan's Island.

"Hey, Roland. How's your day?"

"Oh, it's a pretty great day," he says, without much conviction. If I repeat the question, in fact, there's a good chance he'd say the opposite.

Mrs. Drinkwater, now standing on the chair that she'd been perched upon—she's too matronly to actually sit on the floor—announces that it's time to go to the pumpkin patch. We shouldn't drive caravan-style, she says, because it's not safe. There are printed directions if we don't know where to go. Please be careful exiting the parking lot.

A cascade of overstimulated kids and overwhelmed parents flows out of the undersized classroom, trickles down the undersized hallway, and bursts into the undersized parking lot, with its oversized minivans and SUVs and tripped-out trucks with oversized names like Armada, Avalanche, Sequoia, Galleon, many of which sport the red-blue-and-yellow "puzzle" ribbon proclaiming AUTISM AWARENESS. (Are the ad men just fucking with the auto execs with these big, unwieldy names? A Chevy Avalanche? Really? What's next, the GM Asteroid? The Honda Rigel? The Chrysler Obama's Socialist Government?)

In the mass exodus I lose sight of wee Zara Reid, and her famous father is nowhere to be found.

WHEN WE LIVED IN NEW YORK, THE WEATHER WAS AN AFTERthought. If it rained and you were caught without an umbrella, you bought one for three bucks from the Somalian immigrant who materialized out of the subway exhaust with a cardboard box full of knock-off Totes. Spring and fall were interchangeable; winter was sometimes too cold, summer sometimes too hot; but that was the extent of it. One of the selling points of upstate, for us, was *communion with nature*. We wanted to be aware of the changing seasons. To chart the phases of the moon. To live off the land. To breathe in air that wasn't polluted by bus fumes and Ground Zero smoke.

We were, in retrospect, idealizing Mother Nature, that fickle little whore. Here is a summary of the seasons of New Paltz, New York:

WINTER

Snow removal becomes a major operational expense. Heavy sleet storms knock down branches, causing frequent power outages—dangerous, as the furnace starter runs on electricity. Kids need coats, hats, scarves, mittens, boots, so getting out of the house becomes more difficult. The flu runs rampant in the preschool.

SPRING

The flora and fauna come back to life . . . and so do the bugs, especially the mosquitoes, but also wasps, yellow jackets, horseflies, and gnats, so you can't sit out on the porch, or go down to the swings.

SUMMER

Kids go in and out of wet bathing suits, the metal carseat fasteners are hot enough to brand cattle, and every time you hit the playground, the kids must be slathered in sunscreen like so many spareribs in BBQ sauce. Bug-life tapers off a bit, but bees and wasps ascend to rule the yard. Thornwood is closed for several weeks, so there's no childcare break.

But the fall! O, but the fall is sublime! The foliage morphs from ubiquitous green to a broader palette, browns and yellows and oranges and reds, and the bugs fall dead, and the sun's rays lose their ability to broil your skin, and it's too chilly to swim, but not chilly enough to stay indoors. Football and basketball begin their seasons, and baseball ends. School starts. The Pickle Festival comes to Rosendale, and the New Paltz Halloween parade is one of the year's highlights. A popular fall activity for tourists and local yokels alike is picking fruit at the orchards. Apples, peaches, nectarines, cherries, blueberries, pumpkins—you ride a tractor out to the trees, fill plastic bags with nature's bounty, and head home never wanting to eat another piece of fruit again as long as you live.

Meadow Hill Farms is in Highland, the next town over, a ten-minute ride from Thornwood. Roland spends his ten minutes flipping through the "car copy" of his *Field Guide* and commanding me to repeat-play "Hotel California," his current favorite of the tracks on *The States Mix*. The political signs change, I notice, as we cross Black Creek and leave New Paltz.

Don Henley has just sung about the Mercedes-Benz and the pretty, pretty boys for the second time when we pull into the driveway, which, in keeping with local custom, is half a mile long, crooked, unpaved, muddy, and rutted with potholes as wide and deep as medicine balls. A well-tanned white guy with dreadlocks looks up from the sprinkler system he's tinkering with and gives us a little wave as we drive by. I wave back, and thus do not see the pothole, which appears to be the work of a meteorite. The minivan lurches down and then back up, but the tire holds its integrity. Roland grouses from the back seat. "Ayyyyyyahhh," he whines.

"Sorry," I tell him, using the diversion to kill the Eagles.

"Daddy," he says. "Music!"

"We're *here*, Roland."

"Music!"

"Fine."

I turn the CD player back on and make a hard left. There is no parking lot *per se*, just a clearing of trampled grass and dirt among the apple trees, where many of the ginormous vehicles from the Thornwood lot have clumsily reassembled. I park my Odyssey next to a Ford Excursion with a YANKEES SUCK sticker on the rear panel. (Red Sox fans are some deluded motherfuckers. Yes, the Yankees suck . . . and the earth is flat, Stephen Hawking idiotic, Taylor Swift overweight, Glenn Beck sane.)

I liberate Roland from his carseat and pry the *Field Guide* out of his hands. As I set him on the uneven surface, a burnt-orange and refreshingly bumper-sticker-free Nissan Murano screeches to a stop in the "space" next to my minivan. In the back seat is a brown-haired girl who looks like Pinkalicious. In the driver's seat, black wool hat pulled down to his thick but well-kept eyebrows, is the unmistakable figure of Daryl "Duke" Reid.

I'm seized with panic. Although I have volunteered myself to engage him, Reid's celebrity intimidates me. I don't want to come off like one of the madding crowd of Circle Jerks who emerge when he appears for breakfast at the Bistro (see how they drool). And, I mean, what if he's not in the mood to acknowledge my existence? But then I tell myself that he and I are both here for the same reason: to collect pumpkins that we will bring home, carve, and leave on our front steps to rot. We're both dads. We have common ground. And it's not like I'm asking him for a spare kidney. He might *want* to appear in *Rents*.

But there's more to it than starfuckerphobia. If Joe Palladino, our timepiece of an exterminator, represents the moribund model of masculinity, Daryl "Duke" Reid epitomizes the avant-garde ideal. He is the sort of man I aspire—or, more accurately, aspired—to become (but without so many tattoos). He's successful, he's beloved, he's famous—not Obama famous, but famous enough—he's respected, and above all, he's a dutiful dad who makes a living through his art. By any measure, he's living the dream. How can I not simper in the face of this *we're not worthy* paragon?

I came close. That's the part that's so frustrating. I sold a film script. Not many screenwriters can make that claim. I won money from a game of chance that stymies almost everyone. But that's all I did. Three-of-a-kind on the slot machine, the clang of coins cascading into the plastic tub, a nice haul, but hardly the life-altering jackpot I was hoping for. *You're so talented, Josh*, my mother assures me (she's Jewish; this is part of her job description). *Every day I thank God for your talent*. I don't share her gratitude. Talent is like a lottery ticket: if it doesn't pay out big, it's just a tease. Is it better to be talented and broke, or a rich hack? The young aspiring artist would hold with the former, but anyone over the age of thirty knows better. I should have gone to fucking law school, like my mother wanted.

"Look, Roland," I tell my son, as I fight off my urge to run for the hills. "It's Zara."

What I'm hoping will happen here is, Roland will notice Zara, wave at her, and the exchange will give me an excuse to wait for Reid to get out of the car so I can say hello, assuming my nerve has been sufficiently worked up by then. But the boy is having none of it. He's still in architecture mode, his mind far away, puzzling over the intricacies of Shingle and Stick, French Eclectic and Gothic Revival, dormers and cornices and gables.

Head in the clouds is the Asperger's cliché, but with Roland, a better analogy is that he's underwater, swimming contentedly around the fishbowl of his mind, like one of those large aquatic mammals that only has to come up for air every two hours. He's dimly aware of what's happening above the surface, but does not try to engage, any more than a dolphin would interpose in a conversation between two Sea World employees. Unlike the dolphin, Roland's *capable* of interaction; he just doesn't want to interact most of the time, because in social situations, like a dolphin on dry land, he's out of his element.

Already my feeble plan has failed. The best I can do is take my time closing the door and take the long way around the minivan, which doesn't have the desired effect either, because Roland's noticed the other kids heading for the big wooden platform rigged to the tractor on the other side of the "parking lot," and gives my wrist a surprisingly forceful tug.

"Come on, stupid daddy."

"I'm not stupid. Please don't call me stupid."

We head toward the platform, Roland trying to pick up the pace, me trying to slow us down, his body going limp and then pulling taut, like a kite-string on a windy beach day. I look over my shoulder just in time to see Reid emerge from his orange car. I've seen him before—at school functions, at Lowe's, at the Bistro, where he seemed flattered by the attention of the fawning waitstaff—but aside from the occasional greeting by way of a nod and a "hey," I've never spoken to him.

Reid is a big guy. Not fat, and not particularly muscular—the video for "My Heart Is Hydroplaning," in which he cavorts shirtless in a mosh-pit, his well-inked arms as ripped as a middleweight's, is a good fifteen years old, if you can believe it—just big. He's a legit six-four, but filled out, like a boxer no longer in training. He towers over me (I'm five-eight in my Doc Martens; either average height for an American male or short, depending on whom you ask). And he always wears some slight variation of the same uniform outfit: dark blue Dickies jacket zipped over a bright orange hooded sweatshirt, work pants the same color as the jacket, engineer boots, and on his presumably bald dome, either a wool hat or a bandana, depending on the season. He dresses like a security guard, or a gas station attendant (or how gas station attendants used to dress in my suburban New Jersey youth; we don't have gas station attendants in New York).

Reid is fiddling with his iPhone—I think it's an iPhone; I'm too far away to tell—as he opens Zara's door. The pixie girl bounces out of the orange car and heads for the gaggle of kids over by the tractor, her Dora sneakers lighting up as she runs. Without looking up, Reid closes the door, locks the car, deposits the keys—which dangle from a metal chain, punk rock style—into his pants pocket, and follows her, peeking up from the tiny screen every few moments to avoid banging into a car or tripping over the half-worm-eaten apples strewn around the ruined lawn.

Roland, seeing Zara racing toward us, releases my hand and breaks into a run. She gigglingly follows him, passing me. I could either slacken my pace to wait for Reid or pick it up to catch up to the kids. Not trusting Roland, and feeling shy myself about interrupting the rock star's heated text exchange for something as mercenary as an interview request for a magazine he's almost certainly never heard of, I opt for the latter. No sooner do I start my half-jog than my foot catches in a hole in the grass, tweaking my ankle. Fortunately, nothing gives. While I manage to catch my fall, I can't stop the reflexive f-bomb from escaping my mouth. But the only person close enough to me to hear is Reid, and he's too absorbed in his iPhone to hear me . . . and even if he did, would a punk rock god really get his panties in a twist over a stray *Fuck*?

By the time I get to the tractor and the throng of kids, parents, and teachers, Roland and Zara have already found seats. I climb up rickety stairs to the platform, a crudely constructed plywood rectangle about eight feet wide and twenty feet long, with benches around the perimeter and in the middle, enclosed by a yard-high rail of two-by-fours. Most of the seats are already taken. Although Roland and Zara climbed up one after the other, he decided not to sit with her, instead finding a spot next to Tucker, who is not, best as I can tell, on the spectrum, unless there is an arcane DSM category for Mean Kid Who Doesn't Listen to His Teachers, Stirs up Trouble, and Enjoys Inflicting Pain. Tucker has the face of an angel, a snake-oil-salesman manner, and a collection of hip *Star Wars* T-shirts he wears every day, but make no mistake: the kid is a bad seed. I actively dislike him. On the other side of Tucker is his faithful sidekick, Joey, a fat Italian kid dressed in a gold Nike running suit, matching pants and jacket, like Bobby Bacala from *The Sopranos*. Joey has some sort of speech delay; instead of saying *He hit me*, he'll go with *Him hit me*. He is also the only kid in the class whose parents I've never actually seen.

Roland thinks that Tucker and Joey are a barrel of laughs. He equates being naughty with being funny. He doesn't understand the nuance. This sort of thing worries me. I don't want him to fall in with the wrong crowd, with rotten apples (the metaphorical answer to the ones all over the ground) who will take advantage of his trusting nature. My mind is rife with scenarios of his naïveté getting him into trouble when he's a teenager. *Just put the CD in your jacket and walk out, Roland. The cashier won't even notice. It'll be a gas.* Aspie kids get picked on a lot in school because they often don't understand when their tormentors are being mean to them. Deciphering the motives of a sophisticated bully is beyond the scope of their cognitive abilities. Hopefully he'll stay tall and handsome and interested in girls. Girls will keep him out of trouble. Three cheers for girls! For now, though, the Tuckers of the world are content to lead the Rolands of the world down the wrong path. Like, Tucker will sometimes smack Roland across the face for no apparent reason. Roland will react by slapping him back. Sometimes this gets him into hot water with Mrs. Drinkwater, although to be honest, I'd rather he hit back than just take it with a grin. In any case, I'm not pleased with my son's choice of seat.

Ideally, I'd wait for Reid to sit and find a spot next to him. But he's still on the grass, fiddling with his iPhone, and in no apparent hurry to board the clumsy wooden platform, which lists back and forth like a Shanghai harbor junk. So I take a seat on the middle bench, caddy-corner from Roland, Joey, and Tucker, between Lenore and Ethan's mother, an obese woman given to wearing pastel-colored shirts with pictures of unicorns and fairies on them. Because Thornwood is a special school, the student body hails from towns all over Ulster County: Highland, Plattekill, Milton, Marlborough, Modena, Clintondale, West Park, Port Ewen, and so on, where church attendance is higher, Republican sympathy stronger, mean household income lower, college degrees rarer, gun ownership more common, and NASCAR interest more acute, than they are in New Paltz. And while I have nothing against Jesus, Giuliani, blue collar employment, GEDs, revolvers, or Jeff Gordon, there is not much overlap in the Venn diagram of "People Who Like Those Things" and "My Friends." Thus I have not fraternized much with the other Thornwood parents, who are probably just as put off by my ironic T-shirts, stylish glasses, Doc Martens, and staunch belief, as evidenced by the OBAMA/BIDEN bumper sticker on Stacy's Outback, that the President was not born in Kenya. I smile, I say hello to the kids, I comment on the weather, and that's the extent of my interaction. But there's more to it than simple elitism. To engage at Thornwood means having to talk about The Spectrum. And I don't want to talk about it. The last thing I want to do, when contending with Asperger's for most of the day, is spend my free time discussing Asperger's.

Ethan's mother sits so that that she's turned away from me, her giant ass a veritable Hadrian's Wall between us. Just as well.

"Pumpkins," Tucker says, "taste like *poop*."

This cracks up Roland, who says, "Tucker is so silly." *Silly*, his catch-all word.

I can think of some other choice adjectives to describe Tucker, but I let it go. "Yes," I say. "Tucker is indeed silly."

Reid is the last person aboard the wooden contraption that will carry us down the half-mile length of broken road to the pumpkin patch. He finds a seat next to his daughter, as far from me as you can get on the platform, and across from Olivia's mother, who is dressed to the nines. Salon Mom, Stacy calls her; I don't even know her real name. Lisa? Liz? Lauren? Something with an "L." Tanning-salon tan, perfectly manicured nails, perfectly frosted hair, and an outfit several degrees too dressy and/or revealing for the occasion. Today she's wearing skinny jeans, a form-fitting sweater, and shiny red pumps with three-inch heels. Heels! To the pumpkin patch!

At long last, Reid looks up from his cell, which I'm now close enough to confirm is, indeed, an iPhone. "No reception out here," he says, to no one in particular.

"AT&T is horrible," says Salon Mom, adjusting herself so her small but firm tits are pointed at him. "I didn't get an iPhone because I just didn't want to deal with them."

Before Reid can respond, the owner of Meadow Hill Farms—who is a) named MacDonald, and b) sort of old—climbs onto the tractor. "Hello, boys and girls," he says, his voice disturbingly loud. "Welcome to the farm! Who's ready to *pick some pumpkins*?"

The kids all cheer maniacally, as if prompted to do so by a guy waving a sign on the set of *Leno*. Sort-of-old MacDonald fires up the tractor, which comes to life with a series of clangs and starts, and the entire platform rumbles with its shaky engine.

"Let's go!"

I glance around the platform. Even the parents seem excited about this little adventure. Salon Mom, for one, looks like she might orgasm (in her defense, the throbbing of the platform does add a frisson of tactile pleasure to the experience). Pumpkin picking, I don't get it. Seems to me that if I'm working the fields, harvesting the orange gourds myself, *they* should pay *me*, not the other way around. Apples at least you can eat, or give to teachers, or throw like baseballs. But pumpkins? Heavy, bulky, useless. Beyond that, these field trips make me nervous. Although there are plenty of kids here on the spectrum, and therefore less potential for judgment, that doesn't make it easier when Roland misbehaves. I'm constantly fretting about what he might do. And today, the pressure of landing the *Rents* interview has pushed my anxiety to new levels. It's almost enough to make me forget what Sharon told me, and that little shit Chad Donovan. Almost. But the nagging ache in the pit of my stomach is a constant reminder.

Reid is deep in conversation with Salon Mom, who would, I'm sure, suck him off right there in the tractor bed if he but said the word. Roland seems happy. He, Tucker, and Joey are shrieking with glee as the tractor winds its way down the long path. Up ahead, a big red barn, which can charitably be described as "distressed," approaches.

"So I understand you're a screenwriter," Lenore says.

I was so preoccupied with my own shit that I forgot about the pretty twentysomething speech therapist sitting beside me. "That might be overstating it," I say. "But yes, I write screenplays." *Write,* or *wrote?*

"Cool," she says. I can't tell if she's sincere or just trying to make conversation. "Anything I might have seen?"

God, I hate when people ask that question. I know she's trying to be nice, and for all I know she's genuinely curious, but still. "Not yet."

She seems mildly disappointed. "Well, I'm sure it's just a matter of time."

"Thanks." I change the subject. "I hear Roland's been mean to you."

"No, no. Roland's a sweet kid. He just says some funny things sometimes. He has such an active imagination."

"That he does."

Our conversation ends as the tractor lurches to a stop, every last person on the platform falling forward. Sort-of-old MacDonald stands up on the tractor and holds out his arms like a ringmaster at a circus. "Here we are!" he cries. "One pumpkin each! Last one there's a rotten egg!"

Mrs. Drinkwater, positioned by the stairs, tries to manage the ensuing mass exodus created by the rotten-egg incantation, but in vain. Parents and kids push and shove their way pell-mell and tumble bumble down the narrow stairs, and scamper into the pumpkin patch, a football-field-sized expanse just behind the big "distressed" barn, as fast as four-year-old legs can carry them. "One each," the white-haired teacher hollers, tumbling after, slowed by her long skirt and her brittle legs. "Just one each!"

Tucker is first to the pumpkin patch, Joey and Roland at his heels. I decide not to try and catch up. *Chill out, Josh. Have some trust. Let the boys have their fun.*

I watch my son run—he's fast, faster than I ever was, his build tall and lean, like a cross-country runner's, like my father's—and the others follow him, and when I snap out of it, I realize I'm alone on the platform with Daryl "Duke" Reid. We get to the steps at the same time. A golden opportunity to engage him.

"After you," I say.

"I insist," he replies.

So I go down first, but I wait for him. "Zara's a real sweetheart," I tell him. "My son adores her. I'm, um, Roland's dad."

"I know," he says. "She talks about Roland all the time."

"Nothing bad, I hope." I recall last year's crush, Mollie, with her round face and cute glasses, how Roland used to express his affection by biting her leg and trying to cut her forearm with scissors.

Reid chuckles. "No," he tells me. "Nothing bad."

"Roland can be a handful."

"Zara's used to it. She has an older brother."

"Oh yeah? How old?"

"Six. Almost seven. He's in the second grade."

Elementary school is so far in my future that it feels like science fiction. When Roland is in second grade, there will be spaceships and teleportation devices and phasers set to stun—or so it seems. But of course this is ludicrous. A year from now, he'll be in kindergarten, armed with his IEP and his classification and his milk money, well on his way to the numbered grades of the primary school, to puberty, adolescence, and what lies beyond.

"Seems a long way off."

"It goes quick," Reid says. "Everybody says that, but it's true."

We're almost at the pumpkin patch, approaching earshot of other parents. Now is the time to ask. Now. Right now. *Are you listening, Josh? Now!* But I can't quite pull the trigger.

"You guys in New Paltz?" Meaning the school district, not the town proper.

"We are, yeah, but Wade goes to the Annex."

But the moment is over, the ship has sailed. Here comes Mrs. Drinkwater, making a beeline toward us. "Mr. Reid," she says, "can I speak with you for a moment?"

"Sure," Reid says, and then to me, "Excuse me, man," and off he goes with Mrs. Drinkwater, taking all hope for my first successful freelance pitch with him.

With no one else I care to talk to at the farm, I turn my attention to Roland. He's still with Tucker and Joey, the three of them a bit too rambunctious for my comfort level, although neither Mrs. Drinkwater nor the other aides seem to mind. Not content to simply choose a pumpkin and be done with it, they are racing around the patch, picking up softball-sized pumpkins and dropping them on the ground. For Tucker, this is his first step on the road to juvenile delinquency. Not hard to connect the dots from smashing pumpkins to spray painting swastikas on highway overpasses. Joey, for his part, is too dense to know this is bad behavior. Tucker controls him as surely as Lex Luthor did Otis in *Superman II*. As for Roland, he just thinks it's funny. He doesn't appreciate the destructive nature of what he's doing. He doesn't understand the consequences, the ramifications.

"Roland," I tell him, "we should really just pick out a pumpkin. Like Zara's doing."

Indeed, the Pinkalicious lookalike has found a gorgeous ripe gourd that her father is helping her haul.

"No," Roland says, but kindly, patiently, as if I'm misconstruing what's going on. "We're playing the Pumpkin Drop game."

And back he goes into the fray. I try and relax—he's not hurting anyone; he's not even hurting the pumpkins, really, just handling them a bit roughly—and my main concern with him is always that he'll hurt someone. Plus, none of the teachers seems concerned. So I let it go. But I suddenly feel, out here in the wide-open pumpkin patch, in the wide-open farm, in the wide-open expanse of upstate New York, a wave of claustrophobia come over me. Like I might drown. Why must I, as a father, be subjected to this degree of vulnerability? Why can't Roland and I just stay home, where it's safe, where I can exercise some semblance of control, where if my son screws up, no one will witness the transgression and judge him, judge me? I look up at the sky, only a few stray clouds against a backdrop of bright blue—four cotton balls on blue construction paper; a Maude Lansky art project—and the tops of the trees start to spin through the blinding afternoon sun. I close my eyes, take a deep breath, and the feeling of vertigo *thank God* passes.

At last Mrs. Drinkwater summons the class to gather round her pleated skirts. Mercifully, Tucker decides to heed her command, and Joey and Roland follow him. She instructs them to give their pumpkins to their parents and follow her to the play area, where there are picnic tables, and on the picnic tables, cider and apple donuts for our snack. (Will there be sufficient donuts for the adults, too? I sure hope so. I'm kind of hungry.)

Roland dashes over to me, hands me his pumpkin—a smallish, ill-formed monstrosity that looks a bit like Spookley—as if it were a hot potato, and runs back to Tucker and Joey (whose parents, needless to say, are elsewhere this afternoon). The up-to-no-good duo leads the charge to the play area, my impressionable son whooping it up at their heels.

How I loathe those two little brats! I know they're kids, and kids are innocent, blank slates, and blah blah blah, but man, I really hate them. There were kids like Tucker and Joey when I was little, too, stirring up trouble, ruining the fun for the rest of us. What's the point in them even existing? Why did their neglectful parents even bother conceiving them? Will they ever offer anything positive to society? Because things don't turn out well for kids like this. The Joey of my high school is now in prison; after his Ponzi investing scheme failed, he got drunk one night and set fire to his office. A janitor almost died, had third-degree burns on his face. Arson is serious shit; my Joey will be in jail for a long time. My Tucker didn't make it that long. He died in a drunk-driving accident junior year (he was at the wheel, and, fortunately, had just dropped off his girlfriend, the only other passenger). His mangled car sat on the lawn in front of the high school for weeks afterward, behind a superfluous sign that told us DON'T DRIVE DRUNK.

It's hard not to ponder, watching preschoolers play on a perfect October afternoon, all the bad things that can befall them. Illnesses and generic defects. Allergic reactions to peanuts and shellfish, anaphylactic shock. Car accidents. Fires. Drunk driving. Emotional and psychological breakdowns. Depression. Venereal disease, herpes, AIDS, and genital warts. Alcoholism, drug addiction, sex addiction. Anorexia, bulimia. Obesity. Cancer, lupus, Lyme disease. Murder, rape. Prostitution, drug dealing, petty crime. Prison. Blindness, deafness, loss of limbs. Post-traumatic stress disorder. Post-partum depression. Infertility. Bad luck.

And even if everything turns out okay, even if they make it through relatively unscathed, these little containers of our love, our hope, our belief in the future . . . how many of *us* have a genuinely good relationship with *our* moms and dads? What's the percentage? It can't be more than fifty-fifty; it can't. The odds are against us, as parents. The deck is stacked, the dice loaded. We'll give, we'll give, and we'll give some more . . . and our kids will bitch about us in therapy, if not outright dislike us. Yet here we are at the pumpkin patch, feeding on their youthful glee, pretending otherwise. If that doesn't speak to the inherent optimism of human nature, I don't know what does.

On the other side of the barn, in a little clearing that should be but isn't fenced in, is a series of haphazardly sited wooden playhouses, six of them in all, each big enough to hold about five kids, and each equipped with a door prone to slamming shut. The boys are now running from one house to the other, doors slamming behind them. I close my eyes, but even the slamming sound conjures visions of broken fingers and ER trips. Other kids approach the play area, join in. Eventually, the entire class, sixteen children in all, have joined the game (all except Taylor, who is terminally shy and sits with her just-as-shy mother at the picnic table). Wham! Like claps of thunder, the doors slam. It gets to the point where my body shakes with each slam, like I'm a shell-shocked soldier in a Vietnam movie.

Mrs. Drinkwater and the aides, Lenore and Irene, summon the class to the tables, where the cider and apple donuts are laid out beneath white napkins in big baskets, but no one is listening. The only ones gathering at the donuts are the bees.

"Attention, children," she says again, stepping onto the bench. "The donuts are here."

I detect the slightest loss of confidence in Mrs. Drinkwater. Like she's lost control of her charges, like she doesn't know what to do. A convoy of cars is running the red light, and she's a traffic cop on the side of the road, waving white gloves at SUVs, blowing her whistle vainly over the throb of the gunning engines. If anything, the kids, realizing their collective power, are spurred on by her desperate announcement. The revolution has begun.

Tucker, of course, does not halt, the little shit. He runs faster, more carelessly, from one house to the next, slamming doors on Joey and Roland as they enter with increasing violence. I want to rush into the game and tackle him, like that college football coach who ran onto the field himself to prevent a winning touchdown. But I check my overprotective-parent impulses.

"Donuts," the teacher says again, but her voice trails off. "You don't want donuts?"

Lenore and Irene are both in better physical shape than their boss, and both seem ready to run out and corral the wild horses, but neither, I guess, wants to show Mrs. Drinkwater up, because they don't move.

Meanwhile, the game has changed. The boys are now playing with little Olivia, Salon Mom's daughter, the smallest kid in the class. Although they're not really playing with her; they're bullying her. Tucker is yelling, "No girls allowed," and Roland and Joey are laughing, and Olivia is on the brink of tears. This devolves into a game of chase. They are all running after Olivia, and Roland is at her heels, too close behind her. He has issues with personal space. I'm afraid he's going to trip her, or worse.

"Last call for donuts," yells Mrs. Drinkwater, now in full panic mode. Lenore and Irene have started to move into the fray, doing their best to redirect the kids without actually touching them. The more helicopterly inclined parents begin to remove their children to the picnic tables. Daryl "Duke" Reid has secured Zara, led her to a splintery bench. Salon Mom, too self-absorbed to helicopter, is busy talking to one of the other mommies, and the parents of Tucker and Joey are, as I mentioned, not here.

Roland is out of control now. He gets like this sometimes, his body flailing, his eyes twinkling with mischief. He can't tell what's funny from what's naughty, what's fun from what's dangerous. He runs at Olivia, out for blood, like one of the kids in *Lord of the Flies*. And although I'd rather let it be, I have no choice but to intervene.

"Roland," I call. "Roland, *stop*. Right now. Stop!"

He doesn't listen, doesn't even look at me. So I run—really run, like I'm being chased, the treads of my Doc Martens crushing stray apples in my path—and don't stop till I yank him away from Olivia, who is now full-on crying; away from the truculent Tucker and the fat-assed Joey. I pick him up and hoist him over my shoulders—the same way I carried Maude this morning, although

Roland is considerably heavier. Then I sit down on the ground and cradle him, holding him fast, trying to still his movements.

He doesn't like this. At all. He has a nine-point-nine-on-the-Richter-scale meltdown in my arms. He's screaming and crying and yelling and flailing. He's speaking to me, but his words are incoherent. He's had tantrums before—sometimes the oddest things will set him off (see also: the incident with Maude's poop yesterday morning)—but never to this degree. I half expect Max von Sydow to show up and sprinkle holy water on him. *The power of Christ compels you, the power of Christ compels you.*

I hug him tightly, as still as I can, for a long time. This is not easy, like trying to tamp down a volcano. It takes every ounce of strength I possess to contain him. *The power of Christ compels you, the power of Christ compels you.* He has a slight build, and he's physically weaker than his sister, despite the age difference, but he's throwing everything he's got at me. I half-expect his head to rotate completely around, for bile to spew from his mouth, for him to start talking backward. *The power of Christ compels you, the power of Christ compels you.* His face is deep red, glistening with his tears.

"It's okay," I tell him, stupidly. "It's okay."

By now, the others are where they're supposed to be, sitting at the picnic table in neat rows, drinking their cider, munching on their apple donuts. Reid sits next to Salon Mom, not looking at us. No one looks at us. Even the teachers stay away.

Finally he calms down sufficiently to speak (English, not Hungarian). "Daddy," he says, "I was playing a game."

That's what it is, then. He was *playing*. He doesn't understand what he did wrong. What he does understand is that I've embarrassed him in front of his friends.

"Do you want to sit and have a donut?"

This sets off a new round of wailing and crying. No, he does not want to sit and have a donut. No, he does not want apple cider. He wants to leave. He wants to get out of here, to leave the scene of his humiliation, his mortification. He does not want to be with me, the Bad Daddy. He wants his Mommy. Where is Mommy? He wants her *now.*

And the irony of all this is that, from a developmental standpoint, his outburst is *good.* This is what we want. This is why we have him at Thornwood, so he learns to pick up on social clues. So he learns what behavior is inappropriate. So he recognizes when he misbehaves.

So he feels bad when his father embarrasses him in front of his friends.

His humiliation constitutes progress, if not triumph.

Why has this disorder befallen him? Why does Roland—why does *our son*—have Asperger's? Why so many like him, now, at this moment in human development?

Baron-Cohen's "mind-blindness" theory, seductively attractive though it may be, doesn't really explain anything. Scientists are adept at figuring out *how* things happen: how leaves turn brown, how sperm penetrates the egg, how metal rusts when it gets wet. When it comes to the question of *why*, however, science falls mute. *Why* is the provenance of the poets and the philosophers, the artists and the mystics, the rabbis and the priests. Wherefore the spike in autism? Something environmental . . . or is it larger than that?

Julian Jaynes, in *The Origin of Consciousness in the Breakdown of the Bicameral Mind*, which I happened to be reading when he was diagnosed, argues (convincingly, in my view) that what we know as consciousness is a relatively recent phenomenon in human development. Only in the last few millennia, he suggests, did the human brain acquire the ability of interior monologue; before that, the ancients heard "voices" that told them what to do, voices they attributed to gods—the characters in the *Iliad*, for example, make no decisions on their own, but are slaves to the commands of flawed deities—but which were actually ideas generated from a right half of the brain that had yet to properly fuse to the left. Is the autism spike another mutation, the next step in the Jaynesian evolution of consciousness? Whatever his social deficiencies, Roland has the potential to see the world in ways no one has before, and the raw brainpower to make something of what he sees.

Perhaps the answer is metaphysical. Aquarius, the zodiacal sign of the "New Age" astrologers have awaited for at least a century, is the most evolved of air signs. Air, the element that rules the brain, that governs the way we think. Is this fundamental reorganization of collective human thinking—and whatever its origins, the autism spike represents nothing less—an indication that the Age of Aquarius is at last dawning?

I like to think of Roland's condition as a blessing, a gift. When he's in high school, he'll kick ass in mathematics and science courses. He'll ace his SATs. He'll go to some brainiac college for engineering or physics or, if his current interests hold, architecture, and he will be well-compensated in his professional life. Will he have difficulties making friends? Most likely. But then, he won't need them in the way Maude and the other neuro-typicals will. The truth is, I'm not worried about his future. I'm only worried about his present. If he can make it through kindergarten unscathed, the boy will be unstoppable. I firmly believe that.

Other parents are starting to leave—there go Daryl "Duke" Reid and his daughter, hand in hand, strolling back to the car like normal people—and still Roland sobs gently in my arms. He's stopped fighting back now, resigned himself to the prison of his father's arms, but his cheeks are still red, his face still glassy.

So now I've missed my chance with Reid, I've paid a babysitter for nothing, I still have no idea what Sharon meant about Stacy having an affair, and, worst of all, I've shamed my son in front of his classmates. I'm a complete failure, the worst father in the world.

To get back in Roland's good graces, I resort to the tried-and-true method: bribery. "Roland," I ask him, running my fingers through his thick sandy-blond hair, "would it make you feel better if we went to Lowe's and got a floor-plan book?"

It works. Thank fucking God, it works. He snaps out of it. His body stills, his sobs cease, the demon is exorcized. A smile crosses his face. He sits up, still in my lap, and looks me straight in the eye (he's always a few inches too close when he does this, making it hard for me to focus). "Daddy, I would like to buy a new floor-plan book," he says, sniffling.

"Then that's what we'll do."

Mrs. Drinkwater averts her gaze as we walk by—she, too, is ashamed by what happened—but Lenore says, "It's okay, Roland. You'll have a better day tomorrow," and Irene gives him a little wave.

By the time we're in the car, he seems to have forgotten all about the outburst. But I remember.

"Daddy," he says. "Music!"

You can check out any time you like but you can never—

INT. ULSTER COUNTY COURTHOUSE, KINGSTON, N.Y. - DAY

In a large courtroom, a bevy of Ulster County residents, a diverse sea of humanity, at jury duty. Some are reading books, others chatting, still more staring silently at the big flag behind the unoccupied judge's chair.

DARYL "DUKE" REID, sporting a dress shirt, tie, and snazzy suit pants, looks up from the battered copy of *Ulysses* he's reading and squints at the pretty woman sitting one chair away from him: STACY.

REID

Excuse me. Sorry to bother you, but you look incredibly familiar. Do we know each other?

STACY

(*sighing*)

Mary-Louise Parker.

REID

Huh?

STACY

Sorry. It's just people always mistake me for Mary-Louise Parker.

Reid takes the opportunity to size her up.

REID

I don't see it. Parker *Posey*, maybe. But I've *met* Mary-Louise Parker, and you look nothing like her. Not that you should take offense either way. Mary-Louise is really pretty.

STACY

So you're saying I'm a slightly less attractive Mary-Louise Parker?

REID

(*laughing*)

Not at all. You're both very pretty, and there are some similarities, but I would never mistake you for her. I'm Daryl, by the way.

STACY

Stacy. Wait, are you Daryl "Duke" Reid?

REID

Yeah.

STACY

Oh my God. I didn't recognize you with the suit on. You're *Zara's* father, right? I'm Roland's mom. Our kids are both . . .

REID

Both at *Thornwood*. Of course. *That's* why you look familiar. It's your husband who usually drops him off, though, right?

STACY

Yeah. He's a writer, so he works from home. Although I don't know how much *work* he actually does. Mostly he just mopes around the house.

Before Reid can respond, a BAILIFF appears at the front of the room and quiets the crowd.

BAILIFF

Attention, everyone. I've just been informed that the one case on the docket has plea-bargained. Your civic duty has been done, and you're free to go.

Collective sigh of relief from the crowd, which begins to file out.

REID

Hey, do you want to maybe go get coffee or something? I'm dying for another cup.

STACY

Sure, I'd love to.

In the mass exodus, their bodies are pushed closer together.

STACY

So where did you meet Mary-Louise Parker?

REID

Friend of a friend. Actually—this is kind of embarrassing—I used to date her.

STACY

Ha! How'd that go?

REID

She's fucking batshit. But what can I say. I have a type.

STACY

Fucking batshit?

REID

No. Beautiful.

As they're pushed together through the wave of people leaving the courthouse, he puts his arm around her waist. Stacy smiles.

STACY

You know what we should get instead of coffee?

REID

What?

She turns to face him, stands on tiptoe, kisses his cheek.

STACY

A room. The Holiday Inn's right down the street.

REID

Now you're talking!

They exit the now-empty courtroom, and we . . .

FADE OUT

THEY BUILT THE LOWE'S ON 299, JUST OVER THE NEW PALTZ border in Highland, a few years ago, over fierce opposition from the town's vocal BUY LOCAL faction. There was a slew of angry letters to the paper—although there are always angry letters in the *New*

Paltz Times, whose editors seem to delight in fanning the flames of incendiary municipal conflict, no matter how small—defending the monopoly of the local True Value, lamenting the evils of the parent corporation, and predicting that the presence of the Lowe's would grind to a halt the traffic on Main Street (this last charge was, and is, preposterous; it's a hardware store, not a Dead show). But the opponents were in New Paltz, and the store is in Highland, so the plan was approved. It has saved me untold hours of time driving to Kingston for items unattainable at True Value, and, on rainy days, is a convenient place to take the kids for a ride in the big car-shaped shopping carts. Plus, Roland loves Lowe's, even more than Toys "R" Us. If left to his own devices, Roland would stay here for days. He would live here. He could while away the hours leafing through the floor-plan books, but he also likes to walk the aisles, especially the ones dedicated to lighting, and to explore the kitchen sets on display in the back—opening every cabinet, testing every drawer.

Right now, we're in one of the lighting aisles. Roland is taking boxes off the shelves, reading what kind of light it is, and telling me where it will go—"This is the Plymouth wall sconce. This one we can hang in the *master* bath."—although he would be talking about where it will go even if I wasn't standing beside him, making sure the box doesn't slip from his shaky grip and fall on the floor. My function here is twofold: to keep the merchandise from smashing and my son from being struck by a stray forklift. Otherwise, I'm useless.

The only sign that Roland has endured the single worst meltdown of his young life is the redness in his cheeks. But then, his cheeks have always been unusually red, even when he was little. (A few years ago, some busybody came to our table at the Plaza Diner and asked if he had measles. Stacy almost threw a butter knife at her, ninja-style.) But aside from the ruddy cheeks, he's totally fine. No trace of the tantrum.

As we stroll slowly down the aisle, I'm struck by the fact that Roland is *walking*, rather than riding in the cart: a recent phenomenon. This is only the third or fourth time he's actually set foot in Lowe's, although he's been here countless times. Kids grow up so gradually, you sometimes don't notice the milestones.

"This pink pendant lamp can go in Maude's room," Roland says, glancing over his shoulder but not actually looking at me.

We've been here for maybe half an hour, and covered only about a quarter of the lighting stock, when who should come down the aisle but Peter Berliner, his three kids in tow. He doesn't look like a cuckold, that's for sure. He's a handsome guy, strong chin and cheekbones, wavy hair falling in his face. His kids are flat-out gorgeous. Even Ernest, who's autistic and looks it, is devilishly handsome. The three of them together, with their dashing dad, look like the Cullens, from *Twilight*. When they run in the sunlight, their skin sparkles.

Peter slows down his cart as he passes by and gives me a "Hey, Josh."

The poor guy. He has no idea, none, that every mommy in town is talking about him right now, that his cheating wife was just busted *in flagrante delicto* at Dia:Beacon. I could remedy that, of course, pull a Sharon Rothman, but I would never. It's not my place. Or is it? Am I doing him a disservice, not telling him? Why must I have to make this sort of decision? It's not like I asked to be told. Now the challenge is getting through this conversation without revealing what I know. Like not blowing a surprise party, but with much more dire consequences should I fail.

"Peter. What's the good word?"

We execute an elaborate frat-boy-style handshake that ends with us snapping fingers.

"Cynthia sent me to pick up some bins. Exciting, right?"

"Very." Long pause as I search for something to say. "I heard you were pretty hammered last night."

He eyes me quizzically. "No . . ." he says, drawing out the word to form an implicit question. "Ernest, put that back."

The boy has picked up a curtain rod and is swinging it like a baseball bat, which Roland of course finds hysterical.

"You weren't out with Soren last night?"

"No, I was at HoeBowl, down in Pine Bush. Last night was the semis."

"How'd you do?"

"Shitty, but we won anyway."

"So you weren't with Soren."

"No." His face is the picture of suspicion. He must encounter a lot of this lately—remarks from people that don't quite make sense, clues dropped anonymously at his doorstep. His subconscious must be catching on, even if his waking mind remains oblivious. Just like I dream of mice before I consciously hear them. "Haven't seen him all week."

This is strange . . . if Soren wasn't out drinking with Peter, then who *was* he out drinking with, and why did he lie to Meg? *The more you dig, the more you find.*

"I guess Meg had it wrong. Or Soren was so drunk he thought he was with you, and it was actually Earl Anthony."

He snickers, acknowledging my obscure bowling reference. "Maybe. The guy can put it away. Ernest, I said no!" He turns his attention to his son, the other kids more or less behaving, and I realize that Roland is gone.

"Shit, I lost my kid," I tell Peter, racing to the end of the aisle. "See you around."

"See you around."

Roland hasn't gotten far—he's in the next aisle, working his way methodically through the boxes of lights. I decide not to bother hollering at him for straying—he's had enough rebuke for one day. Instead, I coax him out of the aisle with the promise of a new floor-plan book—we go with *One-Story Homes and Garage Apartments*, a real page-turner—and after a trip to the bathroom, we're back in the vast and mostly empty parking lot (so much for the prophetic abilities of that Cassandrine letter-writer to the *New Paltz Times*).

As I'm strapping Roland into his carseat—he's too distracted by the new book to do it himself—I catch a last glimpse of Peter Berliner, shepherding his brood into a green Ford Windstar. He moves slowly, almost sadly, as if he already knows.

Friday, 2:24 p.m.

Vanessa is in the driveway, leaning against the side of her gold Escort, puffing on a cigarette but not, best as I can tell, inhaling it. The tableau of a twenty-six-year-old coed with lowcut jeans, a form-fitting top, and a decent-looking face sucking on a Camel Light *if she smokes she pokes* while draped on the soft contours of an American-made automobile should be provocative, sexy, alluring. How many ads for how many products have exploited this sort of image through the years? And yet Vanessa manages somehow to look ridiculous, like a child who's raided her mother's wardrobe and appropriated her cigarettes, which she (and Vanessa) does not know how to wear or smoke.

"Oh, hi," she says as I get out of the car, taking another puff, but otherwise making no move to hurry.

"Um . . . where's Maude?"

"She fell asleep watching TV?"

Stacy has made it clear to Vanessa on numerous occasions that the television is to be used only as a last resort, that we're paying her to *play* with the kids, not just watch over them in case aliens hell-bent on abduction and anal probing zip over from Pine Bush. This is why we hired Vanessa to begin with; she impressed upon on us how, as a ceramics major, she would do arts and crafts with the kids. Never happened. It may as well have been a New York mayoral campaign promise to build the Second Avenue Subway.

"Right. Do me a favor, then, and stay out here and keep an eye on Roland. He's in the car, reading a book."

"Oh, okay."

After tripping over Steve the cat, who has appeared out of the ether as soon as the screen door opens, I enter the house to find that Maude is not, in fact, asleep in front of the TV, but on the toilet, where she has just birthed one of the stinkiest poops of her young life (which is saying something; my daughter can really stink up a room). She's already used half a box of baby wipes in a vain attempt to clean herself. Her right hand is caked in brown, and there is a streak of fresh crap on the blue ceramic wall tile.

Fatherhood is shit.

Back in high school, during my stint at McDonald's, I worked the grill. I used to assemble the cheeseburgers. The way you assemble cheeseburgers is, you put the tops—*crowns*, in the Golden Arches parlance—of twelve buns upside-down on a metal tray. You add the ketchup and mustard, the pickles, the chopped onions, and the slice of cheese. You then clip the tray to the grill and slide the patties onto the crowns. The last step is, you take the twelve bun bottoms—or *heels*—out of the toaster on a giant spatula. The training-video way to do this without spilling any bun heels is by hand—you move the heels one at a time from the spatula to the respective patty. The pros, the guys who really knew what they were doing, had a quicker way of unloading the heels. They'd just swipe them off the giant spatula with one fell swoop of their arm, and *voilà*, the heels would land where they were supposed to go. This was a risky maneuver, because more often than not, you lost a heel or two and had to start from scratch, and you wound up wasting time rather than saving it. But if you were feeling it, and you executed the maneuver—especially at lunchtime, when the stakes were so high—the effect was like pulling a tablecloth out from beneath a set table without disturbing so much as a fork. The first time I did this successfully, during the busy one o'clock hour . . . well, let's just say there's a reason it's called the lunch *rush*.

I often think about those days sweating over the grill at Mickey D's when I am called upon to do something like my current task. Because this is where, as a father—and not to toot my own horn here—I really shine. As quickly as possible, I take a baby wipe and wipe the brown goop off Maude's little hand, before she decides to pick her nose or suck her thumb. Then I pluck her off the toilet and deposit her in the tub, and before she can so much as protest, I've washed her thoroughly with soap and a wet washcloth. I plop her on the bathmat and wrap her in a yellow duck towel. Then I fish the baby wipes out of the toilet, throw them in a plastic bag along with the soiled washcloth, flush the toilet, spray some cleanser on the stain on the tile, wipe it down, add the paper towel to the shit-stained wipes already inside the plastic bag, tie off the bag, throw it out the window, wash my hands, and carry her to her room for a change of clothes. The whole process takes less than three minutes. And when I'm done, I feel as giddy as I did when executing the Magical Heel Trick at McDonald's circa 1989.

No sooner am I back in the living room than the phone rings. I'm expecting Stacy or Sharon, but no, it's Meg. Meg, whose husband has a secret.

"Hey . . . Josh," she says, her voice slow and stoned-sounding as usual, "what are you guys up to?"

"Oh, the usual craziness. Roland had a meltdown at the pumpkin patch, so we had to leave early, and when we came home, Vanessa was in the driveway smoking a cigarette while Maude was taking a monster dump."

"Oh. My. God. You *have* to get rid of her."

"I know."

"What are you guys doing now? I'm thinking of maybe heading over to Hasbrouck."

"I just got home."

"Come back out! I've got some gossip."

"Yeah, fine, what the hell. You going now?"

"In a few minutes."

"Okay. Oh, Meg? You don't happen to have Sharon Rothman's number, do you?"

"I think so. Why?"

"Oh, we were . . . discussing something at the playdate, but I had to leave, and we never got to finish."

"You know what? I do have it, but it's in my phone. I can't get it until I hang up."

"It's okay. I'll get it when I see you."

"You sure? I can call you right back."

"It's fine, really. It's not a big deal," even though the deal couldn't be bigger. "See you in a few."

I throw some juice boxes and Pirate's Booty in a plastic bag, grab Maude off the couch, and head back outside, locking the door behind me. Roland is still lost in his book and his garage apartments. Vanessa has apparently fired up another cigarette, and is staring listlessly at the trees, the remaining leaves of which are glorious shades of yellow, orange, red, and brown. Ignoring her, I install Maude in her carseat.

"Oh," says the babysitter, finally finished with her nicotine fix, "I wanted to talk to you about something?"

I give her a look that suggests she should continue. She doesn't pick up on it. So I say, "Shoot."

"I was talking with some other babysitters, and they get twelve dollars an hour instead of ten? Twelve is the going rate now. And I think, you know, I've been with you for a while now, and I think I should be paid the going rate."

The only time Vanessa comes down to earth, the only time she doesn't raise her voice at the end of a sentence and turn every statement into a question, is when money is involved. When she negotiated the job, she had a dizzying list of demands: ten dollars an hour, twenty hours of steady work per week, no Saturday nights, and so on. It was shocking. This drippy girl who would later ask if we had *water* she could borrow was transformed into the reincarnation of Samuel Gompers. This generation, man, I tell you. All these twentysomethings who came up in the boom-boom eighties, they act like they're so *entitled*. And yet so many of them are functionally useless. It's really something.

And there I go, sounding like *my* father. May the Lord have mercy on his crotchety soul.

"Speaking of money," I tell her, "here." I dig into my wallet and hand her a twenty.

She eyes it with what can only be contempt. "You said I'd be here for three hours?"

"Well," I tell her, "you were here for two." Less than two, actually, since she was ten minutes late, but I don't press the point.

"Yes, but you *said* it would be three." She crosses her arms. "I was really kind of depending on that extra ten dollars."

"Were you."

What I should do is call her out. Fire her. Let her know how I *really* feel about her sorry babysitting abilities. Vanessa isn't in a union; I can dismiss her at any time. I'm under no obligation whatsoever to pay her another dime. That said, babysitters, they do hold a certain power. At the end of the day, we need them more than they need us. Babysitters are Saudi Arabia, we parents are the United States, and the hours they spend watching our children are the barrels of oil deep beneath the desert sand. What if I read her the riot act, tell her to buzz off, and then there's an emergency, and I need her to come back? You can't fire a sitter without a replacement lined up. You just can't. On the other hand, the notion of paying her ten dollars for doing absolutely nothing, especially since I've already paid her twenty for doing absolutely nothing, is infuriating. The more I think about it, in fact, the angrier I become. But I'm just not up for a confrontation. So with a long sigh that is probably wasted on her, I again take out my wallet. All I have *shit* are twenties.

"Do you have change?"

"No," she says, without checking her wallet. "I only have the money you gave me."

"Fine," I tell her, my voice sharp. "Consider this severance." I hand her the twenty, hop into the Odyssey, fire up the engine, and peel out of the driveway.

Vanessa runs toward the minivan, waving her hands.

I pull back into driveway and roll down the window. "*Now* what?"

I'm expecting her to grovel, to apologize, to beg for her job back, but no. "My bag," she says. "I left it on the piano."

Maybe she doesn't know what *severance* means.

"Of course you did."

So I have to park, and kill the engine, and walk back to the porch, and open the door—Steve runs back out as I do, a black-and-white blur bursting into the woods—and wait for Vanessa to collect her things, which she does with zero sense of urgency.

As we wait in awkward silence, the mail truck drives by. The mailman—who is not a mail*man* at all but a heavyset woman named Fawn, who will beep incessantly when she delivers a package that can't be stuffed in the roadside mailbox, lest she be compelled to remove her ample bulk from the truck and deposit said package on the front porch—gives me a wave as she motors down the hill to deliver my neighbor Bill his McCain/Palin propaganda and NRA membership newsletter.

"I'll give you the change next time," Vanessa says, stepping onto the porch.

"There's not going to be a *next time*, Vanessa," I explain, bolting the door. "This is it. We're done. You're not worth twelve dollars; you weren't worth ten dollars. You're a lousy babysitter, and my kids can't stand you. Now get off my fucking porch."

I jog back to the driveway, collect the mail, and hop back into minivan. I don't look back at her, not once.

I have to admit, it feels pretty good.

ANOTHER COP ON BLACK CREEK ROAD, EATING A DONUT—How cliché! At least go for a cruller, officer!—as I pass. Then, dashing across the street as I approach, a blur of burnt orange: a fox, a real live fox! Pinky Dinky Doo's catchphrase comes to mind: *Now there's something you don't see everyday.* In New York, you have celebrity sightings. Leo on his mountain bike, Jake and Maggie at the West Bank Cafe. Here, you catch glimpses of creatures well-represented in fable literature, animals that, as a child of the suburbs and a man of the city, I'd never laid eyes on before relocating upstate: foxes, giant turtles, newts, hawks, even bald eagles. The sense of wonder and excitement I feel upon spying this creature, a red-haired thing that seems half-cat, half-dog, on Black Creek Road, is no different than what I felt when I happened to ride the Rock Center elevator with Heidi Klum ten years ago. A fox is a fox, after all.

At the red light at Ohioville and 299, I flip through the mail. Cablevision bill, Central Hudson bill, Chase Visa bill, Waste Management bill, Netflix (it's either *I Love You, Man* or *He's Just Not That Into You*, my selection or Stacy's, and the contents of that red envelope will determine what I wind up watching tonight, assuming I have any energy left over to watch TV after putting the kids down), and the new *Us Weekly*, the cover of which startles me to the degree that I almost pull a Lizzie Grubman and hit the gas instead of the brake.

On the cover is Fergie of the Black Eyed Peas (as opposed to her older-but-cuter blue-blooded namesake across the pond) and her husband, the famous-for-reasons-beyond-my-understanding Josh Duhamel. At first glance they appear to be together, perhaps attending an exclusive premiere party, but it's actually two different photos juxtaposed to create that illusion. Fergie, on the left, with her Grecian-goddess hair and canary-yellow dress, is a spring flower, a vernal nymph (and not at all the hip hop fly girl of the "My Humps" video). Duhamel, wearing three days of scruff and a black leather sports coat over a black shirt, could not look more villainous. Below their celebrated visages is the terrible headline:

CHEATING SHOCK

FERGIE BETRAYED

Accused of cheating with a stripper, Josh denies it and races to be with his wife. The tawdry truth about that night and why Fergie is standing by her man.

To the bottom right, occupying her own little rectangle, is THE STRIPPER, a bottle-dyed blonde with a plain-Jane face—she sort of looks like Vanessa, in fact—in a blue-and-white-striped bikini, jutting her boobs out and forcing a smile.

That celebrity marriages have the shelf life of organic deli meat should surprise no one. After all, celebrities are drawn to other celebrities primarily because the other celebrities are celebrities. Was Jennifer Aniston in love with Brad Pitt, or was she in love with *Brad Pitt*? There are two problems with this. The first is, the novelty of celebrity wears off quickly, especially if you're a celebrity in your own right. Pitt, for example, married the star of *Friends*, the most popular TV show of the moment, and wound up with an image- and career-obsessed diva with zero percent body fat who made him spend weekends with David Arquette. The second problem is that celebrity is not static. When Brad and Jen tied the knot, his career was still ascending, while hers was at its zenith, but at that exact instant in time, they had roughly the same Q rating. At the altar, their celestial bodies were conjunct. Then *Friends* was canceled and Aniston's career nosedived, while Pitt starred in the *Ocean's Eleven* films and a string of other critical and commercial successes. Their marriage could not withstand the celebrity disparity, not when Aniston is so clearly the jealous type . . . and certainly not with Shiva the Destroyer on hand to accelerate the process, in the sexpot form of Angelina Jolie.

Want to know how Fergie and Duhamel hooked up? He caught a Black Eyed Peas show in Miami and put out word through celebrity channels, including the pages of various tabloid magazines, that he wanted to *ahem* taste something Fergilicious. This is not, needless to say, how the rest of us come a-courting. Here's what Josh Dumbbell "dished" to a "reporter" at *InStyle* magazine five years ago: "My recurring dream involves the lead singer of the Black Eyed Peas. Oh, my God, I've got the biggest crush on her. God, is she hot!" How can a marriage that began like *that* possibly stand the test of time? I mean, plenty of people are hot. Anne Coulter is hot. That doesn't mean I want to marry her. Let's just say that I don't envision Josh and Fergie as the latter-day Paul Newman and Joanne Woodward.

But here's why the headline is so jarring: Fergie's real name is Stacy Ann Ferguson, which also happens to be my wife's full maiden name (and why she can't use it at SAG). Not only do Josh Duhamel and I share a first name, we were also born on the exact same day: November 14, 1972. I'm possessive about both my name *and* my birthday, so right off the bat, I don't like the guy. Throw in that he's not only an enviably handsome dude, but the sort of enviably-handsome-dude-who-knows-he's-an-enviably-handsome-dude, stir in his lackluster IMDB page (*Win a Date With Tad Hamilton!*, *Las Vegas*, *Transformers I* and *II*), sprinkle in the fact that he escorts Fergie to exotic beach locales where he *knows* paparazzi lie in wait like piranha, Nikons at the ready, and as his hard-bodied wife reads YA paperbacks and works on her tan, Josh Duhamel—or *J.D.*, as his friends call him; because Josh isn't a cool enough name for this big swingin' dick—breaks out the oils and brushes, and a fucking *palette and easel*, and starts painting a fucking *seascape*, right there on the beach in the Bahamas, or whatever *Girls Gone Wild* hotspot they've chosen for their little getaway, because, he's, like, an *artist*, you know? . . . and it's sort of impossible not to fucking loathe the guy. I mean why is *he* always in the magazines? Who gives a rat's ass about *him*? And then we find him porking—excuse me; *allegedly* porking—a stripper.

The kids are quiet; too quiet. When I glance in the rearview, both Roland and Maude have their fingers up their respective noses. They're really going at it, excavating like seasoned archeologists. As a parent, I'm supposed to discourage this. Nose-picking is not something that's smiled upon in civilized company. But how logical it must seem—no; how logical it *is*—to insert an index finger in the index-finger-sized hole at the tip of your nose, inside which there is a fingertip-sized ball of goop that needs removal! How unnatural, to check that very sensible and biological impulse! And yet I somehow have to explain to my kids that this is something they shouldn't do.

Ah, fuck it. Let them pick. At least they're quiet. I'll just pretend I didn't notice.

The *Us Weekly* cover is a bad omen.

Josh and Stacy.

Cheating shock.

Somewhere Eugenia Last is laughing.

INT. SOUND STAGE, LOS ANGELES - DAY

STACY sits on a bench, reading a script. She's reading for the part of Slut #1, so she's dressed scantily. We see her mouth some of the dialogue silently. Then, JOSH DUHAMEL, an impossibly handsome movie star, rounds the corner. He's wearing a black leather jacket, black V-neck T-shirt, black jeans, and hasn't shaved in two days.

JOSH DUHAMEL

Why hello.

STACY

Oh my God. You're Josh Duhamel.

JOSH DUHAMEL

I am. But it's, um, *DUM-ull.* Two syllables.

STACY

Oh. I'm so sorry. I didn't know.

JOSH DUHAMEL

No worries. It's cool. You mind?

STACY

No, please.

He sits next to her.

JOSH DUHAMEL

Yeah, so I'm Josh Duhamel. *The* Josh Duhamel. But my friends call me J.D.

STACY

(*offering her hand*)

I'm Stacy. Stacy Ferguson.

JOSH DUHAMEL

(*taking her hand; not letting it go*)

Holy shit, dude! That's my wife's name!

STACY

Yeah, I know. Do you call her Stacy, or do you call her Fergie? I always wonder about stuff like that.

JOSH DUHAMEL

Lately, I don't call her anything. She's way pissed at me.

STACY

Sorry to hear that.

JOSH DUHAMEL

No, it's cool. It's just, you know, she thinks I had this one-night-stand with a stripper.

STACY

Did you?

JOSH DUHAMEL

Well, yeah. But I'd rather my wife didn't think so.

STACY

She's nice-looking, your wife. She's got lovely lady lumps.

JOSH DUHAMEL

Ha! Yeah, well, she's not as nice-looking as you. Nor are her lady lumps as lovely.

STACY

You flatter me.

JOSH DUHAMEL

I'd like to do more than that.

STACY

You're funny.

JOSH DUHAMEL

I'm not joking.

STACY

You know, my husband can't stand you. He won't watch your movies and hates when you're on a magazine cover. I think he's jealous. But I gotta say, you're a really hot guy.

JOSH DUHAMEL

Thanks. You're not so bad yourself. I know this seems sort of sudden and out of left field, but, you wanna go back to my trailer?

STACY

Will we be alone?

He nods; she gives him a come-hither smile.

STACY

Then yes.

JOSH DUHAMEL

Sweet.

They walk off hand in hand, and we . . .

FADE OUT

Bounded by Village Hall, St. Joseph's Church, the SUNY campus clocktower, and a row of modest houses on Mohonk Avenue, Hasbrouck Park occupies a single block of sodden land a short walk from the center of town. There is a gazebo, and a rugged baseball field, and a rudimentary basketball court, and a wide expanse of wet, clover-strewn lawn, which is the setting for, among other municipal events, the annual Pride Day festival. In the southwest corner is the playground: swing sets, seesaw, sandbox, and the highlight, a vast splintery wooden maze of stairs and slides and turrets and blind alleys and chainlink bridges approximating a castle keep, complete with its own fence, which kids love because they can easily hide from their parents (and parents fear for exactly the same reason). If it hasn't rained recently (Hasbrouck is sited in a marsh area, and takes weeks to dry out after a big storm), and if it hasn't been defaced by teenagers and SUNY students (all those kid-tested-mom-unapproved hiding spaces make it an ideal spot for drinking, smoking, fucking, vandalizing, urinating, and vomiting, so before you unleash your children, you have to check for spent beer cans, cigarette butts, used condoms, curse words scrawled on wood in black Magic Marker, piss stains, and puke), and if it isn't recess at Mountain Laurel (the local Waldorf school, a veritable *madrassa* of fundamentalist crunch, doesn't have its own playground, instead dispatching its student body to the public park every school day after lunch: sad-faced, long-haired, grass-fed seventh and eighth graders in organic-cotton tie-dye shirts, running roughshod over the wooden castles built for younger children, reveling in a schoolyard kingship that will end once ninth grade rolls around, and the bigger, meaner, street-smarter New Paltz, Kingston, Highland Central, or Rondout Valley high schoolers beat them up and steal their hippie lunch money), and if it isn't too crowded (Roland especially can be unpredictable if there are too many other kids around), Hasbrouck gets my vote for best playground in the area, narrowly edging out Majestic Park in Gardiner (where, on the weekends, you can watch the bright parachutes of thrillseekers from Skydive: The Ranch falling softly back to earth). This late in the afternoon, this late in October, the playground is almost deserted.

The spot on Mohonk with the busted meter is open, so I park there, saving myself a dime. My mother would be proud. Meg's green Jetta—she has one bumper sticker, SAVE THE RIDGE, in big red letters on a white field; Save the Ridge was a big deal when we first moved here, an ultimately successful grassroots movement to stop a cabal of nature-raping developers (a group said to include Robert De Niro, a Hudson Valley weekender, whose alleged involvement evaporated his reservoir of local goodwill) from erecting houses on Shawangunk Ridge; in New Paltz, we're big on *saving* things—is two spots ahead of me, left wheel jutting out a good half-foot beyond the yellow line. The twins play on the seesaw, although they seem more intent on climbing it than achieving any semblance of balance. Meg leans against the fence, zoned out, her iced Starbucks almost done.

"Sorry," she calls, killing the iced latte with a final slurp of the big green straw. "I should have asked if you wanted one."

"I'm good," I tell her. "It's the time of day where I generally switch from caffeine to alcohol. Let me unleash the monsters."

Roland has not yet mastered the ability to unbuckle himself from his carseat. He could probably do it, if he set his mind to it, but he'd rather just wait for me. He can be lazy that way. If he were a sultan of old, he'd have no problem being ferried about on a pillow-strewn sedan. I take him out first, because he sits behind me, and then fetch Maude, who, by the time I get to her side, is bitching about not being the first one out of the car. They scamper down the little hill to where Beatrix and Brooke are taking turns slamming the seesaw as hard as they can onto the ground. The wooden plank is splintered, and looks like it might split in half, which, I suppose, is the goal.

"How was the rest of the playdate?" I ask, but before Meg can answer, Brooke decides she wants to partake of the sandbox, and the twins take off, running away from us and into the playground proper. Maude follows them as fast as her stout little legs can carry her, which is pretty damned fast for someone two-and-a-half feet tall. Soon, both of the kids will be able to outrun me. What will I do then?

"But Daddy," Roland says, tugging at my sleeve. "I don't want the sandbox. The sandbox is *too boring*. I want something that interests me."

I know he means the swings, so I suggest the swings, although I don't want to be stuck at the swing set.

"Swings. Yes, swings would be fun. Come on, Daddy," giving me another tug. "I need a little push."

The main problem with Hasbrouck Park—other than the aforementioned soggy ground, lack of shade, overgrown Waldorf kids, penchant for overcrowding, and SUNY fratboy vomit—is that the wooden fence partitions the swing sets from the rest of the playground. If you're here with two kids, and one of them wants to use the sandbox and the other wants to swing on the swings, you can't tend to both of them, unless you're that creepy guy on *Heroes* who can be in two places at once.

"Why don't we do the sandbox? Or the castle?" I try and infuse my voice with enough enthusiasm to change his mind. "*I* know! You can do the slides!"

"No," he says. "That's *too boring*. Swings!"

"Damn it," I mutter.

He laughs gleefully. "You said a bad word, Daddy."

"It's okay," Meg tells me, moseying toward the sandbox, which rests in an enclosure within an enclosure, surrounded by wooden planks, and is the best place to ensconce the kids if you want to hang out with another grown-up. "I'll watch her."

"You sure?"

"Maude's a snap."

So I head with the boy over to the swing set. Seven of the eight swings have wet mud beneath them; the only one suspended above a giant puddle is, of course, the one Roland decides to use. I somehow manage to persuade him to try a different one, and after a few false starts—"No, Daddy, you pushed me *too hard*! I want a *little* push!"—we fall into a pleasant rhythm, punctuated by the high-pitched squeal of the rotating chain.

Across the soggy field, over by the gazebo, three SUNY hipsters toss around a Frisbee. A couple huddle on the low bleachers behind third base, sharing a cigarette; I'm pretty sure the woman is Wendy, the manager at McDonald's, in street clothes—this constitutes a celebrity sighting, of sorts—but she's too far away for a positive ID. In the playground proper, on the other side of the wooden fence, a father—shaved head (corporate shaved, not punk-rock shaved; the shiny pate of a vain captain of industry), clunky rectangular glasses, well-pressed lavender dress shirt, face you want to punch, barks into his cell phone while his son, who is three-and-a-half, tops, and desperate for his old man's attention, climbs up the slide. The corporate-bald dad (is he from New Paltz? Not many guys like that up here) is facing me, his back to the slide, and doesn't see the kid come *this close* to falling. The sandbox is beyond the castellated turrets and out of my line of sight, but Maude has a way of making her displeasure heard, so I assume she's fine.

"You okay, Roland?"

When he doesn't answer, I ask again. He's off in La-La Land, swimming in the vasty Asperger's deep. I know he's happy, soothed by the swing's rhythmic sway, and that makes me happy, too—this, right here and now, may well be the most relaxing part of my day—but then I start to worry that I'm not doing enough, not engaging him enough, not trying hard enough to draw him out of the watery depths of his mind. I need to check in. To be sure. Especially after the incident at the farm. So I ask a third time.

Finally he comes up for air. "I'm *okay*, Daddy," he snaps. "Stop asking that. No more asking that."

The bells in the phallus of the clock tower (bells which are, incidentally, digital and fake; the originals were lost in a fire decades ago and never replaced) awaken, whip into a frenzied tintinnabulary foreplay, and erupt in a three-chime climax.

Three o'clock? That's it? Shit. I thought it was later.

On the sidewalk, a voluptuous SUNY coed struts by, heading up the steep hill toward campus. Her Ringwaldian get-up—skin-tight dress with bright, wide stripes; engineer boots over ripped fishnet stockings; bottle-dyed red hair; a *Pretty in Pink* fedora—is retro-eighties, but with a 2000s twist: no shoulder pads or baggy blazer to obscure those sumptuous curves. Yum. As eye-candy goes, she's a box of Godivas. She's sashaying right by us, Lady Godiva, her hips swaying sinfully, so I can't *not* look that way. Because I'm wearing sunglasses, and because I'm a dad pushing his kid on a swing, and because, above all, she's too busy chatting with her boyfriend (one of those young punks with big, round, black buttons *the buttons Toad lost and Frog helped look for?* in each ear; a new Cincinnati Reds baseball cap, bill perfectly straight, set on his head at a just-so hip-hop angle; his underpants pouring out the back of his torn jeans like Roland's do after he uses the bathroom; cigarette between his black-nail-polished fingers; the sort of degenerate who congregates in front of the scuzzy coffeehouse on Main, blocking foot traffic on the narrow sidewalk, begging quarters off tourists) to take notice of me, I gobble up her image. If I were a Manhattan construction worker—heck, if I were me and it was fifty years ago—I'd wolf whistle. I'd hoot and holler. But Lady Godiva doesn't see me; I'm invisible to her, just some middle-aged loser at the playground; I don't register any more than the swing set does. The boyfriend *does* notice, though. Glaring at me, he takes a final drag on his cigarette, and flicks it menacingly onto the sidewalk.

"Ooh," I say. "Tough guy."

By then they are past me, well out of earshot. I watch Lady Godiva's glorious gluteus maximus wiggle its succulent way to campus, not even averting my eyes when Fall Out Boy shoots one last dagger over his shoulder.

A little girl—South Asian or maybe native South American; dolled up in a princess dress; probably adopted—comes over and sits on the swing next to Roland's. "Push me!" she yells, but whoever is in charge of her is nowhere to be found (her guardian's probably in the sandbox, where the action's at). "Mom! I need a push!" When this tactic does not get the desired results, she turns her attention to me. "Can I have a push, please?"

This puts me, as a grown man at a preschool playground, in a delicate position. I could, of course, easily grant her request. But to give her a decent push, I have to touch the small of her back; should I be touching the small of the back of a girl I don't know, whose parents, for all I know, may be litigious assholes who see pedophilia everywhere? What if they accuse me of molestation? Or another dire possibility: she falls off the swing, and I get sued. That I am actively worried about these outcomes, unlikely though both may be, does not reflect well on our society. What have we become?

And there I go, sounding like Andy Rooney.

I decide to compromise. "Do you know how to swing?"

"Yes."

"Okay. Hold on tight."

Instead of pushing her, I reach well over her head *keep your hands where I can see 'em*, grabbing a chain in each hand. I pull the swing back as far as I can go, count three, and release. She pumps her legs—she wasn't lying about knowing how to swing. Same result, no physical contact. Problem solved.

"Daddy!" Roland calls. "I need a push!"

"Thanks," the little girl says.

"You're welcome."

"Daddy . . . "

"I'm coming, Roland."

Now I'm starting to get bored. And, as always happens when I come to the playground, I have to pee. There's no bathroom at Hasbrouck—after Labor Day, the Port-o-Potty they keep on the grounds during the summer, one of the more disgusting Port-o-Potties you'll ever donate bodily waste to, flies south for the winter—so I'll either have to take Roland across the street to the well-appointed men's room at van den Berg Hall, or just hold it. I decide to hold it. We won't be here that much longer.

"Roland, should we go see what your sister's doing? And the twins?"

"No, no sisters. No twins. No girls."

"Five more minutes," I tell him. "I want to talk to Meg."

"Oh, okay . . ." he says, drawing out the word like a long sigh. "We can go see Maude."

He drags his feet along the ground, his toes sliding through the mud, until he slows down sufficiently to jump off. Then he races into the playground proper, tumbling once in a hole in the grass but catching himself before falling. By the time I catch up to him, he's already in the sandbox, mud-caked Merrills off, right in the middle of the entryway. Brooke—who, while only four, operates as the leader when the kids are all together—has integrated him into the game, which involves piling sand into a broken orange bucket. Maude, her legs practically buried, rakes up big piles of sand with a miniature rake that was once bright yellow but is now the color of watered-down lemonade. Beatrix is in the far corner, pouring sand from a broken green bucket into a hole some older kid—or, more likely, some overzealous dad; maybe the corporate-bald guy—must have dug. Too advanced for this crew.

"You made it," Meg says.

"At long last." I pick up Roland's shoes, clomp them together to get the mud off, set them beside the other three pairs. "How's Maude doing?"

"Oh, she's having fun."

"Maude, honey. Give me that passie." I snatch the thing out of her mouth—it makes a pronounced popping noise like after the third *lollipop lollipop oh lolly lolly lolly lollipop*—and put it in my pocket. She makes no move to resist.

I collapse into the bench next to Meg.

"Oh my *God*," Meg says. "*Wait* until you hear the latest gossip."

"Is this about Dia:Beacon? Because Jess told me that this morning."

"Dia:Beacon? What about Dia:Beacon?"

I tell her an abbreviated and euphemism-laden version of the story: Cynthia Pardo and Bruce Baldwin, her pants down, his dork up.

"Sheesh. You know, she didn't use to be this way," Meg says. "But nothing she does surprises me anymore. Especially when *he's* involved."

"He" would be Bruce, Meg's prom date, the charmer who forcibly groped her at the post-prom party. If he hadn't been so drunk, he might have raped her. Does Meg know that I know that story? I lose track of what I'm supposed to know and what I'm not.

"So what's your gossip?"

"Well," she says, "I had lunch with Cathy DiLullo this afternoon. She'd just come from Cynthia's office, and *she* told me Cynthia's *pregnant*. Can you *believe* that shit? Like this isn't going to be hard enough on her kids."

"Bruce knocked her up already, huh? No big shock, I guess."

"No. That's what's so crazy. *Peter's* the father. She's, like, sixteen weeks, and she's only been with Bruce for a month."

"Didn't Peter Berliner get a vasectomy?"

Vasectomy: a fatherly rite of passage. Fourteen minutes of discomfort, a day of ice-packed boxers, and you're home (and condom) free. I've been snipped; so has Soren, and Dennis Hynek, and Chris Holby, and pretty much every other dad I know. The choice between vasectomy and another kid is no choice at all.

"Yes! That's the other crazy thing. *God*, those two are fertile."

"Wow." I kick a hole in the sand with the heel of my Doc Marten. "What a mess."

"I know, right? Brooke! Knock it off."

Brooke, who had been flinging sand at her sister, grudgingly complies.

"And—get this—*Peter* doesn't *know.* She doesn't want to tell him. She knows he'll want to keep the baby, and she wants to get rid of it. That's why she told Cathy—she wanted Cathy to get her the morning-after pill. Like that would work!"

"That's . . . man. I don't even know what to say."

"Brooke!" She turns back to me. "I know, right?"

"We just saw him. At Lowe's. He looked so . . . sad. So defeated. He *must* know something's up."

"Brooke! I mean it!"

"So is Soren recovered from his big night out?"

"I guess. I haven't talked to him all day, the fucker."

At the curse, the only word in our entire exchange that Meg does not mumble, the other adult in the sandbox area, a slovenly middle-aged woman with a pot-gut and a faded tattoo of indeterminate design on her bicep—incarnate proof that the tattoo fad is on its last legs (and arms); it's over, people! really, if you're going to get inked in the tens, the only appropriate design is of Fonzie jumping a shark—gives us the Evil Eye. This is the same trucker grandma who was smoking a Newport Light when we first arrived—and probably the negligent guardian of the little girl I pushed on the swing.

If Meg notices, she does not react. "I don't care what he does," she says. "I really don't. Soren can suck it."

I'm reluctant to disclose the truth about her husband—that he wasn't out drinking with Peter Berliner, that he lied to her—because the last thing I want to do is unleash the Headless Whoresman upon Meg's mind, too. Then again, if she really *doesn't* care what he does, there's no harm in telling her. Tall, ruggedly handsome, and blessed with a Danish accent, Soren was quite the ladies' man in his bacchanalian bachelor days—he once confessed to me, nonchalantly, that he'd bedded seventy-two women before meeting Meg—so an affair is certainly in the realm of possibility, but if he'd been out with a secret mistress last night, chances are, he wouldn't have come home that knockered. And even if he was, then the sting of betrayal is something Meg and I could go through together. Misery loves company.

"Listen, I have to tell you something."

"What?"

"Soren wasn't out with Peter Berliner last night."

She doesn't say anything. She doesn't react at all. Shit. I should have kept my mouth shut. In situations like this, messengers turn up dead. But I already opened the can of worms, so now I have to empty the damned thing. "Yeah, Peter was at HoeBowl. Tournament game. He bowled like crap, he said, but they still won. I just . . . I don't know. I thought you should know."

Finally, Meg makes a face. "That little *shit*."

With another grimace in our direction, the trucker grandma scoops up the plump toddler she's presiding over *Come on, Jakey, let's go* and hightails it to the baby swings, leaving in her wake an invisible cloud of burnt menthol.

"Christ," Meg mutters, once she's safely past. "Large Marge."

"I'm sorry, Megs. I probably shouldn't've . . . "

"No, it's fine. I know where he was. He was out with fucking Bruce Baldwin. They're, like, *friends*. Which of course is not something I'm thrilled about. So when he goes out with him, he doesn't tell me."

She shakes a few Late July cheese crackers out of their red box, then tilts it toward me.

I grab a handful. "Thanks." The crackers taste good. Really good. "Soren is friends with Bruce Baldwin?"

"They met at the gym. They hit it off. I guess he's a pretty cool guy," she shrugs, "when he's not drunk and horny on prom night. I just think it's disrespectful, you know? I don't want to make a big stink about it, but the guy did things to me that were not very nice. My husband should want to slice his balls off, not buy him a beer. Fuck Soren."

I'd never looked at Sharon Rothman in a sexual way before this morning, and my feelings toward Meg are even less libidinous. She's pretty (a younger, curvier, crunchier Michelle Pfeiffer), she's smart, she's funny, she's cool, I love her, sure—but I could make the same claims about my sister. Hooking up with Meg would feel like incest . . . and yet . . . and yet . . . if Stacy rode off into the sunset with her Headless Whoresman, and Meg and Soren broke up, wouldn't it make perfect sense to . . .

"Would you ever, you know, leave him?"

"So I can be a single mom, consigned to a life of poverty, with sleazy men marking me for easy nookie? No effin' way."

Not that I'm eager for this to happen. I'd prefer to dance with the lady that brung me, and keep Meg in the CLOSE FRIENDS & FAMILY column, where she belongs. But if the towers collapse, something must be built at Ground Zero.

"What if there were a better alternative?"

"Who? David Rothman?"

She laughs, but the mention of Sharon's husband makes my stomach lurch.

Across the playground, the corporate-bald dad is now overcompensating for his endless cell phone call, chasing after his kid, his arms up over his head Godzilla-style, making too-loud monster noises, running too fast. He's having QUALITY TIME, or thinks he is. He'll go back to work tomorrow—a guy like that works on Saturdays, too, probably spends sixty hours a week in some office where the secretaries are leggy and willing—and feel good about himself, that he kicked off after lunch to spend a nice afternoon with his kid. Never mind that the boy looks legitimately terrified.

"You know," Meg says, "this place would be perfect if there were a tiki bar. I could really use a mai tai right about now."

"Me, too," I tell her, eager for a change of subject. "How great would *that* be. A playground–slash–tiki bar?"

"Specializing in yummy girlie drinks. Cosmos and Bellinis . . . "

" . . . Harvey Wallbangers . . . "

" . . . Sex on the Beach and Blowjobs . . . "

". . . but with toddler names. The Dora, the Diego, the Elmo . . ."

" . . . the Buzzed Lightyear . . . "

"Ha! We should draft a business plan. We'd make millions. All we need's a catchy name."

"Why not The Playground?"

"That's not bad."

"No, wait—I got it: Mother's Little Helper."

"Perfect! I mean, unless the Rolling Stones object."

"There's a Ruby Tuesday; why not a Mother's Little Helper?"

"Why stop there? We could open a whole block of Rolling Stones–inspired businesses. A youth hostel called Gimme Shelter. A coffee shop called Brown Sugar. Make your own pottery at Paint It Black."

"Right. Vanessa could manage it."

Meg's made funnier jokes, but I'm a bit punchy, and the dig on my drippy babysitter's choice of major convulses me with giggles. Really, who the fuck majors in *ceramics*? I laugh so hard that all four of the kids—who are, for once, actually getting along; the meltdown at the pumpkin patch behind him, my son has reassumed the persona of Good Roland, dutifully playing with the twins and Maude—stop their game and look at me.

"Daddy's being silly," Maude says.

"Meg made a funny joke."

"What is the . . . excuse me . . . what is the funny joke, Daddy?" asks Roland.

"It's too hard to explain. Go on. Keep playing."

After another beat, they mercifully do. I use the diversion to appropriate the cheese crackers. "Do you mind? I'm ravenous."

"Go for it."

"I don't want to take food from your kids' mouths."

"It's fine. I have another box in the car."

"Thanks."

Most of the culinary staples my children regularly consume nauseate me—I would rather eat deep-fried shit, for example, than ravioli—but these Late July cheese crackers? *Man*, are they good. I don't know what they put in them, but they have achieved cheese-crackery perfection. Even Steve the cat has been known to feast upon Late July cheese crackers, if we happen to leave an open box on the counter.

"I fired her. Vanessa. Gave her the heave-ho."

"What happened?"

I stuff my face with cheese crackers and tell her the story.

"Good for you!"

"You know," I say, "it *would* be great to have a bar here. I really do think that's an inspired idea. I'm not even joking."

"It's the new thing, in Park Slope," Meg says. "Seriously. Hipster parents bringing their toddlers to bars in the afternoon, so they can get knockered."

"What's a toddler supposed to do at a bar? Play darts? Come on, now. Just make a wine spritzer in your bottle of Vitamin Water and go to a playground, like the rest of us."

"Don't tell anyone," Meg says, a guilty look crossing her face, "but I totally poured like two shots of Baileys into my Starbucks."

"Really?"

"Really. I've got a nice little buzz going right now." Through my laugh, she says, "Half a glass of wine when I get home, and I'm good through bedtime."

"I'm really dreading bedtime today."

"Oh, I dread it every day. If I was a gazillionaire, I'd hire a live-in nanny *just* to put the twins to bed. I could deal with the rest of the day, if I could somehow skip bedtime. I'm not even joking. If I won the lottery, that's like the *first* thing I would do."

Out of nowhere, Maude rips a fart that sounds like a minor earthquake. "I fart," she announces, as if anyone didn't hear her. The other kids freeze, look at her, and then burst out laughing, as do Meg and I.

"What do you say?"

"Excuse me!"

More laughing, and then the kids resume their game. Thank God for the sandbox.

"I know it's hard," Meg says, "that Stacy travels so much, and I know it's hard for you to, you know, keep the home fires burning and all, but I tell ya, I envy you guys. I really do."

The notion of *my* so-called life—the lack of sleep, the lack of sex, the lack of money, the lack of social status, the lack of a social life, the lack, really, of almost everything—being enviable, even without factoring in the alleged affair, is so preposterous that I can't help but chuckle.

"I'm serious. You love her, she loves you, you respect each other, you get along great. You *communicate*. Soren," she says, "he's just not *like* that. He's a typical *guy*. He *sucks* at communicating."

We get this a lot, Stacy and I. People comment on what a *perfect couple* we make, how *right* we are for each other. Even Rob, who must, by virtue of his job as a couples counselor, view long-term unions with pessimism (and must recognize that the central premise of every romantic comedy that ever was—namely, that there is such a thing as One True Love—is total crap; that just as there are any number of restaurants where we could enjoy a sumptuous meal, there are any number of people with whom we could, under the right circumstances, fall in love and live with more or less happily ever after; that love, as Eugenia Last and every astrologer worth her horoscopical salt well knows, is, above all, about *timing*) never fails to mention how in love we seem and how much we seem to genuinely like each other. Is it all an illusion? Are we just good actors (I know *she* is), playing time-honored roles in a time-honored play? The last session with Rob, Stacy said, *It's just . . . I'm afraid we lost something . . . a spark . . . something . . . and it's just . . . I'm just worried that it's gone forever, that we can't ever get it back*. I laughed that off, assured her it wasn't the case . . . but she's always been more perceptive about matters of the heart than her out-of-touch husband. Was Stacy right? Has the flame of our love smouldered to nothing? And what then? Divorce? Some Femi-Nazi judge denies me custody because I must, by virtue of my penis, be the subordinate caregiver, and my kids are taken from me, my house is taken from me, and I wind up in one of those sad bungalows on the outskirts of town, where the truffula trees are all chopped down, where the divorced dads go? No fucking way. She can take her love to town all she wants; I'll be the cuckolded albatross around her neck, impairing the view of her cleavage; I'll be human baggage, if that's what it takes to keep the kids. No way I grant a divorce. And in New York, I'd have to. Harder to get a divorce in New York than any other state in the union. Blue laws. Blue *ball* laws.

"He's either lobbying me for sex, or he's brooding in the basement," Meg says. "There's no middle ground. The only time we really talk, I mean *really* talk, is at Rob's."

Maybe *I* should give Rob a call. He might have some insight into my predicament. It's been months since we've been to see him—late July, I think (like the crackers), when Stacy made that grim the-spark-is-dead pronouncement—but he always said we could contact him if we ever needed to talk something through "in a pinch." And doesn't my wife cheating on me, and my entire life threatening to collapse like the WTC, constitute a pinch? If not that, what?

"I mean it," Meg says. "You and Stacy, you have it easy. Or as easy as you can have it, when you have kids."

She's *serious*, I realize. Meg really thinks Stacy and I are . . . are . . . shit, I can't even think of an *example* of a solid couple. Barack and Michelle Obama? Ari Gold and Mrs. Ari? Tom Cruise and Katie Holmes? She must not know about Stacy's affair. But I decide to press her, carefully, just to double-check.

"So you don't think she'd ever cheat on me?"

"Stacy? No way. I mean, *anyone* might be tempted to cheat, in the right situation, but unless she's trapped in the trunk of a car with George Clooney, I'd say you're safe. Why? Do you *think* she's cheating on you?"

"No," I tell her. This is the truth. I don't *think* she's cheating on me—and the fact that Meg is in the dark about the supposed infidelity is welcome news; if Stacy's L.A. trip were a Chad Donovan booty call in disguise, Meg would know—but I can't say for certain. And until I can kill him, the Headless Whoresman will ride on.

"Hey Meg . . . what's the deal with Sharon Rothman?"

No sooner does the question escape my lips than a wasp—one of the last remaining wasps of the season, the lone-wolf Rambo who didn't get the memo that the summer is over, that autumn is here, that he should hole up in whatever papery flophouse wasps hole up in for the winter—flies out of a nest somewhere in the woods and stings Beatrix on the cheek. The poor girl starts wailing, and Meg and I, our moment of fun ruined, jump to our feet and hustle the kids out of the sandbox, which is a lot harder than it sounds, because none of them is wearing shoes, and no one, not even Beatrix, wants to leave. Meg consoles her injured daughter, I help the others find their footwear, and, pell-mell and tumble bumble, we make for the safety of our cars.

"Is she allergic?"

"I don't know. I sure hope not."

"Are you okay to drive?"

She laughs. "Alas, yes."

The corporate-bald dad and his son pass us on the sidewalk, although he doesn't so much as glance at me. I'm as invisible to him as I was to Lady Godiva. The boy is half-running to keep up with his old man's Midtown Manhattan pace, and looks distraught, as if his father might tire of him, release his hand, and leave him behind. "Godzilla two, Mikey zero," the corporate-bald dad boasts, lording his hollow victory, in a game of his own invention, over his overwhelmed three-and-a-half-year-old, who, although the dad might not realize it, is on the brink of tears.

I install the kids in their carseats—Roland first has to sit in Maude's and get a rise out of her before moving, the same "game" we play every time we get into the minivan—and take my place behind the wheel. I put on my seatbelt. I fire up the engine. I watch Meg's SAVE THE RIDGE Jetta drive away.

Her VW has already disappeared around the corner before I realize I forgot to ask her for Sharon's number.

Friday, 3:41 p.m.

The States Mix STARTS SKIPPING. *WELCOME TO THE H-H-H-H-HOTEL Cal-cal-cal-cal . . .*

"It's broken," I tell Roland. "We have to listen to something else."

"Wah!" he cries.

"I'll make a new *States Mix* when we get home, okay?"

We're driving around now, listening to music, killing time, the Odyssey cruising south on 208, toward Gardiner. I'd stopped at Dressel Farms, where the Port-o-Potty is still operational, and took a leak. Was leaving two children unattended in a locked automobile for three full minutes a violation of federal, state, and local law? I don't know, but I couldn't take them with me, nor was holding it an option. It was Port-o-Potty or empty Poland Spring bottle; should I have whipped it out in the minivan? I think not.

"Wah!"

"If it's broken, it's broken. There's nothing I can do."

Here's my plan for the rest of the day: When we get to the light at Ireland Corners, I'll bang a left on 44/55, and another left on

Ohioville, just before the Thruway overpass, and take that to 299, thus completing a big backroads circle—then head over to Pasquale's, a souped–up pizza joint at Cherry Hill Plaza, near Meg's house. I'll fortify my meatball hero with a mug of beer, and possibly two (the Mother's Little Helper talk with Meg was inspiring). Then we'll go home, watch Noggin for an hour or two, and, with any luck, put the kids, and this wretched day, to bed.

"But Daddy," Roland says, "I want music."

I switch over to the radio.

. . . true love won't desert you . . . you know I still love you . . .

Journey? Fucking *Journey*? You've got to be *kidding* me. Why are they still playing Journey on the radio? Why do I hear Def Leppard at least four times a week? Can we all agree to have a moratorium on AC/DC for the next year? Seriously, guys—I've been shook all night long long enough.

I know there's good music out there; it just never gets played on the radio. You'll hear three minutes of white noise before you hear, say, "Chicago" by Sufjan Stevens, my pick for best song of the last decade. Radio stations either play tried-and-true hits, like "More Than a Feeling" or "Fly Like an Eagle" or (please shoot me) "Radar Love," pre-packaged tween-marketed acts, or, worst of all, the slick studio work of an alumnus of that staggering monument to mediocrity, *American Idol*. Even a legitimate rock star like Daryl "Duke" Reid gets very little airtime. You never hear Circle of Fists on the radio, even "My Heart Is Hydroplaning," which was clearly written with a general audience in mind. And Reid is that rare commodity in today's music scene, a guy who actually makes enough money from his art that he doesn't have to hold down another job. Radio has gotten so bad, so predictable, that when I hear a song from the eighties that I didn't particularly like at the time—"I Want a New Drug" or "Let's Hear It for the Boy"—it just about makes my day. The (guilty) pleasure I got last week, in hearing that crappy Huey Lewis song . . .

And yet, loath though I am to admit it, there is something magical about Tom Petty, and Led Zeppelin, and my dad's favorite, the Rolling Stones, and the other perennial classic-rock greats. Regardless of how you feel about "(I Can't Get No) Satisfaction," it's a song that everybody—and I mean *everybody*—knows. There are African bushmen, there are Papua New Guinea primitives, there are aliens with radio scanners on Alpha fucking Centauri, who try and they try and they try and they try and still can't get none. Mick Jagger and Keith Richards are human synapses through which music and mass adulation are exchanged. How exhilarating it must have been to have purchased *Let It Bleed* at the record store the day it came out in 1969 (as my father did), put the needle to the record, and listened with astonishment to the opening strains of "Gimme Shelter"! What a powerful communal experience that must have been, to have bought the album on faith, without hearing a note, and been rewarded with such aural sublimity.

As great as Sufjan Stevens is, his melodies are not in that stratum, and probably never will be. Not everyone knows "Chicago," just as "My Heart Is Hydroplaning," cult hit that it is, is just that: a cult hit. New music is about the long tail. Niche markets. Small audiences. That's why they keep playing the Stones on the radio—there just aren't any new bands who can fill those blue-suede shoes. The wattage of Radiohead, Coldplay, Green Day, even U2, all pales in comparison to such incredible starpower, like so many yellow main-sequence stars next to Betelgeuse (or *Beatle*geuse, as it were)—and besides, none of those acts is exactly new. Who's going to seize the mantle from Mick and Keith and John and Paul? The fucking Jonas Brothers?

I'm contemplating the death of the rock star, connecting the dots to the decline of Western civilization, when I pass yet another cop on the side of the road, this one hiding behind a billboard for State Farm Insurance. Instinctively I pump the brake, but there's no need: it's fifty-five on 208, and the needle's on forty-five as I pass him.

Nevertheless, he pulls out behind me, tires squealing, and flips on his takedown lights, the red and blue streaming menacingly off my rearview. I hit the brake, jerk the minivan to the side of the road. He comes up behind me slowly, ominously. Something about the tableau of aggressively macho cop-car detaining passively effete minivan suggests a prison tough about to make a bitch of the new inmate who just dropped the shower soap.

"Daddy," Roland says, "why are we stopping?"

"We got pulled over," I say. "By a police officer."

"But why?"

"I honestly don't know."

State troopers all look the same. Lean frame, ramrod posture, mirror shades, Stetson hat, narrow mustache, shiny boots. Is there some sort of internal memorandum that instructs them to dress like Tops from gay bondage porn?

My heart is an 808 drum as I roll down the window and kill the engine. My morbid fear of cops rivals my musophobia in intensity. Cops bring out the Kafka in me. I must have been Jean Valjean in a past life. I can't even bring myself to watch movies about men sent to prison for crimes they didn't commit; I get too upset. *In the Name of the Father*? No, thank you.

For the sake of the kids, I try and remain calm. Like K. in *The Trial*, I've done nothing wrong. Forty-five in a fifty-five is not a ticketable offense. Even at the end of the month, when quotas must be reached.

The cop takes his sweet-ass time coming to the window. He ambles over all bow-legged, like he's wearing chaps. O, the repressed homoeroticism of the policeman's lot; O, the unrepressed sadism! He doesn't take off his mirror shades as he peers into the window—rude, if you ask me—gruffly requesting the usual documentation.

"What seems to be the trouble, officer?" I ask, as pleasantly as possible.

"You were speeding, sir." He talks like Friday on *Dragnet*, so much like the stereotypical, no-nonsense cop that it's a self-parody. I resist the urge to laugh.

"Daddy," Roland says again, "why are we stopped?"

"Hold on, Roland."

"I clocked you at sixty-eight."

There is no way I was doing sixty-eight. No fucking way in hell. "Really? Are you sure?"

This is not, evidently, a prudent question to ask a policeman. He interprets my genuine puzzlement as belligerence, collecting my license and registration with stony silence, and ignoring the two kids in the backseat.

"I don't mean to question your authority or your judgment or anything like that," I tell him, trying to keep my voice pleasant. "It's just that I drive this road every day, and I don't like to go fast. My daughter won't let me." I gesture to the back seat, but he continues to ignore the kids. "And I'm not in a hurry. Quite the opposite, in fact. I mean, is it possible your radar gun isn't calibrated correctly?"

Again, not a savvy question to ask. Already he doesn't like me; now I've questioned his cop instincts, his ability to read a fucking speed gun, and his dislike has blossomed into full-blown hatred.

"This isn't the place to discuss that," he tells me, his voice even more robotic than before. "We'll talk about it in court."

"I'm sorry, but, I mean, I just don't understand how it's possible that I was doing seventy."

"I didn't say you were doing seventy," he says. "I said you were doing sixty-eight."

Okay, then.

He ambles back to his car, my license and registration clenched in his fist. I turn around and check on the kids. Roland is perusing his new floor-plan book. Maude is slurping on her passie, her sippy cup in hand. They seem calm enough.

Personally, I think he should have a bit more sympathy for my plight. He should at least acknowledge the kids in the back—I don't want their first experience with a police officer to be this unpleasant—and, I mean, come on now. I'm a dad in a Honda Odyssey with a MOMS ROCK! bumper sticker, chauffeuring around two little kids on a workday. I'm not a drug dealer. I'm not a tailgater. I'm not a drag racer. *How fast could I have been going if my speedometer read forty-five when I passed him?* I'm not the menace to society; I'm the one he's supposed to *protect* from the menace to society! Let me off with a warning, Officer Stalin, and be on your way.

But then, he's a police officer, and that's what police officers do: they assert their authority, like the schoolyard bullies they once were. They get off on their power. If the Tuckers and Joeys of the world manage to stay on the straight and narrow, they wind up driving patrol cars. This joker probably has just as little respect for me—*a man, in a minivan, with two kids, on a workday!*—as I have for him.

Five minutes into whatever it is he has to do with my license and registration while I'm parked on the side of the road, and his cruiser is fishtailed into the southbound lane, fucking up traffic in both directions—five minutes, it must be said, of stellar behavior from the Lansky kids—Maude spills water on her pants and starts bawling. The white stopper thingy fell out of the sippy cup lid—maybe the lid itself is cracked; one of the green ones is, I now recall, and her lid is green—to disastrous effect. What I need to do is comfort her, dry her off, and change her pants. But I can't do that without getting out of the minivan. Is it legal for me to get out of the car? I don't know. But he didn't tell me not to.

I open the door and step onto the gravel on the side of the road. I look behind me, where the trooper sits in his Crown Vic, its lights spinning their bright carnival colors onto the road, and gesture to the side of the Odyssey, so he knows where I'm going. I don't want him to be surprised, come at me with his weapon drawn. I walk around the back of the minivan, open the big side door, and start to dab up the wet spot on Maude's pink pants.

"Get back in the car!" Officer Stalin's shouting into his CB radio mic, and his voice blares through the PA. "Sir, get back in the car, *now*!"

"My daughter is screaming," I respond, raising my voice so he can hear me, but careful to keep calm, to not swear. "She's upset."

"I don't care," comes the blaring voice. "Get back in the car. For your own safety!"

I don't see how it's unsafe for me to be here on the gravel, what with the entire bulk of the minivan—not to mention his own fish-tailed cruiser—shielding me from the actual road. A road that is not exactly the Santa Monica Freeway when it comes to traffic.

"Now!"

I do what he says. But before I get back in, I shout, "You're making a three-year-old cry! That's unconscionable!"

Back in my seat, I'm trembling. My fingers are shaking so bad I can barely keep them on the wheel. How I managed to engage the cop without dropping an f-bomb is beyond me. I didn't think I had this much self-control.

"Sorry, Maude," I tell her. "You just have to wait."

So Maude is crying, and Roland is yelling at her to shut up, and I have so many conflicting emotions surging through me—anger, frustration, humiliation, indignation, more anger; basically, I feel like I've been violated—that I want to rip the steering wheel clean off and throw it like a Frisbee through the fucker's windshield. Which, now that I mention it, is the sort of thing Roland, whose interior monologue is devoid of neuro-typical censorship, says all the time when he gets this mad.

This is the state of things when Officer Stalin finally returns to my front window, his mirrored shades giving him the look of that shapeshifting cyborg from *Terminator 2*. Again, he ignores the crying three-year-old and the irritated four-year-old, and speaks in the same robotic tone: "It's unlawful to leave your vehicle during a traffic stop. In addition, raising your voice at a state trooper constitutes disorderly conduct. That's an arrestable offense." He gestures back to his cruiser. "I have it all on videotape."

Arrestable? Really? I can already see it on the AP wire: FATHER ARRESTED FOR GETTING OUT OF HIS CAR DURING TRAFFIC STOP TO TEND TO CRYING DAUGHTER. That would trump the story about the mother in Texas who was arrested in front of her kids, taken away in handcuffs, for not wearing her seatbelt. I'm Facebook friends with the editor of the national desk at Fox News, who I know from my days in HR, and if the whole you-only-get-one-phone-call business proves true, she's my one call. On the other hand, getting arrested is probably not the best recourse right about now. Nothing good could come of that. So, humiliating as it is, I go into groveling mode, which is what the sadistic fucker wants—to break me, to make me cry *uncle*, to apologize even though I'm not in the wrong. Quite like the prison shower rapist. "I'm sorry, officer. I was only trying to help my daughter."

Still he doesn't acknowledge Maude's crying, which has subsided to mucousy grunts and sniffles. Instead, he says, "The best way to help your daughter is to stay in your seat during a traffic stop, especially on a busy road such as this. You could get hit by a car, and then she'd *have* no father."

There's a better chance of me being struck by lightning—that actually happened last year, to a man in Highland, the next town over; a father of two, my age, outside in a sudden storm, struck dead by lighting—but I don't press the point.

"Maybe your daughter was crying because you were so clearly irritated when you were detained," Officer Stalin continues, returning my license and registration with a little white print-out that is, in popular parlance, the ticket. "Maybe she was picking up on your cues. You're her role model, remember. You have to be a good one."

My cell phone, on the passenger seat, picks this moment to ring. The ringtone is called Old School; it sounds like a rotary-dial phone from the fifties, something from a film noir. I ignore it.

What I should do now is end this conversation. Apologize one more time, and be done with him. But I can't seem to let it go.

"She spilled water on her pants," I tell him. I've managed to conceal the boiling rage in my voice, but I still sound shaky. "That's why she was crying. They were fine until then. They're *little* kids, and they've been sitting back there for a long time."

He doesn't like this. Again, he takes this as an attack on his competence. "You've been here for the eight minutes necessary to process the paperwork," he tells me, "and not a minute longer."

I know that further engagement will only get me in deeper

trouble. He clearly hates my guts; I should just accept my ticket and the stinging humiliation that comes with it. Anal rape is worse when you resist, right? But I can't stop myself. "Do you *have* kids? My son is four; my daughter is three. Eight minutes on the side of a road is an eternity, when you're that little." As I talk, my cell phone makes a bleeping noise, indicating a new message. I ignore it. "Can you please at least *acknowledge* them? I don't want them to be afraid of police officers."

He stands there for a moment, perhaps searching his mind for some statute I've violated with this modest request, some arcane blue law he can book me with. Then, finding none, he leans in a bit, gives a two-fingered wave, and says, with all the warmth of one of those animatronic animals at Chuck E. Cheese, "Hi, children. You be good, now."

"Thank you, officer."

He knocks three times on the hood of the minivan, marches back to his Vic, and is gone, off to harass some other innocent driver, leaving me on the side of the road, exposed and upset and thoroughly ashamed.

And I'm struck by a sudden thought: *Is this how Roland felt when I pulled him away from his game at the pumpkin patch? Did he flip out because he felt I abused my power, punished and humiliated him when he'd done nothing wrong?*

My tears come quick and loud, in big wet sobs; the raw emotion built up during the course of the day, a liquid cancer that won't come out of my body any other way. My reaction to Officer Stalin here is not all that dissimilar to Roland's to me at the pumpkin patch.

In the backseat, the kids have gone silent. They know something's wrong. I can see the terror in their eyes. Maude has stopped sobbing, her sippy-cup mishap forgotten. Even Roland has picked up on the discomfiture. No one likes to see Daddy cry.

"Sorry, guys," I say, trying to stifle the sobs. "It's okay. I'm okay. It's going to be okay."

"Daddy," Maude says, "was he *bad*?"

"Yes, honey. He was bad." I meet her concerned glance in the rearview, the caregiver look she generally reserves for her dollies and Steve the cat. "Not *all* policemen are bad, but he sure was."

"It's okay, Daddy."

"Thanks, honey."

"I want to break him," Roland says. "Stupid idiot cop."

"So do I." I fire up the engine. "But you can't break a police officer. You'll go to jail."

Glancing at my phone on the passenger seat, I remember that someone left a message while I was talking to Officer Stalin. I check the call log: Stacy. Three out of five bars here, good enough reception to check the message:

> *Hey, it's me. Just calling to check in. I'm off to yet another meeting—fun fun fun. I can't wait to come home, you have no idea. This has been a fucking nightmare. The work has totally sucked, we haven't been able to leave the hotel even though we're like so close to the beach it's torture—why come to L.A. if we can't go outside?—and then I don't know if you remember my old boyfriend, Chad? He's, like, stalking me. He called me yesterday, out of the blue, and asked me to dinner, and he won't take no for an answer. He keeps calling the hotel and leaving these weird messages, and posting weird shit on my Facebook wall. Ever since he left Promises, he's been a totally different person. He's, like, all into Jesus now. It's kind of creepy. Anyway, love you. Talk to you later. Bye.*

Again the Fish in the Pot in my head reminds me that Sharon may have bad information, that of course Stacy loves me, that of course she's been true, that all the anxiety of this suck-ass two-star day has been much ado about nothing, a product of *caught in a trap* suspicious minds. No smoke, no fire.

One thing for sure: we can safely cross Chad Donovan off the list of suspects.

And yet the Headless Whoresman is only wounded, and will not die.

INT. SQUAD CAR – NIGHT

The car is parked on the side of Route 299 in New Paltz, hidden behind a billboard. A COP sits in the driver's seat, presiding over a radar gun. A car zooms by doing sixty.

COP

Should I? Ah, fuck it.

Instead, he plops a Munchkin into his mouth. Confectionary sugar winds up on his otherwise immaculate moustache. Another car speeds by. CLOSE SHOT of the radar gun: 69.

COP

Sixty-nine. Excellent.

He turns on his takedown lights and peels out after the car, a silver Subaru Outback with an Obama/Biden sticker on the bumper.

COP

Another proud supporter of the Muslim socialist. No way I let this guy off.

The Subaru pulls over; the cop pulls behind it.

EXT. SIDE OF ROUTE 299 – MOMENTS LATER

The COP saunters over to the driver's-side window, where STACY fidgets.

STACY

Good evening, Officer.

COP

You in a hurry, ma'am? Because I clocked you at sixty-nine.

STACY

No. No hurry. I guess I just wasn't paying attention.

COP

Not a good idea to not pay attention when you're behind the wheel, ma'am.

STACY

No, it's not. You're right, Officer.

COP

Have you been drinking, ma'am?

STACY

I had a beer.

COP

A beer?

STACY

Two beers. Maybe three. But, you know, over the course of several hours.

COP

Get out of the vehicle, please.

STACY

Yes, Officer.

She does. She's dressed to kill. The cop ogles her admiringly. His eyes stop at the wedding band on her left hand.

COP

Where's your husband?

STACY

Home. Home with the kids.

COP

I see. Maybe you're in a hurry to get back to him?

STACY

Not particularly.

COP

Trouble at home?

STACY

I wouldn't call it trouble.

COP

What would you call it?

STACY

Boredom. No, that's too strong. Ennui? I don't know. We're in a rut, Officer. We're just in a rut.

COP

I might be able to help with that.

STACY

Really.

COP

Do you like a man in uniform?

STACY

As long as handcuffs come standard issue.

COP

You're a nasty one, huh?

STACY

Guilty as charged. Was I really speeding?

COP

You were.

STACY

Am I really under the influence?

COP

I'd hate to have to find out.

STACY

Is this the part where I offer to do something for you in exchange for you forgetting all about this?

COP

I don't know if I can completely forget about it. I might want to take you to dinner.

STACY

Yeah?

COP

Sure. We should probably get out of New Paltz, though, go out in Fishkill. That's where I live.

STACY

Then you can take me back to your place.

COP

If all goes well.

STACY

I have a feeling it will. I've always had a thing for cops.

COP

Yeah?

STACY

I have a recurring fantasy about fucking a cop. In uniform. In the back of his squad car. Or maybe sprawled on the hood. But I guess you're on duty.

COP

I am. But it's Tuesday. It's a slow night.

Grinning, the cop reaches into his belt, pulls out his handcuffs. We hear them CLICK open. Then we . . .

FADE OUT

CRYING AND DRIVING PROVED DIFFICULT, SO I SWUNG BY PHILlies Bridge Farm, our CSA, not far from where I was pulled over, to gather my composure. (*CSA* stands for Community Supported Agriculture, but people up here use the abbreviation as a synonym for *farm*. When you join a CSA—and everybody in New Paltz does, just as every student wizard joins one of the Houses at Hogwarts—you come to the farm once a week to collect your share of fresh organic produce, a sizeable percentage of which you wind up throwing away six days later because you don't know how to cook it and it goes brown and limp in your refrigerator.)

Harvest Days, when the unpaved parking lot fills up with the Subarus of CSAers picking up the week's take, are Thursday and Saturday; on Friday afternoon, then, the farm is empty, just a handful of crunchy college-kids-on-leave watering the rows of sunflowers. Roland and Maude are playing in a sandbox, not as elaborate as the one at Hasbrouck, but elaborate enough for my purposes. They're playing happily, interacting well, enjoying each other's company, as they often do in the late afternoon.

It really turned out to be a gorgeous day. The sky is big and blue, the sun low over the farmhouse, bathing with light the red and orange and yellow of the autumnal trees. To the west, the mighty Shawangunk Ridge—a layer-cake of glacier-hewn bedrock, ugly and beautiful all at once, on which is perched, improbably, a manmade hard-on of stone: Skytop Tower, part of the famed Mohonk Mountain House resort complex—presides over the valley. SAVE THE RIDGE. Bucolic splendor, the lure of upstate New York. A lovely tableau, a picture postcard (literally, as Skytop Tower is our Liberty Bell, our Mount Rushmore, adorning our GREETINGS FROM NEW PALTZ, N.Y. postcards). So much beauty to behold, *don't know why there's no clouds up in the sky* and it could not be more antithetical to my *stormy weather* state of mind *keeps rainin' all the time.*

The hint of red under the new *Us Weekly* reminds me that I forgot to open the Netflix. Carefully tearing the reusable envelope—how many did I destroy before figuring out the clever trick?—I withdraw the smooth white sleeve. It is not *I Love You, Man*, but Stacy's uninspired selection, *He's Just Not That Into You.* This means I will be channel surfing later; if I watch *He's Just Not That Into You* tonight, by myself, I might as well donate my balls to someone who can actually use them.

Shaky reception here, but I'm able to get through. The plan is to catch Stacy before her meeting, but the call goes straight to voicemail. I leave a perfunctory message, *kids are fine, miss you, love you, can't wait to see you.* Then I check the home voicemail, an oh-so-convenient process that entails dialing (but not really *dialing*; no one *dials* anymore) a mere twenty numbers, plus the obligatory pound key, and then waiting for the automatronic woman *the auto-matron?*, whose changelessly cheerful tone of voice is the telephonic equivalent of the old biddy doing forty-five on the Thruway, delivering her news with all the urgency of a corpulent carrier pigeon. Get to the point!

You have . . . one . . . new message.

A message, a message! Knots in my stomach, bad ham doing its dread work. Sharon, the dreaded follow-up call, a nuptial oncologist phoning with the biopsy results of the invisible cancer in my marriage? Stacy, with benign news about her scones, her chopped salads, with what she ate for lunch *with who ate her for lunch*?

New voice messages. Playing . . . new voice messages. Call answering message from . . .

I click the number key, bypassing the chipper auto-matron, and skip right to the message:

"Jawsh," comes the familiar voice, as lugubrious as the auto-matron is sunny. "Haven't heard from you all week. Just wanted to see how you were holding up. Call me when you get a chance, okay? Um . . . okay, bye."

I've always been close to my mother, but lately, I find her difficult to talk to. She doesn't understand, and therefore doesn't approve of, my lifestyle. She can't wrap her brain around the fact that not everyone of consequence has a job in the legal or medical professions. I should have a law degree by now, I should be a partner. I should be married to a nice Jewish girl who stays at home and cares for the children, who balances the checkbook and manages the dry cleaning. I should be a *success*, not in the bullshit screenwriterly way, but using the traditional yardstick of such things, net worth.

(My net worth, needless to say, is less than zero. Red-inked ledgers, spreadsheets with five-digit numbers in parentheses, credit scores lower than what I got on my SAT verbal. When I finally do address the Chase Visa bill looming on the front seat, perhaps after a few Rolling Rocks, it will inform me that if I continue making the minimum monthly payment, I will pay off the balance in a mere ninety-eight years. Untenable debt, the bane of my generation. Just in time for the trough of Social Security to run dry. A nation in default. We are so fucked. Barring some unexpected windfall, next month, maybe the month after, I will have to undergo the profound humiliation of beseeching my mother for financial aid. Fatherhood is one long slog to Canossa.)

Never mind that the former Linda Silverman didn't even follow her own advice. *My* father wasn't Jewish—people assume Lansky is a Jewish surname, because of the notorious Jewish underworld kingpin, but it's actually Slovak in origin; Meyer Lansky's real last name was Suchowljanski—and owned, as I mentioned, an auto body shop, at which his role was more than administrative; working with your hands is hardly the stuff of the Jewish-American dream. And while he wasn't a staunch Catholic, he insisted I learn about the church; I was the only kid I knew who went to both Hebrew School *and* C.C.D. (Mom rectified that deviation from her faith with her second marriage—he goes by Frank, but the name on my stepfather's driver's license is Israel Frankel.)

Why did she have to call today, of all days? The very lilt to her voice puts me on the defensive, destroys my confidence, undermines my sense of well-being. She makes me feel like I'm eight years old, a child. Not that she intends to do this. Not consciously. She means well, my mother; she worries about me something awful, and why would she fret so if she didn't care deeply? And I know she's proud of me; I know she brags about me to her friends at temple. If *Babylon Is Fallen* ever made it to the local cineplex, they'd never hear the end of it. But for all her love, for all her pride, for all her worry, she doesn't trust me. She doesn't. You can tell by the tone of her voice, she's waiting for the other shoe to drop. She's Chicken Little. Every misstep is a crisis, every wrong turn a sign of the Apocalypse.

Roland and Maude are now throwing sand at each other. "Stop it! Guys! Stop throwing sand! Come on, now."

I am seized with a feeling I've had throughout my life in times of turmoil, a powerful urge to confide in someone, to seek counsel, coupled with the realization that, with Stacy unavailable (and even my wife, far and away my closest friend, has her limits in this regard), I have no one to fill that role. A chronic loneliness. Part of the male condition.

I settle upon my sister, who usually answers her phone no matter what, but I hang up when I remember she's in Pisa at the moment, on a deferred honeymoon with her new husband, filling her Facebook feed with photos of the Leaning Tower.

I can't call Meg; wasp.

I can't call any of my guy friends out of the blue, my drinking buddies from the city, my old chums from college, and cry into the phone. Guys don't do telephone, and we certainly don't cry into our Nokias.

I don't have Sharon's number, and I can't call Meg right now to get it.

I scroll down the CONTACTS list on my phone. Most of the numbers belong to pediatricians and schools and take-out restaurants and landscapers and snow removal companies and car services. I used to have more friends. I don't know what happened.

With no one else to turn to, I decide on Rob, our therapist. Maybe we can set up a time to talk this evening or something. The number usually goes right to voicemail, so I'm surprised when a live human being—a woman with a thick Irish brogue—picks up. When I ask to speak to Rob, I'm told that this is his answering service. (She has a brogue, then, because she lives in Ireland; outsourcing is the new black.)

"I didn't know he had an answering service."

"Dr. Puglisi is attending a mental health conference in Los Angeles this week, but he is checking his messages. Can I have your name, please?"

The phone cuts out just then—shaky reception at Phillies Bridge Farm—which is just as well, because there's no reason to keep talking.

I have all the information I need.

Rob's been in Los Angeles all week.

Stacy's been in Los Angeles all week.

Rob and Stacy have been in Los Angeles all week.

Well now.

I had not considered Rob Puglisi as a suspect. I don't think of him as a real person—or to be more accurate, as a viable candidate for intercourse of any kind outside the hallowed walls of his Balinese-decorated office—because I have too much respect for the work. But why *not* Rob Puglisi? He's older, yes, but he's a handsome dude—tall, with fashionable glasses and a carefully trimmed beard, always dressed in tweed coats of the kind worn by members of the British royal family. He sort of looks like Phil Jackson, but if the Lakers coach were reincarnated as a professor of nineteenth-century British literature. He has a deep, hypnotic speaking voice—he does hypnotherapy, of course he has a hypnotic voice!—that with the slightest modulation could come off as intensely seductive. He's smart, he's enlightened, he's funny . . . and he always *did* seem to take Stacy's side.

Furthermore, from a purely logistical standpoint, he's a therapist; his job involves the keeping of secrets. He knows how to keep his mouth shut. If your intention is to have a discreet affair—one that doesn't ruin your marriage—this is vital. Your lover, after all, is your partner in crime. You don't want the guy you robbed the bank with flashing money all over town, and you don't want your Monica Lewinsky blabbering to every Tom, Dick, and Linda Tripp in town.

This assumes, of course, that Stacy is only scratching an itch and doesn't intend to leave me outright.

I tuck my phone back into my jeans, watch the kids laughingly throw sand—I've given up trying to stop them—and try to focus on that, to lose myself in their simple joy, to feel grateful for all that I have, to not feel sorry for myself.

I'm three deep breaths into the meditation when Roland and Maude simultaneously hit each other in the eye with sand, and it's time to go.

EXT. LAKE MINNEWASKA, NEW PALTZ, N.Y. - DAY

The pristinely set lake, surrounded by mountains of white stone and pine trees, twinkles in the sunlight. STACY sits on one of the rocks, looking down at the water, alone in her thoughts. She's wearing workout clothes, but she still looks hot. She gets up to continue her hike, and who should she bump into, coming in the opposite direction, than her former therapist, ROB PUGLISI.

ROB

Stacy! How nice to see you.

STACY

Hey, Rob.

They embrace, for perhaps a touch too long, given the clinical nature of their relationship.

ROB

Curious that I ran into you today. I was literally just thinking about you.

STACY

Yeah?

ROB

It's been months since our last session. I wondered how things were going.

STACY

Well, they're going, I guess.

ROB

That doesn't sound promising.

STACY

I wanted to come back to you and talk about everything, but Josh refuses. He thinks it's too expensive, that we can't afford it.

ROB

And what do *you* think?

STACY

That he's using that as an excuse. That he's afraid to come to terms with how bad things really are.

ROB

I'm sorry to hear that. But I can't say I'm surprised.

STACY

Really?

ROB

I shouldn't really say this, given our therapist/patient relationship . . .

STACY

We haven't seen you in six months. Can't we just be regular people now?

ROB

I suppose.

STACY

What were you going to say?

ROB

That he doesn't appreciate you. That he takes you for granted. That every single session, I had to fight off the urge to reach over and throttle him.

STACY

You seemed so calm.

ROB

I'm good at my job.

STACY

He always did think you were on my side.

ROB

Well, he was right about that. How could I not be on your side? All the sacrifices you've made for him, for your family . . . how can I not admire that?

STACY

Thanks, Rob.

ROB

Are you serious about us being like regular people? About stepping away from our previous relationship?

STACY

Yes.

ROB

Then I should tell you that I'm in love with you. That I've loved you from the moment you stepped into my office. And that if you leave that nebbish of a husband, I will take care of you in ways you always dreamed about.

STACY

Rob, my God. I don't know what to say.

ROB

Then don't say anything.

He kisses her; she returns the kiss with equal ardor.

STACY

This is such a romantic spot. Do you wanna . . .

He nods. She takes his hand, leads him to a secluded part of the rock, and lies down.

FADE OUT

THE WALLS AT PASQUALE'S ARE WHITE BRICK, WITH PLENTY OF plate-glass windows overlooking the Stop & Shop (correction: the *Super* Stop & Shop; in addition to providing the freshest produce and meats, it wears a cape and fights crime) on 299, and roomy booths of green vinyl, and a mural of the Amalfi seascape on the wall by the restrooms, and a little statue of a big-mustached pizza guy, the *paesan* stereotype, that greets you as you enter, and red-green-and-white paper placemats with a clumsy drawing of the Italian boot, with the caption BEAUTIFUL ITALY in English, but the major cities written in Italian: Roma, Firenze, Venezia, Napoli.

Two booths away, a troika of Goth-arrayed SUNY coeds, none of them particularly cute, has gathered for pizza. As I gorge on meatballs, I eavesdrop on their conversation, which, far as I can tell, involves Eighties Night at Cabaloosa.

" . . . and it's like, they play, you know, oldies. Like, you know, Madonna, and Prince, and Culture Club."

"Culture Club?"

"You don't know Culture Club?"

"Never heard of them."

"Boy George?"

"Um, no?"

"Don't they sing that song? The *comma-comma-comma-comma-comma come-ee-lee-un* . . . "

"I think so?"

"I have, like, no *idea* what you guys are talking about?"

"It's kind of a dumb song."

"Ya think?"

"I have *never* heard that before in my *life*. You guys are like total dorks."

She's maybe eighteen or nineteen years old, hip enough to dress Goth, smart enough to be in college . . . and she's never heard of "Karma Chameleon"? Never heard of Boy George, who's only the Lady Gaga of 1982?

Shit, I'm getting old. Not *getting. Am.*

"What's this?" I ask Roland, showing him the placemat.

"Italy," he says.

"Aunt Laura is there right now." I pronounce it the Jersey way, like the insect; Stacy says *ont*; the kids usually hold with me. "Did you know that?"

"She's in Pisa. She saw the Leaning Tower."

"Right."

"Wait," Maude says. "Because . . . because . . . where is Aunt Laura?"

"In Italy. With Uncle Michael."

"In Italy, you stupe," Roland says, smacking her.

"Hey! Enough of that!"

I take another big gulp of my beer. You don't think about having a draft beer at a pizza place, or at least I don't, but the Bud at Pasquale's is crisp, cool, and refreshing—just like they say it is in the commercials. The Clydesdales would be proud.

"There's only one interstate highway in Nebraska," says Roland, the Crown Prince of the Non Sequitur. "Interstate 80."

When I get home, I'll verify this, but I don't have much doubt that he's right.

Roland is polishing off the last of his ravioli. Maude is gnawing on breadsticks, pausing between bites to re-insert her pacifier. They haven't been *not* naughty—we can't go to a restaurant without them moving seats three times, or peeling the wrappers off the crayons, or getting fingerprints all over the windows, or fucking around with the blinds, or lying down on the bench, or crawling underneath the table to get from one side of the booth to the other (as it now stands, Maude is next to me, and Roland is by himself across from us), or bursting into song—but the naughtiness is at an acceptable level. There is less misbehavior than I was expecting. It's almost like they both recognized, on some level, that their old man'd had it—the last day of a long tour of duty in Parenting Afghanistan—that another outburst would put me over the edge, and I'd wind up in the back of a squad car, an ambulance, or a hearse, and they'd have no one on hand to ply them with ice cream when they got home, or cue up their favorite shows.

"Do you like your bread, Maude?"

"I like it, Daddy," she says. "I *very* like it. It's *so* delicious."

"Good."

Idly, I take out my phone to check the time—4:47—and am about to try Stacy again when I hear a tiny voice call out, "Roland! Hey, Roland!"

The next thing I know, Zara Reid, in the same blue-on-blue dress she wore to the farm, slides beside Roland at the big booth, and a heavy hand rests on my shoulder.

"Hey, man," comes a deep voice. And then Daryl "Duke" Reid, still wearing his blue Dickies uniform and his ski cap, still impossibly big, pulls up a chair and plops down at the head of the table. "Mind if we join you for a minute?"

"No," I tell him, trying my best to disguise my shock at such a stroke of good fortune, "please."

"You're Josh, right?"

"Yeah. And this is Maude."

"Maude. I like that."

The dude can fill a room, and not just because of his size. Charisma fairly radiates off him. Maybe one day he'll run for office. It's not unprecedented; John Hall, former leader of the band Orleans, is now a congressman a few districts downriver.

"And you already know Roland."

"That we do. I'm Daryl, by the way." He extends his hand, which is almost twice the size of mine—and that's not including the brass-knuckle-sized ring on his middle finger—and gives me a surprisingly gentle shake.

"I know. Although I wasn't sure if you preferred Daryl or Duke."

"Duke's just a stage name," he says, as if embarrassed. I didn't know such a big, self-assured guy was capable of bashfulness. "The idea was that it would make me more mysterious. It worked, I guess. But now I'm stuck with it. The days of Duke are kind of behind me, you know? These days, I'm pretty much a stay-at-home dad. Not much punk rock about that."

"Oh, I don't know. There are certainly days when I have the urge to smash things."

"There are days," he says, "when I do," and we both sort of chuckle politely, although neither of our jokes is all that funny.

"Anyway, I'm glad we bumped into you," Reid says. "I've been meaning to call you." *He's* been meaning to call *me*? "Zara's been talking about Roland nonstop, and I promised her I'd arrange a playdate."

Idiot that I am, it did not occur to me that Roland's affection for Zara might work both ways. The boy *is* adorable. He's got that going for him. And that's an objective observation, not just the opinion of an admittedly biased father.

"That'd be great. Let me tell you, Roland *loves* Zara. We'd love to. Unless you're having second thoughts after today's little incident at the farm."

"What incident?"

"You didn't notice the nuclear meltdown?"

"Oh, *that*." Reid swats that notion away with a wave of his giant paw. "That was nothing, believe me. It always feels terrible when it's your kid, like you're the worst parent alive, but, I mean, they're four. Shit happens."

All three of the kids erupt into paroxysms of laughter.

"Papa," Zara says, once the laughing fit has worn down, "you said *shit*."

"Yes, I did. Papa said a bad word. Don't you go talking like that, okay, pumpkin?"

"Okay, Papa."

"Yeah, my son—he's in the second grade now, but he did his time at Thornwood—he was really a handful. He'd have a meltdown like that at least once a day, usually more, and always at the worst possible moments. A tantrum at the class field trip you can deal with; at the departure gate at JFK, dude, that's another story."

"Oh, *man*."

"Everybody looks at you, because you can't control your kid, and you're totally mortified, and it's really hard to keep your composure. You just want to scream. My wife, she took it all really hard. It was hard for her to leave the house with him. Because, I mean, in our society, if a kid misbehaves, it's always the mother's fault, right? We love to tee off on the mother. She's either withholding her love, or else she coddles him. Either way, it's all on her. The mother always takes the blame. And it wasn't Céline's fault; it wasn't my fault; it was no one's *fault*. It's just how Wade is, how he's wired. The things that sometimes make him difficult are the same things that make him special, that make him *him*." He leans back, gives his knuckles a loud crack, and laughs. "I'm sorry, man. I do this. I just start talking. My wife hates it."

"No, no, it's cool. It's good to talk. Do you guys just want to stay and eat with us?"

"You don't mind?"

"I mean, I may have to beat a hasty retreat if they get jumpy, but until then . . . "

I flag down the green-eyeshadowed waitress, who runs back to the kitchen to fetch sodas and slices of pizza.

"So how is Wade doing in school?"

"Really well. He's doing really well. He loves his school, loves his teacher. But, I mean, we have him at the Annex. They know how to handle him there."

"The Annex . . . "

Before I can formulate my question, Reid answers. He's seen this movie before. "It's a school for children with, you know, autistic spectrum disorders. Wade's what they call PDD-NOS. Pervasive

Development Disorder Not Otherwise Specified. That's what they call it when you have *some* autistic symptoms but not, you know, autism as such."

"Papa," Zara says. "I'm hungry."

"I know," he tells her. "That's why we're here."

"You want some bread?" I offer.

She takes a garlic knot out of the basket, gnaws on it.

"Thanks," Reid says. "Yeah, PDD-NOS. It's a stupid name. I really wish they'd come up with something better."

"At least it doesn't sound like *assburger*."

When he doesn't so much as smile at my joke, it dawns on me that Daryl Reid may not realize that Roland is on the spectrum. I glance at my son, but he's too busy making eyes at Zara to eavesdrop. There will be a day when Roland realizes that he has Asperger's, but he doesn't know yet, and I see no reason to hurry that epiphany along. "You know that Roland is, uh, A-S-P-I-E."

Reid's eyebrows shoot up. "No, I didn't," he says. "I had no idea."

"He can be very unpredictable. Although right now, he's on his best behavior. The services, they help. And he seems to behave better when Zara's around." This makes sense, I see now; if her older brother is at the Annex, Zara is used to handling volatile boys. "That's what Mrs. Drinkwater said."

"Mrs. Drinkwater." Reid shakes his head, and his Sid Vicious scowl looks like one of the faces he makes in the "My Heart Is Hydroplaning" video. "Wade had Mrs. Burns. She's the best. We *love* her. We got really lucky with that. Mrs. Drinkwater, she's . . . "

"Overmatched."

"Exactly. She's nice and all, and she cares, but . . . "

The green-eyeshadowed waitress returns with their pizza.

Reid pats the excess oil off both slices, gives Zara hers, and takes a giant bite from the crust of his own. He looks at Roland, shakes his head in wonder. "Really. I never would have known."

That he didn't know is, in a way, good; it means Roland can pass as "typical," which is ultimately what you want as a parent:

your kid to function in society, to not stand out all the time. On the other hand, his condition is very real, and if people don't know about it, his brusque manner can be confused with rudeness. It's a double-edged sword, the spectrum. To reveal or not to reveal.

"So what do you guys do?" Reid asks. "I know that's a lame question, but I'm curious."

"No, it's cool," I assure him. "My wife—her name is Stacy—she's an actress, and she works in marketing at IBM. I'm a . . . screenwriter." I swallow the word, as I always do. It's a ridiculous thing to say with a straight face, like telling people that you're an astronaut.

"That's a tough racket," he says. "Almost as bad as the music industry."

"Tell me about it. But, you know, at least I don't have to lug around heavy equipment. Or leave the house."

"Have you had any luck?"

"I sold a script once. And for about a day or two, it looked like it might even get made. George Clooney was interested, or so I was told. But that was five years ago—right before we moved here, when Roland was a baby—and it doesn't look like anything will ever become of it. I'm sure George has moved on."

I decide not to mention the crippling writer's block.

"Still," he says. "Pretty impressive."

"I guess." If I'm ever going to bring up the proposed interview, now is the time. The iron is hot. *But tread carefully, Josh; be subtle.* "I also do some freelance writing. For *Rents* magazine. Do you know it?"

"Sure. Céline has a subscription, so I wind up reading it in the can. What stuff do you write for them?"

"Whatever they tell me to." Not strictly a lie. "Little wrap-ups, mostly. And the occasional celebrity interview."

"Did you write that profile of Amanda Peet?"

"I wish."

"Yeah. That was pretty good."

Now or never, Josh. Shit or get off the pot.

"I don't suppose *you'd* like to be interviewed? You know, about fatherhood and stuff?"

The bashful look returns. If I didn't know better, I'd think he was blushing. "Oh, I doubt they'd want to talk to me. No one cares about Circle of Fists anymore. There's some heavy hitters in that magazine. I can't compete with Nicole Richie and Ashlee Simpson-Wentz."

Before I can bust his chops for knowing who Nicole Richie and Ashlee Simpson-Wentz are—and for using the latter's married name!—the three girls at the opposite table, the not-that-cute Goth chicks ignorant of the Culture Club experience, approach us, all giggly. "Excuse me," says the nose-ringed leader, the one who insisted that she'd never heard "Karma Chameleon," that her friends were total dorks, "but are you Daryl 'Duke' Reid?"

Reid says that he is, and that he's flattered that they recognized him, and they tell him they think "My Heart Is Hydroplaning" is like the best song of all time ever, and he thanks them, and they ask about his new album, and he says it won't be out till next year, and they ask for his autograph, which he provides in crayon on the back of one of the BEAUTIFUL ITALY placemats. Then they thank him profusely and quit the restaurant, giggling all the way to the parking lot. Not once during the entire exchange do they so much as glance in my direction. Not even a rock star's reflected glow can get three homely college chicks to notice me. Super Stop & Shop, meet the Invisible Dad.

"You were saying?"

"Disaffected Goth teenagers don't read *Rents* magazine," he says. "Totally different demographic. I highly doubt your editor has ever heard of me."

"Alright, I'll come clean," I tell him. "I already asked. Just on the off chance I wound up talking to you. And they definitely want you."

"Papa," says Zara, sliding into his lap.

"Really?" Reid seems genuinely delighted—not at all the reaction I was expecting. "To do a parenting interview?"

"That's what they told me. You game?"

"I'd love to. Really. Thanks for thinking of me."

"Papa," Zara says again.

"What is it, pumpkin?"

"Can Roland come to our house for a playdate?"

On the magic word *playdate*, Roland comes up for air, reentering the general conversation. "Daddy," he says. "I want to go to Zara's house. And I want Zara to come to our house."

"Oh, we'll make that happen," Reid assures him. "We'd love to have you over, Roland."

"Do you have a ranch?"

"A ranch?"

"We have a Cape Cod home, but I like ranch homes better because ranch homes don't have stairs."

"Oh, a *ranch*. No, our house is what's called a Queen Anne."

"A Queen Anne!" Finding this amusing, Roland guffaws. "Zara's house is a Queen *Anne* home! There are a number of Queen *Anne* homes in Buffalo, New York. Also in Louisville, Kentucky; Rolla, Missouri; Cleveland, Ohio . . . "

"Daddy," Maude breaks in, as Maude will. "Can we have *hice* cream?"

" . . . New Albany, Indiana; Richmond, Virginia . . . "

"When we get home," I tell her. "If you're good."

"But what's for me?" Roland says, suddenly irritated. "Maude gets hice cream and I get *nothing*!" And he throws back his head and brays like an injured animal.

This makes Reid laugh.

"I better go," I tell him.

"Yeah, me too. Have to fetch Wade. He's at a chess lesson, of all things."

We get the check—Reid insists on paying, and I acquiesce only when he agrees to let me leave the tip—and we exchange numbers and e-mail addresses, and we all head to the parking lot together.

Two days from its apogee, the moon, a plump yellow crescent, hangs above us like a pendant lamp from one of Roland's lighting catalogs. Nature's nightlight. You feel like you could reach up and shut it off. The sun, ready to punch out and quit his eleven-hour workday, has already vanished over the Ridge. There have been UFO sightings over those naked rocks—we're not far from Pine Bush, where Whitley Strieber was whisked heavenward in alien communion—and the orange glow of sunset *the dying ember of another day* gives the range a decidedly otherworldly quality. If not for the trees and the tower, the Gunks, bathed in the twilight's last gleaming, could grace the surface of some lesser Uranian moon.

We say our goodbyes. Zara climbs into the burnt-orange Murano, and Roland and Maude hop into the Odyssey, and with a tentative-if-vague plan to get together early next week, the rock star and I part company.

Bagging the interview is great and all; but I really like the guy, and it looks like we might become *friends*. I'm so psyched about the prospect—I'm desperately in need of cool dad friends, and Daryl "Duke" Reid is, without a doubt, a cool dad; more than a cool dad, a paradigm for how I want to live—that I momentarily forget about the day's many troubles, about Stacy's alleged infidelity, about Roland's breakdown, about the altercation with Officer Stalin, about the Headless Whoresman. Instead my mind concentrates on the immediate future—the kids going to sleep in another two hours, the return of my wife tomorrow afternoon, the playdate with Daryl and Zara Reid next week—and it's not a stretch to say that, at this precise moment, my heart is hydroplaning.

PART III

hi-ho, the derry-o,

the wife

takes

a

lover

Friday, 7:47 p.m.

FATHERHOOD IS PRESSURE, AND GOOD FATHERS DON'T WILT IN the heat. They manage the day's chaotic demands with grace, with poise, with calm, cool detachment. Like Tom Brady operating a two-minute drill to win the big game *slant to Moss, curl to Welker, move the chains* but without the thrill of victory, or the ESPN highlight reel, or the diamond-encrusted Super Bowl ring, or the ticker-tape parade in the Canyon of Heroes, or the celebrity endorsements, or the contract bonuses, or the waiting arms of Gisele Bündchen.

BEDTIME: THE MOMENT OF TRUTH.

In the Great War, they say, soldiers on the front lines went out of their way to avoid killing their counterparts in the opposing trench. The German infantrymen would give ample warning before opening fire, so the Brits could get out of the way; the latter happily reciprocated. Horrible enough to be mired in mud on some apocalyptic wasteland, Siegfried Sassoon'd so far from home; why make it worse with excessive bloodshed? This was the mind-set of many of the soldiers. But paperwork had to be filed, reports had to be written, by officers far from the foxholes, for superior officers even farther from the foxholes, and so, once a day, the rat-a-tat of gunfire *the hi hi hee of the field artillery* would pierce the Flemish stillness, and all would not be quiet on the Western front. This was battle, and battle, for reasons that need no elaboration, comprised the most stressful part of the soldier's day.

Bedtime is battle; battle, bedtime. This is what I'm thinking as I march my charges, *left . . . left . . . left right left* after much flustered cajoling *I don't know but I been told (I don't know but I been told)*, up the stairs to the battlefield of Roland's room *Make my sippy cup juice cold (make my sippy cup juice cold)*, where the Bed Wars saga begins.

The late afternoon was easy: the calm before the Katrina of night. Tired from their long days, Roland and Maude supped on cottage cheese and apple juice and hung out in the basement, one on each couch, taking in the Noggin fare (*Max & Ruby, Olivia, The Fresh Beat Band, Dora the Explorer*).

Then they started fighting for no good reason, and the initial transgression—Roland smacking Maude across the face, in this case, although both parties were equally responsible—was the assassination of the Archduke that lit the Balkan powder keg of full-on conflict that kicked off the Great War of bedtime.

And here we are.

My mission, should I choose to accept it (as if! Like Ethan Hunt, I'm not really allowed to decline):

1. Wash hands and faces.
2. Brush teeth.
3. Put on pajamas.
4. Turn on noise machines.
5. Make sure Roland has a sippy cup and Maude has at least three pacifiers.

6. Give Roland a book to read; beg him to stay in his room while I put Maude to bed.
7. Read Maude a few books.
8. Sing Maude a few songs.
9. Read Roland a few books.
10. Sing Roland a few songs.
11. Hug and kiss and say goodnight.
12. Turn out the light.
13. Get the fuck out of there before they make me go back to Step 6.

Thirteen steps lead down.

On paper, it doesn't look difficult. How hard can it be to turn off a fucking light? In practice, however, it's the sort of operation that would confound Danny Ocean. And Danny Ocean had his band of merry men; with Stacy in California, I don't have a single accomplice, let alone eleven. I'm on my own. Again. For the fifth night in a row.

Although they were in a state of near catatonia during ninety minutes of PRESCHOOL ON TV, Roland and Maude recover their second wind as soon as they hit the stairs. They bound around the rooms like uncaged puppies, wrestling on the ground, kicking each other, smacking each other, and laughing their proverbial heads off. If they had tails, they'd be wagging.

A father uninitiated in the ways of *Healthy Sleep Habits, Happy Child* (long live Marc Weissbluth, M.D.!) would interpret this as a sign that they are not really tired *I don't know but I been told (I don't know but I been told).* That father would be wrong *Sleep behavior's hard to mold (sleep behavior's hard to mold).* What I'm witnessing is the last gasp of fight before the long night's slumber, the part at the end of the horror movie where Jason or Freddy or whoever the villain of the *Saw* movies is comes back to life one last time, for the ultimate scare. The trick is to have the kids already in bed, with the lights out, at the instant they realize they're zonked. Makes it harder for them to change their minds, to fight through it.

I don't mind the roughhousing—although I'm always afraid someone will get a chipped tooth, or a black eye, or some other injury that looks, to the casual observer, to the teachers at Thornwood, to the instructors at Barefoot Dance, to the other playdate mommies, like evidence of child abuse—because they enjoy it, and it burns off excess energy. The key is to quiet them down before the play fighting disintegrates into real fighting, like what just went down in the basement. Tonight, the transition goes smoothly. After two minutes of frolic—I watch as the numbers on Roland's clock move from 7:48 to 7:49 to 7:50, mainly to avert my worried eyes while they thrash about—I'm able to lure Maude into the bathroom, where she makes a big show of washing her hands.

"By myself," she admonishes me, when I try to turn on the taps. "I can do it!"

With the girl thus occupied, I'm able to turn my attention to the boy, who has rediscovered *Wonders of the World*, a children's picture book I picked up at Oblong Books over in Rhinebeck. He's going through the various landmarks with his index finger, naming them: Dome of the Rock, Angkor Wat, Leaning Tower of Pisa. What a gift from the universe! Understand, last night, Roland and I read through an entire floor-plan book, determining who among his friends and family would occupy each bedroom:

—And who will sleep in the *Master* Bedroom, Daddy?
—Me and Mommy.
—And who will sleep in Bedroom Two, Daddy?
—Roland and Zara.
—No, I think I want to sleep in Bedroom Three. It has dormers.
—Okay. In that case, Maude is in Bedroom Two.
—And where will Wade sleep?
—Wade? Who's Wade?
—Zara's brother.
—Oh. He'll sleep . . . I guess we'll put him in Bedroom Three with Maude.

—But Daddy, I'm in Bedroom Three. With Zara. Remember?
—Of course. How could I forget? Then he'll sleep in Bedroom *Two* with Maude.
—*Dah*-dee. You're for-*get*-ting someone.
—Who?
—A member of the *fam*-i-lee.
—A member of the . . . oh, right. Steve. Steve can sleep in the Master Bedroom with me and Mommy.
—Okay. And *this* house, Daddy. This is a nice ranch home. It has *three* beds. And who will sleep in the *Master* Bedroom, Daddy?

There are a hundred and twenty pages in that book, two floorplan designs per page (and sometimes more). I insisted we stop after half an hour of reading, but he would have gone on until the book was finished; I think he did, after I left the room. So you can imagine my delight that he picked out *Wonders of the World*. I would much rather discuss the Great Wall of China and the Sydney Opera House than great rooms and garage apartments.

"Roland," I tell him, "take your clothes off."

"But Daddy, I have to wash my hands first."

He's right, as he always is with matters of routine, with trainspotting. I don't usually put his pajamas on until *after* his face is washed and his teeth are brushed, because nine times out of ten, he spills water on his pee-jays and I have to change him. Instead, I don't change him until he's washed and brushed. But I'm flying solo tonight, and I want to accelerate the process.

"It's okay. Maude's in there now. Let's just get your pee-jays on."

By some miracle, Roland actually listens to me. He begins to remove his shirt—one of those one-piece deals designed to look like a T-shirt over a long-sleeved white undershirt; on the front, in a heavy-metal-looking font, is the inscription SOLD MY SOUL FOR ROCK 'N' ROLL, only *soul* is crossed out and replaced by the word *sister*; ah, the comedians at Target—but he has trouble with it, as he does with most unpracticed acts that require decent motor skill, gross or fine. He flails his arms and contorts his body like Houdini attempting a straight-jacket escape.

"Wah," he yells out, almost falling over as he extricates his head from the shirt. "Stupid shirt!" He hurls it toward the window, in the opposite direction of the hamper, where it should go. Then he starts to move toward a pile of Thomas tracks that's attracted his sudden interest.

"Roland," I remind him. "Take off your clothes. Pants *and* underpants."

"But I like these underpants."

"They're dirty. We have to change them."

"But Daddy . . . "

"Pants and underpants."

"How about we make a deal? How about pants but no underpants?"

"No. Pants *and* underpants."

If he persisted, he could probably win this particular battle. The world will not spin off its axis if he doesn't put on clean underwear until the morning. But he doesn't. The fight vanishes from his eyes, as if he shut off a remote control, and he quickly and more or less gracefully kicks off his pants and underpants. Then, without me having to issue an edict, he plucks off his socks.

Now that he's ready for getting ready for bed—it's such a fucking *process*—I check on Maude. She's still at the sink, her hands so full of lather they look porcelain.

"That's enough, Maude. Rinse, now."

"No," she says. "I need . . . I need more soap."

I take away the bar of Dove—which is about half as big as it was five minutes ago—and over her vocal protests, hold her hands under the water.

"Too hot! Too hot!"

It's not too hot; it's not even lukewarm; she's just saying this as a form of protest. But I kill the left tap anyway, humoring her.

"Rinse."

As if granting me a major concession: "Okay, Daddy."

While I wait, I do a quick inventory: two juice cups, check; three pacifiers, check; Roland's star blanket, check; Maude's frog, check. The prop master has done his job. I turn on the noise machines.

"Now we have to brush."

"No! I don't want to brush my teeth."

"Do you want to get corn teeth?"

I'm fuzzy on the origins of the *corn teeth* concept—it was Stacy's invention—but the notion terrifies our neat-freak Virgo daughter. She does what I tell her. I take her toothbrush—an electric one with Hello Kitty on the handle—and move for the Disney Princess toothpaste.

"No, Daddy!" she screams, in what can only be described as horror. "I don't like that kind!" As if I accidentally grabbed a tube of Preparation H, or mixed up the Smart Rinse with Mister Clean.

"Oh, right. Sorry."

Roland likes the Princess toothpaste; Maude prefers the Little Bear kind. Duh.

She runs the motorized bristles across her teeth for approximately thirty seconds, then flips off the switch, hands me the toothbrush, grabs the two pacifiers on the vanity, and is gone.

"Take off your clothes," I yell after her. "Time to put your pajamas on."

She follows the first directive at once; like her mother, she likes to prance around in the nude. It will take some doing to get her into her pee-jays, but for now, I let her be.

"Okay, Roland. Your turn."

Roland is old enough to get himself ready for bed. He knows how to wash his hands, knows how to brush his teeth. But he hates doing these things. So every night he fights me tooth(paste) and (dirty finger)nail.

"Come on, Roland. Now!"

Why does raising your voice not work? Is it because they know that we're full of shit, that the limit of our anger is an increase in volume and a reddening of the face? Carrot and stick doesn't work so well to begin with, but when there's no stick, and they know it, you're kind of screwed.

No sticks, but here are carrots, in the form of chewable vitamins. I usually forget to dole out the vitamins—that's more of Stacy's purview—but the kids love them. They love them enough that, like dogs and puppy treats, the promise of a vitamin will generally compel them to roll over, play dead, give me paw. Like lollipops and dishes of ice cream, vitamins are the prison cigarettes of young childhood, the currency that buys favors.

"Who wants vitamins?"

As if by magic, two butt-naked children appear in the bathroom. *That* was easy.

"I want vitamins!"

"No, *I* want vitamins!"

"But what's for *me*?"

"You can *both* have vitamins," I tell them. "*After* you finish getting ready for bed. Roland, wash your hands and brush your teeth. Maude, let's put your pajamas on. Come on." I give the bottle a shake for Pavlovian emphasis.

The ploy, incredibly, works. Roland does his thing in the bathroom, and although Maude refuses to put on underpants—"I want to air out my china!"—I'm able to coax her into her pale green Tinker Bell nightgown.

I bring the vitamins into Roland's room, shaking them teasingly, like the Pied Percussionist. The kids follow. I put the bottle on the shelf and open the dresser drawer to find a pair of pajamas when the fight starts.

What happens is, Roland reaches into Maude's mouth, plucks out her precious pacifier, and hurls it across the room. Maude slaps him in the face, hard, and then runs behind my leg for cover. He reacts like a prodded toreador bull. If he were a cartoon, smoke would shoot out of his nostrils. He runs at her—at me—swinging his arms wildly, trying to land a punch.

"Stop." I put my body in between them. "Just *stop*."

"I want to hit her! I want to break her!"

"Maude should not have hit you. Maude, you shouldn't have hit him. But Roland, you provoked her. You threw her passie."

"She hit me! I have to hit her back!"

"No you *don't.*" I shake Maude off my leg and pick up Roland, hugging him. "You need to let it go, okay? I know she hurt you, but that doesn't mean you can hurt her. We can't have vitamins if you guys are going to fight."

"Maude is bad! She's bad! Bad sister!"

But his anger dissipates with my hug, and I'm able to calm him down.

"Let's put on your pajamas, and then we can have vitamins, okay?"

I'm back at the dresser, digging in the drawer, when Maude decides, imprudently, that she wants to read the *Wonders of the World* book. "That's *my* book! *Mine*!" Roland runs at her from across the room, again like the bull, and lands a vicious kick right in her abdomen. Maude keels over, crying.

"Roland! Jesus Christ!"

I move to separate them, to push him away, but he swings at me, too, connecting a (thankfully) glancing blow to my crotch. "What the . . . " My reaction is instinctive, involuntary. I swing back, smacking him on the arm. I'm able to temper the force—I don't hit him hard, and I don't hit him where I can hurt him—but I hit him just the same. I can't stop myself.

"God *damn* it."

Now Maude is crying, and Roland is crying, and there's a palm-shaped red mark on his left forearm, and my mood, already precariously dark, has gone completely black. I want to get into my car and drive off the Mid-Hudson Bridge. This is my nightmare: losing control, hurting him. Behaving like a savage. How can I teach him to check his violent impulses when I am unable to check my own? That the temptation to slap an unruly child is universal—Gandhi shared a bed with hot virgins to gauge his willpower; a better test of his self-control would have involved watching a four-year-old boy with Asperger's for a few weeks—does not make me feel any less like shit, nor does the fact that I've managed to not come close to doing so during the rest of Stacy's long absence. I'm waiting for the sirens, for Officer Stalin to come back and make good on his threat of arrest, for the cold metal handcuffs, the rough hand on my head as he stuffs me into his squad car.

The red mark on my son's arm, a scarlet letter, my shame.

"I'm sorry," I tell him. "I didn't mean to do that. I shouldn't have done that."

"No," and his voice is wild, "you shouldn't, you stupid Daddy!"

I fall on my knees, and I hug Roland, and I hug Maude—who hasn't stopped crying; me slapping the resident bully doesn't make her pain go away, any more than frying a murderer brings the victim back to life—and I rock them back and forth, back and forth, and like the little old lady in *Goodnight Moon*, I whisper, "Hush . . . hush . . . hush."

"I want Mommy!" Roland says.

"She'll be back tomorrow."

"When we wake up?" Maude asks.

"Yes, when we wake up."

"I want her *now*!"

"So do I. But we have to wait one more day."

None of us is badly injured, so Roland and Maude eventually stop crying, and when they do, I give them their vitamins, which they choke down through post-tears aftershock hiccups. After another round of apologies—and another round of demands for Mommy, this time intended to hurt my feelings (it works)—I help Roland into his pajamas, set him up with *Wonders of the World*, and promise him a new floor-plan book if he doesn't disturb us while I put Maude to bed.

Back when Britney Spears was in the throes of one of the more egregious periods of self-destruction ever chronicled in the tabloids—despite the best efforts of Lindsay Lohan and Mel Gibson, the photograph of the bald-headed Brit flailing her folded umbrella at a phantom paparazzo remains the gold standard of Celebrity Gone Mad—*Us Weekly* ran a story about how she once barricaded herself in the bathroom with her two young sons for many hours, causing Kevin Federline, gold-digger-turned-father-of-the-year, to call the police and, ultimately, the high court to deem her unfit to manage her own affairs.

Of all the crazy details and angles in that trainwreck of a story—and there are too many to count, starting with, Spears managed to make *Kevin Federline* seem like the paragon of parental stability—what really struck me was how she'd managed to keep those boys locked quietly in the bathroom as long as she did. My kids are about the same age as Sean Preston and Jayden James, and there's no way Roland and Maude would tolerate being confined in a bathroom, even one as palatial as Brit's must be, for more than a few minutes, now matter how many folded umbrellas were trained on them. What was her secret? According to the tabloid report, what Brit did was, she plied both kids with generous doses of NyQuil, which had a sedative effect on them.

Not a night has gone by since reading that article that I have not fantasized, during the Herculean labor that is bedtime, about giving Roland and Maude a hearty shot of NyQuil to hurry the process along.

The Nightime Sniffling Sneezing Coughing Aching Stuffyhead Fever So You Can Rest Medicine! Of course!

Maybe Britney Spears wasn't so crazy after all.

Written by Virginia Kroll and mawkishly illustrated by Fumi Kosaka, *Busy, Busy Mouse* is, for a preschool book, high concept. It tells parallel stories: a little girl and the titular mouse going through their diurnal routines—with the realistic twist that, since the mouse is nocturnal, he is just getting up when the little girl is ready to say goodnight. Maude loves this book. We've already read it twice, eschewing *Guess How Much I Love You* (just as well, as I can't narrate Sam McBratney's heartwarming tale of Big and Little Nutbrown Hare without bawling at the end) and *Biscuit* (the aw-shucks pooch whose increasingly desperate bedtime demands mirror Maude's own), the remaining books in our stack (we've already made it through *The Cat in the Hat* and *Maisy Goes to Preschool*).

" 'Up comes the sun. Good morning, everyone.' "

As the nameless heroine, a brown-haired girl with tiny black circles for eyes, yawns and stretches in her bed, our friend the Busy, Busy Mouse, wearing what appears to be a yoga outfit, careens into the mouse hole beneath her nightstand.

"Turn the page?" Maude asks (she's in my lap, in the glider). I nod.

" 'Baby crying. Eggs frying.' "

On one panel, the little girl and her apron-clad dad fry up an egg, as her little brother fusses in the highchair. Opposite, the Busy, Busy Mouse sits at his own kitchen table enjoying a snack of milk and cookies, his twitching tail visible behind his chair.

"Turn the page?"

"Go for it."

On the next few pages, the girl and her kid brother get into the groove of their day as the mouse goes through his bedtime routine, the latter falling asleep as the former are at their busiest. How exactly is it *cute* that this poor girl has a fucking mouse hole in her room? Are her parents unaware of steel wool and plaster of paris? I'm convinced that all these literary vermin are meant to make children more amenable to the inevitability of mousely cohabitation. *Don't be afraid of me! I'm cute! I'm cuddly! I'm just like you!* As video games desensitize kids to violence, the Busy, Busy Mouse makes rodent infestation seem like a blast.

Before I can continue, Roland bangs on his door—because of the child safety knob, he's imprisoned in his room—shouting for me, his voice cutting through the din of the twin noise machines.

"What are you *doing*?" I open the doors, first Maude's, then his. I don't want to get mad at him again, but it's hard not to, when he's so blatantly disobedient.

"I was going to stay in my room," Roland explains, "but I have to poop."

"Oh." I calm down. "Well, in that case. Sorry. Hold on, Maude."

But Maude doesn't want to hold on. Or rather, she does want to hold on—to my jeans. So the two of us wait in the hallway while Roland does his business. He insists on the door being closed, for privacy, which suits me just fine.

"Okay, done!"

I open the door to find the boy in downward-facing dog, pants at his ankles, his reddish butthole winking at me, and in the bowl, a black-brown turd the size and shape of my fist. Seriously: it looks like a miniature version of that Joe Lewis monument in downtown Detroit, only made of shit.

"Oh my *God*," I exclaim. "How did *that* come out of your body? This is the biggest poop I've ever seen!"

Roland blushes with pride.

"*I* want to see," Maude says. "*I* want to see."

"Hold on a sec."

I grab a baby wipe and clean Roland's behind—it's a no-wiper, as his poops tend to be; not a speck of brown on the wipe—and help him pull up his pajama bottoms and underpants. Then the three of us stand around the bowl, like the witches from *Macbeth* over their bubbling cauldron, admiring the big stink.

"Wow," Maude says. "That's a gi-*nor*-mous poopy."

"Thanks, Maude," says Roland.

He flushes it away, and returns to his bedroom, and I bring Maude into her room, sing through the eclectic list of songs I've appropriated as lullabies—"The Boxer," "Fire and Rain," "Piazza, New York Catcher," "Tom's Diner"—and lie with her on her futon mattress (the only thing she'll sleep on other than our bed or the floor) until she conks out. Then I go back to Roland's room, read him *Wonders of the World*, and then, as an encore, *The Cat in the Hat*.

"Is your arm okay?"

"It's fine, Daddy."

"I'm so sorry I hit you."

"It's okay, Daddy."

"I was wrong to do that."

"I know."

I tuck him in.

"Can we turn off the light?"

"No thank you, Daddy. I'd like to sleep with the light on."

"Okay."

I sing him his favorite lullaby song—"Thunder Road" (or "Screen Door Slams," as he calls it), which he prefers because it's long—and kiss him goodnight.

On the way out, my hand on the child-safety doorknob, he detains me with a question, as he often will. "When are we having the playdate at Zara's house?"

"Next week," I tell him. "I'll go arrange it now. Go to sleep!"

"Okay, Daddy."

I make it as far as the kitchen, where I set about cleaning the coffee pot, when Roland calls for me in the monitor. I grab a container of blueberry yogurt and a spoon—usually what he requests at this hour—and head upstairs.

But he's not hungry.

"There's a noise," he says. "It's making me afraid."

"Noise? What noise?"

Then I hear it, too. Scratching. The unmistakable crackle of mice in the wall.

Shit. I've never heard them up *here* before, although his room is over ours, so it makes sense. But I try and show no fear. He's not adept at reading facial expressions, which works in my favor, as I'm able to disguise my own pulse-pounding terror. More loud scratching.

"You mean *that*?"

"Yes, that."

"That's nothing to be afraid of," I tell him. Not a lie. The mice can't get out, and even if they could, they won't harm him or even go near him. "It's just . . . it's just the heater."

"The heater?"

"That's all it is."

I kiss him again, hoping that he believes me, that my musophobia won't be passed from father to son, like anemia or male-pattern baldness.

"When are we having the playdate at Zara's house?" he asks again, as I'm about to close the door.

"I'll find out," I tell him. "But we can only do it if you go to sleep now."

"Okay, Daddy." He sighs. "I love you, Daddy."

Right up to the moon.

"I love you, too, Roland. I love you, too."

Right up to the moon . . . and back.

Friday, 9:23 p.m.

THE CHILDREN ARE NESTLED, ASLEEP IN THEIR BEDS (OR, IN THE case of Maude, the futon mattress on the floor). In the baby monitors, I can hear, over the whir of the white noise and the throb of the steam train engine, their relaxed breaths—Maude's softer and slower, Roland's louder and more herky-jerky. Not a creature is stirring, not even a mouse (as far as I know).

Victory! Success is mine! I want to shout from the rooftops, to scream for joy, but instead I am utterly silent.

No matter how miserable I feel during the day, no matter how hopeless my life seems at four in the afternoon—and today the misery and hopelessness were particularly acute, as the Headless Whoresman could attest; if he had a head, he'd nod—my mood always lifts when I realize that the kids are asleep. *I can see clearly now the rain has gone*. I've never done smack, but this must be what heroin feels like, the immediacy of the mood shift; one minute you're a ball of stress, but as soon as that opium works its way into your bloodstream, ooooooo ahhhhhhhhhhh mmmmmmmm-mmmmmm.

No doubt about it: this the best part of the day

I change from my lone pair of jeans to my lone pair of sweatpants. I make myself mac and cheese (my default meal when Stacy is away; I don't even waste time wondering what I'll have for dinner), dig a Rolling Rock from the way-back of the fridge, behind Stacy's bottles of Magic Hat #9 (it's literally ice-cold; the container of cream cheese back there is frozen solid), and pop it open. I carry food and beer to my desk, and eat like a starved animal.

I check my e-mail: a rambling missive from Laura, sent to me, Mom, Frank, and Michael's parents, with several attached photos, about the day they spent in Pisa; a form letter from Cynthia Pardo, in her guise as broker at Coldwell Banker, advising me to *get to know my Realtor*™ (Bruce Baldwin, for one, has followed her advice to a T); a "friendly" reminder that my Chase Visa payment is due; and a short note from Meg, who had to take poor Beatrix to the ER on account of her reaction to the wasp sting.

Nothing from Stacy. Nothing from Sharon, whose number I have not managed to procure.

I check Facebook. Neither of them has updated their statuses. But Chad Donovan's cryptic post, I see, has been removed from Stacy's wall. I look up his page (on Facebook, as in life, I'm not friends with him), and sure enough, beneath his creepy-looking picture—drug addicts who find Jesus in rehab tend to have a certain crazed glint in their eye—is a long passage from Matthew, something about fishermen, the whole thing in unreadable caps. Yeah, cross him from the list. Stacy's lover, if such a person exists, is not the Second Coming of Chad Donovan.

After fortifying myself with the last swallow of amber Latrobe goodness, I type "Rob Puglisi" in the Facebook search bar. Three Rob Puglisis pop up (one of them, surprising given the Italian surname, is black), but none is my dapper therapist. Rob's not on Facebook, or else he's hidden himself from the search engines; probably the former. As I'm mulling over the significance of this—and I'm now convinced that if Stacy has gone Bathsheba on me, Rob Puglisi is King David to my doomed Uriah—a new notification pops up. A friend request. Chances are, a long-forgotten classmate from Livingston High, an underwhelming acquaintance from Rutgers, or else an unloved colleague from my time at News Corp.; the percentage of friend requests made by people I actually care about is miniscule. But I'm wrong:

> *D. W. Reid has requested to add you to their [sic] friends' list.*

Wow. He really *does* want to be friends!

I click ACCEPT.

AT THE VERY BOTTOM OF CABLEVISION'S ON DEMAND MENU IS A heading marked ADULT, where you might order up such cinematic masterpieces as *Eat My Box*, *Ram My Rack*, *18 & Easy: Barely Legal Schoolgirls #4*, and that beloved Oscar nominee, *MILFs Get Freaky*. I'm on the basement couch now, nursing a second Rolling Rock, the purring Steve in my lap, making dough on my flannel shirt. I'm trying my damnedest to distract myself from my interior monologue. Should I indulge myself with a little girl-on-girl action? Some *Amateur Moms Come*, *peut-être*? Nah. I'm tired as hell, and I'm not feeling particularly lusty. Plus, Stacy returns tomorrow, so I should recharge the ol' nine-volts, on the remote chance that she wants to get busy—that *I* want to get busy; that both of us want to get busy; that both of us want to get busy *and* have the opportunity to do so—tomorrow night. But it's more than that: this business with the affair has made me not want to contemplate sex at all, even sex involving barely legal schoolgirls.

Instead, I flip on the basketball game. Nets at Knicks, preseason "action," a replay of a game played two nights ago (tip-off for the 2009–2010 season is not till next week, when the Knicks travel to Miami to take on the Heat). I try to identify all the players—New York has traded virtually its entire roster in the last two years—but the only player I recognize is the slothful center Eddy Curry, the embodiment of the team's bloated salary cap. I'm well beyond eyeball level in debt, while he gets paid fourteen million dollars a year to sit on the bench and look bored.

Commercial: the Dos Equis Guy, holding court with the ladies, fencing, powering along in his motorboat. A gentleman who cares more about women, sport, and adventure than beer—what a novel concept! No wonder the ads are so popular. The Dos Equis Guy represents what we men aspire to be (an active participant in life who, when he deigns to consume beer, drinks the imported stuff; Daryl "Duke" Reid), not what we too often are (pathetic, chauvinistic armchair quarterbacks with a weakness for cheap domestic swill and the bloated guts to prove it; Joe Palladino).

The Dos Equis Guy bears more than a passing resemblance to Rob Puglisi.

I try Stacy again. Straight to voicemail.

Stay thirsty, my friend.

A jarring cocktail of fear, panic, and desperation explodes in my heart and radiates throughout my body. In the window, I can swear I see the Headless Whoresman, peering in, checking on me.

SOMEHOW—THE BEER-AND-A-HALF PROBABLY HAS SOMETHING to do with it, as does the fact that the Knicks are putrid; and, of course, the criminal lack of sleep in the last five days—I manage to nod off during the telecast. I dream again; not a full dream, just a Coleridgean snippet: a mash-up of the couch, the basketball game, and the Mystery Woman from this morning's interrupted vision. We're not at Meg and Soren's house this time; we're at Madison Square Garden, The World's Most Famous Arena, and the Janel Moloney Mystery Blonde is one of the Knick City Dancers. I'm sitting in Celebrity Row, next to Spike Lee, and Walt "Clyde" Frazier, the longtime Knicks color commentator, whose talent for mangling SAT words rivals his Hall of Fame abilities on the hardwood, keeps saying, "Things are starting to *percolate* down low." Spike Lee tells me to get my ass on the court and talk to the Mystery Woman, but there are too many dancers in the way, and I'm intimidated by the presence of the coach of the Los Angeles Lakers (that's who the Dream Knicks are playing), who is not Phil Jackson but Rob Puglisi. *Things are starting to percolate down low.* Then the buzzer sounds . . . and sounds again . . . and sounds again . . .

Still half asleep, I pick up the phone.

Glancing at the cable box—all of the clocks in the house, I realize, are attached to a device whose primary function does not involve time-telling: cable box, coffeepot, microwave, range, cell phone—I see that it's a little after ten. It's got to be Stacy, so I answer without bothering to check the caller ID.

"Hey," I say, in the brightest voice I can muster.

"Josh. Hey. It's, um, it's Sharon?"

For a brief instant, I'd almost forgotten about Sharon, and infidelity, and bad tidings, but no—I'm trapped in the house now; the Headless Whoresman knows this, and he's coming for me. Like Dracula to Mina, he's coming.

"Oh. Hey."

"I'm glad you're home."

"Where else would I be?"

"I called a little while ago and no one answered."

"Really? I must have fallen asleep."

"Shit. Sorry to wake you."

"No, no, it's cool. I want to talk to you. Obviously."

"Good. Because I'm on your porch."

"No shit?"

"No shit."

"I'll be right up."

Had I known she was coming, I'd have put on a clean shirt and brushed my teeth—my breath smells like fetid Velveeta. At the very least, I wouldn't have taken off my jeans. As it is, my hair is sticking straight up, I'm wearing sweat pants (nice sweat pants, but still) and a flannel shirt over my NEW JERSEY: THE ALMOST HEAVEN STATE T-shirt that doesn't quite match. I kill my television (Gloria would approve), bound up the stairs and into the bathroom, put a dollop of Aquafresh on my index finger, jam it in my mouth, swish it around, and swallow it. Better than nothing. My heart is pounding so hard I feel like it might burst through my ribcage and fly away, like it would in an episode of *Tom and Jerry*, as I get the door.

The woman standing on my front porch is not someone I immediately recognize. Her black-coffee hair is un-scrunchied and immaculately straightened, a "Rachel" sort of cut that swoops onto her shoulders, accentuating her gorgeous brown eyes, which, framed by the straightened hair, gleam even more brightly. Gone are the baggy sweater with the ridiculous turtleneck, and the baggy jeans, and the duck boots, replaced by a tight black sweater whose deep V-neck highlights both an intricate pendant necklace and the cleavage in which the pendant rests; a knee-length black skirt, black patterned stockings, and, on her feet, patent-leather pumps with a significant stiletto heel.

"Come in."

The morning's awkwardness a distant memory—we're friends now; circumstances have thrust us together—we greet each other with a firm hug and double cheek-peck. The firmness is welcome, as I feel like I might keel over from nervousness. Her lustrous hair smells like the inside of a hip hair salon I used to go to when I lived in Hoboken. Aveda, I think, although when it comes to olfactory identification of feminine beauty products, I'm no Hannibal Lecter.

"Sorry to burst in on you," she says, as the embrace breaks off. "I tried calling first, but I was going out anyway, and I really wanted to talk to you, so I figured I'd just drop by."

"No, no, no, it's cool."

She does a gander around the living room. She's never been to our house before.

"You look nice." An understatement. "Where are you off to?"

"Oh." She looks down at what she's wearing, as if she's forgotten, and gives an apologetic shrug. "An opening at G.A.S."

"G.A.S.?"

"Gallery and Studio? In Poughkeepsie? Franc Palaia's place? A friend of mine has an exhibition there. Here," she says, handing me a bottle of shiraz. "I thought you might need this."

"Thanks." I take the wine. "It's not Paul Feeney, is it?"

"Please. G.A.S. is a little out of Paul Feeney's league."

Relieved that someone else has uttered a thought I've always kept to myself—not all of New Paltz worships at the Paul Feeney altar—I laugh. "Yeah, I'm not a big Feeney fan, either. I'm going to open this now, if you don't mind. I'm really . . . I'm kind of a wreck. You wanna sit down?" I gesture toward the seldom-used living room sofa, which is piled with coloring books, clothes, Maude's dollies, and at least one empty juice box. "Wait. Let me move this shit out of the way."

"I'll do it. You pour the wine. I could use a glass myself. It's been a day."

Working quickly—the lunch rush experience at McDonald's has prepared me well—I uncork the shiraz (St. Hallet; Australian). I find two long-stemmed glasses, rinse them and dry the rims on the tail of my flannel shirt, so there are no fingerprints on the glass, and put them on a tray. I dig a hunk of gouda out of the crisper drawer and throw it on a tray with some crackers and a knife. I carry the tray and the bottle into the living room, resting it on the (small) section of the coffee table not occupied by Roland's stack of *Pottery Barn* and *Lamps Plus* catalogs. Then I pour off two generous glasses of the shiraz—turning the bottle like a sommelier, I still manage to drip some wine on the side of one of the glasses—and hand the neat glass to Sharon, who is sitting on the edge of the now-clean sofa, her legs tightly crossed, her posture perfect, like she's the guest on a Sunday morning talk show and we're about to debate the Middle East peace process.

"This is a cute house," she says, taking the glass. "The porch is really lovely."

"Thanks. Yeah, it's nice out there, as long as the mosquitoes stay away."

(At the bay window, the Headless Whoresman taps on the glass with his scythe, ready for the kill.)

Smalltalk concluded, she gets down to brass tacks. "I'm so sorry, Josh. I never should have brought that up at a playdate. I just . . . I wanted you to know, and I figured we'd have a few *minutes*, at least, to talk."

"It's okay."

"I must have really put a damper on your day."

"You know, my day was destined for dampness no matter what. Cheers."

"Cheers." She gives my glass a reluctant clink. We both take a healthy guzzle of Aussie vino. It's probably really good. I can't really tell right now. It's hard enough to sit down. It's hard enough to breathe.

"Anyway, as I was saying this morning, I think Stacy is having an affair."

"You *think* she's having an affair, or you *know* she's having an affair?"

"I think. But I'm pretty sure. I mean, I'm almost positive."

"With *who*? That's what's been bugging me all day. I can't figure it out. At first I thought it was with Chad—her old boyfriend from college, this asshole tennis pro—but then Stacy left me a message that sort of put that notion to bed. No pun intended. Now I think it might be Rob . . . you know, Rob Puglisi, our therapist?" Her eyes betray nothing. "But the truth is, I have no idea. Because frankly, I find the whole thing kind of shocking. So, I mean, who is it?"

Sharon takes a deep breath. Her eyes drift to her fingers, which fondle the stem of the glass.

"And *please* don't tell me you don't know, or you can't say."

"Soren," she says finally, as the scythe comes down with a thwack.

"Soren? Soren Knudsen?"

"Yes."

My breathing is so tortured that for a moment I think I might hyperventilate, but I'm able to pull myself together. Curiosity is all that's preventing me from fainting. Soren Knudsen! Well, he *was* out drinking last night with someone other than Peter Berliner, probably Bruce Baldwin, although I'm not sure; either way, he lied to Meg. And Soren is a handsome, charming, artsy, and—although I'm loath to admit it—sexy motherfucker. Chicks dig Euro-dudes. Seventy-three chicks, in his case. (Seventy-four, counting Stacy.) Furthermore, his sex life is unsatisfying, something his wife has not been shy about broadcasting. And if it *is* Soren, well, that would also explain why Meg doesn't know anything.

But how could he have gotten loopy with Stacy last night if Stacy is in Los Angeles? Unless . . . unless she *isn't* in Los Angeles. Do I have any proof that that's where she is, other than her worthless word? I call her cell phone, not the hotel—I don't even know which hotel she's staying at, come to think. She drove *herself* to the airport. Maybe she and Soren both took the week off work, repaired to that B&B in northeastern Dutchess County I read about in *Hudson Valley Magazine*, and have spent the last five days fucking like bunny rabbits while Meg and I mind the store. It's not beyond the realm of possibility—although, let's face it, it's certainly in possibility's outer suburbs. I'm not sure I buy it.

I wind up asking Sharon the same question I asked that asshole cop. "Really? Are you *sure*?"

"No. But I've seen them together a lot. At odd times. In weird places. Did you know they had lunch last week at the Bonefish Grill?"

I shake my head. I drink more wine, although my stomach would rather I didn't.

"You know how it is. No one from New Paltz hangs out in Poughkeepsie. They probably figured they wouldn't bump into anyone they knew. But I was meeting one of my girlfriends from Vassar, who lives out there, and I saw them. They didn't see me, but I saw them."

Stacy and Soren both work in Poughkeepsie—my wife for IBM, Soren for the *Journal*—so it would make logistical sense for them to have lunch. But why would she not tell me about it?

"A few weeks later," Sharon continues, "I saw them again, at the bar in the Grand Hotel. It was five thirty in the afternoon, happy hour. They were cozied up in one corner. They weren't just sitting there like friends. They were really close; their knees were touching. That time, they *did* see me. And both of them turned white as a sheet. I'm guessing Stacy didn't mention that to you."

"No," I tell her, after another long guzzle of shiraz. "No, she didn't."

"I've also seen her leaving his house. I know she's friends with Meg, but she was there to see *him*. I could tell. *He* walked her out to her car, not Meg, and his arm was draped on her shoulder, and she was sort of leaning into him. And that night, I happen to know that Meg was out with Cathy DiLullo."

"That was, what, two weeks ago?"

"Yeah."

"I remember that. Stacy said *she* was going out with Meg and Cathy DiLullo."

"Well, she was with Soren."

My glass is empty. Sharon pours me a refill, then tops off her own glass. Neither of us moves to drink. Neither of us says anything. Outside, a car screams down the hill, a sudden crescendo in the nocturnal symphony of crickets and owls, and slams on its brakes. Deer in the road, probably. Lots of deer up here, especially at night. Hazard of country life. Inside, the only sound is the dueling noise machines, white noise and train, from the upstairs bedrooms. My heart dies silently.

"Like I said, I don't know for sure. But I have a good eye for this sort of thing."

"Are you cold? I'm cold."

"I'm fine."

"It's cold. Let me turn up the thermostat. Hold on."

I'm right—it *is* cold. Sixty-six degrees on our digital thermometer. This explains my sudden but all-consuming chill. I crank the heat up to seventy. The furnace rumbles to life beneath me, just as something ill rumbles in my belly. I lock myself in the bathroom, and I barely make it to the toilet before torrents of purple acid erupt from my throat. Again it comes, then a third time, and when the contents of my stomach are emptied sloppily into the bowl, I dry-heave four or five times, just to be sure.

My body is trembling as I drag myself to my feet; my cheeks flash with heat. I flush away the wine-dark spew, wipe away the residue with fistfuls of Charmin, and flush again. I empty the spray bottle of Lime Mate; the pungent citrus scent almost makes me wretch again. I wash out my mouth with Cool Mint Listerine, spit violently into the sink. I run hot water over my hands until the heat is too much to handle.

God, I look like shit. Two days of stubble accentuating the double chin, like rows of puny shrubs on the side of a bulbous mountain. Unfathomable tiredness in my eyes. No wonder Stacy cheated on me. Soren is a rock star by comparison, a Danish Daryl "Duke" Reid. And it's not like he and I are pals exactly. I've always found him a bit standoffish, if not outright cold. I always attributed this to his Danishness, but maybe there's another reason; maybe he didn't want to get too chummy with the cuckold schmuck whose wife he had designs upon.

When I return to the living room, Sharon is carving a hunk of cheese, piling it atop a cracker. "Sorry," she says, her mouth full. "Didn't really eat any dinner."

"That's what it's there for."

"How are you? Are you . . . are you okay?"

"I guess."

"You should have more wine."

I shouldn't, but she pours what's left of the bottle into the two glasses, and I take a sip. It goes down easy, and it stays down. Thank God.

"I shouldn't have told you. It's just . . . I've *been* in that position. And I really wish someone had told *me*."

The hint of a past, a chequered backstory. As I suspected: Sharon has secrets, and unlike most of New Paltz, manages to keep them.

"No," I tell her. "I'm glad you did. I mean, I'm not *glad*, but I prefer to know. I would've found out sooner or later. The last thing I want is to be Peter Berliner, everyone staring at me like I'm a fucking leper. The last one to know."

"Cynthia," she says. "Jesus."

"You can maybe forgive someone for cheating on you. I can see that. But humiliating you in front of the whole town? That's not something you come back from." I start, my body snapping to attention like a senior officer walked into the living room. "You didn't tell anyone else about this, did you?"

"Of course not." She slides a touch closer; our knees glance. Her skin is warm beneath the stockings. "Even David doesn't know."

"Good. Thanks. Really. I appreciate your discretion."

"Oh, I'm very discreet."

I can feel the emotions churning again, deep in whatever overtaxed recess of my body feelings are generated from. Anger, sadness, grief, frustration, disbelief—maybe even a smidgen of relief, now that I know the *darkest hour before the dawn* truth. Can they all be explained by chemicals, feelings? I don't hold with that. Emotions have to be more than a cocktail of amino acids and neurotransmitters, a dry martini that can be shaken-not-stirred in some laboratory off the New Jersey Turnpike. Have to be. But if feelings *are* a cocktail, mine, at the tail-end of this interminable day, is a batch of Everclear punch some frat boy cooked up in a trash can; strong shit; you have to pour the juice in first, or the grain alcohol will eat through the plastic bag.

I don't want to feel anything right now. I don't want to rage, I don't want to cry, I don't want to puke again. I want to be numb. I take another hit of wine. "Was it David?"

"Was what David?"

"The one who cheated on you. The one no one told you about."

"God, no. David would *never* do that. My husband's a rock. That's why I'm with him. That's what he provides. David supports me, not just financially but emotionally. He makes me feel safe."

"Must be nice."

"Like everything, it's a trade-off." She uncrosses her left leg from her right, crosses her right over her left. Now I feel her toe—she's doffed those shiny black pumps, made herself comfortable—on my calf. "I love David, I love him very much, but I don't know if I'm *in* love with him. I don't know if I ever was, really. I was in a very dark place when we met. He saved me. Without him . . . "

She goes to drink, but her glass is empty, as is the bottle. We killed it quickly.

"I have another bottle, I think," I tell her. "Let me get it."

"I really shouldn't," she says.

"Oh, right. The opening." I'm suddenly desperate for her to stay. I don't want to be alone right now. I know the breakdown's coming. The towers have been hit, but they haven't collapsed yet. And collapse they will. No way around it. This is too big. The news is too grim. I want to prolong the darkness indefinitely. I want to keep talking, I want to keep drinking. The wine will stave off the abyss. For now. "Are you okay to drive?"

"Probably not."

"I could make some coffee."

"You know what? To hell with it. Get the bottle."

The fine shiraz of St. Hallet *patron saint of drunks?* has impaired my McDonald's-lunch-rush efficiency. Like Briar Rose and the spindle, I prick my finger on the tip of the corkscrew while peeling off the label. Fortunately it doesn't bleed, although it smarts. The corkscrew itself goes into the bottle crooked, so the cork breaks apart, pieces falling into the wine (Columbia Crest merlot; nothing fancy). When I finally manage to extract it from the neck, purple droplets rain all over the counter. I hurry back to the living room, stepping on a lost Lego brick as I approach.

Finally I make it back to the sofa. I pour two glasses—my aim is even worse now; wine sloshes off the rims onto the coffee table, where it is absorbed by a loose page from a *Shades of Light* catalog—and slide in beside her, a touch closer than before.

"Wine," she sighs. "I don't know how I'd manage without it."

"I'll drink to that."

The Columbia Crest is not as good as the Aussie shit, but I'm in no condition to play sommelier. Without food to soak it up, the wine has gone right to my head. Yeah, I'm a bit loopy. Which only makes me want to keep drinking, so full-blown loopiness can be quickly achieved.

"What are you going to do?"

"I don't know. Talk to her, I guess, and go from there."

"It's hard," says Sharon. "I know it's hard. But if you live in denial, I mean, you wind up . . . you wind up like Peter Berliner."

"Please please *please* don't tell anyone, okay?"

"I would never."

We fall silent for a moment. Sharon cuts more cheese. I nibble on a cracker.

So all we can do is to
Sit!
Sit!
Sit!
Sit!

The noise machines duel, the crickets and owls continue their night-music. The wine and cheese ease my stomach. And the Headless Whoresman, his job done, seems to have disappeared.

Finally, Sharon breaks the silence. "I understand wanting to have sex with other people. I don't even think it's that big of a deal, as long as it's done openly and honestly—and as long as you don't fall in love."

My (admittedly impaired) sense is that she's speaking from experience.

"Well, apparently my wife has fallen in love with Soren Knudsen."

"Maybe, maybe not. It could cut the other way. It could wind up making her love you more."

"Yeah, I don't think so."

"Think about it. The unknown commodity, the forbidden fruit, the greener grass on the other side: all of it serves to inflame desire. You're attracted to someone, you sleep with them, you get it out of your system. It's never as good as what you imagine it will be. Not that you should run around shagging anything that moves, like that Felicia Feeney. But there's so little in this world that's emotionally and physically satisfying in the way that sex is. Why deny yourself the pleasure?"

"Well, how about because you swore not to?"

"Wedding vows," she says, "seem a bit outmoded to me. A bit patriarchal."

"That's the Vassar talking."

"Or the wine."

We honor its mention with another gulp.

"You want a more pragmatic reason?" I tell her. "Fine. Here are three: disease, pregnancy, not embarrassing your kids. I can't even *imagine* what Cynthia's son, the oldest one . . . "

"Konrad."

" . . . has to deal with at school. What's he in, fourth grade? I mean, the whole fucking town knows; you think the kids at *school* don't? And kids are merciless. It's a trade-off, like you said. I don't hook up with whoever my heart desires, but, on the other hand, I don't have herpes."

"I'm not saying you should knock up big-mouthed syphilitics." She's looking directly at me, her face a few inches from mine. Her eyes, which despite their beauty have, until this moment, communicated nothing but ennui—Sharon has the comportment of an amnesiac, like she's on a desperate quest for something but has forgotten what it is she's looking for—glow with a passion I did not know she possessed. "Stacy sleeping with Soren, that's not cheating on you. What's cheating on you is *not telling you about it.* That's what fidelity means. Fidelity means no secrets."

The shiraz might have something to do with it—it's certainly advocating on her behalf—but I find myself being wooed by her *I'm always true to you darling in my fashion* cold logic. New Paltz is a liberal town; why should I raise an eyebrow when that liberalism extends to the *yes I'm always true to you darling in my way* bedroom?

Whatever the movies have us believe, love and lust are not indivisible. Yet we insist that to secure the former, we must temper the latter—a futile attempt to impose order on the chaos of nature. Is this hubris? Naïveté? Or rank stupidity? Sharon has a point, I'll grant her that; sexual monogamy, like the wedding vows that proclaim it, seems dreadfully old-fashioned, if not outright retrograde. Consider: when Maude borrows one of Roland's floor-plan books—which she does only to get his attention and approval, but that's another story—and he goes apeshit, yelling, *But it's mine! It's mine, Maude!* I calm him down and try and explain that possessions are better when shared. What I do all day long, as a father of two, is try and instill in my children the virtues of *sharing*. Sharing, it can be said, is the very backbone of civilization. If we don't share, as a society, we perish. It takes a certain level of maturity to understand this. And yet, when it comes to sex—and *only* when it comes to sex—sharing is forbidden. There's a disconnect there, seems to me. My getting indignant with Stacy for sleeping with another guy is no different, fundamentally, than Roland fuming at Maude for daring to leaf through one of his floor-plan books. Initiating divorce proceedings because of infidelity, to extend the metaphor, is a miffed child taking his ball and going home. Going home *alone*. Going home alone rather than do what the civilized world, in virtually every other arena save the marital bedroom, celebrates and venerates: share.

Share, sharing, Sharon . . .

Maybe the divorce rate wouldn't be so high if our expectations weren't so unrealistic. Open marriages don't work, they say; maybe they don't work because they are the exception and not the rule. Certainly Gloria and Dennis Hynek seem quite happy. Maybe an open marriage is something we *evolve to*. In five hundred years, human beings might look at rigid sexual partnerships with the same mixture of horror and surprise that we now view chastity belts.

Sexuality, perhaps, is best thought of as a carnal Hasbrouck Park, a playground of delights at which Stacy and I have ridden the seesaw of monogamy for the last decade. Maybe what I need to do is let her down gently from the seesaw and indulge her desire to take a turn on the swing set, rather than let her fall to the stony ground *a marriage on the rocks* by maliciously jumping off myself. Maybe our marriage will improve, maybe we'll get out of this rut, if we evolve from seesawers to *ahem* swingers.

"Your teeth are purple," I tell *share sharing* Sharon.

Her hand finds my knee. "So are yours."

Without moving her hand, she leans over and plants one on my lips.

I could not be more shocked at this turn of events. I'd be less surprised if Steve emerged from the bedroom on his hind legs and began to recite the Hamlet soliloquy. But then, I've always been slow on the uptake.

"Sorry," she says, her lips centimeters from mine.

If I were in my right mind I'd push her off, make her leave, but I'm drunk and confused and devastated, and I'm also suddenly and excruciatingly horny—When *was* the last time Stacy and I had sex? Has the entire month of October been one long dry spell?—so I'm all too happy to respond in kind.

IN JUNE OF 1999, STACY WAS DATING A GUY NAMED GREGG, WHO was also an actor—a pretentious jackass who liked to expound upon *the craft*, as if he were being interviewed by James Lipton, even when discussing a suburban dinner theater performance of *Bye Bye Birdie*. Gregg's friend Lee used to date Roberto, a playwright friend of mine from college. Broke his heart, actually, and was the subject of at least one bitter one-act. One silver lining of the doomed Roberto-Lee union is that Gregg wound up acting in some of Roberto's plays, which is how Roberto met Stacy, and cast her as the lead in *The Line Waver*, Roberto's one-act (not the bitter one), which was performed at the Bond Street Theatre for two weekends that summer. She was tremendous in that, just tremendous, although the script was unworthy of her talents, as even Roberto would admit, if he still took my calls (he's since gone Hollywood, writing teleplays for second-tier HBO shows).

That's how Stacy and I met. I saw her in the play—even though she was in her late twenties, she played a character who would now be called a cougar, and played it with aplomb—and I sort of developed a crush on her, as I sometimes do when I see a play and the leading lady blows the roof off the place. At the after-party at 2A, a bar located at *go figure* Avenue A and East Second Street, I found myself sitting next to her on one of the cushy vinyl couches on the upstairs level. She was drinking a vodka tonic, extra lime. Her hair was pulled back, so I could see the contour of her shoulder blades, and every last detail of her (very pretty; actressy pretty; Mary-Louise Parker pretty) face. She was sitting maybe a bit too close on account of the busted springs in the couch and the three vodka tonics she'd already consumed, a fact she mentioned six or seven times, and Gregg was on his soapbox, pontificating to Frank and a few of his gay playwright friends on the genius of Pinter. Pinter, whom I despise. Gregg was wearing a flouncy white shirt two removes from the one Seinfeld famously ridiculed, unlaced almost to the navel, like a romance-novel hero, his long wavy hair smacking of Fabio. He looked like a Calvin Klein Jesus. During our conversation, Stacy mentioned that Gregg only wore Tom's of Maine deodorant, which explained why I could smell his rank reek from clear across the room. (Living in New Paltz, I've since come to appreciate the Tom's of Maine fragrance.)

We had a great talk. We talked about how Shakespeare was overrated, and how film and stage acting differ, and how her favorite actress of all time was Eva Marie Saint, who was so fantastic in *On the Waterfront* and *North by Northwest*. And then for whatever reason the subject of *The Big Lebowski* came up, and we wound up throwing quotes at each other for the rest of the night. *We should have coffee sometime*, she said. I replied, "The Dude abides."

We never did meet for coffee, but on New Year's Eve—the Y2K New Year's Eve, when the new millennium did not begin and the world did not end—I went to a party at Roberto's apartment, a massive industrial-chic Williamsburg loft. New Year's Eve, like Valentine's Day, is a holiday that tortures the unattached, and if I lived somewhere other than New York, where the Times Square craziness is impossible to ignore (not the case in New Paltz, one of the myriad benefits of living here), I might have stayed home watching Charlie Chaplin movies and gone to bed before midnight. Instead, I went to Roberto's. At two o'clock in the morning, I found myself on the fire escape with Stacy. She and Gregg had just gotten into a horrible row—the *coup de grâce*, she feared, of their star-crossed love—and she was lamenting the end of yet another relationship, the hopelessness of being single at her advanced age (she was twenty-nine at the time; I was twenty-six). We stayed up all night, shooting the shit, and we had breakfast at Dark Odessa, and after the sun came up on the new year, I walked her back to her apartment. We kissed on her stoop, one of those magical *Princess Bride* kisses. It took a few weeks of stops and starts—Gregg wound up apologizing, and the rumors of the demise of their relationship were exaggerated—but by Valentine's Day, we were a couple, and have been ever since.

Another thing that happened at Roberto's party on December 31, 1999: when the ball dropped, and we all reveled in our miraculous deliverance from surefire destruction, I wound up making out with a woman I didn't know—she sort of looked like the Mystery Woman from my (prophetic?) dream, in fact—who just happened to be a) alone, b) in need of a make-out partner, and c) standing next to me at the stroke of midnight. I don't even know what her name was; I never asked, and by the time I found Stacy on the fire escape, I no longer cared.

I mention this because it's been nine years, nine months, and twenty-two days since I swapped spit with someone other than my wife (I'm not including Roland, who occasionally slips me the tongue when he kisses me goodnight). That's a significant period of time. When Sharon kisses me now, almost a decade later, her tongue lapping against mine like a cat *a Cat with a Tat!* greedily drinking up a saucer of milk, I feel like Charlie Brown's Christmas tree after they string the lights on it and plug it in. *See? All it needed was a little love.* I crackle with energy. I *am* the body electric. All the day's conflicting emotions, good, bad, and ugly, they all find release in that high-voltage kiss.

My left hand slides behind her neck, my right finds the small of her back. I pull her close to me, her breasts rubbing hard against my chest. I know this is morally gray territory—Stacy cheating on me does not give me carte blanche to cheat on her; two wrongs don't make a right—but the fact that I'm committing my own act of transgression, that I'm being *naughty*, only adds to the intensity of my primal hunger. My cock is a murder weapon, *and then something went* BUMP*!* hard as a bludgeon.

I break off the kiss for a moment, just long enough to pull off my flannel shirt (my chill, my nausea, any sign of illness, are long gone). Sharon does the same with her sweater. Now she's in her bra, and her breasts, bubbling out of the top of that black lace brassiere like giant champagne bubbles . . . I can't even tell you. Big, round, firm as a Sealy Posturepedic. Stacy has great breasts, too, but Sharon's are . . . well, they're not Stacy's, and that makes them, at the moment, preferable. *A bird in the hand.* I want to squeeze them, I want to manhandle them, I want to tear them apart like overripe melons, but I restrain myself. I'm gentle. I caress, I explore. I trace little circles over her nipple with my index finger; Sharon moans; she likes that. *I know it is wet.*

"Oh my God," she mutters. "Oh my God."

The next thing I know, her brazen hand dives into my sweatpants—which, while a Fashion Police violation worthy of the back page of *Us Weekly*, do make for easier access than button-fly jeans; today, function trumps form, no matter what the Fug Girls say—and . . .

"Why, we can have lots
Of good fun with this trick—
A game that I call
UP-UP-UP with your dick!"

. . . then it's *my* turn to take the Lord's name in vain.

The first person to touch my penis in a sexual way—I'm giving Rabbi Weiss, the mohel who did my briss, the benefit of the doubt here, although he did wind up being arrested on child molestation charges not long after the ceremony; contrary to popular belief, Catholics don't have a monopoly on perverted holy men—was Sarah Hoyle, back in seventh grade. I don't know that anything can quite equal the thrill of that initial touch, but this comes close; and Sharon's practiced fingers, unlike Sarah's, know exactly what scales to play.

When was the last time my cock was handled by someone other than me or my wife? The temptation is to romanticize one's oat-sowing bachelorhood, but New York, for all its eight million inhabitants, is a lonely town, or was for me. Before Stacy, there was a long period of no sex, few dates, and countless hours surfing Internet porn; the young Warren Beatty I was not. I've been with Stacy since I was twenty-six; for the entirety of the two-thousands. My last hand-job occurred when I was probably twenty-four, and it was almost certainly a drunken encounter. So yes, the novelty of Sharon's deft fingertips on my leaden cock is something of a revelation.

"Have no fear!" says the Cat.
"I will not let it fall.
I will get you more hard
As I cradle your balls."

The little guy is not in game shape; shit; this will be over too soon.

I take the time-honored advice and THINK ABOUT BASEBALL. The umbrella term "baseball" somehow finds human form in the person of retired Baltimore Oriole shortstop Cal Ripken, Jr., holder of the record for consecutive games played. Which calls to mind my own streak: the not-quite-ten years I've been exclusive to Stacy. Do I want it to end? Do I want a black mark on my perfect record? Then again, records only matter if you *care*, right? In the grand scheme of things, let's be honest, what difference does it make that Cal Ripken gutted out more ballgames than anyone else? He was paid millions and millions of dollars to play a kid's game; so what? Ripken reminds me of another bald-domed icon, John McCain, *choosing* to rot in that terrible Viet Cong prison, to subject his broken body to unspeakable tortures, instead of hopping the next flight home, as he easily could have, as the fortunate son of a senator. He stayed in 'Nam for *honor*, because it was *the right thing to do*. But was it? Would anyone really have faulted him for bailing (anyone but his father, that is, which is probably why he remained; but that's fodder for his Rob Puglisi)? I wonder if McCain would make the same choice, if he could do it all over. Would he trade in his medals and his presidential run and his honor for fully functional arms and a face that isn't scarred? Was his *heroic sacrifice*—words we heard again and again on last year's campaign trail, words we dared not question—worth it? When he is not calling for the deployment of still more troops to the euphemistic battlefield of Harm's Way, or the repeal of gay rights legislation, or the "reform" desperately needed in *War*shington, does the Gentleman from Arizona, in moments of quiet reflection, lament not checking out of the Hanoi Hilton early? Does he curse his obdurate pride, or is he at peace with the choice? Probably he is ambivalent. Probably it depends on the day. How will I reflect upon this tryst with Sharon ten, twenty years from now? Will I regret doing it? Will I regret *not* doing it? Why are these decisions never easy?

My Fish says, "No! No!
Make that Cat go away!

Tell that Cat with the Tat
You do NOT want to play.
She should not be here.
    She should not be about.
        She should not be here,
Not when Stacy is out!"

My lips have worked their dilatory way south, and I'm now nibbling on her neck, sucking on the supple skin, working my tongue around and around. She tastes as good as she looks. Her head is flung back, warm wet breath on my earlobe, and she's moaning, "You're so hard . . . you're so *hard* for me . . . you're so fucking *hard*," as she plies her prestidigitational magic, and all that's preventing me from shooting all over her dainty fingers, from oozing spent desire onto her multi-carat marquise-cut wedding ring, is the erection-killing image of the distended pink face of Senator John McCain.

But how quickly the close-up of McCain on the TV screen of my mind pans to his comely running mate—who would be gazing at Russia from the portico of the gubernatorial mansion in Anchorage still if he'd gone with Romney—and while I abhor her politics and her opportunism and her choice of baby names, I must concede that the image of Sarah Palin's hot-librarian glasses, her attractively bitchy face, her long slender legs, combined with the smooth rhythm Sharon's fingers have now found on the instrument of my longing, is insufficient to ward off a potential sticky mess in my sweatpants. Only a matter of time.

Sharon, sensing this, releases me. She pulls away, stands up, turns around—affording me a lovely view of the tattoo on her lower back; the same place Vanessa has hers, but unlike Vanessa's deformed butterfly, Sharon's intricate red-and-black scorpion inspires drool—unzips her skirt, and lets it slide to the floor.

The stockings don't come all the way over her panties, but stop at mid-thigh, and are held in place by a garter belt. *A garter belt? She was wearing a fucking* garter belt *to a gallery opening?* This has now become a scene from a porno I decided not to watch on Cablevision.

And then she stands up.
And then—oo la la!
The Cat with the Tat
Doffs her blouse. And her bra,
A silky black bra,
It is shut with a hook.
"Now look at my rack,"
Says the cat.
"Take a look."
Then she gets up on top,
And she straddles my lap,
And I feel I might blow
If she gave one more tap.
"I'll unfasten the hook.
You will see something new.
Two things. And I call them
Thing One and Thing Two.
These Things will not bite you.
They want to have fun."
Then out of the bra
Come Thing Two and Thing One!

But it's gone too far, way too far, and I'm starting to have second thoughts.

There is a line between fidelity and infidelity, a line I am dangerously close to crossing. Necking is one thing; nuzzling is another; fondling could conceivably be excused, under the circumstances; but the marital-vow Rubicon will be crossed, no doubt about it, if I come. Sharon can play at semantics all she wants. Secrets, schmecrets: if another woman makes you spooge . . . *that's* infidelity.

"She should not be here
When Stacy is not.
Get her out of this house!"
Says the Fish in the Pot.

On the other hand, I mean, Stacy *is* fucking Soren. Why exactly am I clinging to our hollow vow of monogamy when she isn't? Like poor John McCain, I'm making a *heroic sacrifice* in the name of *honor.* I'm *doing the right thing.* Feh. Honor and heroic sacrifice seem not so important next to the tangible bounty of Sharon's C-cups.

But it's my temptress who pulls away. She leans back on the other side of the couch, her legs spread. "Oh my God I'm so . . . "

"Have no fear, little fish,"
Says the Cat with the Tat.
"These Things are good Things."
And she gives them a pat.
"They are pert. Oh, so pert!
They have come here to play.
They will give you some fun
On this wet, wet, wet . . . "

" . . . wet." The same hands that so skillfully kneaded my cock Sharon jams down her black silk panties. Her head rolls all the way back, her yogic abs as buff as a nubile starlet's in the *Us Weekly* "Beach Bodies" issue, her neck exposed like a vampire victim's (Did I make that mark on her neck? Oops). Her voice, already breathy, is an Enigma album. "I'm so *wet.* I'm so fucking *wet* for you. Oh, Josh. I'm so fucking *wet* for you."

If you'd told me at five thirty this morning that in less than twenty-four hours I'd have a MILF Getting Freaky in my living room, declaring her wetness for me, I would have laughed in your face. The whole situation is so absurd, in fact, that it almost makes me laugh out loud even now. The funniest part—or, if you will, the most absurd—is how closely Sharon, in the throes of (real or imagined) ecstasy, resembles Stacy. *Ecstasy, ex-Stacy.* I'd never noticed this before, but in Sharon's half-naked, take-me-I'm-yours pose, they look eerily similar. I am in the larval stages of cheating on my wife with a woman who could be easily taken for her sister.

Easily taken. Too easily.

"But that is not ALL we can do!"
Says the Cat . . .

Wait a second . . . did she *plan* to do this? Did she make up the whole thing—Stacy's affair, Soren, even the gallery opening at G.A.S.—just to seduce me?

I can't do this.

Just as that flash of insight cuts through the darkling muck in my thick, wine-addled skull—with Sharon lying before me wearing only stockings and a garter belt, plumbing the depths of her desire with ready fingers; with the tent in my sweatpants so tall Ringling Brothers could use it for a sideshow; with the temptation to ix-nay my decade of fidelity at its absolute zenith; with matters about to escalate to the point of no return—*that's* when the dulcet soundtrack of white noise, steam train, baseboard-heater clang, cricket-chirp, owl-hoot, and seductive I'm-so-wet-for-you incantation is cleaved by an awful scream, like when the feedback-thick guitar comes in heavy over the dreamy synth at the beginning of "My Heart Is Hydroplaning."

One of the kids is awake.

USUALLY WHEN MAUDE WAKES UP IN THE MIDDLE OF THE NIGHT, she flips on the light switch and stands by the door, sometimes pounding on it, until I rescue her from the prison of her bedroom.

So I'm surprised to open the door to a dark room, the dull incandescent glow of the nightlight losing its battle with total blackness. Closing the door behind me—don't want Roland to wake up, too—I turn on the light to find Maude on the futon, sitting up but otherwise just where I'd left her, crying hysterically, her entire body convulsing with each tortured breath. Tears stream down her face, and her curly hair is a wet mop of sweat, which indicates fever, nightmare, or both.

"Maude, honey. What's wrong? What's wrong?" I scoop her up, embrace her; her legs wrap around my body as I rock her back and forth.

"I . . . I . . . I . . . "

"It's okay. It's okay."

I ease into the rocking chair, taking care to arrange her body so that it doesn't come anywhere near my still-semi-erect penis. I run my hand along her cheek. Her skin, while damp, is not any warmer than usual; she doesn't have a temperature.

"Did you have a nightmare?"

She tries to say yes but can't find the words, instead expressing her affirmation in a long, low wail.

"It's okay, honey. It's just a dream. It's not real. It's just a dream."

The night of the Academy Awards, Maude woke in a similar state of hysteria. Her nightmare involved Roland throwing up in her crib—a vision so real that she never again slept in that elevated baby cage. She wound up staying up and watching the show with us—Hugh Jackman hosted, and Maude was riveted by him; his demographic extends, we joked at the time, to two-year-olds. That began a rough sleep patch in which we tried toddler beds, real beds, and even the Pack-N-Play of her infancy, to no avail. The only place she would sleep, other than our bed, was the floor. And Stacy or I had to lie there with her until she conked out. After a fitful night of floorsleeping, I dismantled the crib and put down the futon mattress, and she's slept there more or less comfortably ever since.

So I know she's not going back down easily, not after this sort of night terror. Resigned to spending the rest of the night in here, I fall into a gentle rhythm on the glider, and work my way through the second set of lullabies: "Oh, What a Beautiful Mornin'," "Winter Wonderland," "Hotel California," "Chicago." Her breaths start to slow, and she calms down, but does not fall back asleep. I can feel her eyes moving, alert, terrified. Like mine when I hear the mice. When I tire of singing, I fall silent, rocking back and forth, patting her back, and watch the slow progression of numbers on her clock: 11:35 . . . 11:41 . . . 11:53. I am conscious of Sharon Rothman down in the living room, perhaps drinking more wine, perhaps eating more cheese, perhaps asleep herself on the sofa, but hopefully gone.

Then I said to the cat,
"Now you do as I say.
You re-bra these those Things
And you take them away!"
"Oh dear!" said the cat.
"You did not like our game . . .
Oh dear.
What a shame!
What a shame!
What a shame!"

I was so close to ruining this, to destroying everything, and for what? One night of drunken pleasure? A weeklong fling, perhaps? What the fuck was I thinking? Thank God Maude woke up!

"I love you so much," I whisper in my daughter's tiny ear. "I love you and Roland and Mommy so much."

Maybe her nightmare wasn't random. Maybe there were metaphysical forces at work—ESP, some father/daughter mind-link, a subconscious cry for help that Maude . . . perceptive, sensitive, nurturing Maude . . . somehow picked up on, as she slept. Maybe my internal distress call manifested itself in her bad dream, and rang out in her cry. I mean, it's been more than half a year since her last major nightmare; why tonight, why at that precise moment, did she wake up screaming?

Maude picks up her head, looks at me. "I know, Daddy," she says through her pacifier.

"Do you want to go back to bed now?"

This scares her. Her leg begins to kick involuntarily, like she's being electrocuted. "No," she says. "*Your* bed." And her half-cry returns: "I . . . want . . . to . . . sleep . . . in . . . *your* . . . bed."

"Okay. My bed. Fine."

I'm a bit concerned that Maude might notice Sharon on the couch; if she sees Iris's mommy here, she might mention it to her mother, and I'd rather keep this visit under wraps, for obvious reasons. Holding her in such a way that her face is pressed against my chest, I carry her carefully down the stairs.

Sharon isn't in the living room. I'm hoping she's gone, but when I round the corner, I see that the bathroom door is closed, the light on. The coast, as they say, is clear. I bring Maude into our room—she crawls happily into the dead center of the bed, where she will occupy as much space as her small body allows—cover her with blankets, and kiss her goodnight.

Glance at the alarm clock: 11:58. Two minutes left in my two-star day.

Friday, 11:59 p.m.

FULLY CLOTHED, SHARON SITS ON THE COUCH, FLIPPING THOUGH the new copy of *Us Weekly* she found in the bathroom—the one with yellow-gown'd Fergie and black-clad Josh Duhamel on the cover.

"Is she okay?"

"She's fine." My buzz is gone, devolved to stout headache. "She had a nightmare."

"Poor thing. I hate when Iris has bad dreams." She closes the magazine, taps the cover. "Stacy and Josh. Just like you guys. Weird."

I want to counter with, *That makes you* THE STRIPPER, but all I can muster is, "Yeah."

We hold our positions for a moment, Sharon sitting on the couch, me standing in front of her, not really looking at each other. Once again the house is quiet.

"I should probably go," Sharon says. But she does not move. "If you want me to."

She says this so I can stop her, reassure her, implore her to stay, to finish what we started. Soap-opera dialogue, just like this morning. What she doesn't realize is that I also don't want her to stay.

"Yeah," I tell her. "That's probably for the best."

"I'm sorry," she says, tossing the magazine on the stack of Roland's catalogs—it opens to the page about the cheating Josh Dumbbell—and slipping back into her four-inch fuck-me pumps. "I shouldn't have come. I shouldn't have told you."

She moves toward the door, toward me. She hugs me—a different kind of hug than the one she offered when she arrived; a lover's hug; a hug that bespeaks of intimacy—and kisses me again on the mouth. This time I don't kiss her back.

"Are you okay to drive? We drank a lot."

"I'll be fine."

"You sure?"

"I'll take the back roads. It's not that far."

It *is* far, everything up here is far, and the police are as ubiquitous as they are overzealous, as I well know. I should probably insist that she wait, that she sober up more, that she have a cup of coffee, a glass of water, a handful of Altoids, but Sharon is a grown-up, responsible for her own actions, and by now, frankly, I'm ready to be rid of her. "If you say so."

"We can pick up where we left off," she says. "Whenever you like. David won't mind. We have an arrangement."

Well, well. That explains Old Man River, doesn't it? For once, *I'm* the one armed with gossip, with fresh grist for the mill. David Rothman, the willing cuckold, the *mari complaisant*. Another version of Dennis Hynek. Not quite as shocking as sex in an art museum, but juicy gossip just the same. This particular tidbit, however, I'll keep to myself.

"Well, Stacy and I don't. She's not having an affair. No matter what you say."

"I hope you're right." She kisses me again on the cheek and is gone, leaving in her wake two empty wine bottles, a tray of cracker crumbs and cheese rinds, and the faint scent of whatever wonderful product she puts in her hair.

Then she shut up the Things
In the bra with the hook.
And the cat went away
With a sad kind of look.

From the living room window, I watch the BMW X-5 back out of the driveway, watch the red tail-lights vanish over the hill. Quiet descends on Plutarch Road, and I feel like I got away with murder. Like I dodged . . . more than a bullet—an airliner screaming toward the tall steel tower of my life. I fall on my knees on the hardwood floor by the front door, and I offer up a prayer of thanks to whatever Unseen Hand has steered me clear of the potential plane crash.

"Thank you," I say aloud. "Thank you, thank you, thank you."

Not that I'm blameless. I realize that. One day, I'm sure, I will feel guilty about my misadventure with Sharon—I'm hardly innocent; I returned her kiss, I nuzzled her breasts, I did not shy from her expert caress down below—but now I feel charmed, like I passed a test. I feel like Vincent and Jules in *Pulp Fiction*, when that kid bursts in, gun blazing, and every bullet misses them. Given the choice—and that's what tonight represented: a choice—I doubled down on my marriage. I kept my chips on Stacy's number. And I feel good about my decision. Lady Luck was on my side. And from the looks of things, she's going to hang around for a while. I don't need to check Eugenia Last's column to know that today (it's Saturday now, a few minutes past midnight) will bring five stars.

One more thing: for all the circumstantial evidence, for all the cogence of Sharon's argument, the thing is, *Stacy's not having an affair with Soren*. She's not. I know this now. Even *if* she'd cheat on me, which is unlikely, there's no way she'd also betray Meg, one of her best friends. But even if it were all true, even if she was fucking

Soren in art installations like Cynthia Pardo, that doesn't make it kosher for me to mess around with Sharon. It just doesn't. If sharing is a virtue we teach our kids, so is the notion that in life, things don't always divide evenly down the middle; there are days when Roland will eat one more cookie, days (like today) when Maude will partake of one more lollipop. The wisdom of King Solomon. It's not a fucking contest (nor is it a *fucking* contest). John McCain was right about that—fuzzy and intangible though the concept might be, honor is what separates us from lesser life-forms, be they animals or Feeneys.

But I'm not in the clear just yet. Time to make like Winston Wolf (speaking of *Pulp Fiction*) and clean up the scene of the crime. That's what the living room feels like—a crime scene. Class A felony: attempted adultery. Hide the evidence. Invent an alibi. Take a long cold shower. Pray for the best.

I close the *Us Weekly*, stack it with the lighting catalogs on the coffee table. I bring the wine bottles outside—Steve tries to door-dash, but I stop him; coyotes prowl at night—toss them in the recycle bin. They land with a loud glass-crash, momentarily deafening my left ear.

Cassiopeia is directly overhead, its five brightest stars limning a celestial "W." Dubya has his own constellation; oh, the irony. I take a moment to drink in the night sky—one of the many boons of life in the country, away from New York's eternal daylight, is the vault of stars on pristine nights—and am searching vainly for the Seven Sisters when a car comes over the hill and slows to a crawl, blinding me with its high beams.

Sharon returning, to sober up some more, to try her hand again at seduction? No—it's not an SUV. The roof isn't high enough.

Panic seizes me. What if this is an intruder, a team of thugs hell-bent on butchering me and my family, *In Cold Blood* in upstate New York? It's not like terrible things don't happen now and then; witness the unspeakable horror of the home invasion and murders in Cheshire, Connecticut, last year. And here I am, outside, caught in the headlights like a scared deer, unarmed, vulnerable.

But no, it's not an intruder. Once my eyes adjust, I recognize the car: a 2003 Outback. And I *should* recognize it; I'm the one who bought it, used—excuse me; *pre-owned*—at Colonial Subaru in Kingston, when we first moved here.

Stacy.

She must have taken an earlier flight.

A sobering though hits me: had Sharon stayed . . . *my wife would have walked in on us.* Thank God thank God thank *God* that I turned her down, that I sent her away! I try to quiet the noises in my head, to appear calm, but Stacy is very adept at noticing when I'm acting funny. Which I'm obviously doing right now, because it's after midnight, and I'm standing in the driveway for no apparent reason. A suave and seasoned philanderer might explain this away with ease, but I feel like she caught me presiding over a bloodied corpse, murder weapon still in hand. And I have one of the worst poker faces in the English-speaking world. I'm the anti–Lady Gaga.

Stacy gets out of the car, slams the door shut, and comes to me. She's wearing her travel clothes—oversized college sweatshirt, jeans, red Sauconys, her hair pulled back in a red bandana—and a big smile.

"Hey you!"

"Hey!" I squeeze her tight, drinking in her familiar scent—God, I love how my wife smells!—and hope that she doesn't detect the strong fragrance of Another Woman on my clothes. She feels so right pressed against me; even dressed down, tired, after a long flight, she looks perfect.

"They let us out early, and I was able to hop an earlier flight. I was so psyched."

"I missed you. Man, did I miss you." But my brain is still in detective mode—it's harder to shift mental gears than emotional ones—and I find myself asking the question that pops into my head. "Why didn't you call?"

Hard to tell out here in the driveway, but I'm pretty sure her face blushes slightly. "Don't get mad."

I grin. I'm happy to keep the tone playful. "What did you do?"

"I dropped my cell phone in the toilet."

"Again?"

Stacy goes through cell phones like they're tampons. It's a running joke.

"It wasn't my fault."

"I'm just giving you shit. Really. I'm so glad you're home. You have no idea."

I move away from her and to the trunk, where I collect her bags. With a night of sleep—or at least a shower—separating me from the Sharon imbroglio, I could better disguise my culpability. As it is, there's not enough time. I feel like the guilt is a second head that's sprouted on the back of my existing one, like Voldemort in the first Harry Potter movie. How can she not notice something so obvious? There's a fucking *head* on the back of my head!

"You're acting funny," she tells me. "Have you been drinking?"

"I had a few beers. To relax."

"You don't seem relaxed."

"I'm just surprised to see you. And I'm really tired. It's been a long day." I'm walking toward the house now, carrying the bags, and thus able to avoid direct eye contact.

"So why aren't you in bed?" She's half a step behind me. Literally and figuratively. "Why are you outside?"

"Maude had a nightmare." This is the truth, but it sounds like I'm improvising an elaborate ruse, like Jon Lovitz on that old *SNL* sketch. No way she'll buy this, even though it's true *she reads my she reads my yes she can read my lame poker face.* "She's in our bed, and I wanted to give her time to conk out. So I figured, it's a clear night, why not come look at the stars." We step through the door. Steve, happy to see her, arches his back; Stacy leans down and pats him. "It's hard to spot those constellations. I suck at it."

"You should try it without the lights on." She kills the driveway flood lamps.

This is a decent set-up line for a bawdy rejoinder, but I'm not feeling it. The clever part of my brain—if, in fact, there exists a segment of my gray matter that can generate something approaching cleverness—is in panic mode, trying to cover my bloody tracks.

I let the bags drop on the floor. Stacy immediately notices the magazine on the coffee table. "Ooh. Is that the new one?"

If I can make it to the morning without her giving me the third degree, I'll be in the clear. I still have to confront her about Soren, tell her what I was told and who told me, but that will be a difficult conversation, and I don't have the energy for it right now. All I want to do is pass out on the bed with my wife and daughter. *Get to bed, and we'll live happily ever after.*

"Yeah. With Josh and Stacy on the cover."

Will she notice the remains of the cheese and crackers on the coffee table—the smoking gun of near-adultery—as she takes the *Us Weekly*? Nope. She grabs the magazine and heads to the bathroom. I move to clean up the mess, but before I can get to it, she returns, the rolled-up mag in her fist.

"Was someone here?"

I try and make my voice as nonchalant as possible, which does not work well. She's a much better actor than I am. "Yeah. Sharon Rothman stopped by."

Four quick words, a magic spell. The floodgate damming All Hell bursts, and just like that, the Pandemonian contents break loose.

"Really."

"She was on her way to Poughkeepsie. To a gallery opening. So she stopped by."

"She stopped by."

"For a drink. She brought a bottle of wine, so we had some. Some wine."

"In addition to the beer you drank to relax."

"What's that?"

"You said you had a few beers, to relax."

"Oh, right. Yes. In addition to a few beers."

"That explains why your breath smells like a garbage dump." Stacy's face contorts as she processes this information. Then she crosses her arms over the CARNEGIE on her college sweatshirt—her attack pose. "I don't know if I like the idea of you entertaining other women in my house when I'm not here," she says finally, indignity and accusation creeping into her voice.

Stacy and I rarely fight. Not that we don't ever have cause for quarrel; it's just that I will go to great lengths to avoid outright conflict, because I suck so royally at one-on-one, out-in-the-open debate. My arguments, however well-thought-out before the clash, and however correct, degrade to emotional grunts the minute I'm attacked. In short, I avoid rows with Stacy because Stacy always wins. Always. She's Jerry to my Tom. I find it easier to acquiesce *surrender surrender but don't give yourself away* than to take up arms. The Neville Chamberlain route, peace at all costs.

Yet tonight, I have no choice. I've already ceded the Sudetenland, and now the tanks have rolled into Poland. I have to fight. I have no choice. The very future of our marriage depends on it. I can't just laugh this off (although I probably should). I have to have out with it, all of it; to defend myself, and by extension my marriage, or die trying. "Well," I counter, "I don't know if *I* like the idea of you meeting *Soren Knudsen* for lunch and not telling *me*."

Her expression is difficult to read. Guilt? Surprise? Anger? I don't know. "Who told you that? Sharon, I suppose?"

"I'd rather not say."

"You think, what? You think I'm *cheating* on you? Is that *really* what you think?"

"I didn't say that."

"But Sharon did. That little whore." She flings the magazine across the room and scowls at me. "What did she say?"

I stand there dumb, a moron. I don't want to talk about this, not now, not ever; it's clear from her reaction that she's *not* having an affair—with Soren Knudsen or anyone else. Her arms are still crossed, and now she's tapping her foot on the hardwood floor, which would be more effective if she weren't wearing her Sauconys.

"What did she *say*, Josh?"

So I lay out the evidence. The lunch at the Bonefish Grill, the conspiratorial meeting at the Grand Hotel, the glimpse of her leaving Soren's house one night two weeks ago.

"And from *that* she deduced that I was having an *affair*?"

"Well . . . " It does seem sort of stupid, phrased this way. "Yes."

"She's seen too many episodes of *Y&R*. That bitch. Why can't people in this fucking town mind their own fucking business?" She bends over to get the magazine off the floor, then barricades herself in the bathroom. Like Britney Spears did, but without the kids. She comes out a few minutes later, toilet flushing behind her. She glowers at me, her eyes seething, and without a word, marches down the hall toward the bedroom.

"Shhh. Quiet," I tell her. "Maude's in there."

But she's wearing the sneakers, and Maude can sleep through earthquakes once she's out. Stacy vanishes into the room, closing the door on me (and the cat, who has followed her every step of the way since she walked through the door; he prefers her). After a minute, Steve gets tired of waiting and slinks back to the couch.

Two minutes later—I watch the time pass on the microwave clock, every second like a fresh knife wound to my heavy heart: where is this going? What is she doing in there? Have I ruined everything? Can our marriage recover from this stupid, awful, hideous, two-star day?—the longest two minutes of my life, Stacy returns, carrying a shoebox. Without looking at me or speaking, she makes for the couch, sits, and motions for me to join her. I have no idea what to expect. What's in that box? Her diary? Divorce papers? Gwyneth Paltrow's severed head?

"I was saving this for your birthday," she says. "*Some* of us know how to make those occasions special." This is yet another dig on her craptastically bad fortieth, which she will be giving me shit about until the day I die, and possibly also during my funereal eulogy—but her voice is softer, more forgiving, so I relax ever so slightly. "But you might as well open it now."

Inside the box is a stack of black-and-white five-by-seven photographs—gorgeous, artsy photographs of my gorgeous, artsy wife, wearing a variety of naughty undergarments (negligee, bra, garter belt, and in one shot, just her hands covering her pert breasts), in an array of sexy and seductive poses. It looks like the sort of photo shoot a celebrity who doesn't want to bare all would submit for *Playboy.*

"Holy fucking shit."

It's hard to believe that the alluring model in these five-by-sevens is my wife, the same woman I've shared a bed with for ten years, the mother of my two high-maintenance children. We take for granted how attractive our wives are, I guess, or I do; sometimes it takes looking at her from a different lens to appreciate her beauty anew. She's prettier than Sharon Rothman, prettier than any of the other mommies in town, prettier—yes!—than Mary-Louise Parker. "These are . . . these are great."

"Yeah?" Her eyes fall to the floor, hair falling in her face. Even now, after five days of work and a long flight, in her Carnegie Mellon sweatshirt and Guess jeans, she's still a hottie. "You like them?"

"Of course! I mean, look at you! You're so fucking *hot.*"

"Soren is very talented. And Meg was there when we did the shoot. Just so you know. She didn't meet us for lunch at Bonefish to discuss it, and she must have been in the bathroom when Sharon saw us at the Grand Hotel. That's when Soren showed us the prints."

"Oh my God," I say, hugging her as hard as I can, tears welling in my eyes. "I feel like such an idiot."

She pats my head as I stifle my tears. "You've been alone with the kids all week. That would make anyone feel that way."

"I never believed her . . . but Sharon, I mean, she was so *convinced.*"

"Did she put the moves on you?"

I don't answer, but my weep-wet eyes give me away.

"Oh my God! She put the moves on you! You didn't *fuck* her, did you?"

Then Stacy came back.
On an earlier flight.
Should I tell her
The things that went on here tonight?

"No. No, of course not. I'd never do that."

Which is the truth, right?

"Good."

Should I tell her about it?
Now, what SHOULD I do?
Well . . .
What would you do
If your wife asked YOU?

I could elaborate. Maybe I should. But, given that I answered Stacy's question to her satisfaction, I decide against rehashing the play-by-play of Sharon's almost-successful seduction attempt. I love my wife more now than I did when the day began, and when the opportunity presented itself, in all its garter-belted glory, in the end, I did not betray her. That should be enough.

"She *does* that, you know."

"Does what?"

"Hits on married guys."

"Really."

"She modeled for Soren a few months ago, and at the end of the session, she basically offered to blow him."

"I didn't know that."

"She and David have an *arrangement*, is what she told him. Please. She's a fucking homewrecker. Like Angelina Jolie. They have the same puffy lips."

The idea that anyone would select my home as wreck-worthy seems ludicrous—I feel like the least sexy man this side of Barack Obama—and I tell her so.

"Are you kidding? You're *totally* cute. You are. You're, like, a total FILF."

I laugh. "You're biased."

"Just a little."

I hug her again, as tight as I can, trying to merge our bodies into one. I'm a *Titanic* survivor kissing dry land. A clumsy metaphor, I realize, comparing my wife to dirt, but that's how I feel—like I've been saved. "I really missed you. I can't tell you how glad I am that you're home."

"Me, too."

"These pictures are great. Really. This is, like, the best birthday present of all time ever."

She looks down at her fingers, plays with her wedding band. "We're in sort of a rut, you know? I thought this might, you know, be the spark we needed."

We embrace again, and I kiss her deeply, desperately, as if trying to make up for lost time. And then I'm making out with my wife on the same sofa, in front of the same platter of cheese, where I (briefly, but still) made out with Sharon less than two hours earlier.

"I love you," I tell her between kisses. "I love you so much."

She gets this sly grin on her face—a grin I know well from the early days of our marriage, but haven't much seen of late. "You wanna?"

"Of course."

"Shit. Maude's in our bed."

"Damn it."

"We could just do it here."

"On the couch? It's like we're in junior high."

"We could go upstairs, to Maude's room." We both reject the proposal silently, independently, and simultaneously. "Yeah, bad idea."

"I'm actually really exhausted."

"Me too."

"Tomorrow," she says. "Date night. And by 'date night,' I mean 'whoopee night.' "

"About Vanessa . . . "

"Screw Vanessa. I planned this already. I got one of Meg's sitters. Abby. If she can handle the twins, she can handle Roland and Maude. She's coming at six."

"Yeah? You planned it?"

"I figured we could use a night out."

"Where should we go? The Would? Global Palate?"

Her eyes twinkle with mischief. "I was thinking we'd do something different. Something naughty. Mix it up. Check into a motel, under an assumed name. Pretend we're having an affair."

"Cynthia Pardo and Bruce Baldwin did it at Dia:Beacon. We could always go there."

"They did *what*?"

"See, you go away for five days, you miss stuff." I hold her close, kiss her forehead. "There's that motel in Balmsville, near the strip club. That might make for a good hideaway. We could go get lap dances first."

"Sold." She kisses me hard on the lips, a final stamp of approval and possession and commitment. "And for the record . . . I would *never* cheat on you, you *stupe*."

Stupe. Roland's word. "Me, neither." I now know this to be true.

We sit for a while on the couch, as we've sat so many times before, holding hands, quiet and content.

"Wait," Stacy says, "they did it at Dia:Beacon?"

"Yeah. The cops came and everything. But that's not even the half of it. Cynthia's *pregnant*."

"What?" Stacy shakes her head. "This place," she says. "The more you dig . . . "

" . . . the more you find."

And the word *find* triggers the iPod in my brain. As I wash my face and brush my teeth and take one final leak, and as we crawl into bed, Stacy and I forming parentheses around the asterisk of the slumbering Maude, I can't get the song out of my head, the chorus playing on a loop, over and over and over, until I finally fade into sleep:

Good love is hard to find.

Saturday, 5:03 a.m.

I WAKE UP. NOT FROM A CHILD'S CRY, OR A KICK FROM THE SLEEPing and flailing Maude, or a nightmare, or a pressing and urgent need to void my bladder (although I do have to pee, I always have to pee), or the invasive scratching of rodents trapped in the walls. I wake up because my body has decided that now—5:03, the same time Roland roused me yesterday; precision of the internal clock—is the time to wake up.

Stacy faces the wall, a jumbled mess of arms and legs, snoring loudly, chainsaw snoring: the blessed soundtrack of home. Maude occupies the center of the bed, limbs splayed out like she's being drawn and quartered. Roland is asleep, too; in the monitors, nothing but the whir of the twin noise machines. Peace, quiet. My loved ones, my family, tucked safely into bed. There is something deeply satisfying, something almost magical, about watching over your sleeping wife and children. I'm fulfilling an ancient paternal role, one that *hasn't* changed with the times: Father as Protector.

I should be exhausted—I only slept for five fitful, wine-drenched hours—but I'm not. On the contrary, I feel as alert and refreshed as I've felt in ages; I feel alive, inspired, even powerful. They were an efficient five hours, I guess, a productive half-day at the office. There certainly was a lot of paperwork to process. Oddly, of all that went down yesterday—the anxiety of the alleged affair, Stacy's return and my titillating birthday present; the run-in with the law; the babysitter stand-off; Roland's pumpkin patch meltdown and the subsequent breaking of bread with Daryl and Zara Reid; Cynthia Pardo and Bruce Baldwin, Cynthia Pardo and Peter Berliner; and, yes, the delicious caress of Sharon's fingers on a part of my body that no one has touched in ten years except my wife and the urologist who performed my vasectomy—what I wake up thinking about is something relatively minor. I'm rehashing the remark made by Joe Palladino, my goateed exterminator, he of the mouse bait and the blind-date blow job:

Just you and the kid on a Friday afternoon. A little Mr. Mom duty today, huh?

It's time for an update, it occurs to me, a *Mr. Mom* for the new millennium: a groundbreaking film about a dad who *isn't* a cipher, who isn't thrust haplessly into the primary-caregiver role, but who courts it, and who excels at it. Brad Pitt could star—heck, if the tabloid photo spreads of him hauling Maddox, Pax, Zahara, Shiloh, Vivienne, and Knox from Lake Como to Los Angeles are to be believed, he won't even have to act. Maybe it's time for Hollywood to catch up. Maybe I should stop writing derivative vampire thrillers and bang out a screenplay about my own absurd life. Maybe then my agent would respond to my e-mails. Maybe he'd do even more. Maybe—

A little Mr. Mom duty today, huh?

See, the days of *Mr. Mom* are over, no matter what my benighted exterminator might think. The paradigms have altered. The gender roles have blurred. The distinction between Mother and Father is all mucked up. And that, more than anything, is why Joe's comment sticks in my craw. For hundreds of thousands upon hundreds of thousands of years, in almost every culture that is or was, women have cared for the children, and men have not. Right here, right now, we are experiencing a cataclysm of domesticity, a tectonic shift in how things are and how they will be going forward—and there is nothing, *nothing* in the language that adequately reflects this sea change. *Mr. Mom* affixes a masculine title to a feminine noun—arguably the *most* feminine noun going. *Mr. Mom* is defined by its antithesis, by what it's not, by how it's unusual, extraordinary, queer, risible, ridiculous, possibly malefic. Compare: *undocumented, illegal, illegitimate, Antichrist.* What we need is a new term for what we are. A word that is *positive*, something we stay-at-home dads, we SAHDs, we Y-chromosomed co-parents *Co-parents! As if fathers actually participating in raising their kids has to be specified! As if doing so is encroaching on the mother's side of the parental line of scrimmage!* we evolutionary Mr. Moms, can be proud of. A word like . . . like . . .

A clatter from the living room disturbs this train of thought: Steve playing with a catnip toy? Somehow I know better. With my heart in my throat, I creep down the hall to investigate.

One of the mice has at last found its way beyond the wall. Steve—who perhaps heard Joe Palladino's lecture this afternoon; perhaps one of an exterminator's functions is to light a fire under his housecat ally, to play Knute Rockne to the resident four-pawed mouse-killer—has discharged his feline duty, and has the li'l varmint trapped under the sofa; the same sofa where Sharon and I partook of our wine and cheese. Was it the smell of cheese that drew the brazen mouse from beyond the wall? Do mice *really* like cheese?

For all the times I've read, heard, or used the hackneyed phrase "cat and mouse," I've never actually beheld a real cat toying with a real mouse. I always assumed that the cat, with its superior cunning and quickness, would pursue the mouse relentlessly *with paws but without pause* until the disgusting little poop machine was dead. But it's not really like that. The chase comes in stops and starts, like the action in a football game. Cat pounces upon mouse, catches him, then releases him, as a fly fisherman and his prize trout. Mouse retreats, but knows better than to attempt a full-fledged escape. Both creatures wait without moving for many minutes. Then, without warning, the cat strikes. He bats the mouse around with his paws, like a one-named Brazilian midfielder dribbling a soccer ball, and for a few moments, both animals are a blur. Then Steve pins him by the tail—predator and prey are in the middle of the floor now, nowhere for the little fucker to hide—and I get a good look at the cause of my nightly autumnal terror. The mouse—who must know his days of haunting my interior walls are over—breathes furiously, the whole of his body expanding contracting expandingcontracting, like a tiny billows, his flaxseed-sized heart pounding furiously in his tiny ribcage. And as I watch him anticipate the end—an end Steve, master of suspense that he is, a feline Hitchcock, seems determined to prolong—I actually feel pity for the poor thing. The mouse, he's like me—more like me than the cat, certainly. He's small, this mouse: insignificant, vulnerable, afraid, in over his head; and though his desires may be great, his needs are modest. And here he is, pursued without relent down dark hallways by a fierce creature of the night, a sharp-fanged monster, an embodier of unquenchable cruelty, as we are in our dreams.

After yesterday's encounter with the Headless Whoresman, after those twenty-four hours of torture, the red-alert threat of the destruction of my marriage and my entire way of life never more real, this puny, terrified ball of fur seems not so scary.

Crossing the living room, I open the front door, admitting the night's chill. "Over here, mouse," I tell him, as if he knows what this means. "Here."

Then I walk casually toward the chase scene, the set piece from a Mickey and Minnie horror film, and scoop up the cat.

"Go, mouse. Go!"

I give him a little kick. He scurries for the door, slowly at first, as if expecting to be stopped, as if this is merely an elaboration on the same old game, a hazard on this mini-golf course of rodentine death; as if he has already succumbed to his fate and doesn't trust his two-footed savior. Once it dawns on his stupid vermin brain that he's in the clear, he picks up speed. He zigzags to the wall, creeps along the baseboard, and runs out the door. Steve, flailing in my arms, can only watch as his prize bursts free into the night. He lets out a long howl of displeasure *What the fuck are you doing, Josh?* and not wanting to disturb the kids, I throw him, too, into the dark and chilly night, bolting the door behind him.

No sign of a hangover, a hangover I surely deserve, as I make my way into the bathroom and take a long, satisfying leak. Fergie and Josh Duhamel, the allegations of his dalliance with THE STRIPPER still hanging over their collective and Photoshopped-together head, eye me uneasily from the magazine cover on the floor. I've had it with *Us Weekly*, with Heidi Montag and that asshole Spencer Pratt, with Rihanna and that asshole Chris Brown, with Bristol Palin and that asshole Levi Johnston, with Jennifer Aniston and Jessica Simpson and that asshole John Mayer (*do we detect a pattern here?*). I'm tired of affairs with strippers and nannies and cocktail waitresses, of leaked sex tapes and risqué phone messages, of Hollywood marriages that implode in a matter of weeks. Just because they pump gas and doff their Manolo Blahniks for airport security and buy paper towels in Target does not mean that stars are *anything* like us.

Oops! I've been a mite careless with my piss stream; a few drops of urine have found their way onto the luminous faces of the celebrity Josh and Stacy. So sad, too bad. After the requisite shake—this time I aim for Duhamel's smug, five-o'clock-shadowed mug—I roll up the magazine and toss it in the trash.

A little Mr. Mom duty today, huh?

Joe Palladino, of all people—the most artless Philistine in the Hudson Valley—has sparked something in me, the dormant creative force, the slumbering King of Wands. If not the mice, who remain, Paladin Pest Control has managed to exterminate my writer's block. After filling the coffeemaker with cold water and Kenyan Gold, I wake up my laptop, open a NEW PROJECT in Final Draft (When was the last time I even clicked on the app icon? A good year ago, I think, last fall, the wretched attempt to craft the vampire script), and begin typing:

1. EXT. JESS'S HOUSE - DAY

A McMansion, not quite as gaudy as the others. Several cars in the driveway, including a dark blue Honda Odyssey. In the yard off to the side, an enormous swing-and-slide set, unused.

2. INT. JESS'S KITCHEN - DAY

STEVE, 36, handsome but tired, pours himself a fresh cup of coffee. We hear happy SQUEALS of small children from off camera. SHARON, 32 and pretty, enters, mug at the ready. As he tops her off, she looks at him with grave concern.

SHARON

I don't know how to tell you this, Steve, so I'm just going to tell you.

At the first whiff of brewed coffee, that incense of the Muses, it hits me: the word! The Mr. Mom upgrade! The updated term for what I am, what all we stay-at-home dads are. I open the "title page" in Final Draft, type out the twelve letters. Then I go pour my coffee. I reclaim my seat, and I sip the Kenyan Gold, and I admire the word I've written on the screen . . . but only for a minute. Roland's awake now—I can hear the clatter of Thomas tracks tumbling over—and he's calling for me, and loudly (loud is his only volume). Time to deploy. Leaving my laptop open on the title page, I turn off the baby monitor, so he doesn't wake the mother-and-daughter sleeping beauties, and I march up the stairs, mug in hand, to report for duty.

Such is the life of the fathermucker.

Acknowledgments

Jen Schulkind: thanks so much for giving me another crack at this. As I've now come to expect, your editorial insights have markedly improved this book. It's a privilege to work with you.

Mollie Glick, my agent of almost ten years: bless you for taking the long view. You rock, as does the rest of the Foundry crew (mercy buckets, Stéphanie Abou).

Robin Antalek, who read this novel in serial form, Dickens-style, before anyone else did: your encouragement and support have been priceless. I can't thank you enough.

Big love and thanks to everyone in the TNB universe, especially Jessica Anya Blau, Susan Henderson, Jonathan Evison, Lenore Zion, Zara Potts, Jeffrey Pillow, Nick Belardes, Kimberly M. Wetherell, Gina Frangello, Tawni Freeland, Gloria Harrison, Quenby Moone, Cynthia Hawkins, Megan DiLullo, Erika Rae, Richard Cox, Simon Smithson, Matt Baldwin, Sean Beaudoin, D. R. Haney, and the great Brad Listi.

Lauren Cerand: you are a genius.

Mad props to: Carrie Kania, Cal Morgan, Teresa Brady, Nicole Reardon, Robin Bilardello, Erica Barmash, Mary Sasso, Maggie Oberrender, Jennifer Hart, Aaron Murray, Lelia Mander, and everyone else at Harper; Christine Preston, Michael Preston, Olivia Abel, Cathy Serpico, Charles Sterne, Caitlin Welles, Liz Eslami, Jeff Bens, and Meghan O'Neill Currier; Jess Walter, Jerry Stahl, Colleen Curran, Jim Othmer, Thelma Adams, Steve Almond, Maria Semple; Molly Jong-Fast, Ruth and Terry Quinn, Liz Pickett and Les Castellanos, Elizabeth and Tim Hunter, Shari Lynn Goldstein, Keith Karchner, Jen Papataros, Erica Chase-Salerno, and the rest of our friends (both grown-ups and kids) in New Paltz.

Kathy, Lorrie, Belkis, Olga, Sandy, Charley, Cindy, Rachael, Marcia, Joan, Christine, Brieann, Toni, Deanna, Danielle, and Inge: if every preschooler had you as teachers, the world would be a much happier place. Your positive influence on our lives is impossible to overstate.

Janice and Greg Olear, Franklin and Lorraine St. John: you are patrons of the arts, whether you know it or not. Love and thanks to you and the rest of the family, especially Jeremy Olear and Lou and Diane St. John (and C. J., my niece, who is such a great artist).

To my children, Dominick and Prudence: you are a daily source of inspiration and joy, even on days when Dad is grumpy. I am blessed to have such wonderful, smart, and dazzling children.

Finally, to my lovely, talented, and no-doubt-about-it faithful wife, Stephanie: only thirteen more years till we can go to Europe for a month! Without you, I don't know where I'd be . . . someplace colder, shallower, less meaningful, less supportive . . . Brooklyn, maybe? But seriously: this book doesn't exist without you. I love you more than you know.